By Anne Baker and available from Headline

To find out more about Anne Baker's novels visit
www.annebaker.co.uk

Anne Baker

THE ORPHAN'S GIFT

HEADLINE

First published in 2019
by HEADLINE PUBLISHING GROUP

First published in paperback in 2020
by HEADLINE PUBLISHING GROUP

1

Cataloguing in Publication Data is available from the British Library

ISBN 978 1 4722 6405 3

Typeset in Baskerville by Avon DataSet Ltd, Bidford-on-Avon, Warwickshire

Printed and bound in Great Britain by Clays Ltd, Elcograf S.p.A.

HEADLINE PUBLISHING GROUP
An Hachette UK Company
Carmelite House
50 Victoria Embankment
London EC4Y 0DZ

www.headline.co.uk
www.hachette.co.uk

To my editor Clare Foss with thanks for the help and advice she has given me over countless years

CHAPTER ONE

December 1932

AIMEE KENDRICK WAS WAITING with Frankie Hopkins for their teacher to come to the old schoolroom and give them an art lesson. Frankie opened up his portfolio and put his latest watercolour up on one of the easels. Aimee said, 'We aren't going to paint this morning. Miss Rathbone's going to give us a talk on history of art.'

'I know, but what d'you think of my latest effort?'

'I like it, it's very good, but you keep on painting the same view.' She turned to look out of the window and across the Mersey to the magnificent Liverpool skyline. 'This is it.'

'Yes, it fascinates me and I keep trying, but I haven't got it quite right yet. Miss Rathbone will be able to tell me what it needs to put it right.'

'You've already signed it as though it's ready to go to the saleroom,' she giggled. 'Francis S. Hopkins. What does the S stand for?'

'Sebastian. That's how my mother taught me to write it.'

She laughed outright. 'Nobody could say that wasn't a posh name.'

'Everybody laughs. I don't know why they think it's funny.

After I'd done that, I had second thoughts about the perspective.'

'It's perfectly all right. I think it's a lovely picture.' Aimee was bored with it. 'I'm beginning to get excited about Christmas, are you?'

'Not particularly,' he said. 'Christmas comes and goes but doesn't bring much excitement for me. You don't know how lucky you are to have all this.' He waved his hand to encompass the comfortable house and large garden in Rock Park.

Aimee wasn't having that. 'You sound like a disillusioned old man,' she said, though she knew he was only two years older than her and had just had his nineteenth birthday. 'I'm not lucky at all because my mother lives in France and I hardly ever see her.'

'Aimee! What d'you mean, not lucky?' Frankie's laugh had no mirth in it. 'Your mother is the famous painter Micheline Durameau Lepage.' He let her name roll across his tongue. 'She's at the forefront of French art, and creates lovely sunlit scenes of rural France. Everybody has heard of her, and she's had her pictures hung in the most important galleries in France and England. You must be tremendously proud of her.'

'I am,' Aimee said, 'you know I am, but I hardly see her, and my father was killed in the war. My mother married again and she's very wrapped up in painting and her new husband.'

'Of course she is. She's had to concentrate hard on her career to be the success she is. What's wrong with that?'

Aimee adored her mother. Usually she spent all her summer holidays in France with her, but this year Maman had wanted to stay in Paris to prepare for a display of her paintings in her husband's art gallery in September.

'Sorry, *ma cherie*.' She had smiled at Aimee. 'We'll still have three weeks together in August, and how about coming for a couple of extra weeks at Christmas? Would that make amends?'

Aimee had said yes, though she'd felt resentful at the time, but now she had the long Christmas holiday in front of her.

Frankie said, 'I don't have a mother at all. She died when I was seven.'

'But you have a father.'

'No, I call him Dad, but really he's my mother's dad, my grandad.'

'I thought I was short of relatives, but you have even fewer.'

'I'm short of most things. You've got two grandparents to take care of you.'

Aimee's grandma believed she'd inherited real artistic talent from her mother and praised her pictures highly. She had asked Maman to arrange for Aimee to have extra art lessons at home, even though she had them at school already.

'I can't see that you have much to complain about.' Frankie sat down at his desk.

'You're right, compared with you I don't. Sorry, I'm moaning, aren't I?' Aimee went over to the picture he'd put up on the easel. 'I think this painting is really good.'

Poor Frankie did have almost nothing. Everybody felt sorry for him. Miss Rathbone thought he had real artistic flair and had suggested that he share Aimee's lessons. He had a passion for painting and she'd said his presence might encourage Aimee to strive for the right effect.

Grandma did not agree. 'What does that lad know about art?' she'd said to Aimee. 'Your pictures are better than his. Much better.' Neither did she approve of Frankie as a companion; she thought it would have been wiser not to allow him in the schoolroom at all. Aimee liked Frankie, though, and thought Miss Rathbone was right about his talent, and he was good company too.

Long ago, before many people had cars, Frankie's grandfather had kept the stables in the road behind Rock Park. Those of their neighbours who did not keep a carriage of their own used to send for Bob Hopkins to drive them across town. He'd probably never had much business, as it was a short stroll to Rock Ferry pier, from where a pleasant ferry trip would take them to Liverpool, and his family had fallen on hard times. Nowadays he had a cart instead of a carriage and would take suitcases to the station or collect packages. He also did odd gardening or painting jobs for his neighbours, or anything else he could pick up that would bring him an hour or two's work. Since he'd left school, Frankie had been doing much the same, but he'd set his sights on working in a shop or an office.

He turned from his picture. 'You'll be going to France any day soon, won't you?'

'Yes, next Tuesday.'

Her grandparents took her to France for the Christmas celebrations, but they stayed only for four days as Gramps needed to get back to take care of his business. Aimee would usually be brought back to England in the new year by one of Maman's friends. This year it was to be Miss Rathbone.

'Here she comes,' Frankie said, and stood to attention by his desk as the teacher came in.

'Good morning, Aimee. Good morning, Frankie.'

Miss Rathbone had been Maman's best friend when they

were younger. They had trained together at the École des Beaux-Arts in Paris. Aimee liked her – she was kind and generous – but she looked older than her thirty-seven years, and time had etched deep lines of disappointment and dissatisfaction from her nose to her mouth. Her wardrobe was limited, though her clothes looked as though they'd once been expensive. In the declining economic climate it appeared that, like many others, she'd fallen on hard times, and she no longer had money to spend on luxury items. She still painted in oils and watercolours, and Aimee knew she would have liked the success that Maman had achieved.

'Let us look again at the Impressionists of the nineteenth century,' she said, unpacking her folder of large-scale prints. 'Today we'll start by studying Monet's work.'

Aimee sometimes felt she was two quite different people. In France she was Aimee, and life was luxurious, nothing too expensive for Maman to provide. At school her friends spelt her name A-m-y, and she was totally English.

Frankie Hopkins was fascinated by all Miss Rathbone could tell him about art, and he settled back to listen. He couldn't get enough of it. He was immensely grateful to both Aimee and her teacher. They had encouraged him to paint and had shown him techniques that really helped.

He saw Aimee as a friendly face in a world that was very different to his own. Her family could provide her with extra teachers as well as a posh school. She'd shown him the paintings she was doing in her classes and he'd said, 'I'd love to try that.' One wet Saturday afternoon she had brought down pencils, paper and paint to their greenhouse and they'd painted together; afterwards she'd given him the materials to take home.

When Frankie was young, he was often left to amuse himself while his grandad was working, but once he'd had his eighth birthday, Dad had taken him along to help, and taught him to do the same sort of work. Nowadays, if he hadn't found a job for himself, he worked as Dad's assistant. Once he had heard about Micheline Durameau Lepage, though, he'd been fired with ambition to be an artist, and told his grandad of all she'd accomplished.

'She'd have had all sorts of lessons to learn how to do that,' Dad had said. 'The only art lessons you'll get are what they give you at school.'

Frankie knew that at school he'd get nothing but chalk and a slate to draw on. Aimee told him about her lessons and he could see that he'd need tuition like that if he was to succeed. It took him a long time, almost three years, before he plucked up the courage to say, 'Will you ask if I can come to your art lessons and learn to paint too? I'd love to know how to do it properly.'

She'd stared from him to the painting of the beach he was working on. 'You can paint as well as I can,' she said, sounding surprised. He watched her put her head back and think about it. 'They'd say no,' she told him. 'My mother pays Miss Rathbone to teach me, and I'm afraid Grandma doesn't like you much and would see no reason for you to benefit from my lessons.'

What he liked about Aimee was that she always took him seriously. They'd spent that afternoon devising a plan that just might work. 'Candida Rathbone talks about natural talent,'

Aimee said. 'She says I've got mine from my mother. You'll need to impress her with your talent and show her how keen you are. If she thinks you're really good, she'll want to teach you. She used to teach a whole class in a school once, but she's given that up.'

'I could paint a dozen pictures to show her,' he said eagerly.

'No, one or two – three at the most,' she said. 'Make one a portrait and one a scene of the beach or a boat, and do your very best work. She's very kind so she just might agree, but don't tell anyone I had anything to do with it.' Miss Rathbone came from Liverpool and walked to Rock Park either from the ferry or the train station. 'You can meet her on her way here and show her your paintings,' Aimee added.

Frankie went home with one of her folders and a fresh supply of paper and paint. He had several attempts at painting the very best pictures he could. Two weeks later, he met Miss Rathbone at the park gates and persuaded her to stop and look at his work. Unbelievably, she was impressed. 'You've a lot to learn by way of technique,' she told him, 'but with the right teaching, you could be good.'

He'd told her he was Aimee's friend and knew she'd assumed he lived in a neighbouring house. He felt he had to tell her of his circumstances and that he couldn't pay for lessons. 'Let me think about it,' she'd said.

Frankie was bursting with hope – if it had been possible for Micheline Durameau Lepage, surely it must be possible for him? – but his grandad had been less impressed. 'You're becoming obsessed with painting,' he said. 'You should stay away from that girl. It's all right for the toffs, especially the ladies, a nice hobby for them, but it won't do for the likes of you. You'll have to earn your living.' Frankie knew then that his grandad didn't believe he'd have a dog's chance of earning anything from his pictures.

A week later, Aimee came rushing over to his house. 'Candida thinks you have talent and you're worth teaching,' she said breathlessly. 'She asked me if I knew you, and she's asked Gramps if you can come to my lessons, so it's all agreed.'

Frankie took her in his arms and whirled her all round their living room. He'd never felt so exhilarated. 'Marvellous, wonderful, I can't believe my luck.'

Aimee was laughing with him. 'Next lesson is two o'clock on Tuesday. I'll come to the pear tree to get you, because you won't know the way up to the schoolroom.'

'Thank you, thank you, Aimee.' He kissed her cheek. 'I couldn't have done this without your help.'

She giggled and spun him round. 'We did it together. I can't stay now because Gramps will be home soon, and then it's dinner time. See you Tuesday if not before.'

Frankie did another jig, intoxicated with joy. Dad had been watching them from his chair by the fire he'd just lit. 'No good will come of this,' he said in doom-laden tones. 'I can't believe Mrs Kendrick is going to allow it.'

Aimee knew Grandma would not approve of Miss Rathbone taking Frankie into her art class, but as she was bound to find out sooner or later, she went home and told her. Grandma was old-fashioned and set in her ways, and Aimee knew that if she was kept in ignorance until she saw Frankie coming upstairs, it would involve him in an almighty row.

Minutes later, Gramps came home from work. Aimee watched with horror as Grandma drew herself up to her full height of five foot two and went to meet him in the hall, incandescent with rage. 'Walter, I'm told you've given Candida Rathbone permission to teach that Hopkins lad in our house? What on earth possessed you?'

Gramps spoke slowly and calmly. 'Candida says he has talent and it would be a shame not to encourage him.'

'Not in our house,' Grandma barked. 'I don't want him here. I don't want him near Aimee. Candida can do that in her own place if she wants to.'

'I'm sorry, Prue . . .'

'Well put a stop to it now before it goes any further.' She turned on Aimee. 'You're not to go round to his house,' she said. 'You're not to encourage him. I forbid it.'

'Grandma, please.' Aimee wanted to say that Frankie was her best friend, but she knew that would only make matters worse.

'I feel sorry for him,' Gramps said. 'He's a nice enough lad, polite and well mannered, and Aimee likes him.'

'For goodness' sake, that's what I'm objecting to. He's quite unsuitable as a companion for her.'

CHAPTER TWO

AIMEE AND FRANKIE HAD gravitated together from a very early age. The old stable where Frankie lived was in the road behind Rock Park, and a five-foot brick wall separated his garden from that of Aimee's house. A convenient apple tree grew close to it on her side, and she soon learned to climb it to get onto the wall. It was a shorter drop down on his side, and Frankie kept a wooden box there to make climbing up easier. It was quite a long way round by road, and even Bob Hopkins came and went over the wall when he worked in the Kendricks' garden. Frankie said he was going to build a few permanent steps on their side, but he'd never got round to it.

Years ago, Frankie had been helping to collect the grass his grandad was cutting in the Kendricks' garden when he'd said to Aimee, 'Dad could make you a marvellous swing on this old pear tree. You could make it go much higher than the swings in the park, because the only branch on this side is twice as high as they are.'

'It grows a big crop of little yellow pears every year,' Aimee said, 'and if there was a swing there I could jump up and down on it to bring them down when they're ripe.'

'Yes, late summer, lovely juicy pears,' he agreed, 'and they weren't easy to get down last year.' Alongside it there was another pear tree that cropped sparingly, and the fruit had to be kept for months until it ripened.

'I'll tell Gramps I'd like a swing,' Aimee decided.

A week later, she found that Bob Hopkins had bought all the things needed to make one. Frankie came with him to help. Aimee watched as they tied a piece of string round a stone and attached the other end to a length of chain. Bob Hopkins threw the stone over the high branch of the pear tree and then pulled on the string until the chain went over the branch. He attached the wooden seat to the bottom of the chain and called, 'How high off the ground do you want the seat?'

Frankie went to demonstrate, and they soon had the other side fixed on in the same way.

'OK, Frankie,' Bob said. 'Stand on the seat and jump about on it. Let's make sure it's strong enough.'

With mounting excitement, Aimee watched Frankie try the swing out, pushing himself higher and higher. 'I can almost see over your house,' he called down to them. When it was declared safe and she was allowed to try it, she was absolutely thrilled and swung on it until she was called in to eat her dinner.

Later that summer, when the pears were showing yellow between the leaves, Aimee jumped up and down on her swing to bring the ripe fruit down. She soon discovered that it could be painful if the pears hit her, so she encouraged Frankie to take over. Then they would sit on the grass and gorge on them. Sometimes there were so many that Frankie was able to take some home.

One wet winter Saturday, they spent a cold morning painting together in the greenhouse. Frankie said, 'I've heard there's a good cowboy film showing at the Palace Cinema for the children's matinee this afternoon. I'd love to see it.'

'So would I. I've never been to the cinema.'

'I wish you could come. It's more fun if you have a friend to go with, but I don't have enough money to pay for you.'

Aimee went to ask Grandma for the tuppence entrance money she needed, while Frankie waited on the kitchen door-step. She was back in moments shaking her head. 'Grandma said no, not with you.'

'She doesn't like me,' he said, pulling a face. 'She told me I mustn't hang about your house. Your grandfather doesn't seem to mind me playing with you. He's quite friendly and always speaks to me if he sees me in the garden.'

'I wish I hadn't spent my weekly penny on sweets. It'll be miserable here on my own.'

The kitchen was empty. 'Look,' Frankie said. 'I can see a freshly washed-out jam jar on the draining board. You can return it to the shop and they'll give you a ha'penny. Do you have any more?'

Aimee opened a large cupboard under the sink where there was a whole shelf full of gleaming jars. 'Grandma wants them saved for jam and chutney making, but she doesn't do much of that.'

'Big jars,' Frankie whooped. 'They're worth a penny each. Bring two and let's get going.'

'Are you sure?'

'Course I'm sure. I always do it. The boys in my class at school eat jam by the spoonful when nobody's looking to empty the jar as soon as possible. Jam jars are as good as money in the bank.'

They were walking to the cinema when Frankie bent to pick

something up from the pavement. 'Look at this,' he said, pushing it into her hand. 'A ring, though it's not much good. It's lost its stone.'

Aimee slid it onto her finger. 'It must have been a diamond solitaire once, and quite a big one, I think.' The prongs that had held the stone were still in place. She laughed. 'It fits me. Is it gold?'

'Might be.'

'I think it is.'

'You keep it.'

'No, if it is gold, it's still worth something. Shouldn't we take it to the police station?'

'I suppose so. We've still got time, and the station is on the next corner.'

Aimee took the ring off her finger and pushed it back at Frankie as they went inside. 'You do it.'

The constable looked at it dubiously. 'It does look like gold and it has something stamped inside. All right, I'll log it in as lost property. What's your name? You know that if it isn't claimed in a month, you can have it back.'

'I won't want it,' Aimee said. 'It's broken.'

'I do,' Frankie said. 'I think it could be gold.'

Aimee was amazed at how much Frankie knew, and she thoroughly enjoyed her visit to the cinema. 'We could do that again next week,' she said afterwards. 'There's loads of jam jars in our cupboard.'

CHAPTER THREE

AIMEE GREETED HER GRANDFATHER as he was taking off his hat and coat to hang in the hall wardrobe. 'Have you had a busy day?' she asked. She got out his slippers and followed him into the sitting room, where he yawned and settled back in his armchair. She brought his whisky bottle, filled a cut-glass jug with water and set them with a glass on the table beside him, then went to the kitchen to help Grandma get the evening meal ready, as she did most evenings.

She carried the steaming tureen to the dining room, and while she waited for Grandma to ladle the soup into three bowls, her eyes went to the two pencil portraits hanging side by side on the dining room wall. One was of her father in his uniform as a second lieutenant in the Great War; the other was a self-portrait of her mother. Her grandparents revered them, although they were yellowing now even behind glass.

Gramps had told her all about her father. In November 1914, they'd been officially notified that he was missing, believed killed in battle. Grandma had never accepted that he was dead. 'As his mother, I knew he was still breathing. I could feel it in here,' she would say, patting her heart. Later they learned that he had been injured in battle at Arras and left for dead. Local French civilians had found him and taken him to hospital, where her mother, an art student and volunteer carer, had helped to look after him. He'd fallen in love with her, and when he recovered, they'd been married. Alec had returned to his regiment, but tragically he'd been killed just before the war ended. Aimee felt she knew no more about him than was shown in those pencil drawings.

Of course she knew much more about her mother, and was looking forward to spending the whole of the Christmas holiday with her. They were all immensely proud of what Micheline had achieved. Aimee knew Grandma was always ready to talk about her daughter-in-law, and boasted about her fame to friends and neighbours on every possible occasion.

Aimee had heard many times that once the Great War was over, Gramps had invited Micheline to England so they could meet their granddaughter. 'You were such a smiling and undemanding little girl. As soon as Grandma saw you, nothing else would calm her but that she be allowed to keep you and bring you up in Alec's place.

'I was against it,' he continued. 'I was afraid Prue wouldn't be able to cope and that you would be happier with your mother, but it was what Micheline wanted too. She'd had to put her painting ambitions on hold during the war, but with Alec gone, she'd thought long and hard about her future, and looking after you would have made it impossible for her to return to Paris and continue her art studies.

'Eventually I gave in and agreed you should stay,' Gramps went on. 'When we heard that Alec was missing, Grandma had wept and wailed for months, and she doted on you, smothered you with love. You brought her consolation. You wormed your way into everyone's affections, mine included, and soon neither of us could think of life without you. Micheline paid generously towards your keep, and over the following years we watched her career and fame develop. She made such a success of it that I'm sure it was the right thing for her too.'

Aimee could remember Grandma telling her that when her mother came over to see her on her fifth birthday, she'd been thrilled to find she'd grown into a very pretty little girl with a mop of fair curls. She'd picked her up and pulled her onto her knee to cuddle her, but had been shocked when she'd tried to talk to her. 'She doesn't understand one word I'm saying,' she cried.

'She's too young,' Grandma had said. 'She'll learn French in school.'

'But she should be learning now. At what age will she start?'

'About ten, I suppose. I was that age when I started to learn French.'

'You had French lessons? *Mon Dieu!* You hardly speak French at all.' That had been an even greater shock for her mother. 'French should be her first language.'

Grandma knew that an ability to speak French was considered rather exotic in Rock Ferry.

'Your mother was quite upset. She said, "That makes me feel so guilty for leaving her here. She needs someone to come and teach her on a one-to-one basis. You must find her a teacher straight away."

'Micheline had no friend she could call upon to do this, and we had to ask an agency to find a qualified person. Grandpa interviewed one or two candidates, and he chose Mrs Esther Kerr. I think he felt sorry for her; I know I did. Her father had been English and he'd brought her French mother to live here.

Mrs Kerr had been brought up in England and was teaching French at the local convent school. Her circumstances were similar to your mother's, and that singled her out for him.

'She told us she was married at eighteen and a widow at twenty. Her husband was killed on the Somme. Her mother was now old and ill and Esther needed more income to take care of her.'

'I like her,' Aimee said.

'Yes, we thought it a very happy choice.'

Esther had been coming three times a week for all these years, and as a result, Aimee was bilingual. She brought her books by famous French writers that they read together and discussed. She took her to see any suitable French film that came to Liverpool, and exhibitions that had a French connection. It delighted Aimee that they could talk together and nobody knew what they were saying. French seemed like a secret language here in Rock Park.

Aimee was looking forward to her lesson this afternoon. It would be her very last lesson of the year, and just to think of the Christmas holidays starting tomorrow made her feel like singing. She took the Christmas present she'd made for Esther and put it on the schoolroom table in readiness, then set out to walk to the gates at the entrance of the park to meet her teacher.

Just inside the gates was a toll cottage, and Mrs Potts, the keeper's wife, waved to her from her garden, where she was picking sprouts. Bicycles and motor vehicles were not allowed to come into Rock Park without paying a toll, so the noises of the town were kept at a distance.

Esther Kerr was striding down the road towards her with a wide smile on her face, her skirt swinging and her auburn hair blowing in the breeze. She raised her hand in a wave as soon as she saw her, and Aimee went forward to meet her. '*Bonjour, ma petite.*' Esther swept her into a hug. '*Comment vas tu?*' Esther always seemed to bubble with fun and life. She was about the same age as Candida Rathbone, but she dressed more smartly and looked younger and happier.

Once back in the schoolroom, Aimee presented her with the Christmas present she'd spent the last month making. She had no fancy paper or ribbon, so she'd wrapped it in a sheet of Grandma's tissue paper, but it was still half visible through that.

'It looks exciting. Whatever can it be?' Esther laughed and pulled the tissue away. 'Is it a box?'

'Yes, to keep your handkerchiefs in.' Gramps had been about to throw away a wooden cigar box, and Aimee had covered it with shells she'd collected on the beach. Grandma had told her that shell work was a popular pastime in her youth, and she'd shown her how to glue them together in a pattern. Frankie had found her some varnish in his father's stable, and she'd put a light film of it over the whole box. She was pleased with her handiwork.

'I love it, it's beautiful, far too good for hankies.' Esther laughed again. 'I have a few treasured trinkets, some brooches and a bracelet. I'll keep them in it.'

In return, she brought out a gift-wrapped parcel from her bag. Aimee felt a surge of pleasure, 'Can I open it now, or shall I keep it for Christmas Day?'

'Now,' Esther said. 'You won't be here on Christmas Day. I want to know if you like it.'

It was a big book about the current art scene in France, with lots of photographs. Of course, it was all in French. There was a paragraph or two about Micheline Durameau Lepage, and it showed some of her recent paintings. Aimee was absolutely thrilled and couldn't bring herself to close the pages. At four o'clock, when Esther left, she took the book to show Grandma. It was proof that her mother really was famous.

Walter Kendrick got out of bed feeling tired and worried. His financial responsibilities weighed heavily, both for his loved ones and for his workforce. He wanted to do his best for everybody, but he was very much afraid he was heading for big trouble. The war had brought prosperity to many industries, including his, and 1920 had started as a boom year, with mills being sold for enormous prices, but by the autumn, everything had collapsed. India was a major customer for finished products but the Indian government had imposed an eleven per cent tax on cotton imports to protect its own industry. Since then the tax had increased year by year, and in England hundreds of mills had closed down, causing unemployment to soar. Soon there were thousands of empty houses and shops in Liverpool, and the slump spread across the country and then around the world. The financial crisis brought a National Government to power in Britain, but as far as Walter could see, it wasn't going to solve anything

During the war, obtaining raw cotton had provided him with a huge headache, and there were major problems in the spinning mills and weaving sheds, where the machines they used had become old-fashioned and inefficient. The business he'd inherited was split between the original site in Rochdale and the mill in Liverpool where they dyed and finished the fabric so it could be sold to make clothes and household items such as curtains and cushions.

The fact that it was in two separate parts made it twice as difficult to manage. He made just enough profit from dyeing and finishing to subsidise the spinning and weaving and keep his business afloat. He'd seen it losing profitability over the years and he couldn't blame it all on the economy. He was getting old and could no longer infuse his staff with enthusiasm and drive. If Alec had survived, he'd have been running it by now.

Back in the early twenties, a relative of Prue's called Neville Sanderson had turned up at the office and introduced himself. He said he was on the point of sitting his accountancy exams and was looking for a career in industry, and it had seemed a good idea at the time to take him on in place of Alec and train him up for management. It was a decision Walter had regretted. What he'd needed then, and still did, was a reliable man to run the business, but Neville had been a disappointment.

Another decision he regretted was being persuaded by Prudence to live at Fairholme, her family home in Rock Park, when they married. Being closer to his factory would have saved him all the hours he'd had to spend travelling back and forth.

Now Christmas was almost on them and was bringing other stresses. At this time of the year he always took Aimee over to the mill to choose a couple of dress lengths for Micheline. He'd been taking her since she'd been about eight and had started asking him about his business. When she was small he'd had to ask Candida to come too, to keep an eye on her and take her home when she'd had enough, but she'd always enjoyed choosing material for her mother.

He went down to breakfast to hear Aimee sigh with pleasure. 'Gramps, it's the first day of my Christmas holiday, and going to the mill is a lovely outing to start it.'

Walter was somewhat put out to hear Prudence say, 'I really think I should take Aimee to Liverpool today instead. It's so lazy of us to keep taking Micheline the same thing, and it's such a mean present. Rather cheap-looking cotton.' Walter didn't like her disparaging his products. In any case, he always took care to guide Aimee to the most expensive fabrics. 'Micheline has made a success of her life, Walter; her living standards are higher than ours. She wears gowns made in Paris by top designers. Her parties are extravagant affairs.' Walter liked that even less. 'Both Aimee and I need new clothes; we have nothing to wear for Micheline's Christmas celebrations, and it's time I started to pack.'

His spirits dropped further, and he couldn't help but notice that Aimee was hanging on Prue's every word. Of course she'd welcome new clothes; what teenager wouldn't?

But she said, 'Maman always seems pleased with what we take. She showed me some of the clothes she's had made from the fabric, blouses and dresses. She said they were lovely, and that she wears them a lot.'

'To the beach, I expect, on her summer holidays. Walter, we can't go to France and look like poor relations. Micheline is always so smart.'

'Couldn't you have got your dressmaker to run up some party dresses?' he asked.

'From your fabrics?' Her indignant tone let him know how she felt about that. 'Cotton would be quite unsuitable.'

'But it would suit Aimee. I have some pretty flower prints.'

21

'Absolutely not, not warm enough at this time of year. Bunney's were advertising velvet party dresses in the *Echo* last night. They looked exactly right for Aimee, and I'd find something to suit me there too.'

He didn't like Prudence spending more money than was absolutely necessary. The cost of Christmas was always prohibitive, what with train and ferry fares and presents for everyone. He said, 'The shops will be crowded now; you should have done that weeks ago.'

'Walter, I have very little time to do anything, as you very well know.'

'Only too well,' he sighed. Prudence was always fussing about her present shortage of domestic help, and the necessity for her to do housework herself. 'Never before have I been reduced to one girl, and though Dora is quite a good cook, she's absolutely no good at cleaning. She doesn't notice dirt. This is a big house, Walter, and I'm run off my feet. It needs more maintenance too; it's looking downright shabby, and the back door is almost off its hinges. I'm quite ashamed to say I live here.'

Walter snorted with impatience. Once they'd had a proper housemaid, a full-time gardener and a cook, but he was not sympathetic. He thought Prue had little enough to fill her day.

At that moment Dora, their maid, came in. Prue referred to her as a hopeless teenager, but actually she was over thirty and an experienced cook. 'A telegram, sir,' she said. 'The boy is waiting. He wants to know if there's an answer.'

Walter frowned at the yellow envelope and tore it open. It was in French. It took him desperate moments to work out the gist of the message. The words *Micheline* and *morte* leapt out at him and made him gasp. 'Oh my God,' he said, and looked wildly round at Aimee. It seemed her mother had been killed in a road accident last night, and details of her funeral would follow.

'Whatever is it?' Prudence asked petulantly. 'Who is it from?'

'Armand Duchamp,' he muttered.

'Please,' Dora asked, 'do you want to send a reply? The lad is waiting.'

'No,' he told her. He'd need time to think, and could send it from the office.

Prudence stood up and reached across the table to twitch the telegram from his fingers. 'I do wish they'd use English,' she complained irritably, and handed it to Aimee. 'What do they want?'

'Grandma!' she screamed. 'Maman has been killed.'

Walter was already up and round the table to throw his arms round his granddaughter in a consoling hug.

CHAPTER FOUR

P RUDENCE KEPT SAYING, 'WHAT a terrible shock. I don't suppose we'll be going to France for Christmas now?'

Walter was trying to comfort Aimee, who was sobbing against his shoulder. 'Of course not. Perhaps later, for the funeral.'

'What am I going to do?' Prudence wailed. 'I've told Dora she can have four days' holiday over Christmas, and I've done no shopping. No preparations at all. I'll have to ask her to take it some other time.'

'No, Prue, you can't do that; she's thrilled to be able to spend Christmas with her mother. You'd better go shopping this morning and order a turkey or something.'

'Oh, what a shock! How am I going to manage? We haven't been here for Christmas for years. Oh dear! I'll have to lie down for half an hour before I can do anything.'

'We'll cope, Prue, don't worry. Aimee, go and put your coat on. We need to catch the next ferry if we're going to the mill.'

'There's no point in Aimee going with you,' Prudence said. 'She won't need to choose gifts for her mother now.'

'She'll be better off with me,' Walter said firmly. 'Come on, Aimee, get yourself ready.' He pushed her towards the stairs. 'We'll be able to talk about this on the way over.'

The ferry was tying up, so he had to hurry her to the ticket office, but everybody knew him, and they'd hold the boat up for him. Poor Aimee couldn't stop crying; even on the ferry, the cold breeze in her face didn't do the trick. She probably didn't realise it yet, but her mother's death was going to make a huge difference to her life. He hoped Micheline had remembered her in her will. She was going to need it.

It was starting to rain. 'Shall we go and shelter in the saloon?' he asked. There was a steady stream of passengers heading in that direction.

'I'd rather stay here.' Aimee turned her face into the rain and let the cooling drops run down her cheeks. 'Will we be going to Maman's funeral, Gramps?'

'Yes, but that will probably be after Christmas now.'

'It won't be a happy Christmas this year, will it? Grandma is very upset.'

'So am I.' Walter sighed. 'Your mother was young and healthy. She still had half her life in front of her, and she was making such a success of it.'

This was another of life's cruel tricks. When Alec had died, he'd thought it a bitter blow. He'd expected in time to hand on the business to his son, but retirement wasn't an option now, and he was over seventy. He had to carry on; he knew no other way to earn the income he needed to support his family.

All those years ago he'd been very much against Micheline leaving Aimee with them in England. Even then he didn't feel he could afford to support another dependant.

To have Micheline cut down in her prime was too cruel.

* * *

Aimee clung to Walter's arm as they walked from the Pier Head to the train. The mill was on the outskirts of the city. She looked sad, but she had her tears under control now. 'I wish I knew more about my parents,' she said. 'All I know of them is in those pencil drawings in the dining room.'

'Your grandma never stops talking about your mother, and you've spent more time with her than we have, so you probably know her better than we do.'

'Yes, but I know nothing about my father.'

'You took over all the books and toys that survived his childhood; and Grandma must have shown you the photos she has of him?'

'Yes, but it's a bit unusual to have a French mother and an English father, isn't it?' Aimee said. 'I don't know much about how that came about.'

'We told you, your father was injured while fighting in France during the war, and we didn't know what had happened to him.'

'Yes, he was missing for sixteen months and that's when they got married, but I know only the bare bones of it. A lot more must have happened to him.'

Walter nodded thoughtfully. Sixteen months had always seemed a very long time to be missing, particularly as Alec had turned up fully recovered, a married man with a baby on the way. He sometimes wondered why it had taken so long. Had he found joy and happiness with Micheline and been unable to tear himself away from her? Surely he must have felt guilty at staying away from the fighting for so long? 'I think of your father as a hero who gave his life for his country,' he said eventually.

'So do I, but . . . Please, Gramps, tell me more about him. What did he do before he went to France? What was he like as a person?'

'He was working in the mill with me, I was teaching him the business, but once war was inevitable, he volunteered to fight. I expected it of him, though his mother tried to dissuade him. He did some months of training and then he was sent to France to join the British Expeditionary Force as a newly appointed second lieutenant. He was writing to us regularly and we knew he'd be involved in the fighting near Arras. He was just twenty-three years old when we heard he'd been posted as missing, believed killed. I don't think he'd been in action more than once or twice before it happened.'

Walter sighed. 'That was a dreadful time. Grandma refused to believe he was dead, though I'd given up all hope.' He blew his nose. He didn't find it easy to talk about Alec's time in the army, but he had to tell Aimee all he could about him.

She felt for his hand. 'Then you received those two pencil portraits through the post?'

'Yes, and also a long letter with the first news of what he'd been through. You can imagine how relieved and thrilled we were to know he was alive. By then he was recovering from his injuries and had married Micheline, and you were on the way.'

'How romantic,' Aimee sighed. 'Maman saved him and nursed him back to health.'

'Yes, but then he was killed just before the war ended.' That had been the end of all hope.

'That must have been dreadful for Maman.'

'Dreadful for all of us. I'll give you his letters to read when we get home; there are also some pages torn from his diary, which will tell you what he endured. Now, when we get to the mill, let's try to forget our bad news and put on a brave face. The workers will all be cheerful and looking forward to Christmas. Why don't you choose a dress length for yourself while you're here? I have some fairly heavy fabrics in dark shades, both stripes and florals; they'd make up into a smart dress for you.'

Aimee did her best, but knowing that Maman was dead and she'd never see her again cast a ghastly blight over everything. People had thought it odd that her mother lived in a different country and she didn't see much of her, and now Aimee's conscience pricked her; she could have written to her more often. How she wished she had now.

She walked to school with Lydia Greening most mornings and had often wished for a normal family like hers. The Greenings were neighbours and lived at Pendlebury, a house with a good river view; a position much envied by Grandma. Lydia's father was a doctor and her mother had been a nurse but now kept house for them all. Lydia had an older brother and sister. Grandma thought they were the cream of Rock Park society because they had a car and Jeremy Greening was sent away to boarding school.

Aimee had learned a great deal from Lydia; she'd heard in minute detail all about her boyfriends and those of her sister Emily, who was two years older. The girls in her form at school considered romance very important, and Lydia was able to instruct her in the sort of boy she should choose for a husband. She'd also learned a lot about the monthly curse and having babies, which was a good thing because she had nobody else to tell her, but all the same, there were times when she was glad that she wasn't like Lydia Greening after all.

If Lydia came round, Grandma welcomed her into the house while doing her best to exclude Frankie, though Aimee had told her she had more in common with him. Lydia sided with Grandma; she didn't like Frankie either. 'He's not our class, Aimee, I don't know what you see in him.'

That night, Aimee got into bed to read the pages of her father's diary that her grandpa had dug out for her. They were crumpled and yellowing; they looked as though they'd been handled and read often. It was the first time she'd seen her father's handwriting, and she felt she was entering his world and would soon get to know him. She began to read:

I was shocked to find on the day I arrived at the front that headquarters was planning to mount the first major offensive of the war. I wish I knew more about army life and what is expected of me; nothing has prepared me for this. I found I was in charge of thirty or so men and it was my duty to lead them and give them orders. They all looked frightened at the prospect, which to say the least put me into a state of trepidation.

Before dawn the next morning the enemy lines were bombarded by our heavy guns, and the noise and the explosions hurt my ears. The enemy were firing back and the thought of leading my troop over the top and across no-man's-land put ice in my stomach. I knew I'd have to do my best to hide the terror I felt as missiles exploded all round us. When the order came for me to lead them towards the enemy trenches, I had to grit my teeth and get on with it.

We were massed in one storming herd and succeeded in taking the first line of enemy trenches, and then the second, and even held them for a time, and we were filled with pride that we had been successful.

But the enemy rallied and fought back and the offensive was halted. My next order was to withdraw my men to our previous line. I was doing that when I felt the shock of a bullet shattering my right thigh. I fell and thought it was all over for me. I must have fainted, because I next became aware of hideous pain in my leg and my sergeant pulling me into a shallow shell hole while gunfire burst all round us. I must have passed out again because it was dark when I heard him speak again. 'It all seems quiet now, sir, we'd better move from here and find a better place to shelter.'

I was in agony and my strength was gone. I sensed the sergeant was lifting his head to peer round to make sure it was safe. Suddenly a single shot rang out and he fell back on top of me. I stared at him in horror and disbelief. There was a bullet hole in the side of his head; he'd been shot by a sniper. I knew then that I was on my own. Paralysed with fear, I felt my own life must be near its end too.

I don't know how long I stayed with my face burrowing into the mud of France, because it was daylight again and the gunfire had ceased. My trousers were torn and wet with blood; I thought then that my problem was more than just a bullet in my leg. I tried to get to my feet but I couldn't; the best that could be said of me was that I was still alive.

The grey light of dawn showed a bleak landscape of broken trees and churned-up earth with all the detritus of battle half buried in it: here a length of gleaming barbed wire, there a boot and a British helmet. I had pushed myself away from my dead sergeant, but he wasn't the only one; I could see another body not far away. I felt I had to get away from there. There were distant sporadic bursts of gunfire and I had no idea where I was or which way I needed to go to reach the British lines. If I got it wrong, I'd end up in German hands and I couldn't expect any help from them.

Over to the west there seemed to be the remains of what had once been a farm, though precious little of it remained: just a collection of half-demolished walls. I started to drag myself towards them. I found it hard going. I managed to pull myself to my feet against a shattered tree and tottered on, but almost tripped over a dead cow. I was sure now the place had been a farm. It was starting to rain again and I felt exhausted and vulnerable. I was desperately in need of help and longed to see a roof where I might shelter.

Once on the other side of the wall, I saw an open cart with a tired old nag harnessed to the shafts. There was all manner of bric-a-brac on the cart, old clothes and bedding too. What I wanted to do was to climb up and hide myself amongst it, but though I tried, I couldn't summon the strength and slid back to the ground. I was lying there gasping when I heard voices and footsteps approaching from the other side of the wall.

A man and a woman were standing over me speaking in French. I'd never been any good at languages but I recognised the word '*anglais*'. The next minute they'd hoisted me onto the cart and made me comfortable on the piles of clothes. I showed them my leg, and heard the word '*docteur*', and hoped I was about to get the help I needed.

They covered me against the rain and the cart started to move. There was no spring in it; the jolting caused an excruciating pain in my leg, but I thanked God for the help I was getting.

Aimee's face was wet with tears as she slid the pages onto her bedside table. She wished she'd known her father; she longed to know what had happened after that, and how he'd met her mother.

The next day, she pleaded with Gramps to tell her what else he knew.

'Only what Alec told me,' he said. He opened the atlas on the desk in his study. 'This is the area in France where the fighting took place, but Micheline's home was in the Dordogne, which is down here. She was at art school in Paris when the war broke out.'

'Miles away,' Aimee said; she'd already studied the maps.

'You've heard of Nurse Edith Cavell?'

'Yes, she was shot by the Germans for caring for and helping to repatriate Allied soldiers.'

'Apparently many were injured in battle and trapped behind enemy lines, and she was part of an organisation set up to help them. She was very brave. Alec said he was picked up by French civilians and moved out of the area by the same organisation. He was taken to a clinic in Paris, where he had some pieces of shrapnel and a bullet removed from his buttock and a further bullet removed from his thigh. He was cared for by young students in the attic of a school; Micheline was one of them.

'After a few weeks, she took him to her home in the Dordogne, where her mother helped her look after him and nurse him back to health. It seemed the whole family belonged to that organisation and thought it was their duty to do what they could.'

Aimee asked Grandma what she knew about it, and she said, 'He should never have gone to France in the first place. He should have stayed at home and helped Walter in the mill.'

CHAPTER FIVE

THAT SAME MORNING, CANDIDA Rathbone was making poached egg on toast for her breakfast when she heard the front doorbell. It was an unpleasant surprise to see the telegraph boy. Everybody knew they usually brought bad news. She tore open the telegram he handed her.

'Oh my God,' she said aloud. 'No answer, thank you.' She couldn't get the door closed quickly enough. She felt as though she'd been physically kicked. Her mind had been full of getting her suitcase down from the top of her wardrobe and packing for the visit to see Micheline. She found it almost impossible to believe her friend was dead.

She pulled out a chair; the tears came as she sank down to rest her head on the kitchen table. This was a disaster. Oh heavens, she was going to miss Micheline. She'd been her best friend since their student days, and was currently her benefactor. In the present slump, nobody could afford art lessons. Who would pay her now to teach Aimee and Frankie? She wept for the Christmas visit to France that wouldn't now be happening. She wept with disappointment at the loss of all her hopes. What was she going to do now?

Her family had come from Hungary and settled in Birkenhead before she was born. Her father had decreed that henceforward they'd go by the name of Rathbone, that of a prominent Liverpool family. Their passports and documents with their old name on were locked in a drawer in his bedroom and forgotten.

Her mother had died in the flu epidemic that had swept the world after the Great War. Candida had wept with her father. 'We shall both miss her,' he'd said, 'but we'll have to manage without her.'

Her father had been a gifted painter in watercolours and oils, and throughout his life, painting gave him pleasure, but he'd been unable to gain recognition. If his pictures sold at all, it was for very little. In his youth, he'd gained admission to a prestigious Manchester school of art, but he'd failed to pass the final diploma. In the opinion of his tutors, his work lacked both technical ability and originality.

He'd got on well with his fellow pupils, but not with his tutors. They thought him a foreigner trying to be English, not the right type to be an artist. He tried harder and lost his accent. Perhaps he had been argumentative with them, but to deny him the diploma was grossly unfair; it prevented him getting a teaching post, and gave him no hope that a museum would hire him to do restoration work.

It left him with a grievance, eking out a living on the edge of the art world with an occasional job designing postcards, advertising posters and suchlike, until he found permanent work in an art gallery in Manchester. He was always developing new ideas to expand the business, which made him popular with his boss. He carried on painting while he gained a wider knowledge of the art world, and at last his work began to sell. Eventually he set up a gallery of his own in Liverpool.

He'd encouraged Candida to paint from an early age. She'd attended an art school in Liverpool, but the following year her father had taken on a partner and together they were planning to open a gallery in Paris. He resented the London art world that had belittled his efforts and wanted Candida to come to Paris with him. He told her she had more natural talent than he had and it would be a shame not to carry on and get the best training possible. He urged her to apply to the École des Beaux-Arts in Paris, which was situated almost opposite the Louvre, but she was nervous about her command of the French language. She did have a School Certificate in French, but was fearful she wouldn't understand the spoken word.

She was thrilled and proud when she gained a place there. On the first day she met Micheline, who was considered an outstanding pupil and had been given a bursary to fund her three years' study. They were both boiling with ambition to make their mark as painters. It was from Micheline that Candida gained a grasp of the language. She was the younger by two or three years, and her father provided her with a generous allowance. Micheline was already a widow and coping in Paris on very little money. Candida suggested she share the apartment her father had rented for her, and they became great friends.

In the holidays, Micheline took her to stay with her mother in a village in the Dordogne called Dignac. Her father had been in the French army and had been killed in the war. Their home was a centuries-old farmhouse set in lovely rolling countryside. To Candida it seemed to be in a dilapidated state, and very remote, but they were happy years and at the end of the course they both received their diplomas.

Over the following years, she watched Micheline's career take off, while her own pictures were passed over. It seemed she was sharing her father's fate. She was disappointed, of course, but she went to work for him and helped run his galleries. She was kept busy and fully occupied in the art world and she thoroughly enjoyed it. Her father was providing her with the trappings of success.

It was ten more years before he began to experience problems. For a long time Candida thought he'd been defrauded by his French partner, and even now she couldn't quite believe he'd done the things he was accused of, but after a catastrophic summer, he'd ended up in prison in Liverpool, and two months later he had a major stroke and died.

Two days later, there was another telegram for Gramps. 'Micheline's funeral will take place on the second of January,' he said, 'and Armand has invited us to come over and stay in the house.'

Aimee heard later the same day that Candida would be travelling out with them, but Armand had booked her into the hotel in the village.

Aimee couldn't stop thinking about Maman and was afraid that Christmas this year was going to be an unhappy one. Grandma never stopped complaining about having all the Christmas preparations dumped on her at short notice, though Aimee did all she could to help her. Frankie took her shopping and pointed out the best places to buy a Christmas cake and mince pies, and Gramps brought home a duck for their dinner. Aimee cooked it after looking up the recipe in a cookery book, and it turned out better than she'd expected, but none of them was in the mood to enjoy anything.

'I've never been to a funeral before,' she told Frankie. 'I'm not looking forward to going to France this time either.'

He was sympathetic and brought her some sprigs of holly with plenty of berries. 'To make your place look Christmassy,' he said. 'I picked it in the garden of number five. They won't mind, Dad and I do what's needed to keep the place looking nice.'

Aimee had made the journey to the Dordogne many times before, but this time everything felt different. They crossed on the night ferry and caught the early-morning train to Angoulême. France was grey and freezing cold, colder than England. Gramps was hunched silently in his overcoat; Grandma needed help with everything. Miss Rathbone shepherded them all in the right direction and found porters to help with the luggage. Aimee was glad to have her company.

Armand Duchamp brought his car to the station to meet them; he towered over Grandpa, held his head high and walked with a proud swagger. 'Aimee, welcome. A sad time, *ma petite*, a sad time for us all.' Cool and distant, he shook hands with everybody.

Aimee thought him handsome in a very French way. He came from the south of France and looked permanently suntanned. She'd never felt entirely at ease in his company, had never been close to him, although he'd been her stepfather for six years now. He'd told her to call him Papa, but she couldn't bring herself to do that. Her father had been Alec Kendrick, and nobody could take his place.

Armand earned his living in the art world with a gallery in

Paris. Aimee knew that Candida had kept in touch with her mother, and visited regularly; she sensed immediately that she disliked Armand. He stopped the car outside the hotel in Dignac, unstrapped her suitcase and dumped it on the pavement in an off-hand manner.

'You haven't told us about the funeral arrangements yet,' Candida said, picking it up. 'Where will it be, and at what time?'

'You'd better come to dinner tonight,' he told her ungraciously. 'We can go into all that then.'

Aimee sensed that he didn't much like Candida either.

Candida smouldered as she climbed the steps to the front door of the hotel with her suitcase. Micheline had met Armand in Paris while she was having her pictures hung and was being feted as a great success. His good looks and toothbrush moustache had attracted her, and it was no time at all before she was deeply in love with him and talking of marriage.

From that day, Candida had had to hide her resentment of Armand. She felt he'd come between her and Micheline and pushed them apart. When she'd visited them at La Coutancie and they'd taken her out on expeditions to paint the historic buildings in Angoulême or the local vineyards, he'd set himself up as an art expert and found fault with anything she did, while praising Micheline's work. She thought he disliked her because she'd been Micheline's confidante and friend for so much longer than he had.

The Auberge le Vieux Logis in Dignac was old fashioned and built to withstand the summer heat. The stone floors were uncomfortably cold, but Candida was tired after the journey and climbed up onto the high bed to rest. For years after she'd finished her art course she'd continued to struggle at her easel, but none of her paintings were acclaimed and few achieved a sale. Her tutors had said she produced work of high technical ability but that it lacked richness and quality. Others said she had yet to find her style.

It had taken her years to accept that they could be right.

CHAPTER SIX

SINCE THEY'D DROPPED CANDIDA, Aimee had been craning her neck to catch her first glimpse of La Coutancie. When at last Armand pulled up in front of the house, it seemed at once familiar and yet strange to be here without Maman. Half of her expected to see Micheline come bursting through the door to throw her arms round her, and yet she knew that wasn't possible.

Micheline had added a vast extension to the old farmhouse and it was now a large, elegant and comfortable home. It was set in a huge garden, which looked neat and tidy even at this time of the year, and as though no expense had been spared on it. Armand had more domestic help than Grandma had at home. Francine, his housekeeper, had worked for Micheline for years. She knew Aimee and her grandparents, and greeted them more warmly than Armand had. She showed Aimee to her usual bedroom.

Aimee had that strange feeling again that she'd been split into two very different people. Here she was Aimee and lived in a rather grand house, while in England her friends called her Amy and her home had become rather shabby. Life in each place was completely different: it was tea in England and coffee here, and Grandma complained to everyone that French food was far too rich and gave her indigestion. Aimee had felt perfectly at home in both places, but without Maman, everything was different. As soon as she closed the door of her room, tears scalded her eyes.

At dinner that night, Armand said, 'The funeral is to be private. Micheline would not like a lot of fuss, I have not invited anyone from Paris; it's just for family and close friends. She's here in a spare bedroom – you'll want to see her, won't you, Aimee, to say your final farewell?'

Aimee wasn't sure – she'd never seen a dead person before – but when the meal was over, he took them all upstairs. Gramps felt for her hand as they went into the room. There were chrysanthemums of every colour massed in vases, and their sharp, fresh scent was almost overpowering.

Maman was lying at rest in an open coffin set on a stand. Aimee hardly dared to look, but Gramps was urging her gently forward. When she opened her eyes to peep, Maman looked as though she'd just fallen asleep. She was wearing a high-necked cambric nightgown and looked even prettier than she remembered.

The afternoon of the funeral turned out colder and greyer than ever. Aimee shivered and everybody was subdued. The folk from the villages and farms around had turned out en masse, and crammed the little church in Dignac. The service dragged on interminably, and she felt so cold she had trouble stopping her teeth from chattering. Gramps sat next to her holding her hand, passing her peppermints and once his own handkerchief.

At last the congregation was led out to the graveyard. She'd seen it before, of course, but it had always seemed an alien place, so very different from the peace of English graveyards. It was paved all over, and many of the graves were like little stone houses, faced with fancy marble. Even the ordinary families of the village had them, and all were designed for multiple occupancy. Several displayed photographs and other memorabilia, as well as the names and details of the occupants.

Maman was laid to rest in one of the little houses, her family grave. Last night, Armand had spoken of having a miniature wrought-iron easel made to decorate it. There were chrysanthemums galore in the churchyard too, and Grandma said several times she thought it was all very nice but she preferred the simple headstones in England. Grandma had taken Aimee to church every Sunday throughout her childhood, though occasionally she pleaded to stay at home with Gramps, who didn't care much for organised religion. 'God helps those who help themselves,' he would often say.

Afterwards, they were driven to the hotel in Dignac, where refreshments, mostly alcoholic, were served to all. Aimee thought everybody was more relaxed now the funeral was over, and was surprised that they didn't talk more about Maman. Grandma had a headache and wanted to lie down, and as she had to be driven back to the house, Aimee was persuaded to go with her.

Walter was glad to see them go. Armand's tongue had loosened a little with the drink and he didn't want Aimee to hear this.

'Micheline's first husband was a nervous wreck,' the Frenchman was saying. 'Her team was trying to help him get safely across the German line so he could rejoin his unit and fight on, but she had to nurse him here for sixteen months before she could persuade him to leave.'

'He was my son,' Walter reminded him fiercely, 'and he'd been badly injured in the battle in Arras.'

'Yes, his first taste of war,' Armand said. 'It took only one day.'

Candida came to Walter's side. 'I think Alec was very brave.'

Armand was in a black mood. 'Micheline had to do everything for him for many months, prop him up through everything. He took up a great deal of everyone's time and never achieved much.'

'He didn't have much time,' Candida said furiously. 'His life was cut short.'

'It's your country,' Walter added bitterly. 'Did you fight for it?'

'Of course,' Armand said haughtily, taking another gulp of brandy from his glass and turning away. 'I did my duty and fought throughout.'

'A pig of a man,' Candida said. 'I could never see what Micheline saw in him.'

Walter didn't like him either after that, but he said slowly, 'I have sometimes wondered why it took Alec so long to come home.'

'He was brave,' Candida insisted. 'I was very fond of him.'

Walter had wanted to ask Armand about Micheline's will since they'd arrived, but he hadn't wanted to upset him. Now he didn't feel he needed to take account of his feelings. At dinner he found himself seated opposite the Frenchman at the small table. 'If I might take this opportunity, Armand, I would like to ask if Micheline made any arrangements for Aimee's future in her will.'

'I'm not sure.'

'I can't believe she hasn't.' Walter was not going to be stalled on this. 'I'd like to know more before we leave. It's so much harder to get to the bottom of anything once we go home.'

'I'd like to refresh my memory too,' Armand said shortly. 'I'll try to fix an appointment with her *notaire* tomorrow.'

The sun shone the next morning, and though the air was cold, Aimee found that the Dordogne sun brought cheery golden warmth. At lunch Armand announced, 'We can all go in to Angoulême to see the *notaire* this afternoon. He will explain Micheline's wishes as set out in her will.'

When they gathered at the door at the appointed time, Armand looked at Aimee and said, 'Aimee, there's no real need for you to come. You probably won't understand it anyway.'

She was indignant. 'Of course I will.'

She saw Walter bristle as he helped Grandma onto the back seat. 'It does concern her more than any of us.'

Aimee said, 'I'm no longer a child, Armand.'

He replied tersely. 'Micheline drew up this will when we married. You were still quite young and she wanted to make provision for your care. You're not yet of age, and I know your mother appointed trustees to act on your behalf until you are.'

Aimee had given little thought to her mother's will up to

now, but everybody else seemed greedily concerned about it. It didn't make for a pleasant atmosphere on the journey.

They'd driven some distance when Armand said, 'This is where Micheline had her accident, on the next corner. She went into town from time to time and was coming home when a thunderstorm blew up.'

Aimee froze in her seat. She'd heard about the accident, but to see the actual place was chilling.

The road was narrow and winding, nothing more than a lane, and the corner acute. A little further along she saw the broken hedge and deep skid marks on the torn-up verge. 'It was raining torrentially at the time,' Armand told them. 'She ran into the back of a lorry taking produce to the market. The driver said he'd had to stop because he couldn't see where he was going. She turned the car over into that field.'

Aimee heard Grandma's sharp intake of breath and heard her murmur, 'He might have spared us that.'

The *notaire*'s office was dark and forbidding, with books and documents stacked everywhere. The four of them were seated with some formality in a line in front of his large desk. Aimee had to concentrate on what he was saying. He explained that Armand was to receive the money in Micheline's bank accounts and all her investments, together with the house known as La Coutancie. 'We none of us will be able to have anything yet until the will is settled,' Armand said.

Aimee understood that she was to inherit her mother's art collection, all her paintings and working materials, and any other of her personal possessions that she wanted. Gramps and Armand had been appointed executors, and were also to act as her guardians and trustees. They would hold her inheritance in trust until she reached the age of twenty-one.

'You will be able to have all her art materials as soon as probate is granted,' Gramps told her. 'It's only the more valuable things that Armand and I will control until you are of age.'

Aimee was more than pleased; over the years, her mother had mixed with and admired the work of many other artists. She'd collected some of their paintings and had hung them on the walls at La Coutancie, happily discussing them with her daughter.

When they arrived home, Aimee wandered into Maman's studio. She sat down and gazed round. Everything prompted memories of her mother; she felt closer to her here. Propped on an easel was the half-finished picture Micheline had been working on before she died. Aimee spent time studying it and thought about how it might have looked if she'd finished it. It was to be a café scene in Angoulême, with tables on the pavement and medieval stone buildings in the background, a study in brilliant light and deepest shade from the baking Dordogne summer sun. She would keep it always in its unfinished state as a memento of Maman.

There were masses of canvases propped against the wall; Aimee looked through them. Some were Maman's work, possibly her planning for larger works. Aimee found a few she remembered painting herself on earlier visits, and recognised one of her first attempts in oils. Maman had suggested how she might improve it, and she'd meant to have another try, but not now.

There were dozens of paintbrushes of every sort, along with

drawing tools, sets of markers, pastels, watercolours and oil paints, used and new, all of professional quality. Aimee had craved more and better materials, but with all these she'd have so much she'd be able to give some to Frankie. She knew he'd make use of them and treasure them as much as she was going to. She was excited about her inheritance and ran downstairs to look again at the pictures that would one day be hers. Maman had spoken of them many times.

Her grandparents came down and she took them round the hall and dining room, proud to show off her knowledge. 'This is a Marc Chagall, and so is this,' she said. 'An André Masson here, and I love this Edgar Degas, that's my favourite.'

'I've heard of him,' Grandma said. 'Are you sure they're not just prints?'

'Quite sure. Prints are all flat, but look at the brushstrokes here; you can see the paint standing out. An original oil painting has texture.'

Candida had been invited to join them for dinner, and in the sitting room with a drink in her hand she pointed out a Pierre-Auguste Renoir. 'You're a very lucky girl to have that,' she told Aimee.

'I know. I can hardly believe it.'

'I'm very impressed,' Walter said. 'I had no idea the pictures we've seen here were painted by such famous artists.'

'A very valuable collection,' Armand said. 'The house will look bare when they go.'

'Still,' Walter said. 'Micheline has not forgotten you. This is a lovely house.'

'Yes, Micheline was brought up here and has extended the house over the years. It suited her. The peace and quiet of the countryside helped her to concentrate on her painting, but in this district it won't command a great price, and it's a long way from my work.'

Aimee thought he didn't seem all that grateful. 'You have a home in Paris too,' she reminded him.

'Yes, a small flat.'

'You aren't thinking of selling this?' Grandma sounded shocked.

'I might have to. The upkeep is expensive.'

'But you have her wealth too,' Candida burst out.

'Micheline lived extravagantly,' he said coldly. 'Her pictures sold for high prices but she spent a lot. There's not much left. Look at her choice of art.'

Aimee could feel Candida's envy like a mountainous black cloud. Her gaze went to the Renoir hanging over the fireplace. It was not a picture that demanded attention when you came to warm your hands at the blaze. Not an original subject either; it was a still life of a large bunch of overblown roses in a pink and white vase.

'Not his usual party scene,' Candida murmured, 'but every brushstroke is technically perfect.'

'It would look very nice in our sitting room at home,' Aimee said, still marvelling that Maman was passing on so much to her.

'You will have some time to wait before you can take anything home,' Armand reminded her. 'The *notaire* must have time to settle her debts and taxes.'

'How long will that take?' she demanded.

He shrugged. 'I don't know; six months or so, I expect.' He was silent for a moment. 'Walter, when the time comes, I could sell them for you if you wish. My gallery in Paris is the right place to do it.'

'No,' Aimee said. 'I want to keep them.'

Francine came to tell them dinner was ready, and they all stood up. 'We'll have to see,' Gramps said slowly.

CHAPTER SEVEN

C ANDIDA'S GRIEF AT MICHELINE'S death was tempered by worry on her own account. She'd had several sleepless nights knowing her only source of income had died with her friend. She'd hoped and prayed that Micheline might leave her a small legacy in her will, but she hadn't.

Over the last few years, she'd applied for every teaching post she'd seen advertised, but so far she'd had no success. She was toying with the idea of trying any sort of work; she could run an art gallery, or even a shop, though she knew the competition for jobs like that would be just as fierce. In the meantime, she was economising as much as she could.

She believed Walter Kendrick was the sort of person who could always find money for the things he wanted, and had to hope that he would want her to continue teaching Aimee, but she'd felt she couldn't broach that subject while the funeral was hanging over them. At least Aimee had benefited from the will and would possibly be allowed some funds of her own. She loved painting, but there'd been some mention that as she would be sitting her School Certificate in the summer, it might be better to stop the art lessons to give her more time for revision. Candida was hoping she'd want to continue.

So much hung on that, and she'd worried about it for so

long that her nerves were getting frayed, but she knew the journey home this morning would give her the chance to speak to the Kendricks about it. She primed herself to do it as soon as Armand put them on the train at Angoulême.

Prudence liked to play the grand old lady, and fussed about everything. It was absolutely essential that she have a window seat and travel with her back to the engine, so Candida ran along the platform to find them an empty carriage. Even so, it took Prudence some time to settle into her seat.

When she saw her open her magazine, Candida started with the sentence she'd prepared. 'There's a matter of business I'd like to discuss with you,' she said, letting her gaze drift slowly round the family. 'Micheline always paid me a term in advance and was due to pay me again. I have to ask whether you want me to continue with the lessons.'

Her gaze settled on Walter as he said, 'I still feel a little dazed by the change in Aimee's fortunes.'

'Just pictures and the materials for her to paint more,' Prudence scoffed. 'I'm not sure those will be much help. The house is lovely; I was hoping she'd inherit that. It would sell easily, I'm sure.'

Candida smiled at her. Poor Prudence, she lived in a world of her own. 'Some of those pictures are quite valuable,' she informed them. 'They're by the foremost painters of the twentieth century. Even one would . . . Think of that vase of flowers by Renoir . . .'

'In class you listed Renoir as nineteenth century,' Aimee laughed. 'I remember his dates, 1841 to 1919.'

'So I did,' Candida admitted. 'Well done.'

'Maman told me some of those pictures were given to her

by the artists themselves,' Aimee went on. 'I believe she was quite friendly with Marc Chagall.'

'How much would it be worth?' Prudence demanded. 'That flower picture by Renoir.'

'Well, I don't know exactly; it would have to be examined and assessed by experts in the trade. But a lot of money. Thousands.'

'You're sure?' Prudence was sitting up straighter.

'Positive.'

There was a stunned silence. 'Wow,' Aimee said. 'You mean I'll be able to afford anything I want?'

Walter's eyebrows had shot up. He shook his head and rubbed his face with both hands. 'Aimee, love, I'm delighted for you,' he said, 'and it's only right your mother has given thought to your future, but all that is far ahead. It'll be months before that painting is yours, and even then Armand and I will have to discuss what you can do with it. Goodness knows how long it will take to sell. For the moment, we must think about your school exams this summer. It's important that you do well in them. Would it be better to stop the art lessons for a few months?'

'Please, Gramps, I'd like to carry on. Frankie will too.' That was music to Candida's ears.

'Oh, Frankie!' Prudence said disparagingly. 'What does it matter what he wants?'

'Please, Gramps. I came top in English at the end of term. I'll be all right.'

'But you'll have little time to revise if you paint two evenings a week; and what about your French lessons?'

Grandma spoke sharply. 'We could stop Mrs Kerr coming

for a few months, if not for good. You already speak very good French, Aimee; your mother was pleased about that. You'll have no trouble with School Certificate French.'

'No,' Aimee protested, 'don't stop Esther. I really enjoy her lessons. She's a friend, good fun, and we're studying life in France. She's telling me about the history and the books, and we're doing it all in French. I still have a lot to learn.'

'Nonsense. You're bilingual now, and anyway, you won't be going to France so much in the future, will you?' The venom in Prudence's voice shocked Candida. Walter looked discomforted as his wife went on, 'Look what a career in art did for Micheline. It might be more important to you in the long run.'

'We don't know that yet.' Walter was clearly making an effort to stay calm. 'You can't do everything, Aimee; what about stopping lessons with Mrs Kerr until after your exams?'

'Will she even need to work at all if she's going to have all that money?'

'Don't be silly, Prue! Aimee will want to do something with her life.'

Aimee turned to Candida. 'Couldn't you come on Saturdays?'

Candida took a deep breath. 'What do you have in mind?' she asked. 'I mean . . .'

'All day,' Aimee said, thinking of what Frankie would want too, 'morning and afternoon. It'll give me a break from all that maths and stuff.'

Prudence said, 'We could give you lunch, Candida. Aimee's right, she'll need some relaxation.'

'In that case,' Walter said, 'I'll pay you on the same terms

Micheline did until Aimee can take over. We'll speak on the phone tomorrow when we've got over this journey.'

'Thank you.' Candida felt stressed to near breaking point, but at least that gave her one day's work a week. It wouldn't be enough to cover her rent, let alone travelling expenses and food, so it wasn't going to solve her problems, but it was better than nothing.

'Armand offered to sell those pictures for us in his gallery.' Prudence seemed more confident now. 'We can leave all that side to him.'

Candida saw Walter frown, and this she understood. 'He's right about getting good prices for them in Paris,' she said, 'but . . . I'm not sure I'd trust him. I'd not hand them all over to him.'

'My feelings exactly,' Walter agreed. 'I thought he was disappointed and would have preferred Micheline to have given him the pictures.'

'He knows the value of them.'

'Perhaps he would have liked a greater share of what she had.' Walter was frowning.

'If that's the case,' – Prudence was into her stride now – 'and you don't trust him, are you sure it was safe to leave the pictures there with him?'

'We had no choice about that,' Candida said slowly. 'I'll take a look at the London market, see what prices those sorts of paintings are fetching, but I'd feel better if we'd had time to make a full inventory of all that Aimee has been left. Would it be a good idea for me to write to Armand and ask if we might?'

They all sank back in thought.

* * *

Prudence snored through much of the train journey and felt seasick during the Channel crossing. The hotel in Dover where they spent the night was not to her liking, and then she had to face another exhausting train journey. Candida left them once they reached Merseyside. 'I'll ring you tomorrow evening,' she told Walter as she said goodbye.

Prudence was glad to see her go; Candida made her feel inadequate, though she was more attentive of her needs than her own family were. As the taxi was turning through the gates of Rock Park she said, 'I'm so glad to be back home. I really don't care for foreign parts.'

Fairholme had been Prudence's family home. When she'd married Walter, her mother was already a widow and not in good health. The obvious answer was for Walter to move in with them, though it had taken time for him to see that. Fairholme was a much larger and grander house than the one in the back end of Liverpool, near his mill, that he'd been planning to make their home. Prudence was proud of the fact that it was in a gated park. 'Rock Ferry is a flourishing resort with refreshment rooms and shops,' she'd told him.

'At weekends the ferries bring hordes of day trippers to the bowling greens and pleasure gardens of the Royal Rock Hotel, and you complain about them,' he'd reminded her.

'Mother told me it was a favourite visiting place for royalty; King Edward and Queen Alexandra came several times.'

'The royal yacht might have brought them into the Mersey,' Walter said slowly. 'They may even have visited the Royal Rock Hotel and the Royal Liverpool Yacht Club a little further downstream, but you'd never have seen them strolling round Rock Ferry with the Sunday crowds.'

Seeing her heart was set on it, though, he had agreed to make his home at Fairholme. He believed that having the ferry almost on the doorstep meant the journey to work would be easy and pleasant, but he'd always begrudged the time and energy it took him to get there. It was time he would otherwise have spent managing his business.

Nowadays he was even less pleased with the arrangement. 'Rock Ferry isn't what it was,' he said, 'and neither is Rock Park. The houses are old, and far too big. They were designed for an earlier generation. You're always saying we need servants to run the place.'

'We could still live well if you agreed to having more help in the house and gave it a little maintenance.'

'We couldn't afford more servants even if they were available,' Walter was saying when Dora came in with a tea tray.

'Welcome home,' she said, and put a cup of tea beside Prudence. 'I didn't know what time you'd get here, so I've made leek and potato soup and a salad for your evening meal, and there's cheese and biscuits. I hope that'll be all right.'

'It's a bit cold for salad,' Prudence said.

Walter said, 'Thank you, Dora, for staying late and preparing a meal for us, and also for lighting this fire. We do appreciate it. You run along now. Goodnight.'

'I am glad to be back,' Prudence said when she'd gone. 'Rock Ferry has much to recommend it; it's a lovely spot. There's a magnificent panorama from the Esplanade into New Ferry, and so much to see: the River Mersey is always busy with big ships bustling in and out of the port, not to mention the ferries, tug boats and pleasure craft. And what could be more picturesque than the historic naval ships?'

A deep-water channel called the Sloyne ran close to the Rock Ferry bank and provided moorings for the black and white wooden ship that was once HMS *Nile*, now renamed *Conway*, a school and training vessel for officer cadets; and the *Indefatigable*, an old iron ship that trained orphaned children of seamen for a life at sea.

Prudence liked to boast to those who lived in inferior districts that Rock Park was a delightful place. It had been designed in 1837 and the stone houses were built in a variety of styles round a serpentine driveway surrounded by trees and shrubs. The houses along the waterfront were the first to be finished and were thought superior; all were completed by 1850. Prue's one regret was that her house, Fairholme, was further back, with river views only from the upstairs rooms.

She also had plenty to say about the people who had once lived there. Nathaniel Hawthorne, a famous novelist, had resided at number 26 for several years while he'd been the American consul in Liverpool. He was reported to have said, 'Rock Park provides houses for professional people, merchants and others of upper middling class, and is an improvement on anything save what the very rich could enjoy in America.'

It pleased Walter to hear Aimee say more than once that she was not overly impressed with the grandeur of the place. 'It would look better if the Mersey was blue and crystal clear instead of brown and muddy, and when the tide goes out, that wide expanse of glistening mud between the strip of sand and the river adds nothing to the view.'

'You'll appreciate it more when you grow up, Aimee,' Prue had told her.

* * *

Walter was glad to be home too. It worried him to leave his business for days on end, and he didn't enjoy his Christmases in France. He'd never felt completely at ease there and he didn't always understand what was being said to him, but he'd seen it as his duty to keep Aimee in touch with her mother, and Micheline was his daughter-in-law, after all.

He felt he'd had a hectic year and was barely in control of his affairs. He wanted to do his best with his business for the sake of Aimee and Prudence, but he knew his energy was being sapped by turmoil in his personal life.

It had all started back in the cold, dark winter of 1931. One night the foghorns were blaring all night from the ships on the river, keeping the whole district awake, and the next morning Liverpool was blanketed with fog and the ferries had stopped running.

Walter set out to walk to Rock Ferry station to catch the underground train to work. Visibility wasn't good, but ahead of him he saw a woman pick herself up from the road and try to disentangle her bike from that of a butcher's boy. It looked like a minor collision. The lad was staring at the packages of meat strewn all over the road. 'Sorry, sorry,' he was saying.

'Not entirely your fault,' the woman said. 'Just as much mine. As well as this fog, there's hoar frost on the road.'

It was only then that Walter recognised the woman as Aimee's French teacher. 'Are you all right, Mrs Kerr?' He helped prise the bikes apart and pile the meat back into the carrier on the front of the boy's bike.

She looked down at her knee and shivered. It was grazed and bleeding and she'd torn a large hole in her stocking. 'Oh dear, what a mess.'

Walter saw a café almost opposite them. 'Come in there with me and have a hot drink. You'll feel better if you sit down for ten minutes.'

Esther smiled. 'I could do with it, but no thanks, I'm late for school already.'

He saw her grimace as she straightened her leg. 'It's obviously hurting; you can't just cycle on to work.'

'I'm really all right, but perhaps I'll just walk for now. It's only five minutes from here.'

Walter pushed her bike for her as far as the convent. 'You should get the nuns to sponge that graze.'

'Oh, they will, I'm sure.' She shivered again. 'It's cold enough to freeze a brass monkey, but I'll be fine once I get into the warm. I'm all right, Mr Kendrick, don't worry about me.'

At the gate, she took her bike and he watched her wheel it across the yard. She was stoical, blaming nobody, the opposite to Prudence. Why had he never noticed before that she had a way of looking at him through her lashes? She was very pretty, even in a dishevelled state.

At dinner that night, he told Aimee and Prudence about the incident. 'Mrs Kerr was really shaken up but insisted on going on to work. She's a strong woman.'

Prudence sniffed. 'She's as thin as a rake, puny even, I'd say.'

'I meant strong-willed,' Walter said.

'She's a good teacher,' Aimee said, 'and teachers have to be strong to control a whole class of girls. I really like her.'

'Convent girls are always well behaved,' Prudence sniffed.

Esther came one evening the following week to give Aimee a lesson, and an hour or so later Walter met her in the hall as she was leaving. He made a point of asking about her knee. 'It's grown a thick scab,' she said, and held up the palm of her hand. 'I discovered when I got to school that I had another graze here, but we have a large first-aid box to treat minor cuts, and as you can see, I've had no trouble with either.'

She looked very attractive tonight. 'And you're riding your bike again?' He could see it propped against the lowest step of the flight up to the front door.

She laughed. 'You've heard the advice to people thrown from their horses – get straight back on as soon as you can. Same applies to bikes.'

'Yes.' He laughed too. 'It's another cold night; there could be hoar frost on the road again. I hope you don't have far to go.'

'No, I have a room in Rockville Street. Goodnight.'

He thought about her as he watched her switch on her lights and ride off. She'd been widowed in the war, and if she was in lodgings, that meant she hadn't remarried. He'd thought he was well past the age when a pretty woman could provoke such a stir of interest, but he couldn't get her out of his mind after that.

CHAPTER EIGHT

THE DAY AFTER SHE returned home, Aimee went to look for Frankie straight after breakfast. It was raining; the gardens looked sodden and lifeless, and neither he nor his grandad could be seen working anywhere. Grandma had said she must on no account climb the wall to visit his home, that no respectable young lady would, but she still did it, though the brickwork was smoke-blackened and wet.

When she knocked, his grandad called out, telling her to come in. He was sitting in a sagging armchair in front of a low fire. 'Not much work outside for anybody at this time of the year, but our Frankie's got a job in a shop. It suits him better and we're very pleased.'

'A permanent job?'

'Well, they took him on to cover the Christmas rush, but he's hoping so.'

'Which shop?

'That big newsagent in Birkenhead, opposite Woolworths.'

Aimee knew it well; Grandma bought her magazines there. Without Frankie, the day already felt flat. She went home to find Dora setting up Grandma's breakfast tray. 'Scrambled eggs on toast: that looks nice. I'll take it up to her,' she offered.

'OK. Be sure to draw her curtains; she'll be niggly if she has to ask you to do it.' Dora giggled. 'She tells me a housemaid should anticipate her wishes and not have to be asked to do routine things.'

Aimee found it none too easy to juggle the tray, knock and open the bedroom door. She went in breezily. 'Good morning, Grandma,' she said, and put the tray on the table kept for that purpose before sweeping open the curtains. 'Bit of a grey day today.' She returned to push the table into position.

Prue hastily reached for her false teeth and put them in. She was wearing a thick grey hairnet. 'Where's Dora? Hasn't she turned up this morning?'

'Yes, she made your breakfast.'

'Then why did you bring it up? You're Alec's daughter; you shouldn't be doing the housemaid's work.'

'I wanted to talk to you, Gran. Can you tell me any more about my father? Gramps gave me his diary pages to read. I know he had a terrible time.'

'He did. Gave me nightmares for weeks to think of all he suffered.'

'I want to know more about him. What was he like when he was growing up?'

'Pour me a cup of tea, dear; it's not so easy to manage things in bed. Alec was a delightful boy, always top of his class at school. His father doted on him, but he should never have allowed him to join the army. He should have insisted on him staying here; he had a vital position in the mill.' Prudence was tucking into her breakfast. 'Butter me that other slice of toast dear.'

'What else? Did he like games? Who were his friends?'

'He wasn't all that keen on games, but he had lots of friends; everybody loved him. Really, Aimee, you know as much about him as I do. There's not a lot more I can tell you.'

'Tell me about your own life, then, about growing up in this house. Has this always been your bedroom?'

'No, this is the master bedroom. My parents slept here when I was young.'

Aimee thought it looked as though Grandma had changed very little in it over the last sixty years; the style was late Victorian, with heavy curtains at the windows and too much mahogany furniture. She sat down on a blanket chest at the foot of the large bed. It had a carved top and was acutely uncomfortable. 'Did you sleep in my bedroom then?'

'Yes, dear, it's one of the nicest, isn't it?'

'I'd like to know more about your family. Tell me about your father and mother.'

'My father was an absolute darling and a very successful man. I was his favourite child, you know.'

'Yes, you had a sister, didn't you?'

'Yes, Verity, but she died young, and the less said about her, the better.'

'Oh! What about your mother?'

'I had to look after her in her old age, and she was very difficult. Pull this table back, I've finished now.'

'In what way was she difficult?'

'Aimee, I don't want to talk about my family; they all passed away a long time ago.'

'Do you have any old photographs? I'd love to see them if you have.'

'No.'

'Gran, I'm sure you have. You once showed me one taken on your wedding day with all the family round you. Could I see it again? I think you keep things like that in this blanket chest. Can I look?'

'No! Absolutely not. I keep my private mementoes in there and I don't want people prying into them. Now you can take this tray downstairs and leave me in peace.'

'Gran, I'm sorry, I didn't mean to upset you.'

'Just go, dear.'

Aimee went; she was getting nowhere. Once downstairs, she felt at a loose end. She decided to take the bus into town and try to have a word with Frankie. She needed to tell him that art lessons with Candida would be on a different day.

At the newsagent's, she spotted him behind one of the counters. She took a copy of *Woman's Own* from the magazine rack, and waited until he was free to serve her. 'You look very smart,' she said. 'I don't often see you in a suit.'

'A hand-me-down from one of Dad's customers.' He grinned at her. 'His son grew out of it, and now it's my Sunday best. By the way, while you were in France, I saw an account of your mother's funeral in the *Daily Telegraph* and an obituary in the *Times*. Dad could hardly believe it. He was very impressed, and we both learned a lot. I've kept copies for you at home.'

'Thank you. I told you she was famous. Anyway, I've come to let you know that Miss Rathbone will be coming on Saturdays in future. In the morning we'll have lessons in art, and we'll paint in the afternoons.'

'Oh no!' Frankie was aghast. 'Saturday is the busiest day in this shop; I'll have to work then.'

'What a shame! I am sorry. It seemed the best time for both of us.'

He pulled a face. 'Well, you didn't know I had a shop job.'

'I wouldn't have suggested it if I had. It won't be any fun without you.'

But the following Saturday morning, Aimee was delighted to see Frankie in the kitchen, clutching his portfolio. 'You managed to get the day off after all?'

'Not exactly. I've thrown that job over. This is more important to me.' Up in the old schoolroom he said, 'Dad's furious with me, of course. He can't see the point of art lessons. Not for any man, and particularly not for me.'

'That's a shame; you'll have less money now to buy paints.'

He chuckled. 'Dad said I'd be going hungry if I didn't take care, but I won't. I've got another job. I'm going to work on Friday and Saturday evenings at a restaurant called the Ship Inn.'

'You're a man of many talents,' Aimee laughed.

'I'm hired to do the washing-up and mop the kitchen floor at the end of the evening. I'm expected to leave everything clean and tidy for the next day. I can't rush it because the manager lives upstairs; he'll inspect my work before he lets me go.' He laughed too. 'Nobody but you would think that took talent; it's just a few hours of paid work.'

'But it's the hours you want.'

'Well, it means working late at night, and I had to walk home last night because I missed the last bus, but at least this way I can fit in Saturday lessons with Miss Rathbone.'

* * *

Easter was coming, and so far there had been no word from the *notaire* about finalising Micheline's will, which pleased none of them, least of all Candida. They were all impatient, but she was fearful too; she was sliding further into debt and could see no way to stop herself. She had applied to several schools and art colleges, hoping to get a full-time teaching post in the autumn, at the beginning of the school year. She was also applying to museums in towns along the banks of the Mersey for art restoration work, but in this deep depression there was no money for things that were not absolutely essential.

She was delighted to get a letter from Armand one morning telling her that the *notaire* had written to him saying he'd need an inventory of all Aimee would inherit from her mother. In addition to her personal possessions and art materials, he wanted a valuation of each of the paintings by famous artists. *Would you be willing to do it?* Armand wrote.

Candida felt a huge wave of hope. This sounded like work she'd be paid for, and might be worth the cost of telephoning him. She walked down to the local post office to use a public phone. 'Don't you want to value these paintings yourself?' she asked him. 'Isn't it exactly the sort of work you do?'

'Yes, but the *notaire* says he needs an independent valuation, and I'm a beneficiary of the will. You used to do this sort of thing, didn't you? You're qualified?'

'Yes, I am, and I'll be glad to do it; delighted, in fact.' It would give her a trip to France, which she would enjoy, and several days when she could eat well.

Walking on air, she went to the nearest butcher's shop and bought herself a lamb chop and half a pound of stewing steak to celebrate.

Then she realised that the sooner she organised the trip, the sooner she'd be paid. She went back to the post office to ring Walter at the mill, and he told her he'd received a similar letter from the *notaire*. He sounded exhausted. 'I'll gladly leave this to you and Armand.'

'He said I could stay at La Coutancie while I did it. Aimee will probably want to come with me.' Perhaps Walter would pay a little more if she took charge of the girl. 'The Easter holidays are almost on us. What d'you think?'

'Well . . .' There was a pause while he thought about it. 'Yes, I suppose so. This could be paid for later out of her inheritance. So yes, if she wants to go. I'll cover the expenses, of course, and add a little something for the hours you'll put in as our art expert.'

'I'm sorry to have to ask . . .' anything like this always embarrassed her, 'but I'll need you to advance me something for expenses before I can book.'

She guessed he was finding ready cash difficult too, but he agreed. 'I'll put some money in an envelope and leave it with Aimee. The sooner you get this done and everything finalised, the better.'

Candida thanked him and felt very much relieved.

By the following Saturday, when she discussed it with Aimee, she felt restored to her normal happy self. Aimee was excited at the prospect of another trip to France. 'I've had my nose to the grindstone revising all term. This will be a complete break.' Frankie was clearly envious.

At lunch, Prudence was speculating about how much longer it would be before Aimee received her inheritance. Candida said, 'It could be lack of a current valuation of those paintings that has been holding things up.'

Aimee explained that they would soon be visiting La Coutancie to do it. 'That should get things moving.'

'I could come with you,' Prudence said brightly. 'It will be interesting and I could help; we shouldn't leave everything to you, Candida. I could take charge of this little expedition. I've done the journey many times. Yes, include me when you book.'

Candida was rendered speechless and was more than glad to hear Aimee say, 'Grandma, it's very generous of you to offer, but it's a long way and that train journey plays havoc with your back.'

'It does, dear, but I feel I must do my bit to help.'

'Gran, I'd be worried about leaving Gramps here on his own. You know how tired he is when he comes home from work.'

Candida went home that afternoon feeling somewhat cast down, but a few days later she received a note from Prudence saying: *Walter thinks the journey would be too much for me and would prefer me to stay home.* That restored her high spirits, and she couldn't stop smiling. Aimee was growing up and understood how to cope with her grandma. The next time she went to give her a lesson, they discussed dates for the visit and she found Walter had left her the money, so on the way home that same afternoon, she booked tickets for the journey. During the evening, she wrote to Armand to tell him that Aimee would be coming with her and giving the dates of their visit. Knowing that he'd be in Paris, she politely asked his permission for them to go through Micheline's possessions at La Coutancie.

He did not reply to her, but the following Saturday Aimee showed her a letter written in French that had arrived on the breakfast table addressed jointly to her and Gramps. Armand wrote that they were welcome to stay in the house; that Francine was there and would take care of them. He ended by saying that he was sure Candida was capable of valuing the pictures and reminding them that nothing should be taken away until the will was finalised.

Candida felt slighted that Armand had ignored her and left her to find out this way, but she was thrilled to go. And it was paid work.

Candida went home to pull down her suitcase from the top of her wardrobe and start to pack in readiness. She was thankful she had an interesting trip to look forward to, but she knew that in the long term this wouldn't solve her problem.

She woke up in the middle of the night and was almost overcome by a feeling of desperation. She'd have to do more than this to earn some money. When she'd visited her father in prison, he'd looked cowed and beaten and she'd been horrified by the conditions in which he had to live. She'd vowed never to do anything that might land her in a similar position.

Their trip was to start on the Tuesday after Easter, and at last the morning came. Walter brought Aimee to the station on his way to work and saw them off. Aimee was in high spirits and Candida felt better straight away. The journey out was uneventful, and when they arrived in Dignac, the village was bathed in evening sunshine.

Francine seemed pleased to see them. 'I am preparing duckling for your dinner,' she told them. The telephone rang and she went to answer it. 'It's for you,' she said to Candida. 'Armand wants to speak to you.'

Candida went to the phone, aware that Aimee was close behind her. After the usual greetings, Armand said, 'I wrote to the *notaire* and gave him your name as an experienced and well-qualified independent valuer, and he's happy about you doing it. Go easy on your estimates, though, particularly for those paintings by famous artists, the Renoir, the Chagalls and the Degas. Bear in mind it will add up to a substantial sum and the state may impose taxes on it. That would reduce the amount Aimee will receive.'

'Oh goodness, yes, I'd forgotten about taxes.'

'I've not been able to forget,' Armand said. 'Micheline and I indulged ourselves too well and tax was quite a problem. I'll have to draw my horns in now. You'll let me know how you get on, and the figures you arrive at?'

Candida's head was beginning to spin, but the wine at dinner relaxed her, and afterwards she led Aimee round the pictures, looking carefully at each one. She decided she'd calculate what she thought was a fair figure for each picture, and then deduct twenty per cent, to comply with Armand's advice. They had a peep into Micheline's studio, and Aimee was overcome by the wealth of art materials that would be hers.

They were both tired. 'We'll leave everything until tomorrow morning,' Candida said. But before she went to bed, she jotted down roughly what she thought the paintings could be worth and added it up. The figure seemed astronomical. She deducted the twenty per cent she'd decided on, and then did the same again. Even with forty per cent off, the total was huge.

* * *

Candida was having misgivings about her figures. Were her estimates even likely to be right? She knew next to nothing about the French market for such paintings, and though she took an interest in the London art market, it was years since she'd worked in it. In the present world, depression prices were reputed to be low, yet here she was estimating Micheline's pictures to be worth a fortune. She and Aimee spent another two days valuing her painting materials and personal possessions, then she rang Armand at a time she thought he was likely to be at home.

'Yes,' he said, 'hello. Hold on a moment while I find a pencil.' She read her figures out to him, and sweat broke out on her forehead as he pondered for a few moments. 'Yes, that's about what I thought,' he said eventually.

Candida felt relief flood through her. 'You don't think it's too high?'

'You're the expert,' he said. 'Send your estimate to the *notaire* and let's hope he'll now get on with things.'

'I'll take it to him,' she said. 'Aimee and I are thinking of visiting Angoulême tomorrow. There is so much to see there.'

'Beautiful old buildings,' he agreed. 'Don't feel you have to rush away now you're done the job. Stay and have a few days' rest. How is Aimee?'

'She loves being here, we both do. Thank you.'

They stayed for the rest of the week, enjoying the sun and the luxury of living at La Coutancie. On the train going home, Aimee pulled a face. 'Next week it's back to school for the summer term and exams.'

'We've both had a lovely break,' Candida reminded her.

Personally, she needed to pull herself together now and face what was coming.

It was late when Aimee got up the next morning and she still felt half asleep. For once, Grandma was downstairs before her. 'I do wish Bob Hopkins would come and cut the grass,' she said. 'He's let it get far too long.'

'It was raining in the night,' Aimee said. 'Have you had a spell of wet weather while I was away?'

'Yes, quite unpleasant for this time of year, but the forecast is for sunny spells this afternoon. I'd like to sit outside, but look at the mess the garden is in.'

'He can't cut the grass when it's wet, Grandma.'

'I don't think he's cut it since the autumn. Walter really must have a word with him.'

They were just finishing their lunch when Aimee heard the familiar buzz and drone from the back garden and went to the window to look. 'Mr Hopkins is here cutting the lawn,' she said. 'He'll have the garden tidied up by the time you're ready to sit outside.' Often Frankie came to help him, but today he was alone, which probably meant Frankie had a job elsewhere.

She was getting bored with Grandma's company, so while Dora was making a cup of tea for them, she slipped out of the kitchen door to ask Bob where Frankie was. She caught him just as he'd emptied the box of grass cuttings and was fixing it back on the machine.

He straightened up wearily to mop his face, and she noticed he was sweating and looked far from well. 'Frankie's got a few days' work in that newsagent's again. They've got staff off sick and they asked him to fill in.'

'Good,' she said. 'He likes working there, doesn't he?'

The old man sighed. 'He finishes at five thirty, if that's what you want to know.'

'Yes, thank you.' Aimee decided she felt more like sitting in the sun than going to Birkenhead. 'I'll see him when he comes home,' she said.

Twenty minutes later, Aimee was about to take their teacups back to the kitchen when Grandma said, 'Where has that man gone? I don't hear him cutting any more.' She opened the French window and stepped outside. 'Don't tell me he's gone? Good gracious, he has, and he's left the mower just there on the grass with half of it uncut. This is too bad of him. Walter should look for a replacement.'

'That isn't like Bob,' Aimee said. 'Gramps thinks he's a good and reliable worker.' She went out to put the mower away in the tool shed and arrange two garden chairs on the part of the lawn that had been cut. It didn't stop Gran complaining.

Aimee hoped Frankie might come to see her on the way home from work, as he knew she'd be home by today, but in case that was not his intention, at the appropriate time she strolled through the gates of Rock Park and up towards the main road to meet him. She saw him from a distance and quickened her pace; he was all smiles and threw his arms round her to swing her off her feet in greeting.

'Aimee! I'm delighted you're back. Have you had a lovely time? I've really missed you.' He held her away from him for a moment. 'I see you've had more sun than we've had; you've quite a tan.'

'Yes, I've had an excellent time. How about you? Anything exciting happened here?'

'No, just the chance of more shop work,' Frankie said. 'I've been quite worried about Dad, though. He hasn't been well for the last couple of days, and he's got quite a lot of work on.' He laughed. 'I wanted to refuse the newsagent's and help him, but he wouldn't hear of it, because shop work pays better than gardening.'

'He's been cutting our grass today, but he didn't look well.'

'We've had a few wet days here and that's held him up. Yesterday it was better and he was trying to finish painting the outside of Riverview, but he had to come home at three o'clock because he felt ill. That's not like him; he usually carries on regardless.'

'He went home from our place this afternoon and didn't finish the back lawn. Has he caught that sore throat and cold that was going round?'

'No, he feels sick and says he has a pain in his belly that won't go away. What time did he leave your place?'

'Straight after lunch, half past one or two o'clock.'

'He must be feeling worse. I'd better go home and see how he is.'

Aimee walked up to the stables with him. 'You could ask your doctor to call and see him.' Frankie looked grim and said nothing. 'What's the problem?'

'We don't have a doctor.'

'Oh! What do you do when you're ill?'

'I'm never ill. Do you think I should take him to hospital?'

'Good Lord, Frankie, is he that bad?'

'I don't know, but he looks poorly. Usually if he's off colour he takes a couple of aspirin and goes to bed for a while, but this time he seems to be getting worse rather than better. He doesn't want to get up. I feel I've got to do something.'

It was a long time since Aimee had seen the stables from the road, because she usually climbed over the garden wall. She looked across the cobbled yard to the cottage on the far side. The whole place seemed near derelict.

'If he's no better, I'll go home and ring our doctor and ask him to call and see him.'

'Would you, Aimee? Thank you. That would be a great help.'

Frankie left her in the living room and went upstairs to see his father. She'd been here many times before, but it seemed more untidy and darker than usual. A shaft of sunlight caught the large framed photograph hanging on the wall of a young woman holding a baby. She wondered if it was Frankie and his mother. The woman was wearing a nanny's uniform. There were trees and a big house in the background and a toddler playing nearby.

Frankie came clattering back down the bare stairs. 'I think Dad's worse, and he's not eaten the sandwich I left him for his lunch.'

'Right, I'd better go home and ring for Dr Ellis then.'

'Yes please, Aimee.'

She went home over the garden wall. She was expected to ask permission to use the phone, but Grandma was in no mood today to give permission for anything that would benefit Bob Hopkins. Gramps wouldn't be home for some time yet, so Aimee crept through the kitchen to the study, closed the door softly and dialled the doctor's number. As usual, it was his wife who took the call. Aimee told her of the problem and gave directions to find the stables.

'Not one of our patients?' Mrs Ellis asked, and summoned her husband to the phone.

Aimee felt she knew the doctor quite well, as he came regularly to visit Grandma. She told him the story, and how urgent she thought the situation was.

'I'll go straight round now,' he said.

'Thank you, I'll see you there.'

She went back over the wall to tell Frankie. He'd made a cup of tea for his father and was about to take it upstairs to him, but just at that moment, Dr Ellis arrived at the front door. Frankie pushed the cup and saucer into Aimee's hand. 'I expect you could do with this,' he said and went to let him in. She sat down and drank the tea, deciding she might as well wait to see if Frankie needed any more help.

Ten minutes later, she heard them talking as they came to the top of the stairs. 'Yes, rather poorly, I'm afraid, an acute abdominal problem, most likely appendicitis but not necessarily so. In any event, he'll probably need surgery straight away. I'll arrange for an ambulance to come for him as soon as possible. Put a few things together for him – razor, pyjamas, slippers, washing tackle, that sort of thing.'

The doctor nodded to Aimee on the way out. When Frankie returned from the front door, he said, 'Thank goodness you phoned for him. Dad's really ill. I'll go with him in the ambulance.'

'I'd better go home. I'll see you tomorrow, and don't worry, Frankie.'

'Thanks to you, Dad will soon be in good hands.' He dropped a kiss on her forehead. 'Thank God for that.'

Aimee got up the next morning to have breakfast with Gramps. She guessed Frankie would go to work and hoped he'd pop in to tell her what had happened last night. They'd reached the toast and marmalade stage when he tapped on the kitchen window. She let him in.

'I almost overslept,' he panted.

'Were you up late last night?' she asked.

'Yes, it was after midnight when I got home. They operated on Dad as soon as they could, and said I'd only just got him there in time. If I'd delayed much longer, his appendix could have burst and then he would have been very much worse.' He turned to Gramps. 'I'm sorry, sir, that I had to call on Aimee to use your telephone and your doctor to get help for him.'

'Oh! Aimee told me that your grandfather had been taken ill, but not that she'd phoned for Dr Ellis to visit him. You did the right thing,' he said. 'You too, Aimee. You've got plenty of common sense between you. He came through it all right, did he?'

'Yes, I stayed until they brought him back from the operating theatre, and they told me it had all gone well.'

'That's good news, but poor old Bob, he's no longer a young man, is he?'

'No, sir, he's seventy-eight.'

'Good gracious, older than I am! I didn't realise that. Well, I'm pleased to see you've turned out for work this morning.'

'I was told Dad would be in hospital for some time, so I might as well get on with it.'

'That's the spirit,' Gramps said. 'Did you have breakfast before coming?'

'Yes, a slice of bread and marmalade and a cup of milk.' Frankie grinned. 'All I had time for. I've got to run, or I'll miss my bus.'

Walter said, 'I'll pay for the doctor's visit. Give my regards to Bob when you next see him, and tell him I hope to see him back doing my garden before long.'

Ten days later, Frankie told them he was going to bring his grandad home by taxi. Gramps told Aimee to buy him some grapes, and on Saturday afternoon she took them over to the stables.

Frankie was in the kitchen making tea. 'I'll bring it in,' he said.

She found Bob Hopkins lying in his battered armchair in the living room. 'Grapes?' he said. 'My goodness, such luxury. Thank you; you're treating me like a real invalid.'

She said, 'They're from Gramps; he says he's missed seeing you in our garden, but you're not to hurry back. You're looking much better, Mr Hopkins.' His chin was covered with coarse whiskers, mostly grey and white, which made him look older, but the colour had come back into his cheeks.

'I am better, and I understand I have you to thank for that.'

'Not entirely. All I did was phone for the doctor.'

'Frankie says I'm to thank you and your grandfather for all the help you've given us.'

'You'd have done the same for us, I'm sure,' she said. The large photograph on the wall caught her eye again. 'Who is that in the photo?'

The old man looked up and smiled. 'My daughter Connie,' he said. 'Poor lass, she caught the consumption.'

'I'm sorry to hear that. And she was Frankie's mother?'

'Well,' he said, 'she was and she wasn't.'

Frankie brought in the tea and handed the biscuit barrel round.

Mystified, Aimee looked from one to the other. 'What does that mean?'

Frankie's eyebrows went up. 'I've always thought of her as my mother, but Dad has been telling me things since he came home from hospital. I can't believe he kept me in the dark all these years.'

'Never had much time for talking,' Bob said, 'but I'm getting on a bit now, and before I went into hospital I thought I was nearing my end, so I've told Frankie the truth about our Connie. It's time he knew.'

'Secrets.' Frankie half smiled at Aimee. 'It seems every family has them. Connie left home when I was seven, and Dad has looked after me ever since.'

Aimee was full of curiosity. 'Connie worked as a nanny?'

'Yes, our Connie loved children.'

'In her teens, she made a big mistake,' Frankie said. 'You can guess what that was.'

Aimee nodded.

Bob Hopkins straightened up in his chair. 'And I made an even bigger one by persuading her to give her son up for adoption. She was seventeen and she'd fallen in love with a sailor. He went off to the other side of the world as soon as he knew about the baby. Took a job on a boat going to South America to get out of the way, and she never heard from him again. I told her adoption was for the best. I didn't want to see her struggling in poverty to bring the child up on her own. Neither did I want to work for the next twenty years to do it for her.'

'But that's exactly what you have done,' Aimee pointed out.

'Yes . . . in a way. I didn't realise that our Connie . . . Well, she pined for that child. I thought she'd get over it, but she didn't. She'd hang over every pram she saw, billing and cooing at the baby inside, wanting to lift it up and cuddle it.'

'So you persuaded her to become a nanny and look after other people's children? That seems a logical thing to do.'

'I expected it to help her, but it didn't. She couldn't settle, couldn't keep a job, had three or four in quick succession. Then one day she came home with a strange baby. It was him.' He waved in Frankie's direction.

'Oh my goodness!' Aimee's gaze went to Frankie.

'I was as shocked as you are when Dad told me,' Frankie said. 'I'd always thought Connie was my mother.'

Aimee looked at the old man. 'So where did she get Frankie from? You must have asked her.'

Bob heaved himself up in his chair. 'She told me his parents had died in a fire and nobody else wanted him,' he said. 'She screamed at me when I said we should take him to the police or an orphanage, so somehow he stayed. I was afraid she'd stolen him from his pram while his mother had turned her back for a moment. She made such a fuss that I feared for her mind. She was determined to hang onto him and bring him up; she adored him. Wherever she went, she took him with her. Even to work when she was looking after other kids.'

Bob sighed and stopped. Frankie took up the tale. 'Connie was looking after Dr George's children when she became ill. He sent her for an X-ray, and that was that.'

'Aye, he told us it was consumption and said she had to go away to a sanatorium in Shropshire.'

'I was seven years old by then,' Frankie said, 'and they wouldn't let her take me with her.'

'She made an awful fuss,' Bob went on. 'She screamed at them, refused to leave him, but in the end she had to. They said she was infectious and a danger to the boy and everyone else. I thought she'd get better and come back to us, and I didn't dare take him to an orphanage.'

'No,' Aimee agreed. 'Of course not. '

'Anyway, he was a good kid and I'd grown fond of him by then.' Bob reached for his tea. 'But I didn't realise how ill our Connie was. Same thing had happened to her mother. TB's a terrible thing. Our Betty was taken after four years of marriage, and only twenty-six she was. Poor Connie was following in her footsteps. I relied on her for many things and missed her terribly. Frankie cried for her and became quite clingy. We clung together, didn't we? You were a comfort to me, Frankie. The only comfort I had at that time.'

'We needed each other, Dad.'

Aimee heard the catch in his voice and was blinking back her own tears. 'I've felt the bond between you,' she said, 'and now I understand how it came about. So Connie never came home again?'

'No.' The old man sat up. 'No, that was the end of her; she died six months later.'

Aimee felt they'd deliberately stemmed their emotions.

Frankie said in a matter-of-fact tone, 'So I don't know who I am, or where I came from, and there's nobody I can ask.'

The silence between them deepened until Aimee said, 'Did she leave no clues in her room? She knew she'd be away for some time and that you'd be growing up. No letter?'

'We looked everywhere,' Bob said, 'and I've kept looking.'

Frankie sighed. 'I spent two hours searching through her bedroom again last night, but I found nothing that would help.'

'Did nobody come round asking questions when he was a baby?' she asked Bob.

'If they did, I never saw them. Connie brought him here and he's been here ever since, that's all I know.'

Aimee tried to think. 'There are times when people need to know about your parents. They ask about mine because my mother is French and I live with my grandparents.'

'Aye, there are. When Connie put him into school, she told them he was her own, a mistake she'd made when she was seventeen. So I always say the same if anyone asks.'

'The story everyone believes,' Aimee sighed.

'Because it's human nature,' Frankie added.

Later on, Frankie took her up to Connie's room. Aimee looked round, thinking how comfortless and cold it seemed. 'Is your room like this?' she asked.

'Pretty much.'

There was a full-size cot in the corner. 'I must have slept in that at one time.' Frankie pulled a face. 'I've checked it, but there's nothing hidden in it.'

Connie herself had slept in a narrow iron bed, now stripped down to its horsehair mattress. Frankie said, 'I've turned that over, and the cover has never been split, so there's nothing there either.'

Connie had owned a few books: *Alice in Wonderland*, *The Wide, Wide World*. Aimee flicked carefully through the pages, 'The ideal place to hide a letter,' she said.

'I've done that,' he sighed.

'Frankie, she didn't know if or when she'd be coming back, and she must have known that one day you'd ask about your origins. Surely she'd have wanted to tell you what she knew?'

He shrugged. 'I don't know.'

In the small wardrobe were a few items of Connie's nanny's uniform: a shabby hat and coat and some well-worn shoes. Aimee looked inside the coat pockets and peered onto the shelf and into the corners before turning her attention to the chest of drawers with a mirror on top.

Frankie said, 'I've looked through the contents of all three drawers, but you do it again to make sure.'

Aimee emptied them onto the mattress one by one. There was very little left: a few scarves, a pair of woolly gloves, and a handbag. Her heart ached with pity for poor Connie. The only other thing in the room was a battered chair with wooden arms and a fitted cushion on its hard seat.

'Do you remember her?' she asked.

'Of course,' Frankie said. 'She was a happy person; I remember her laughing, playing games with me, hugging me and talking to me constantly. Dad used to talk to me too; he was always very kind. They indulged me, but it's quite scary not knowing who my real mother was, or where I came from. Dad pretends it's of no importance, but I think he feels guilty that he didn't persuade Connie to tell him more about where she'd found me.'

'Gramps has wondered about you, where your talent for painting comes from. Can I tell him about Connie not being your real mother?'

Frankie nodded. 'He's been very kind to me too.'

There was a small rug on the floor by the bed. Aimee turned it over. 'Nothing here either.'

'I'm giving up,' Frankie said. 'I'll probably never know. I've always thought of Dad as my real family, and I'm quite happy to leave it at that.'

Aimee smiled at him, but she could feel his burning curiosity and suspected that wasn't quite true.

CHAPTER NINE

W HEN AIMEE WENT BACK to school for the summer term, Walter hoped life would go on peacefully without any problems, but one evening she came to him very concerned. 'I can't stop thinking about Frankie not knowing who his real parents are. He doesn't talk about it much, but I know it bothers him.'

She'd discussed the situation with her grandpa more than once, but there was nothing helpful he could add except that he'd settled up with Dr Ellis and she must tell them to call him out again if they needed to.

He remembered Connie, of course, and it had been a shock to hear that she was not Frankie's birth mother. 'Frankie sees old Bob Hoskins as his father, and they look after each other. They're all right.'

'Yes, but the old stable is bleak and comfortless, I don't know how they cope there.'

Walter had never been inside their cottage, but he could see it was in dire need of maintenance. 'He's used to it,' he said. 'It's home to them. You must stop worrying about Frankie's problems and think of your own. Keep your mind on your school work and make sure you pass these exams at the first attempt. They are important.'

'I certainly don't want to re-sit them.'

Over the following week, he was glad to see her settling down to her revision, and he was able to tell her that he'd seen Bob Hopkins tending the lawns of Riverview when he came home from work. 'Frankie was with him, doing most of the work,' he said.

One very hot Saturday, Walter had found it hard to concentrate at work and was glad to return home and sit in the garden. That evening, when the sun was almost gone and the temperature was falling, he suggested to Aimee that she carry out their after-dinner coffee to the garden.

'This breeze is lovely after the heat of the kitchen,' Prudence said, settling back in her chair. 'So peaceful.'

The waves could be heard below, breaking against the promenade and sending spray upwards. From the nearby gardens of the Royal Rock Hotel, strains of music wafted in on the breeze. 'I think it must be a spring tide,' Walter said, 'and it's full in.'

'It's the Pierrot show,' Aimee said. 'I'd love to see it. Gramps, you said you'd take me one day. Couldn't we go tonight?'

'Oh no, dear,' Prudence said. 'It's not a suitable show for you to see.' A loudspeaker was being used to advertise that the programme would start in half an hour. 'Really, this is too much.' She sounded irritable. 'Walter, I really do feel we have grounds to complain. Making a noise like this every summer weekend should be against the law.'

'It brings the crowds across from Liverpool,' he said.

'Exactly, and why should we have to put up with that?'

Aimee pulled on Walter's jacket. 'Gramps, why don't we go

for a little walk? That way we'll be able to see what's going on down there.'

He drained his cup and stood up. 'Why not?' At least it would get him away from Prudence's incessant complaints.

'Just along the promenade,' she commanded. 'I wouldn't take her anywhere near those gardens.'

Aimee took his arm and he could feel her steering him to the gates of the Royal Rock Hotel. They could see several Pierrots wearing their costumes; some selling programmes, others trying to lure the crowds in. A ferry had recently tied up and new customers were streaming in. The band was playing jolly ragtime tunes. 'This makes me feel like dancing,' Aimee said with a wide smile.

Walter felt cheered; there was a sense of occasion about the place. 'Come on then, let's see the show,' he said.

It was held in a marquee in the grounds, and a line was forming at the ticket booth. Aimee was steering him towards it when they saw Esther Kerr heading in the same direction. 'Esther,' she squealed, 'hello. Are you going in to see the Pierrot show?'

'Yes, are you?'

Walter couldn't believe it. He'd walked the streets of Rock Ferry hoping to see her, and quite fortuitously, here she was. Aimee was making much of her, chattering away, claiming her attention, and he was able to feast his eyes on her. Her auburn hair was tied back from her face, and she was wearing a summer dress with a low neckline that showed off her long, elegant neck. She was beautiful.

'Do join us,' he said.

At the ticket booth, he asked for three tickets at the front.

Esther turned to him with a radiant smile. 'I can't let you pay for me,' she said. 'I didn't mean to foist myself on you.'

'Of course you can. We're glad of your company.' Should he have said that? She was having such an effect on him, he could hardly control his tongue, but Aimee was chattering away nineteen to the dozen and he didn't think either of them had noticed.

Inside the marquee, the smell of newly cut grass was overpowering. Unfortunately, Aimee sat down between them. No, perhaps it was for the best. He could see one bare and very shapely foot in an open sandal swinging slightly. Any closer contact would have reduced him to ashes.

Walter could not have said what the show was about, with Esther filling his mind, but she and Aimee seemed to enjoy it immensely. When it was over, he couldn't bear to say goodbye to her and suggested a drink in the hotel bar. He could see her hesitating, but Aimee was breathless with anticipation. 'I've never been in the bar any bar. I'd love to see it.'

He ordered orange juice for her, and Esther asked for the same. He needed beer, a long drink to moisten his dry mouth. Esther sat opposite him and spoke of her class at the convent. It took a real effort to keep his eyes away from her. Aimee must never know how he felt. Eventually she stood up and said she must go.

Walter was on his feet at once. 'It's dark now, we should see you home.'

Esther laughed openly. 'Absolutely not. It's often dark when I leave your house after a lesson with Aimee.'

'Did you come on your bike?'

'No, not tonight, there's nowhere I could safely leave it.'

She looked at her watch. 'There's a special late bus on Saturdays that will leave in five minutes. It will take me to the top of my road. Thank you, Mr Kendrick, it was—'

'Walter, please.' Oh my goodness, he never should have said that.

She nodded, her smile intimate. 'It was kind of you to let me join you. Thank you for everything. Goodnight.'

Aimee was tired now, and said little on the walk home; neither did she swing on his arm. 'Grandma will know we've been to see the show because we've been away a long time,' he said, 'but don't tell her I took you to the bar afterwards.' Prue would have hysterics if she knew about that. She thought that even entering the hotel lobby would smear Aimee's reputation.

'I won't, Gramps. It's been a lovely evening, really exciting.'

He didn't know what to say to her about Esther; probably the less said, the better.

When they reached home, only the hall lights were on. 'Grandma has already gone up,' he said thankfully, 'so I'll say goodnight too.' Prudence appeared to be asleep when he crept through the main bedroom to his narrow bed in the dressing room, so there was no need to tell her anything.

Walter had known from the very first moment that to have feelings for Esther Kerr was wrong. He felt torn between heady delight and shame. He had counted himself well past the age for romantic encounters, but he'd been interested enough to work out how old she was by looking at the letter she'd written at the time he'd hired her. She must be thirty-six now. Many would count him a randy old man.

He knew he shouldn't have invited her to join them at the

Pierrot show. It worried him that Aimee might have noticed something odd in his behaviour; from the magazines and novels she left lying about the house, it seemed she was taking an interest in love, romance and weddings, so he would not have been surprised if she had.

He found himself making sure he was around whenever Esther came to the house so he could exchange a few words with her. He encouraged Aimee to talk about her, but he'd made up his mind quite firmly that he'd go no further. She was too close to his family; much too close. It was the very last thing he should do. It could only lead to trouble. He must resist telling her how he felt about her, and would do nothing but admire her from afar.

But he took to walking about Rock Ferry much more than he used to in the hope that he'd see her again. He'd stroll past the convent and even down Rockville Street where she had her room, but he never caught so much as a glimpse of her.

He knew Esther was interested in him; he could see it in her eyes, and when he spoke to her as she was leaving, she found ways to prolong their conversation. He told himself a hundred times to stay clear of her – it could only lead to trouble – but she seemed more attractive each time he saw her. He fantasised about buying her a necklace and fastening it around her long neck. He was sorely tempted.

Aimee had told Prudence that they'd met Esther that night and gone to the show with her. Goodness knows it had been innocent enough, but just that mention seemed to have awakened Prudence's suspicions, and now if Esther was mentioned she made unpleasant comments about her, which made any liaison all the more dangerous. But Esther had a ready wit and her smile could light up her face, and Walter wanted more.

He found himself suggesting a meeting for tea and cakes in the Central Hotel in Birkenhead, and she accepted with alacrity. Afterwards he took her to the Argyle Theatre, and once the lights dimmed, he leaned across to kiss her lovely neck. She felt for his hand and returned his kiss, and from that moment there was no turning back. He knew he was taking an enormous risk, but he gloried in it. He felt invigorated; twenty years younger. He couldn't stay away from her; he took her to concerts, cinemas and out to dinner at hotels.

It took time, but eventually she invited him to her room. He couldn't stay away, but often it was her landlady who answered the front door, and though she was never rude, and didn't forbid him to come in, she gave him such knowing looks that he hated the thought of facing her. After that, he told Esther what time to expect him, and she'd watch for him at her window and run downstairs ready to open the door for him. It made him feel guilty and uncomfortable.

'We'll have to find you a more private place,' he said, and together they went round the estate agents and found a snug little terraced house in Southdale Road, close to Victoria Park. He arranged to pay the rent and took great pleasure in escorting her to the furniture shops to choose what she would need: a comfortable double bed, curtains and crockery.

'You won't be able to come home from school and find a hot meal cooked for you,' he said, remembering how Prudence complained of the work that involved.

Esther laughed. 'It'll be a pleasure to do that; a house to myself will give me a new lease of life.'

As easily as that, Esther had become his mistress, and Walter felt a new optimism. All tedium and worry was gone. He was walking on air; life was utter bliss. Now they shared a secret that had to be kept from everyone.

One Sunday morning, Walter was in his study when the phone rang. It was Armand. 'I've heard at last from the *notaire*.' Aimee was with him, and he mouthed the news to her. 'He says I can now distribute Micheline's belongings according to her will, after which probrate will be granted. As I'm considered the main beneficiary of this will,' Armand went on, 'the taxes will be paid from the cash willed to me. I have signed and returned the form he sent me saying I am willing to swear under oath that the information I have given is true. I understand he's posted a similar form for you to sign.'

'Yes, it came today. Candida tells me Aimee has done well out of this.'

'Indeed she has. I fear Micheline and I lived too well, and of course she spent heavily on paintings – they were her passion.'

'Aimee is here with me and wants to speak to you. I'll put her on.'

'Is this it?' she asked eagerly. 'Everything's settled at last?'

'More or less,' Armand replied. 'You can now take the paintings your mother has willed to you. Do you want me to hire a firm to pack up your inheritance and dispatch it to you, or will you and Candida go to La Coutancie and do it yourselves?'

Aimee was thrilled and excited. 'Oh, I'd love to visit La Coutancie again. I'll have to ask Candida if she'll come, but I think she'll want to; she loves it there too. I'm so pleased everything has been settled in time for my summer holidays.'

'There are a lot of your mother's things in my flat here that you might like to have too – clothes and some bits of jewellery.'

'Thank you.'

'She willed her personal possessions to you, Aimee.' He sounded awkward. 'Would you like to spend a night or two in Paris on your return journey and see what's here? I have no spare room, but I could book you and Candida into a nearby hotel.'

'Yes, I'd love to do that, thank you. I'm absolutely thrilled.' There seemed no end to what her mother was giving her. 'I've never been to Paris.'

He laughed. 'You'll have a good time here. Let me know when you're planning to come and how long you want to stay, so I can make a booking for you.'

Candida was equally delighted when Aimee told her the news, and began planning their trip right away.

CHAPTER TEN

O N THE APPOINTED DAY, Candida met up with Aimee
and Walter at Lime Street station. As before, he bought
them magazines and saw them onto the London train. She
found Aimee in a buoyant mood. 'I don't yet know how I've
done in my School Certificate exams, but that's me finished
with school. I can relax now that it's all behind me. Most of my
classmates are leaving, and we all agree we feel fully grown up
at last. Thank you for helping me apply for a place at the
Liverpool art school. I've heard from them and I'll be starting
there in September.'

Candida felt like singing as the train sped through the
French countryside. When they arrived at La Coutancie,
the sun burned down, spreading the golden light she knew so
well. She sighed happily. 'I love to feel the heat of the sun on
my face.'

'Too hot,' Francine told them as she helped carry their
luggage inside. 'Much too hot.'

Candida thought the house felt pleasantly cool. She drank
the lemonade Francine had prepared for them and hurried up
to her room to open her case and get out a cotton dress to wear
in place of her heavier clothes.

Aimee went straight to her mother's studio to feast her eyes on what was now hers. Candida joined her five minutes later with the inventory and looked with fresh eyes round Micheline's studio. She felt again a stab of envy that Micheline had achieved so much more than she had, and it had brought her so much more of the world's wealth.

'Up to now, Frankie and I have painted with watercolours on paper,' Aimee said, 'and as children's paints are so much cheaper, we've bought those rather than professional-quality ones. Now we can give up economies like that.' She ran a hand over her vast collection of paintbrushes and pens. 'These make me feel inspired. I wouldn't mind trying an oil on canvas now. Perhaps using Maman's materials will help me to paint as well as she did.'

Candida's mood had changed; now she was all practicalities. 'Aimee, this isn't the time to paint. We've got all this to pack and send off.' She'd ordered packing cases when they'd come out to make the inventory, and they were stacked on the landing in readiness. Francine had told her the gardener would come up and help if they needed him.

They made a start, but Aimee kept whooping with joy at everything she picked up, so they made slow progress. 'I'm tired now,' she said after a while. 'Let's leave it until tomorrow and go down to the river for a swim instead.'

It was bliss to feel the cold water against her hot skin, but Candida found herself brooding on the luxuries that Micheline had bought with her earnings. After what had happened to her father, she'd vowed to stay away from anything illegal. It would be terrible to be locked up in prison as he had been, but she had to have money to live on and she was getting desperate. The wealth of this world always seemed to go to other people, never to her. The only way she could think of to get the money she needed was to do what her father had done.

She shouldn't, of course she shouldn't, and the risks were frightening, but she began to toy with the idea that she might be driven to it.

'Packing is downright exhausting,' she said, 'and these pictures are so valuable that we have to be careful they aren't damaged in transit.' She was very glad that the years she'd spent working in her father's gallery had taught her how it should be done. 'And we must make sure that the crates are properly insured.'

When Micheline's studio began to look bare and the sitting room walls had blank spaces, Aimee rang Armand in Paris to ask if they might go into the bedroom he'd shared with Micheline to see her clothes and personal possessions, and decide what she wanted to take.

'Yes, of course,' he told her, 'but many of her more prized possessions are here in my flat. You will see them when you come here.'

He asked to speak to Candida, and Aimee heard them discussing the Renoir. She understood he was asking whether Gramps might want to sell it to release funds, and offering to do it through his gallery, but Candida was offhand about that. Aimee remembered then that though both were kind to her, they were often frosty towards each other.

She left them to it and went upstairs to her mother's bedroom. It was a large room with a huge high bed, and was furnished luxuriously. There were wardrobes and drawers full of clothes, Armand's possessions mixed up with Micheline's.

The clothes here were what Maman had worn every day, jumpers and skirts for cooler weather, or simple summer dresses, some of which had been made from dress lengths she recognised as coming from Gramps's mill. She liked them and felt she'd enjoy wearing what her mother had once worn. All the same, she was ill at ease in here, and though she'd asked permission to come, she felt like a peeping Tom.

She picked out the clothes she liked best and was about to take them to her own room to try on when she noticed a small stack of photograph albums. She reached idly for the top one, sat on the bed and opened it up. Here was her much younger self, aged about four, with Maman holding her hand. She knew exactly where it had been taken; she could see half the church in Dignac, and the patisserie was just a few yards further down the street. She thumbed through the album, fascinated by her own past, then returned it to the stack and picked up another.

She found herself studying photos of Maman's wedding to Armand. She herself had been a bridesmaid, and had worn a beautiful dress that Maman had bought for her in Paris; afterwards it had been much admired at birthday parties in Rock Park. Candida and her grandparents were smiling out at her from the photos, all looking somewhat younger, but what she really wanted to see were photos of Maman's first wedding, to her father. Even Gramps didn't have any pictures of that.

She delved deeper into the stack of albums and found one filled mainly with photographs of Armand. He was a handsome man now with his pencil moustache, but in earlier pictures he was clean-shaven and even more gorgeous. No wonder Maman had fallen in love with him.

She went on turning the pages. Unlike Maman, Armand had annotated his photos, and she found pictures of him with his family: his parents and his sisters Yvonne and Suzette. Aimee knew she'd met them at the wedding but she couldn't remember them. She knew he came from Port Grimaud, near Saint-Tropez. She'd never been there but would absolutely love to go.

Candida came in. 'I was wondering where you'd got to. Have you found anything here you want me to pack?'

'Well, I need to try on these summer dresses to see if they fit.'

Candida laughed. 'Aimee, you're rich now; you can buy all the new clothes you want.'

'I'm not sure about that. Gramps is going to be in charge of my money until I'm twenty-one, and Grandma says he's got a mean streak and doesn't understand that girls need more clothes than men.'

'He'll let you have all the money you need. What are these old photo albums?'

'This one belongs to Armand. I know very little about him, so it's interesting.' Aimee put it back and picked up another, opening it on her knee and staring silently at the pictures.

'What is it?' Candida came to sit on the bed beside her and pulled the album to her own knee. The photograph showed a romantic scene: a young Armand holding a pretty girl in his arms. They were gazing into each other's eyes. She read the caption; it could be translated as: *Eulalie and I plighting our troth.*

She gasped in astonishment and turned the page. In the

next picture, Armand was standing behind the same pretty girl with his arms wrapped round her, both of them smiling in blissful contentment. This time the caption read: *Alone together at last. Two marvellous weeks in Corsica.*

'I didn't know about this, he kept it very quiet,' Candida said.

'I didn't know either. I've never heard of anyone called Eulalie. Do you think they were married?'

'Yes, look, she's wearing a wedding ring. You can make it out in both photos.' Candida slid the photo out of its corners. 'There's a date here; looks like he was married in 1920.'

'Maman must have known about it; these photos were in her bedroom.'

'Yes, but she never breathed a word to me. I thought I was her best friend, and that we told each other everything.' Candida was put out about that. She pulled the album closer and continued to turn the pages. 'Oh my goodness, he has children! Just look at this! Pierre was born in 1922 and Blaise in 1924, two sons. Here they are, handsome just like him.'

Aimee was counting on her fingers. 'They'll be eleven and nine now.' She was dumbfounded.

'They're your stepbrothers,' – Candida's eyebrows rose even higher – 'and we didn't even know they existed.'

'I don't think my grandparents know either. They'd have said something.'

'Prue would have said a great deal.'

'I know you don't like each other much,' Aimee said, 'but Armand has always been kind to me, protective even.'

'He thinks you're just a child.' Candida slipped another photograph from its corners in the album and handed it to

Aimee. 'Nobody will believe he's been married before unless we show them these.'

Armand's first marriage had taken over Aimee's mind; it was only the prospect of visiting Paris that made it possible to think of anything else. She remembered Esther Kerr showing her pictures and talking about the main tourist sights to give her practice in spoken French. She couldn't wait to see all those places.

She and Candida had spent five busy days at La Coutancie, and now all her new possessions were safely packed and on their way to England. They caught the train north and in Paris changed to the Métro. Candida had no difficulty finding her way round the city to the small hotel where Armand had booked them in for bed and breakfast.

Like all the buildings in that central district, it looked very old. They had to share a room, and the bathroom was communal and down a narrow winding staircase. Armand had left a note for them saying his flat was at the end of the same street and that he'd call for them at seven o'clock and take them to a small bistro for dinner.

Aimee saw that as a great treat, and she loved the French decor and the delicious food, but the subject of his first marriage was an obstacle between them. She wanted to talk about it but couldn't bring it up. It had been kept secret, and somehow that made it seem shameful, something that must remain hidden. She'd never felt close to Armand, and this had pushed them even further apart.

CHAPTER ELEVEN

THAT NIGHT, CANDIDA FELT jittery and couldn't sleep. Thinking about her father had unsettled her.

When she looked back on the years she'd been growing up, they'd been very good ones. Dad had always been happy and seemed to enjoy all he was doing. He regularly took her to the Walker Art Gallery in Liverpool and led her round the paintings there, telling her what the artist was trying to convey. He taught her to recognise the personal style of each artist, the different ways in which they employed paint and colour and the brushes they'd used to get their effects.

He had loved painting his own pictures. He'd used their spare bedroom as a studio and showed her how he mapped out important pictures with pencil and paper before starting on the canvas. Her strongest memory was of him standing by his easel adding layers of paint with quick, confident strokes. There'd been absolutely no sign that he'd had worries; she'd seen no clouds in the sky.

Then suddenly his pictures had begun to sell. She'd always considered him to be a master of his trade, and now, at last, it seemed that his work was being appreciated. Soon he had his own gallery, where she could study the original works of current and as yet unappreciated artists, as well as the lithographs and signed and numbered prints of those who'd already made their names.

When she returned from Paris with her final diploma and was having little success selling her own pictures, he told her that getting started was very difficult. It was a problem faced by many artists at the beginning of their careers, and he'd found himself in exactly the same position, with a wide collection of work he couldn't sell and a complete lack of funds. Except, of course, he'd had the added responsibility of having to see to her needs too. He'd told her she must not forget her ambitions and suggested that she carry on painting in her spare time but come to help him in his gallery.

Candida plumped up her pillows and thought of her time there with him.

The gallery had always fascinated her, and for years it had provided them with every comfort. Life had never been better. Her father held events and exhibitions to which artists, dealers and friends were invited. It turned out to be a huge business success. Soon the gallery was selling pictures by famous artists at fantastic prices: Picassos, Van Dycks, Gainsboroughs and Matisses.

Candida acted as hostess and met their customers, pouring wine for them and enjoying their views on the art world. She loved the social scene and saw the sales that followed. Dad let her choose smart and fashionable clothes and took her to restaurants and the theatre. He booked holidays for them, and bought books and pictures. He believed in enjoying life and said, 'I want you to enjoy it too.'

That had been a marvellous time. Then suddenly their extravagant life had come to an unexpected and very abrupt end. Candida was truly shocked. She had seen her father as an honest and honourable man, popular with his customers, and could hardly believe he was being accused of selling fakes in his gallery. He denied ever copying a picture painted by someone else and swore that all his works were original.

But later he admitted, 'I've been fooling the experts for years, but now they've caught me out. I got careless. I painted a fine picture of Christ turning water to wine in the style of a seventeenth-century Dutch painter.'

Candida remembered him working on that painting. 'Would that be the Vermeer?'

'Yes. I used cobalt paint to colour Christ's robe, but that paint wasn't available in the seventeenth century. It was a stupid mistake and one I should never have made.'

In the nightmare that followed, her father was charged with deception and fraud and accused of selling fakes. She understood at last that he was imitating the styles of famous painters to enhance his own pictures. He could catch the atmosphere of Degas, Vermeer or any other artist by using similar colours, paints and brushstrokes.

He would let it be known that he had found a previously unknown picture by one of the great masters, and offer it to an expert for his opinion and assessment. 'I thought I was being careful to leave no clues as to its origin,' he told her, 'and nine times out of ten the painting would be given a certificate of authenticity. Then it would be sold at auction for a high price, and the expert would be congratulated on recognising such a masterpiece. It's been great fun; I've really enjoyed fooling the experts who said I wasn't much of a painter and knew nothing of art. I've made lots of money and had a great time.'

'You gave me a great time too, but Dad, you didn't tell me it was against the law.'

He sighed. 'I didn't, and I've really messed up this time. I stopped questioning what I was doing. I got careless. Sorry, love, so many artists were doing it and getting away with it that it seemed the only way for me to survive.'

Candida pursed her lips. Her father was no longer a young, ambitious painter seeking recognition for his work. He was a sick and broken man who looked older than his fifty-six years.

'Promise me you'll never try to make money that way,' he said.

'I certainly won't,' she assured him. 'Not now I've seen what it's done to you.'

Over the weeks of waiting for his trial, Candida felt sick. He could talk of little else, and she could see the effect the stress was having on him. He had always been cynical about the art world, and had a very low opinion of experts and dealers. 'I've seen them buy pictures from the artist and then offer them for sale at double the price.'

'So have I,' she said. Working in his gallery had taught her a great deal. 'But it's no good telling me you're not the first artist to turn to faking.'

'The museums and art galleries of the world are full of fakes, and there are hundreds more in the private collections of art connoisseurs who have paid fortunes for the privilege.'

'Dad, is that any justification? It's safer to stick to the old honest ways.'

'There's nothing honest about the old ways, love. Faking in the art world goes right back into history. I heard marvellous stories circulating at those parties we held at the gallery. You must know the one about Leonardo da Vinci. Not only did he create a marvellous marble sculpture of David in Florence, but in his early days he sold a marble Cupid to a cardinal in Rome without telling him he'd first stained and buried it for a while to age it as an antique. He did it to produce much-needed funds while he was struggling to make his name.'

'But hundreds of years have passed since Leonardo's time, so how can anybody really know? I took it as just a jokey story, and everybody laughed, so obviously they did too.'

'I understand at least a dozen excellent replicas of Leonardo's *Mona Lisa* exist, many reputedly by his students.'

'No, Dad, surely not the *Mona Lisa?* When I was at art school, we all used to slip across to the Louvre to stare at that with great reverence.'

'Yes, and from time to time the various owners of these replicas have claimed that their version is the real thing.'

'They couldn't really believe . . . ?'

Her father laughed. 'The Louvre is satisfied it owns the original. Close examination shows the composition was changed slightly below the layer of top paint, and it has an unbroken record of ownership from the time it was painted.'

'Thank goodness for that.'

'But there are fakes in probably every museum in the world. It's all kept quiet, of course, because it's embarrassing for the experts to be faced with proof that they can't tell the difference. Come on, let's go to the Walker Art gallery and I'll point out a few of mine.'

'Dad!'

'I mean it, let's go.'

He took her straight to a Vermeer. 'This one was widely feted and hung in several exhibitions. It's one of the best I've ever done. My composition had to be strong and simple like his, and I had to age it to make it look as though it had been painted in the seventeenth century. All pigments have to appear genuine and must stand up to chemical tests. Everything has to look exactly right.'

Candida was not only dumbfounded but felt sick. Dad really had had a long and successful career as a faker.

He walked her to another part of the museum and stood her in front of a Monet. 'He is an Impressionist that I really admire. Your friend Micheline is a modern Impressionist. Modigliani, on the other hand, I've never been that fond of. His pictures are not unlike a child's drawing, but I find his style particularly easy to copy. I've done quite a few because they took up very little of my time and helped me develop my faking skills.' He smiled. 'With a day or two's work I can produce a fresh master piece by almost any of the famous painters and fool all the experts. Faking is a great game; it gave me a marvellous time as well as a good living, but it is important to fool everybody.'

Later that year, he was sentenced to twenty months in prison, and his gallery and most of his other assets were deemed to be illicit gains from illegal faking and confiscated.

That, Candida knew, was how she came to be in the tight financial corner she was in now.

CHAPTER TWELVE

A RMAND TOLD THEM TO come to his flat the next morning to look at Micheline's belongings. His building
looked equally old-fashioned and had the same small rooms
and winding stairs. He made them coffee when they arrived.
'I've moved all her things to the spare bedroom,' he said, and
showed them where it was.

Aimee heard Candida gasp with admiration when he
opened the enormous wardrobe. 'Gorgeous Paris fashions,' she
said, fingering the silk, the cashmere and the fur. 'Such lovely
evening dresses.'

'She needed them here for events in my gallery,' Armand
said. 'I'm having one this evening; you could come and join in,
see my place. Micheline spent a lot on her clothes; she needed
smart dresses and suits for daytime too. Perhaps you can get
some use from them. Take what you want.'

Aimee thought they looked wildly expensive, but they were
clothes for middle-aged ladies, and not her sort of thing at all.
She sought for words to describe them that wouldn't offend
him. 'They're very sophisticated,' she murmured.

'From top designers,' he said. 'Also, Micheline didn't
much go in for jewellery, but there are a few pieces in this
drawer – a watch and a couple of rings. Take them if you

want. She'd want you to have them.'

'I've already taken her watch from La Coutancie.' Aimee held out her wrist for him to see.

'This one is a cocktail watch, diamonds, rather flashy. She has willed all her personal belongings to you. Those two pink suitcases over there were hers; you'll probably need them to take her clothes away.'

Aimee took one look and her mouth dropped open. 'They're absolutely gorgeous, film-star luggage. Are they really for me too?'

Armand smiled. 'Of course. There is just one thing.' He held out his left hand. 'I'd like to keep this, if you don't mind.' A solitaire diamond sparkled on his little finger. 'It's your mother's engagement ring; she wore it most of the time and it reminds me of her, of what we had.' His lips straightened and his dark eyes clouded with grief and despair.

Aimee felt a rush of sympathy for him and felt for his hand. It would take time to really understand Armand. He was a very private, introverted man, but now that she was getting to know him, she liked him better. He was being very kind to her.

He went to work and left them to it. Candida's eyes shone as she fingered the clothes. 'These are beautiful. Micheline certainly had good taste.'

'You have them,' Aimee said. 'I couldn't wear them; they're nothing like my style.'

'They're for the older woman, but just look at the quality of this material, it will wear and wear. You'll probably love them when you're my age.'

Aimee shook her head. 'No, I prefer Maman's summer cottons. If you like them, you take them.'

'I can't do that. You're a minor and Walter will want to decide on things like that.' Candida was looking at the labels. 'These are haute couture: Coco Chanel, and Elsa Schiaparelli. They're like new and must be worth quite a lot of money. We'll take them home and see what your grandparents think. They could be sold.' They not only filled the pink suitcases to capacity, but Candida had to go out to buy another large bag.

Aimee was thrilled when they walked down the Champs-Élysées to have a light lunch in one of the cafés and see the Arc de Triomphe. Afterwards they went back to Armand's flat as Candida wanted to make sure she'd packed everything Aimee was entitled to take.

That evening, Armand took them to his gallery and introduced them to his assistant, Dominique Dupois. She was in her twenties, a bundle of smiling energy and enthusiasm.

Armand said, 'I'm expecting important clients who I hope will buy from me. One in particular collects Paul Nash, and I have a painting here by him. I have to attend to business, so I'll leave you with Dominique for a while.'

Candida felt immediately at ease as Dominique put a glass of champagne in her hand and led them round the paintings. It was all so familiar. She used to do this job for her father. She also found that she and Dominique shared a similar background; they had both worked their way through art school.

'He has some very important paintings,' Aimee said, 'by artists of high calibre. A Degas, no less.'

'But also lithographs, and signed and numbered prints of many others as well,' Dominique pointed out. 'Most art galleries do; not everybody can afford originals, and many lesser-known artists paint very saleable pictures.'

Candida saw the Paul Nash and several other pictures sell for what seemed fortunes.

They were introduced to painters whose names they both recognised. Dominique told them they had been friends of Micheline's.

Candida said, 'You have to be burning with ambition and full of drive to succeed like your mother.'

'Yes,' Aimee agreed. 'I'm not sure I have that, but it's all very exciting and I feel I'm really living at last.'

It was late when Armand walked them back to their hotel. Aimee kissed his cheek when he was about to leave them. 'Thank you for everything,' she said.

The two pink leather suitcases and the rest of their luggage was lined up against the wall in their room, ready for an early departure the next morning.

CHAPTER THIRTEEN

FRANKIE HAD KEPT THE job in the restaurant at the Ship Inn, although the Saturday art lessons had come to an end. Candida and Aimee had gone to France again and he was missing them. He found the endless washing-up of greasy pans and plates less to his taste than serving in the newsagent's, but he could only get temporary shop work.

Saturday was usually a busy night, and if one of the waitresses dropped or spilled anything in the dining room, it was his job to clean up the mess as soon as possible. Tonight a customer had had an accident with a glass full of red wine, and he was summoned to remove the broken glass and some of the sodden table linen.

Never before had he seen anybody here that he knew, but as he rushed in with his dustpan and brush, he passed a table where Aimee's grandfather was eating. He looked up and Frankie almost said hello but realised in time that Mr Kendrick was looking not at him but at his companion, Aimee's French teacher.

Frankie was all fingers and thumbs as he tried to sweep up the slivers of glass, while the waitress fussed over the customer. The light in the dining room was subdued and he wondered if he'd been mistaken. As he crept back to the kitchen, he sneaked a good look at them. He had not been mistaken, and he guessed from the way they were looking at each other that they were having an illicit affair.

Last week his grandad had been reminiscing about working around the houses in Rock Park. 'Those who have money to spare spend it on entertaining themselves, and getting as much enjoyment from life as they can.' He went on with a snigger, 'I've worked in one house where I know for sure the owner has an additional lady friend and keeps it all very much under wraps.'

'Who is that?' Frankie had wanted to know.

Dad laughed. 'I can't tell you,' he said. 'I need the jobs he gives me in his garden. If he knew I'd let the cat out of the bag, I wouldn't get any more work, would I? I find it safer to keep my mouth zipped.'

The next day Frankie told his grandad about seeing Mr Kendrick in the Ship Inn with Mrs Kerr. He laughed. 'So now I know who you were talking about.'

He watched Dad's mouth fall open in surprise. 'Well I never. I wasn't talking about him.'

'Not Mr Kendrick?'

'Frankie, don't you dare breathe a word about him. He's another that pushes work my way, and he's kind.'

'I wouldn't say a word anyway, except perhaps to Aimee.'

'No! Particularly not to her. He's a nice old gentleman and everybody thinks the world of him. You've got to keep it quiet. Not a word to anyone, promise.'

Walter had not been spending as much time at the mill as he should have been. He wanted to be with Esther, and he couldn't suddenly absent himself from home more than he was already doing without Prudence asking questions. He'd counted himself an honest man but soon realised he couldn't live a double life without telling one lie after another and inventing a facade of imaginary events to cover what he was doing.

Saturday was a half day at the factory, but Walter no longer went in at all that day. It hardly seemed worth travelling over to Liverpool for only a few hours, and it gave him the chance to enjoy some time with Esther. He'd told Prudence he was meeting an old friend from his student days for lunch, and that they attended meetings at the Cotton Exchange on Saturday afternoons. He always had likely details of his fictional day worked out for when he got home, should she ask. Meetings at the Cotton Exchange were often training sessions for new entrants and were held in the mornings, but he thought it unlikely she'd discover that.

As Prudence always went to church on Sunday evenings, he spent some of that day with Esther too, as well as at least one evening during the week. He knew he was taking a terrible risk, but at least he was enjoying life and had a spring in his step.

He couldn't avoid hearing bad news on the wireless and knew it wasn't just the cotton industry that had fallen on hard times; trade of every sort had been in the grip of a deep depression for years. It was just that life with Esther had been cushioning him against that.

While Aimee and Candida were in France, he left work early each day and went straight to Esther's house. She usually prepared a meal, which they ate together with some ceremony. One night he stopped on the way to buy a bottle of wine to drink with it, but when he let himself into her house, he could see she was not her usual happy self. She flung herself into his arms and wept on his shoulder. 'Walter, I think I must be pregnant. I'm overdue.'

He spoke before he could stop himself. 'Are you sure? It's early days to assume that, isn't it?'

'Yes, but I'm scared stiff.'

Walter went cold. 'I've always been careful . . .' He kept a good supply of French letters here and had always used one. 'Could you be mistaken?'

She fought her way out of his arms; he could feel her horror at that. 'It should have been last week; it was only when I looked at the calendar this morning that I realised I'm seven days overdue. I work in the convent; to say the nuns will be shocked is the understatement of the year. I'll have to leave and there'll be no going back afterwards.'

Great sobs were racking her body, making her shake. He wrapped his arms round her and held her tight against him. 'I don't want you to worry, Esther. I promise I'll look after you whatever happens. It is too early to be certain, you know it is.' He opened the bottle of wine he'd brought and handed her a glass. 'We have to forget about it for a few weeks until we can be sure. It's the only way.'

'Yes,' she agreed, and gulped the wine down.

'Esther,' he said seriously, 'we're in this together; I want you to know that if there is to be a baby, I'll do my best to help in every way I can.'

That quietened her, but it was a miserable evening for both of them. Walter went home desperately afraid that he'd landed Esther in big trouble. He couldn't eat and he couldn't sleep. He worried himself sick through the hours of darkness, and found it quite impossible to take the advice he'd handed out to her – forget the problem until they could be sure.

The next time he saw her she said the same thing. 'I'm certain that I am having a baby. I wish I wasn't; I wish I could suddenly wake up and find it was all a bad dream.'

Walter had heard that some doctors would help their patients manage unwanted pregnancies, so he knew there was a way. At one time all the family had been cared for by Dr Greening, a close neighbour of theirs, but Prudence had taken against him. She said he didn't seem to understand her illness and was doing her no good. So for the last year or so Dr Ellis had come regularly to see her, and had also looked after Aimee's coughs and sore throats.

Walter thought Dr Greening rather too close to consult, as Prudence and Aimee were friendly with his family, so although he was embarrassed, he went to see Dr Ellis and screwed himself up to ask if he would help Esther.

Immediately the doctor's gentle bedside manner was gone. 'What you suggest is against the law,' he said coldly. 'I can't help you; I would be open to criminal prosecution if I did.'

Walter fled back to Fairholme and shut himself in his study. Prudence would not take this lightly; it was more than a guilty secret, and Esther was far too close to home for there to be any hope of keeping it quiet. He should never have let this happen; his business barely earned enough to keep one family, and he could see no way he could afford a second, though now he was afraid he would have to.

The next time he saw Esther, he was comforted to find she'd changed her mind. 'I've always thought I'd like to have children,' she said. 'I was disappointed that my marriage to

116

Tom didn't bring any, but most of the time he was fighting in France. This isn't the way I'd have chosen to do it,' she laughed nervously, 'but what else can an unmarried woman of thirty-seven do? I'll get myself a couple of loose dresses to try and hide it. I should count myself lucky to have this last chance of a child.'

Walter was relieved to find she was ready to accept her pregnancy. He hugged and kissed her and told her, untruthfully, that he was happy too. He felt he had to allay her worries, reassure her that all would be well. He knew she was looking to him for financial support and it was his duty to provide it, but recently he'd given little thought to his business.

Walter finally got down to the job he hated and spent a morning assessing the earnings his factory had made that year. He discovered they were down again. That was not his only problem. He had lunch with his friend Charlie Henderson, who had designed his patterns for as long as he could remember.

Last year Charlie had said, 'It's time I retired and put my feet up, Walter.'

'Couldn't you put it off for a while? I shall be very sorry to see you go.' Walter had known then that he urgently needed to do something to prop up his pattern department, but before he could do anything, there had been the tragedy of Micheline's death, and Christmas had been on them. So Charlie had stayed on. It was only now, when he announced that he would celebrate his sixty-sixth birthday next month, that Walter's mind came back into focus.

'I don't know how I'll cope without you,' he said.

'You'll have to. I've no energy left.'

Last year Mrs Caldwell, second in command in the pattern department, had gone off sick with some dreadful disease, and there seemed no likelihood she'd be able to return. Between them, she and Charlie had been responsible for all the patterns that were printed on the curtain and dress-making materials, and for teaching and overseeing the work of the apprentice pattern designers.

They had helped the factory stay ahead of the game with products that had remained fashionable and therefore saleable, but now Walter needed to attract new talent and he could ill afford to pay for the best. He had no idea how he could solve this problem; he'd need to think hard about it. He went home early that afternoon feeling at the end of his tether.

CHAPTER FOURTEEN

WALTER HAD NO SOONER reached home than a taxi was drawing up at his front door with Candida and Aimee inside. He went to let them in. Aimee wrapped her arms round him and said, 'Gramps, we've had an absolutely marvellous time. The only thing I regret is that I was unable to see all the sights of Paris that Esther told me about.' Their luggage was piled up in the porch. 'We've brought home such a lot of lovely things. I feel so lucky.'

Her high spirits lifted his, and the sound of her voice brought Prudence into the hall. Nothing would do then but that the suitcases must be opened to show her Micheline's haute couture clothes. Candida set about doing that while Aimee went to make them all a cup of tea.

When she brought the tray into the sitting room, Candida had the garments spread about and Grandma was examining them closely. 'I knew Micheline had beautiful clothes,' she said. 'Walter, just look at this bronze satin gown, isn't it utterly fabulous?'

'Prue, dear, when could you possibly wear that?' he asked. 'We don't go to fine dinner parties and dances any more.'

'Did we ever? More's the pity.' She was not in a good mood, and he should have had the sense to let it drop then.

'Could you even wear that style? Wouldn't it show rather too much bare flesh? You'd catch a cold.'

'You must have got out of bed on the wrong side this morning,' she retorted, frowning.

Aimee tried to salvage the situation. 'I won't want to wear them. You have them, Grandma, if you like them.'

'I do. Look at this jacket and skirt; it's so beautifully made. I must try it on. I must try them all on and see what suits me.'

'They could be sold,' Candida said brightly. 'There's a market for clothes like these. They could be worth quite a sum.' Her tone had become frosty, reminding Aimee that she'd already offered them to her. 'You won't want them spread round this room all evening. I'll help you carry them upstairs, Aimee.'

'Take them up to the room next to our bedroom,' Prue ordered. 'I'll look at them tomorrow when I'm fresh.'

Later, Walter rang for a taxi to take Candida to Rock Ferry station. When it arrived, he and Aimee helped her carry her luggage out to it.

'What's the matter, Gramps?' Aimee asked. 'I can see you're out of sorts.'

He sighed. 'Trouble at the works. Mr Henderson wants to retire and I must look for someone urgently to design my patterns.'

'Patterns to print on your materials?' Aimee asked. 'I could do that for you; so could Frankie.'

'It's not that easy, love. Everything depends on having colours and designs that sell. There's a lot you'd have to know about the cloth and dyes before you'd get it right. It takes my apprentices three years to learn the trade.'

'If you've got apprentices,' Candida said, still with a touch of tartness, 'I'd say they're in a fortunate position. Can't they do it?'

'Some succeed and some don't. I'm not too hopeful of the current two.'

'Didn't you say you'd already settled on the patterns for autumn?' Aimee asked.

'Yes, they're in production now, but I need an ongoing stream of fresh ideas.'

'Well,' Candida said, 'as you've agreed that I should come and paint with Aimee during the holidays, we could spend our next session on patterns and see if we can be of help. The trouble is, I'm not sure exactly what you want. I've seen some of your materials, of course, but I don't know what we should be aiming for.'

'I have several books of the patterns we've used over the years. Each one is produced in three or four different colour combinations. I'll bring one of the books home tomorrow.'

'Good,' Aimee said. 'Frankie's good at colours.'

They waved Candida off, and when Walter headed for his study, Aimee followed him. 'Gramps,' she said, 'there's something I want to ask you. Did you know that Armand had been married before?'

'No, no, I don't think . . . What makes you say that?' She knew from his face that it was as big a shock for him as it had been for her. 'Are you sure?'

'Yes, we found photographs of his first wife. He also has two sons. Candida didn't know either.'

'Good Lord! Did they divorce?'

'They must have done. Maman must have known; we found lots of pictures of them in their bedroom.'

'Perhaps his first wife died.'

'But where are the two sons? They aren't living with him, and they're still only nine and eleven. I've brought a couple of pictures to show you; they're in my case. Why did Maman keep quiet about this?'

He was frowning. 'A mystery, isn't it? But don't worry about it, Aimee; it doesn't matter now, does it?' He sighed. 'Grandma didn't like Micheline marrying again. In a way, I didn't either; it meant she could forget about Alec while we were still grieving for him. Forget about you too. It took me time to see that she deserved a fresh start; the young can't live on memories. Still, that's all in the past now.'

When Aimee had gone to her bedroom to unpack, Walter propped his elbows on his desk and dropped his head into his hands. Alfred Kendrick and Sons had started as a weaving shed over a hundred years ago, and in all that time had provided a living not only for generations of his family, but for thousands of employees. If it hadn't been for the Great War, Alec would have been running it for him by now. Micheline had been well able to look after herself and Aimee, and now Aimee wasn't going to want for much, so perhaps it didn't matter that the whole of the Lancashire cotton trade was in steep decline.

What caught in his craw was that after the successes of his forebears, he would be the one who couldn't stop the business going bankrupt. It was hurting his pride as well as his pocket.

Prudence spent all the next day examining Micheline's haute couture clothes. The beauty of the materials and the designs made her long to wear them, as her wardrobe had long since grown shabby and out of date. She persuaded Aimee to come up and help her fasten the buttons and zips, and considered carefully whether her dressmaker would be able to let the garments out. When Aimee said, 'It isn't possible, Grandma; Maman was a much slighter build,' she was bitterly disappointed but had to accept it.

She kept only a velvet evening cape, an ermine stole and some Hermès silk scarves. She was tempted by Micheline's hats, but Aimee had laughed when she tried one on, and they were mostly too girlish for her. 'You should keep some of these clothes in the back of your wardrobe until you are older,' she told Aimee.

'They'd never suit the kind of life I have,' Aimee insisted. 'Besides, don't they look a little old-fashioned now?'

She found Maman's clothes on the big side for her, and she certainly didn't want to put on weight, but she picked out a Coco Chanel suit, a simple day dress in blue velvet and a Hermès scarf for herself.

Finally, at dinner that evening, Prudence said, 'Such a shame, you'd better give them to Candida after all. There are so many lovely coats and dresses and suits, clothes for every occasion. I bet she'll get into them or have them made to fit her.'

Walter looked up from his mutton chops. 'Candida has a good figure and she's pretty much the same size as Micheline. So is Esther Kerr. Perhaps you should share Micheline's clothes out.'

A crimson flush ran up Prudence's cheeks. 'Why don't you ask Candida to sell them? Such a waste to give them all away.'

Aimee hadn't seen Esther for a few months, but she knew

what suited her, and she picked out several outfits she thought she would like. She understood how much effort Candida had put into making their trip to France run smoothly, and thought she deserved some reward for that. She'd seen her stroke the satins when she'd packed them, and knew she longed to wear them. She decided the bulk of Micheline's wardrobe should go to her.

Aimee was more than pleased to see the packing cases arrive with the treasures she'd inherited from Maman, and they had been taken upstairs to a spare room near the old school-room. She and Walter were getting up from the breakfast table when the morning post arrived bringing an envelope that she knew would contain her School Certificate results. It looked so formal it gave her sudden misgivings; what if she hadn't passed? She closed her eyes and gave it to Gramps. 'You open it for me,' she said.

She heard him laugh. 'Congratulations,' he sang out, and she saw an enormous smile spreading across his face. 'You've got top marks in art and French as we expected, but also in English as well.' He kissed her cheek. 'Excellent. You've done wonderfully well. Run up and tell Grandma. She'll be pleased for you.'

Aimee bounced upstairs, floating on air. She knocked on Prue's door and flung it open. 'Grandma, I've got the results of my School Certificate.'

The room was in semi darkness; the mound on the bed stirred. 'What's that?'

'My exam results.' She knew Grandma's instructions to Dora were that she was not to be disturbed until after nine, and then only with her breakfast tray. In her excitement, she'd forgotten that.

Grandma was reaching for her false teeth; once they were in she said, 'You'd better open the curtains, dear, and then you can show me your letter.' Aimee put it into her hand. 'My glasses, dear. Yes, thank you. You have done well and I'm very pleased about that.' Poor Grandma, she looked terrible, much older in bed than she did when she was up and dressed. 'What time is it? As I'm awake, you'd better tell Dora I'll have my breakfast right away.'

'Yes, Gran. What would you like this morning, egg and bacon?'

'Oh no, dear, bacon plays havoc with my digestion. I'll have two eggs scrambled on toast, and remind her that I don't like my toast too brown. She often lets it burn, you know.'

Aimee gave Dora an edited version of Gran's instructions, then rushed up the garden to the old stables to see Frankie. She found him chopping onions in his kitchen. 'There's so much I want to tell you,' she said. 'It seems ages since I saw you.'

'You're always going off where I can't follow. When will Miss Rathbone be coming again?'

'Tomorrow morning at nine o'clock, but if you're doing nothing today, the packing cases have arrived from France with all Maman's brushes and paints and stuff. I want to show it all to you and I could do with a hand opening the cases.'

'Exciting,' he said, wiping away an onion tear on his sleeve. 'I'd love to come and help, but Dad's working at Springhurst, and I said I'd get a casserole on for tonight. I'll have to do this first.'

'I'll give you a hand.' Aimee pushed some carrots into the sink and ran cold water to wash the soil off them.

'Thanks. I'm dying to see what you've got. These will be the raw materials of a professional painter; what your mother used to produce the paintings that made her famous.'

'I helped to pack everything up so I know there's loads of paint of every sort, as well as inks and that sort of thing. It's beyond everything I'd hoped for. There's a picture she was working on that's half finished, and some really famous paintings that she collected. There's an original by Renoir.'

'Phew, a Renoir? I can't wait to see that.'

'It's just a small still life, a vase of flowers. There's another thing, Frankie. Gramps is short of staff in his pattern department, so I told him you and I could concoct patterns to print on his cloth. He's brought home a book of the ones he's already used to show us the sort of thing we must aim for. When Candida comes tomorrow, she's going to tell us what she knows about patterns and colour combinations, and we'll all try our hand at it. You'll be there, won't you?'

'You bet.'

Before Frankie opened the packing cases, she took him to the schoolroom to show him the pattern book. They pored over it for a long time. 'I reckon we could produce similar stuff to this,' Frankie said. 'I have one in mind already, but I'll have to buy a lot of new paints; I hope I can find the colours I have in mind. My pattern has sprawling shades of pale to mid green, with enough blue to make it seem like liquid, and it'll need touches of dark green and brown too. I want it to look like the ocean.'

'My goodness,' Aimee said, 'you're well ahead of me. You really do see colours.'

Later, when they'd opened the cases, he said, 'Oh Aimee, you are so lucky. There's everything you could ever need to paint and draw here. Look at all these different brushes . . . pastels and crayons . . . and all these canvases.'

They spread them round the spare bedroom so everything would be to hand when they needed it. 'There are so many things here I've never even thought of, and it's all professional quality. Now you can try anything you fancy.'

'Look at the watercolours; are these the shades you need to paint your pattern?'

'Why yes, these are marvellous.'

'You must pick out what you want and take them home.'

'Will you be allowed to give any of this away?'

'Of course I will. Maman has left it all to me, and Gramps is asking you to make patterns for him. Colours are important in the cloth trade; he'd want you to have them.'

'Oh gosh, Aimee.' Frankie was more excited about her new materials than she'd expected.

'Do you want to try out some of these other things? You said once that you were keen to have a go with oil paints.'

She watched his eyes go slowly round. 'I did get some left-over house paint from Riverview and tried it on a piece of board, but it wasn't a success. I had only three colours.'

Aimee laughed. 'I remember you showing me that. It had a yellow sky.'

'Yes, yellow and black. I was trying to paint a sky threatening snow, a storm coming.'

'I want you to take some of these.'

'I can't, not if I take the watercolours for the pattern.'

'Course you can. Take some of these oil paints in different

colours, and a canvas.' She pulled one out from the pile stacked against the wall.

'It doesn't have to be new, Aimee. Professional painters often reuse their canvases. There are several there that have been used. Are they your mother's false starts or what?'

'I don't know. I don't think she painted this one; it's just broken trees, like no-man's-land in the war. Not her sort of thing at all. Would you prefer it?'

'No, it's a bit too big for me to start on. This smaller one will suit me fine.'

'There are several sorts of solvent over in the far corner that you could use to clean the old paint off.'

'Candida says some artists just paint over an old picture, but I would find that distracting.'

Aimee was collecting together a selection of paints for him. 'I'll help you carry them home.'

'Aimee, you're very generous, but I can't take all this,' he said. 'You must know I could never use it all.'

Aimee ruminated on that. Her mother had used it all and presumably she'd needed it. Not for the first time she wondered if she really had Maman's talent, and whether she could achieve a painting career in the way Micheline had. Sometimes she could see a spark in Frankie's work that she herself didn't possess.

She had been tortured by doubts for some time now. Ever since she was small, people had been telling her she'd grow up to be a famous artist like her mother. At first she'd gloried in such a rosy prospect, but recently she'd begun to feel she didn't have it in her. She'd tried to tell Gramps, but he'd just said, 'It will take time and practice, but it will come.' She wanted it badly and it wasn't that she hadn't tried, but once Frankie came to the lessons and she saw what he could do with so little teaching, she knew she was right.

Aimee had a vision of her future in Gramps's mill. She would design all the patterns he needed. It wasn't painting great pictures like Maman, but it was a job allied to art. She felt she'd be able to do that.

When Candida arrived in the schoolroom the following morning, Aimee and Frankie were waiting for her. She opened the pattern book Walter had brought home. 'I hope you've both had a good look at these. This is the standard we have to aim for,' she said. 'I've had a word with Mr Kendrick about what he's looking for, and it needs to be similar to what he's used before, but also different, and more up to date.

'You have to bear in mind that the pattern always has to be extendable in every direction, up and down and on each side. It has to be suitable both for the material and for making up in garment factories or curtain shops, and also to be used by the home dressmaker.

'I've had a go myself.' She pinned up three attempts she'd made, using watercolour on paper, and went on to talk about the motifs used to make the patterns and how the size differed between dress materials and curtains. 'Now, see if you can do better than I have. Paint a pattern Mr Kendrick will want to use.'

Once her students were concentrating on their task, she went to the next room to look at Aimee's inheritance, which was now neatly laid out. It took her breath away. There were several of Micheline's paintings – not the ones she'd exhibited and put up for sale, but those she'd done during her formative years; and here was the one she'd been working on at the time of her death. A sunlit street scene with café tables on the pavement.

Candida fancied finishing it; it would be easy and she'd do a good job on it. The waiter needed darker trousers and more definition in his features, and . . . No, not that! She pulled herself up with a jerk as she remembered that Walter and Prudence had seen the painting when they'd been at La Coutancie, as had Aimee and Armand. They would all know immediately what she'd done.

She had vowed never to paint pictures and fraudulently assert they were the work of a famous artist, as her father had done. Seeing him in prison had terrified her, but here were all the materials she'd need to paint pictures that would be attributed to Micheline. These materials had actually belonged to her; no expert could find fault with them. If Candida's work was as good as Dad's, she could guarantee that nobody would know the difference.

She'd promised him she wouldn't do this, but she desperately needed cash to pay her rent. She'd thought about it a lot and decided it was the safest way. She was planning two original pictures copying Micheline's style: a large important one and another much smaller. What could be more reasonable than to say Micheline had given them to her?

Micheline actually had given her two paintings, one where she'd used her as a model – she'd hated having to part with that – but she had to eat, so long ago she'd sold both of them to keep herself going. Micheline had been generous and given away quite a lot of her work; Candida had seen the framed pencil drawings in the Kendrick dining room, a very youthful self-portrait together with one of Alec. There were also several portraits of Aimee painted at different stages in her childhood hanging on the wall going up the stairs.

She looked around the room. Micheline had left Aimee a good supply of canvases, some new but many used; also several pictures that were old but worthless. She could easily clean them off or paint over them. At art school they'd been taught to stretch the canvas and prime it with gesso, but it seemed Micheline had found somebody to do that chore for her. Candida decided she'd take what she needed now, before Aimee had time to size up her inheritance and know what was really here.

She often brought her portfolio with her – well, her Dad's portfolio really – to carry the prints and posters she used when she talked about the styles of different painters. She'd brought it today to hold the patterns she'd painted, and had deliberately left it here by the door so she could slip in the canvases when she had the chance to come in here alone.

That moment was on her now. She listened nervously; the only sound was the pounding of her own heart. She was shaking with guilt because this was theft, and though Aimee would give them to her if she asked, she mustn't know she had taken Micheline's materials. Nobody must know she intended to copy her style. That had to be kept secret from everyone.

Packing up at La Coutancie had given her the chance to look everything over and think about what she would need. She selected a large used canvas with some bleak painting on it that she didn't think was Micheline's work, together with a much smaller new one, and hurriedly slid them inside her leather case. As there was still no sound from the schoolroom, she added a few tubes of oil paint. They would give her pictures absolute provenance.

She'd do only two paintings – it wouldn't be safe to make a habit of it – and they had to be absolutely correct in every way. She knew she must be extra careful not to make mistakes. She'd paint beautiful pictures so her friend would be proud to have her signature on them. She didn't think Micheline would begrudge her that.

Micheline's paintings wouldn't bring in anything like the price of a Vermeer, whose style her Dad had been caught fraudulently copying, but they would give her some desperately needed cash and keep her going for a while.

When she had them ready, the easiest thing would be to ask Armand to sell them through his gallery, and if questions were asked, get him to find an expert to authenticate them. Experts had almost always authenticated her father's fraudulent pictures, and she thought they would do the same for her.

But Armand must never suspect they were fakes, and neither must Aimee. Nobody must.

Candida felt another rush of guilt when Aimee took her to the room next to Grandma's bedroom and told her she'd kept most of Micheline's Paris wardrobe for her. She even offered to lend her the pink suitcases to take the clothes home. She hadn't dared hope for so much and felt a surge of delight at the sight of so many gorgeous outfits. 'Thank you, thank you,' she said, but it made her feel a thoroughly bad person. She was taking advantage of Aimee. 'As I have to carry my portfolio, I'll just take one case,' she told her. 'I'll leave the rest here until I come again next week, if that's all right.'

'Of course.' Aimee helped her pack the soft wool delaine and merino day clothes she could wear immediately.

'I'll leave the evening gowns until later,' Candida said. She had always envied Micheline's expensive Paris fashions and couldn't wait to get them home to try them on. They would make her look like a successful woman, even though she was acutely short of cash.

She had to squash the feeling of shame that she was following in her father's footsteps. She was still crossing her fingers and hoping everybody had forgotten his fall from grace. He'd been well known in Liverpool, but in the last months of 1929 it had not been headline news, because the Wall Street crash was happening at the same time. Nobody had mentioned it to her for a long time, and she certainly wasn't going to bring it to anybody's attention. It was hard enough to find employment without that.

CHAPTER FIFTEEN

AIMEE PUT ALL THE patterns they'd made into a folder, and when she heard Gramps come home that evening, she took it downstairs to show him. While he poured himself a whisky, she went to the kitchen to fill his cut-glass jug with water. Prue was there looking frazzled. 'I haven't got the veal on yet,' she said. 'Can you remember how long it takes?'

'I'll be right back, Grandma. Two minutes.'

Gramps added water to his glass, then took a sip and opened the folder on his knee.

'These are the patterns we've done for you today,' Aimee said. 'I need to know honestly what you think. Are we on the right track? If not, can you tell me again exactly what you want? I've got to help Grandma with the dinner now.'

She took the bottle of sherry with her into the kitchen and poured a glass. 'I can't relax and enjoy that any more, can I?' Prue said irritably. 'What use is Dora when she wants to go home at five o'clock?'

'She does get everything ready,' Aimee said gently. 'Is it to be veal chops with mashed potato and cauliflower?'

'Yes, and that means a cheese sauce. I do wish Walter wouldn't keep asking for chops. If only he preferred stew, Dora could make it all before she went.'

'I'll see to it, Grandma, don't worry. Dora has already grated the cheese.' At least she wasn't afraid of having lumps in her sauces, not now that she'd had plenty of practice. And there was never any washing-up; the dishes could be dumped in the sink to wait until Dora came back in the morning.

Over dinner, Gramps said, 'I'm pleased with those patterns you've done. The three of you might be on the right track.' He was in good form, praising the veal chops too. Afterwards, when Aimee had made the coffee, he took the patterns out of the folder. 'We've not done anything quite like this before, but I like these swirling greens and blues. This could work as a curtain fabric. Is it your work or Candida's?'

'You're taking after your mother,' Grandma said. 'I knew all those art lessons were a good thing.'

'That's one of Frankie's.'

'Oh! I quite like it; ask him to do this design in different colourways. I'll need three or four to put it into production. Tell him I'm thinking a fairly heavy fabric with a shiny sateen finish.'

'And the other patterns?' Aimee laid out those she'd done.

'Too much like ones we've done before, and too similar to those other manufacturers have been turning out for years. I need something fresh, something to catch the eye.'

She pulled Candida's out too.

'Not bad for a first attempt,' he said. 'In fact they're all not bad; you just need to try again and keep at it. And particularly that lad Frankie; he might just have the right touch. I do like this one.'

Aimee stared at the swirling greens and blues. 'He'll be delighted.'

'Why don't you all try other things? We usually do a few ginghams in different colours, but I need new ideas beyond stripes and spots. Why don't you try patterns for children's clothes?'

'We will, Gramps,' she said. 'We'll all have another go.'

'Good. If I can produce some really outstanding fabrics and they sell well, the business might just earn a bit more profit.'

Candida gazed with satisfaction at the Paris fashions she'd brought home, now draped round her bedroom. She'd tried them all on and was delighted with the effect. Some needed slight adjustment to make them fit perfectly, but she could do that herself.

She had already planned out the picture she was going to paint and have attributed to Micheline; the setting was to be a pool on the Dordogne where they used to swim. She remembered baking-hot days with the sun coming through the overhanging trees dappling the water, giving a little shade. She'd have two young girl swimmers, one in a scarlet bathing suit and the other in bright yellow, and two young boys in wet shorts and bare feet, with perhaps a picnic hamper on the bank.

She was tired now but she needed to get started because her debts would keep on increasing until she earned some money. She unpacked the canvases and began to clean off the black and grey painting of broken trees. This would take a day or two, because every stage of this painting was going to get the minute care that Micheline had always given to her pictures.

In the meantime, she'd plan her picture out on paper. She taped several sheets together to make it the same size as the canvas, and then sketched the outline in pencil, rubbing out parts of it to adjust the size, bringing the figure who would wear the scarlet swimsuit into the foreground. The next day she adjusted it further, and when it looked right, she transferred the sketched outline to the canvas she'd now prepared with three coats of gesso.

So far, so good. Tomorrow she'd start painting. She was looking forward to squeezing paint out of the tubes and thinning some colours with linseed oil. The smell of paint never failed to delight her, and already it was in her nostrils.

As Walter sipped his after-dinner coffee, he couldn't stop his gaze going to the picture over the fireplace. He was beginning to dislike the Renoir that Candida and Armand said was worth a fortune. He was used to seeing a dark, very formal portrait of his father-in-law by a painter he'd never heard of up there. It had been twice the size of the Renoir and had left a discoloured square on the wallpaper round the vase of flowers. 'That won't do,' Prudence had said immediately. 'It spoils the room, makes it look really shabby.'

'It's comfortably shabby,' Aimee said. 'The Renoir does brighten the place up a bit, though.'

'Daddy's portrait needs cleaning,' Prudence said. 'It's hung over the fireplace for the last fifty years. I think I'll arrange for that to be done. When it comes back, you could move the vase of flowers up to your bedroom, Aimee.'

As one of Aimee's trustees, Walter knew he wasn't paying the attention he should to the fortune she'd inherited. For his own part he could ill afford to support her and pay her art school fees, so he was very glad he no longer had that responsibility, but it had never occurred to him that she would be given original pictures by famous artists like Renoir. He'd seen these pictures hanging on the walls at La Coutancie on every visit, but they had never struck him as being particularly valuable, and that just proved how ignorant he was about art.

Of course Armand Duchamp, her stepfather, was her other trustee, and he had worked in the art world all his life. Or had he? Walter's other problem was that he'd never learned to speak French properly, and hadn't always understood what they were talking about at those Christmas parties. It hadn't worried him then, but now he felt that he hardly knew Armand.

Candida had already mentioned selling the Renoir, and that seemed very sensible to him. Aimee had changed her mind about keeping it. 'I'd rather have a regular allowance to spend on myself than see that in our sitting room,' she said. 'It doesn't look right here.' She was growing up, eighteen now; and besides, she had other paintings that meant more to her.

'Next time Candida comes,' he said, 'will you ask her to wait until I get home. I'd like to have a word with her about selling it.' He could trust Candida; she'd been Micheline's best friend for many years and she understood the art world in a way he did not. She spoke good French too.

Normally Walter spent very little time at home on Saturdays, but today he was home by teatime, before Candida left. 'Come to my study,' he said. She was wearing a very smart outfit, and had a new sophisticated hairstyle too. 'You come as well,' he said to Aimee, 'but perhaps you could make us a cup of tea first.'

'I've had a look at the London market,' Candida told him, 'and I've changed my mind about that. Armand has offered to sell the Renoir through his gallery, and I think he'd get as good a price in Paris as anywhere. I don't suppose he'd charge Aimee much commission for doing it either.'

'Commission? Would that amount to a lot?'

'Quite a lot; it would be a proportion of its value.'

'And the price would be in francs?'

'Of course, but Armand will use a professional currency exchange and have the money paid in sterling into a bank account here. He sells pictures for people who live all over the world.'

Walter considered Candida to be his expert on painting, and was surprised at how much business knowledge she had. He hesitated; he didn't know how to put this delicately. 'I shouldn't feel wary of Armand, I know, but somehow I do.'

'I always have,' Candida agreed, smiling at him. 'He's secretive. I didn't know Micheline was his second wife, or that he had two small sons. Neither he nor Micheline ever mentioned those things.'

'But she knew,' Aimee said quickly, 'and he's been very kind and generous to me, and to you too, Candida.'

'Ye-es.' She was less than wholehearted about that.

Aimee went on quickly. 'He booked our hotel in Paris and paid the bill, and took us out for meals and to his gallery. And he didn't have to give me all my mother's jewellery.'

'He kept her engagement ring.' Candida's tone was cold. 'That was probably the most expensive piece she had.'

'But he must have bought it for her in the first place,' Aimee insisted. 'I like him. You and he were always frosty to each other, but that's no reason to distrust him.'

'He thinks I'm pushy,' Candida said.

Walter thought Armand might be right about that, but he could feel his dislike of the man building up again. He'd been more than rude about Alec. Who but a complete rotter spoke ill of the dead? Even if he was right about Alec being afraid, who could blame him when he'd been fighting on the front line in a foreign country?

He said coldly, 'I hardly know Armand. What can you tell us about him? You've known him a long time, haven't you?'

'Oh goodness, yes, ages. He was at art school in Paris when we first went there, a very handsome fellow, and popular with the ladies, though he hardly noticed Micheline then. We spent most of our time painting; she was ambitious.'

'Wasn't he?'

'I suppose he must have been; we all were. We didn't see him after he left, though I heard plenty about him when she met him a few years later. It was only after they were married that I began to see more of him, and it would only have been when I went there on holiday.'

'He looks older than you and Micheline.'

'Yes, but only a couple of years. He must be at least forty, and has had an art gallery in central Paris for a long time.'

'You don't know what he did before that?'

'He told me that he once worked on the streets doing quick pastel portraits of tourists, but many art students try that. Micheline told me he also did some illustrations for magazines.'

'I expect he got a job in a gallery and enjoyed it,' Aimee said. 'Like you.'

'He would have met artists there and befriended them, hoping that if he stayed close their success would rub off on him,' Candida said unkindly. 'No doubt he learned a good deal about the French art world and knows many people in it.'

'I don't like the fact that Micheline was his second wife and that he's never mentioned being married before,' Walter said. 'You didn't know about that, did you?'

'Not until we saw the photographs of his first family. That was a shock.'

'But that doesn't mean we shouldn't trust him to sell the Renoir,' Aimee said. 'You are going to ask him to do it, aren't you, Gramps?'

'Yes, if that's what you want.'

'I do.'

'Then I'll ring him this evening.'

'The problem now,' Candida said, 'is that it's here over your fireplace. We should have left it where it was. Armand could have taken it from there to his gallery.'

'We can send it to him, though.'

'Yes, but we'll need to speak to him first. Did you keep all that packing material?'

'No,' Aimee said. 'Dora arranged for the bin men to take it away.'

'Then I'll have to get some more and send it with a courier firm.'

'That sounds expensive,' Walter said.

'Yes, but it's valuable, and we are shipping it to another country. Armand will pay all the expenses and deduct the cost from the money he collects when it's sold.'

'We should have thought about this before it was brought here,' Walter said. He had a lot of important decisions to make and he mustn't be indecisive about this. Indecision was one of his problems.

* * *

If there was one thing Aimee really wanted to do, it was to help Gramps make more profit from his mill, so straight after breakfast the next morning she went round to find Frankie. 'Gramps likes your pattern of swirling greens and blues and thinks it might work as a curtain fabric. He said you might just have the right touch.'

Frankie's face lit up. 'Did he? That's marvellous; he liked it better than yours?'

'Yes, better than Candida's too, though he thought ours were quite good for a first attempt.'

He came straight back with her to the schoolroom to paint different-coloured versions of the same swirling pattern, while she finished off an oil painting she'd already started of the two historic training ships moored in the Sloyne. She wasn't at all satisfied with it. It had an amateurish look about it.

She ate lunch with Grandma, and afterwards Frankie came back and together they tried their hand at patterns for children's clothes. She gave him more paper and watercolours to take home so he could carry on painting in his bedroom.

That evening when she brought Gramps his pre-dinner whisky and water, she said, 'Frankie and I have been painting patterns all day, trying to do what you suggested.' She showed him what she had done first. He looked through them slowly and carefully. 'I haven't got the magic touch, have I?' she said.

He sighed. 'They're not bad.'

Aimee sighed too. 'That's not the same as saying that they're good and I can expect to see them printed on fabric any time soon. For years everybody has been expecting me to show the same talent as Maman, but I haven't got it, have I?'

'Well, Candida's the best judge of your skill at painting scenes, but I don't know about your patterns.'

'I'm sure, Gramps. I enjoy painting and I love hearing about the famous masters from Candida, but I really haven't got the talent that puts that extra sparkle into my pictures.'

'Maybe after a few years at art school you will have. Micheline was very keen that you learn everything you could.'

Aimee shook her head. 'Even art school will never give me the talent she had. I'm disappointed, but I feel I have to face facts. Seeing what Frankie turns out has taught me that, and it's better if I accept it now.'

'But you're starting at art school next week,' he said. 'It's what you said you wanted. Grandma is convinced you have what it takes.'

'I know, but I'm afraid Grandma is wrong. Everybody praises what I do, but only because Micheline Durameau Lepage is my mother. They expect it, and they want to encourage me, but they're wrong. Take a look at these patterns Frankie has done. I know they're nearer what you want. He's also better at views and portraits.'

Aimee laid out on the floor the same swirling pattern in shades of yellow and orange, black, white and grey, several different shades of purple, and also blues from sky to navy.

'What d'you think of these? Would they be more the sort of thing you would use?'

'Oh my goodness! Yes, this is more like it.' Walter picked up the blue pattern. 'I like this, midnight blue and all these lighter shades. Except blue isn't a popular furnishing colour.'

'Frankie's very keen; he's been working hard today,' Aimee told him. 'We tried patterns for children; he's done this one of toys printed on different-coloured backgrounds, everything from balls and books to toy trains and dolls.'

'That's not bad either. Yes, stylised toys, simple outlines, bright colours.'

'Here he's changed the colour of the background but kept the toys the same.'

'That makes it easier and cheaper to produce in a range of colours. Yes, toddlers might like it and therefore manufacturers will. I can see this in flannelette made up into children's pyjamas.'

'Isn't flannelette made from wool?'

'Can be, but I have machines that make it from cotton. It sells well too. Old people like to have bedding and nightclothes made from it. It's cheap, and warmer than ordinary cotton.'

'I don't see how a machine can turn plain cotton into flannelette.'

'It's a staple of our business. We start with a loosely spun yarn, then a fine metal brush is used on the fabric to raise fibres and create what we call a nap. There's a good market for it to the small clothing manufactures in Birkenhead.'

'Frankie's got lots of ideas for patterns, Gramps – horses or other farm animals, for example, or yachts – but he thinks they're too much like those in the book you brought home and you'll have used them.'

'Well, they don't have to be very much different. This lad has more idea of what's needed than the apprentices I've employed for the last couple of years, but he's got a lot to learn. The dyes I use aren't true to the colour of the paints you have, and he really needs to know about those – their various costs, whether they fade or run when washed, and how some work better on one type of fabric and others on another. Leave these patterns with me and let me think.' Walter refilled his glass. 'And *you'd* better think carefully about your future. I suggest you go to art school as planned; it's never right to change direction on a whim. Besides, I've paid a term's fees.'

'All right, I will. It's just that I'm having doubts about whether a career in art will be right for me.'

'Even if you have an adequate income, you'll need a career of some sort. Everybody has to have something to do in life.' Walter sighed. 'You'd better go and see if Grandma needs a hand with the dinner.'

Aimee started her course at the art school and found it brought huge changes to her life. She'd always had breakfast with Gramps, but now she caught the ferry over to Liverpool with him and really did feel grown up.

She thought at first she was going to enjoy it, but it didn't take her long to discover that her new classmates were brimming with enthusiasm and ambition and had talent that more than equalled hers. Worse, she'd been brought up with encouragement from the family and one-to-one teaching from Candida and had believed she could do as well as her mother. She found nothing new in the teaching at art school and soon realised she was bored with it.

It upset her, but she'd anticipated this and felt she had to face it; no point in burying her head in the sand. She'd made her choice: she wanted to work in the mill, learn how to manage the business. She wanted to help Gramps, take her father's place at his side. All she had to do now was convince him she could do it.

Chapter Sixteen

From somewhere, Walter dragged up the energy to think about the mill and concentrate on his urgent need for patterns. He'd hoped and half expected that Aimee would be able to do it, as so much of her education had been focused on art, but what Frankie Hopkins was turning out surprised him. It was nearer to what he wanted. The boy seemed to have a flair for it.

He could start him as an apprentice to learn the technical details, but he was turning out usable patterns already and would not need the full training; he might even get bored with a long apprenticeship. In any case, Walter needed patterns now, and had nobody else who could provide them. He must be careful not to lose Frankie's services. Perhaps it was a good thing that he was friendly with Aimee. But where did a lad like that get his talent for art?

Walter thanked God that Aimee's mother had left her those valuable pictures; they would give her money to live on, because she was getting restive and beginning to question the future that had been laid out for her.

Teenagers were much inclined to change their minds, but that had never been Aimee's way. He couldn't believe she didn't want to carry on with art school. It was what

Micheline had wanted for her, and nothing else had ever been considered. Aimee had always agreed, but it seemed she didn't really know what she wanted. The income she'd have if she sold one of the pictures she was about to inherit would guarantee a comfortable future for her, and it eased his mind that she'd have it.

That evening he said to her, 'You can tell that friend of yours that I think his patterns look promising. How would it be if I took him as well as you to the works to show him how a pattern works out on fabric?'

'He'd love that, Gramps, and he could see all the different dyes you use.'

'Perhaps we should take Candida too, if you think she'd like to come.'

'She would, I'm sure.'

'Well, let me see, what about this Thursday? You could let the art school know that you won't be in, couldn't you?'

Frankie was thrilled and couldn't stop talking about it. Candida was pleased too and said she'd join them at Liverpool Central; she turned up in one of Micheline's Paris fashions looking extremely chic. Aimee had put hers to the back of her wardrobe because they were too large for her, and wore her Sunday dress. Frankie looked smart in his only suit.

Aimee always enjoyed her visits to the mill, and knew the set-up and some of the staff. Gramps introduced Candida and Frankie to his manager. 'Douglas Tate has overseen our production for many years,' he told them. 'He's worked here most of his life. That's right, isn't it, Douglas?'

'Yes, sir, over thirty years.'

'This is Francis Hopkins and Miss Rutherford. I want you

to show them round, and tell them what they need to know about the pattern process,' he said.

When all the machines were working, Aimee could barely hear what was being said, but she found it fascinating. Frankie was leaning closer to their guide so as not to miss a word, but it was the way the machines could print block patterns on fabric that kept him spellbound. He asked questions about everything. 'This material doesn't look like cotton,' he said at one point.

'It's glazed cotton,' he was told. 'Stiffer and with a pleasant shine, very popular for curtains.'

'It's not at all how I imagined it.' He shook his head. 'It's all so much more mechanised, more advanced. I understood the textile industry was falling behind.'

Douglas said, 'In the early years of the century the industry was revolutionised by new techniques and new machines, but now, in this depression, Mr Kendrick can't take on new innovations.'

'Why not?' Aimee wanted to know. 'Is it because it would be very expensive to buy new machines?' Perhaps she could invest some of her money from the Renoir sale and help him that way.

Frankie's brow wrinkled with concentration. 'Wouldn't it be worth it if it made the operation more efficient?'

'It would; it would mechanise the mill and we wouldn't need to employ so many workers, but Mr Kendrick is reluctant to do that because it would put quite a number of our workforce on the dole. They have family responsibilities and would find it very difficult to get other jobs. Come and see what's going on in our laboratory. We are doing lots of research into fibres. We hope that it'll soon be possible to create synthetic fibres from chemicals and make cloth from them more cheaply than from natural materials. That would free us from having to rely on importing raw cotton.'

'Why, that's marvellous,' Aimee said. 'So there will be a future for a mill like this?'

Douglas laughed. 'Of course, but that depends on so many things and it's all in the future. Nobody knows how long it will take or if it will happen at all.'

Aimee's mind was buzzing. Gramps was always telling her the cotton industry was in decline, but it seemed there could be a way forward.

He took them to a nearby café where he often had his lunch. Aimee had been there with him before, but this time they were quite a merry party as they tucked into steak and kidney pie followed by rice pudding and stewed plums.

Frankie was thrilled with what he'd seen in the mill; it was opening new vistas for him. As they walked back from the café, Mr Kendrick said, 'I'd like a word with you, Frankie; come to my office. Aimee, take Candida to the dispatch room and show her the finished products.'

Frankie followed him, wondering why he was being parted from the others. His hopes soared when he saw his patterns laid out across Walter's desk. Walter took a seat and waved him to the chair opposite.

'I like your work,' he said. 'I'm going to put this swirling pattern into production in four different colour schemes for curtaining, and also this children's toy pattern on flannelette. They'll be part of our stock in the spring.'

Frankie gasped and had to resist the urge to throw his arms round him in a grateful hug.

'You seem to have a natural bent for what I need,' Walter continued. 'These are different and will bring a touch of freshness to our products. Mr Tasker, our sales manager, thinks they should sell well.'

'Thank you, sir.' There were so many things Frankie wanted to say, but he could hardly get his words out.

'But I need a continual supply of new designs and there's a great deal you really should know if you are to keep producing usable patterns. Would you be willing to come here as an apprentice? There isn't much of a wage, but since you're showing more promise than the average apprentice, I'll pay you a little extra plus a bonus for any of your patterns I use.'

'Willing?' A huge smile spread across Frankie's face. 'You must know I'd jump at a chance like this. It's a marvellous opportunity for me.'

'Good, I like to see enthusiasm like that. I'll add the cost of a third-class rail ticket for the first year.'

'Thank you, sir, I'm very grateful. In fact I'm over the moon.'

'Right, it's nine to five and you can start next Monday morning. John Hampton has done two years already. Come with me now and I'll introduce you and ask him to show you the ropes.'

Frankie looked round the room he'd be working in, saw the equipment he'd use and felt he was flying. He walked on air as he was taken to rejoin the others in the sales department. Aimee and Candida were fingering fabrics and talking to the foreman.

He took a deep breath, savouring the smell of new cloth.

'Your grandfather likes my patterns. He's offered me an apprenticeship here.'

He felt Aimee's arms come round him in a congratulatory hug. 'That's marvellous.'

He wanted to hold onto her, keep her close, but the foreman's eyes were on them. 'Didn't he tell you?' he asked.

She was laughing. 'He said your patterns were the sort he wanted, but he didn't mention that he wanted you in here every day. He had to ask you first, didn't he? Make sure you'd agree.'

'Of course I'd agree. I can't believe my luck. I'm absolutely thrilled. He's going to pay me for painting patterns? Doing something I really enjoy? My dad will never believe this.'

Candida said, 'I'm pleased for you, Frankie. I'm sure you'll do well. I wish you all the luck in the world; I just wish Mr Kendrick liked my patterns too.'

'I can't believe he prefers mine.' Frankie felt his beaming smile would stay on his face for the rest of the day. 'I'm very grateful to you, Candida. You've taught me all I know.'

'Every teacher hopes for pupils like you,' she said. 'Talented and keen.'

When Candida left them at Liverpool Central, Frankie said to Aimee, 'Most of all, I'm grateful to you. Without your help, I couldn't have done this.' He leaned across and kissed her cheek. 'You've opened doors for me into your world.'

'I wanted your company. You're far more fun than Lydia Greening.'

He laughed. 'We've got on well since we were kids, haven't we?'

Frankie was bubbling with his good fortune. In the privacy

of Aimee's back garden, he threw his arms round her and pulled her close. 'Oh Aimee, this has really been my day. Thank you for everything you've done to make it happen. I'm thrilled with the way things are going.' His lips came down on hers and he held her tight. Then he rushed for the apple tree and was up over the wall in a flash.

He knew he shouldn't have done that; he knew Mrs Kendrick thought he should stay away from Aimee. She was an heiress, and even though he was allowed to work in their mill, he would definitely not be acceptable as her boyfriend. Not in a thousand years.

Aimee let herself into the house still tingling from Frankie's kiss. She thought about him a lot. Lydia Greening was always boasting about her boyfriends and belittling Frankie. 'I'd give him the push if I was you,' she'd sneered. 'Not good husband material. He'll never be able to earn enough to live on.'

But now that Gramps had taken him on, Aimee could see no reason to believe that. All Frankie had needed was a chance.

When Gramps came home later that day, he said, 'Frankie's a nice lad, brighter than most. Perceptive. I hope he's able to continue turning out new patterns.'

That pleased Aimee. 'If he can draw patterns you can use, he'll be good for your business, won't he?'

She'd suspected for a long time that Frankie had more talent than she did. It was a bitter pill to swallow, but it seemed that she'd never be a top-class artist. She was trying not to be envious. Frankie was her friend and he had so little; nobody needed this piece of good fortune more than he did.

* * *

Once Frankie started to work regularly at the mill, everything began to feel a bit flat to Aimee. It was a wet autumnal afternoon, and Grandma had tried to persuade her to go to a meeting in the church to help raise funds for orphans in Africa, but she didn't feel in the mood for it. She had not seen Esther Kerr since the night of the Pierrot show, but she still thought of her as a friend, and on Gramps's suggestion she'd put aside some of her mother's Paris fashions for her.

She decided that now was the time to get in touch with her and hand them on. She went to her grandfather's study, lifted the receiver and dialled the number she found in Gramps's address book. Hearing Esther's voice filled her with pleasure at the thought of seeing her again.

'It's Aimee,' she said. 'How are you? My mother has left me all her personal possessions and her clothes, and they've arrived here at last. Some are by Paris designers but they aren't for young girls, and Gramps suggested I give them to you and Candida. She's taken hers and I'm wondering if you are free to come over and collect yours now.'

There was a stunned silence. 'Esther, are you there?'

'Yes, hello, Aimee. How nice to hear from you after such a long time.' Aimee realised immediately that Esther was struggling for words, which was quite out of character for her. 'My circumstances have changed somewhat,' she managed at last. 'I'm expecting a baby.'

'Oh, what a surprise! I didn't know you were married.'

Again she felt the hesitation. 'Yes – this summer.'

'You didn't tell me.' She couldn't understand that. She'd thought they were close.

'Could you possibly come and see me at my place?'

'Well – yes. It's Rockville Street, isn't it?'

'No, I've moved. It's Southdale Road now.'

'I don't know where that is. How do I get there?'

She had to concentrate on what Esther was telling her. 'It's not all that far. Walk up Bedford Road and turn right into Old Chester Road; you'll come to it along there.'

'Can I come now?'

'Yes, I'd love to see you. Come and have a cup of tea with me. I made scones this morning.'

'I'll have to put the clothes in a suitcase first, but I'll come as soon as I can.'

Aimee was excited; this would be much better than staying in by herself. She had the feeling she'd caught Esther on the hop, because she'd hardly known what to say to her. But by the time she arrived at the terrace of small Edwardian houses, she seemed to have recovered.

On this damp afternoon, it was comfortable and cosy inside. Esther was still the same as ever, and after ten minutes in her company, it was as though the months they'd been apart disappeared. They laughed together, shaking out the Paris fashions and gasping with wonder at each outfit.

Aimee was curious but didn't like to pry. She noticed Esther wore a wedding ring and asked about her husband. Esther told her that he was a teacher. She made tea and they had the buttered scones; Aimee stayed rather longer than she'd intended.

When she was leaving, Esther said, 'I'm very grateful for the lovely clothes and we've had a great afternoon. You must come and see me again.'

Grandma was home before her. 'Where have you been?'

she demanded. 'You didn't tell me you were going out.'

'No, I'd had enough of painting patterns by myself, so I decided to take Esther's share of Maman's Paris fashions to her. I had a very interesting afternoon. She's married now and expecting a baby.'

Aimee was shocked to see Prue's face flash with anger. 'Don't you ever go there again.' She almost spat the words out. 'It's not a suitable place for you to visit, and don't you dare invite her here either.'

'But why not? She lives quite nearby, in a comfortable terraced house, and she's very good company.'

'Don't you understand what I'm saying to you?' Grandma's eyes bored into her. 'You are not to see Esther Kerr again. She is not an appropriate person for you to know. She is an unmarried woman with a baby on the way.'

'She *is* married, Grandma; she told me her husband's a teacher.'

'Then it's not just her morals that are at fault; she's a liar as well.'

With that, Grandma strode upstairs to her bedroom and slammed the door. Aimee leaned back against the sitting room door and took a deep breath. She was always aware of the need to keep Grandma calm and unruffled, but now, unexpectedly, she'd really upset her. She didn't understand why she'd suddenly turned on her in fury.

CHAPTER SEVENTEEN

WHEN WALTER GOT HOME, he found Aimee was not her normal cheery self. She fetched him his glass of whisky as usual, but he could see she was upset. 'Where's Grandma?' he asked.

'She's gone to bed in a huff. I took Esther some of those Paris fashions as you suggested I should, but Grandma was really cross about it. Furious, in fact. It quite shocked me.'

Walter had to suppress a gasp of horror. She'd been to see Esther? He was more than shocked; he didn't know what to say.

'She's married to a teacher and they're expecting a baby. Grandma rushed up to her room and it looks as though she's going to stay there, so I'd better start the dinner.'

Walter felt numb. This was a catastrophe, but he had to appear normal. 'What is it tonight?'

'Steamed cod with mashed potatoes and parsley sauce, peas and carrots,' she said. 'Dora has made the sauce, so it's easy.'

Once he was alone, he took a gulp of whisky and tried to unwind. He should have kept his wits about him and had more sense than to suggest Aimee give some of those fancy Paris fashions to Esther. He might have known that would cause trouble. Come to that, he should have had the sense not to become involved with Esther in the first place, but she'd brought him so much joy, he couldn't wish that it hadn't happened.

He had no idea how he was going to cope with this, but he couldn't sit here; he'd hear more if he went and talked to Aimee.

'I've come to help you cook,' he said, sitting down at the kitchen table with his whisky. He felt as though he was falling apart at the seams. He could see she didn't need help, so instead he talked about the new patterns Frankie had made for him.

Aimee set a tray for Prue. 'She might as well have it while it's hot,' she said.

'I'll take it up,' Grandpa offered, 'while you dish up and take our plates to the dining room.'

'We'll eat here if it's just you and me,' she said. 'I haven't set the table in there.'

'All right, it's warmer here anyway.' He was careful to close the door behind him, though he found it difficult while holding Prudence's tray. 'To keep the warmth in,' he said to Aimee over his shoulder, but really it was to reduce the risk of her hearing the abuse he was expecting Prudence to scream at him.

He quaked as he opened the bedroom door, but he found she was distressed as well as angry. 'That woman! What were you thinking of, sending Aimee to her house? She's your mistress, isn't she? I saw the way you used to look at her. A fallen woman. I can't believe you were such a fool. Don't you care about Aimee's reputation?'

'Don't upset yourself, Prue.' He closed that door too; she was shouting loudly enough to raise the dead. 'Aimee has cooked dinner and I've brought yours up for you.'

'You can take it straight back. I can't possibly eat a thing.'

He stayed for a few moments trying to soothe her. 'Try a little while it's hot. I'll leave it in case you change your mind.'

'Don't bother,' she screamed. 'I don't want it.' He left it on a chair and went back to the kitchen.

Aimee was waiting for him. Once he'd sat down, she picked up her knife and fork. 'Poor Grandma, she's got it all wrong about Esther, hasn't she?'

That shook him to the core; he had no idea how much Aimee had heard or understood. It might all be quite obvious to her.

'I really like Esther,' she went on. 'She's no floozy.'

'Of course she isn't. Where have you heard that word?'

'They used to call Lydia Greening a floozy at school because she had one boyfriend after another, though Grandma thinks she's lovely. She is very good-looking, though.'

Walter thought of the Greening girls with their white-blonde hair and very fair complexions. 'Raving beauties really,' he said, pushing the mashed potato round his mouth, unable to swallow.

Aimee sighed. 'Yes, that lovely hair. I wish—'

'Aimee, you have the most beautiful hair.'

'It's brown.'

'It's full of life, it's thick and curly and it swings back and forth when you walk. And it has red and gold lights in it just like Micheline's.'

'You said I was more like my father.'

'He had brown hair too.' Walter could see she wanted to be like Alec. 'You're tall and slim like he was and have quite a boyish figure.'

'I really don't care for the Greening family,' she went on, 'and I don't go near their house when Jeremy is at home. He's a groper, can't keep his hands to himself, but Grandma believes he's more my type than Frankie.'

Walter felt confused. Aimee seemed to know something of the facts of life, and he couldn't understand why his relationship with Esther wasn't blatantly obvious to her. He laid down his knife and fork. He had no appetite for cod and parsley sauce.

'Gramps! Don't you like the dinner?'

'Yes, love. I'm just worried about Grandma.'

Later on, Aimee said to Frankie, 'Gramps thinks I've got a boyish figure. Do you?'

'Boyish? What's he mean?' He laughed. 'No, I know you're all girl underneath those clothes.'

Prudence wept until she was exhausted and her eyes were sore and red. This was rejection; she'd seen it coming, of course. Over the last few months Walter had rarely spent time at home with her and always had some plausible lie ready about where he was going and what he was doing. He'd treated her like an idiot without brains or feelings. He'd concentrated on Esther Kerr and neglected everybody and everything else in his life, even the mill, and he used to be very involved in that.

She sat up and felt for a clean handkerchief in her bedside cabinet. Hadn't she always done her best for Walter? Looked after him and run this house in the way he wanted it run despite his falling income. That must be due either to incompetence or to neglect of his duties at the mill. Perhaps he no longer cared, and though she'd always looked after the pennies, he certainly had not.

No, he'd set Esther up in a house, a cosy house according to Aimee. And it had all been a big secret until he'd got her pregnant. Prudence felt full of hate for both of them. Esther was no better than she should be; she'd seduced Walter and stolen him away from Prue. Walter had cheated on her, and she wouldn't let him forget that in a hurry.

Aimee couldn't stop thinking about Esther's pregnancy; it bothered her so much it kept her awake into the night. Grandma had been shouting so loudly, she hadn't been able to avoid overhearing. She was suggesting that Grandpa was the father of Esther's baby, and he was very upset about that. Aimee hadn't wanted to believe it either. Lydia Greening had said romance and falling in love was not something old people did, not people as old as their parents, and Grandpa was a generation older than that, but he had looked almost guilty.

He wouldn't do that, though; he always did the honest and upright thing, so it must be something else. All the same, Esther was attractive and good fun and she didn't look all that old, although she must be getting on a bit now.

Grandma didn't get up in the days that followed. She told Dora she'd hurt her back and the only way to ease the pain was to rest in bed. Aimee saw little of Gramps except at mealtimes, and though he was making an effort to eat and be sociable, she could see he was still upset. It was making an atmosphere and casting a blight over everything.

Nothing had changed by Saturday, and after sharing a lunch tray in Grandma's room, Aimee went into the back garden and sat on her old swing watching the falling leaves. Now that Frankie was working at the mill, he had a half-day on

Saturdays, and she hoped he'd see her and come for a chat. It wasn't long before he climbed onto the wall and dropped down through the apple tree.

'Hello,' he said, taking some letters from his pocket and handing them to her. 'Mr Sanderson the accountant asked me to bring these over. He said Mr Kendrick might like to have time to think about them over the weekend.'

'Was the post late or something?'

'No, your grandpa doesn't come in on Saturday mornings any more.'

Aimee was surprised. Gramps hadn't told her that, and he'd left as usual after breakfast. 'I understood he worked on Saturday mornings and then went out to lunch with friends.'

'He told me he needs to take things easier now he's getting near retirement age.'

'Well he's not here. I'd better put these on his desk. Come indoors, I'd like your opinion on a painting I'm working on.' She took Frankie up to the schoolroom. 'I'm not pleased with this. Is it the perspective that's wrong?'

Frankie studied it. 'Perhaps it's slightly out. You could solve it by changing the line of the riverbank just here. It's a good picture, I like it.'

'You've painted this view often enough.' It was of the Liverpool waterfront. 'How are you getting on at the mill?'

'Like a house on fire.' Frankie was full of enthusiasm for all he was learning about the cotton trade and the patterns he was drawing.

It made Aimee even less content with her lot. 'I think I've grown out of painting and drawing; it makes me feel I'm still at school. I'd like to do something quite different.'

'Such as what?'

'I'm thinking of asking Gramps if he'll take me on to help him in the mill. I did put it to him the other day, but he suggested I train to be an accountant. I told him that would take too long, then he recommended a year at a commercial college to learn typing and shorthand, but he's already got a secretary, and he says she's very efficient.'

'Yes, Miss Bennett.'

'Anyway, that's not the sort of work I want to do at all. He's always telling me how my father would be in charge of the mill by now if he hadn't been killed in the war. I want to help him.'

'Wow! You want to run the place?'

'I think it's getting too much for Gramps, and he wants to hand it on to somebody else.'

'Do you think you could do it?'

'Ye-es. I'd have a lot to learn, but I could do it if he showed me how.'

'Well why not? You'll have to have another word with him.'

'I will.'

Frankie was studying her. 'But that's not the only reason you're feeling low, is it? What's upset you?'

Aimee sighed. She found it hard to talk about it, but now that she'd got to this point, she had to. 'I told you Esther is having a baby? Well, the other day when I told Grandma, she was furious, absolutely breathing fire. I heard her having a terrible row with Gramps about it. She seems to think he's the father. I find that very hard to believe. I mean, he's so set in his ways and so old. But could she be right?' Aimee could see that Frankie was uncomfortable. He didn't want to talk about her family and was pretending to study her painting.

'Possibly she could be,' he said at last. 'I saw Mr Kendrick with Esther when I was working in that restaurant, the Ship Inn, in the summer. They were there having dinner and seemed very engrossed in each other.'

'What? They looked as if . . . as if they were in love?'

'Well . . . yes.'

'Why didn't you tell me before?'

'How could I? Dad warned me never to breathe a word about it.'

'But you could have told me. He's my grandfather.'

'I couldn't.' Frankie wouldn't look at her.

Aimee said, 'I thought we'd agreed to have no secrets between us?'

'We did, but I was afraid you'd be upset, and Dad was worried he'd no longer be required to cut your grass. We have to see things from a different viewpoint if we're to survive.'

'For heaven's sake, you should have told me. I'd have understood what was happening then.'

'I couldn't, Aimee. What your grandfather does is none of my business. I'm grateful to him, I owe him a good deal and I didn't want to start rumours about him.'

'Telling me wouldn't have started rumours. Don't be ridiculous.'

Frankie flung his arms round her and pulled her close. 'Don't let's quarrel about this, Aimee. I think you're wonderful and I don't want to upset you. I wish I hadn't seen them, but I did.' He held her tight and kissed her. 'We all have our secrets.'

She tried to smile. 'What secrets do you have?'

'They wouldn't be secrets if I told you.'

'Frankie . . . you promised.'

'Well, I've been longing to hold you like this for ages. I've been in love with you for years and trying not to let it show. I love you. I didn't dare tell you.'

'Why not? I could see it in your eyes and I can feel it too. It's there for us both, drawing us together.'

'You mean . . . ?'

'I love you too, of course I do.'

He laughed. 'That's marvellous, but I can hardly believe it.' He ran his hands through her hair. 'You're so beautiful,' he murmured.

'When you kissed me the other day, that's when I knew. I've been thinking about it ever since. I wanted to hear you say it.'

He pulled her close. 'So now it's a secret we share but nobody else must know.'

She smiled up at him. 'I'm so happy I want to shout it from the rooftops.' She laughed. 'But Grandma would have a fit.'

'And my grandad would never forgive me if he lost the work he has here.'

They stayed out in the garden until it grew dark, but when it began to drizzle, Frankie gave her a final kiss and said, 'I'd better let you go indoors. I'm thrilled, Aimee, delighted to know where I stand with you. I've always loved you but I was afraid you were beyond my reach.'

'No, no, I'm right here beside you, with you all the way on this.'

'I want you to know that a love affair is not all I'm looking for. I want more than that. I want to spend my life with you; I want you to marry me and I want you to be happy.'

'If I could have that, I couldn't fail to be happy,' she whispered.

'One day,' he promised.

A few days later, after they'd eaten dinner, Aimee followed Walter to his study instead of clearing the table and helping Gran to make coffee. She'd tried to tell him she'd changed her mind about a career in art, but she knew she hadn't convinced him. 'Gramps,' she said, closing the door behind them, 'I want to leave art school and work in your mill.'

He sat down at his desk and opened a file. 'So you've said, but if you don't want to draw patterns—'

'I don't. Frankie has the talent for that, not me, and I don't want to do office work either. I want you to teach me how to run the business. You keep telling me my father would be running it by now if he hadn't been killed. I want to take his place.'

'What?' His eyebrows went up and he sat back in his chair, staring at her. 'You've met my departmental managers and foremen; they're all old enough to be your father and have had years of experience. I can't see them listening to a slip of a girl like you.'

'I can learn to speak to them so that they do.'

'And as for carrying out your orders . . . well, they won't take you seriously.'

'My father must have been young when he started, but I bet they took him seriously because he was your son. I'm your granddaughter, and it may take me a bit longer because I'm a woman, but eventually I'll make them listen to me.'

He looked the picture of doubt. 'Well, I suppose, if you really want to try . . .'

'I do, Gramps, I've been trying to tell you that for months, but you won't accept it.' Aimee could see that even now he didn't believe she'd stick it for long. 'How did you set about teaching my father?'

'There's only one way to learn. I arranged for him to spend three months or so working in each department so he would understand the work that was being done there. You'd need to learn from the bottom up.'

'A sort of apprenticeship?'

'Yes, though nothing formal.'

'Then that's what I want to do. Can I finish art school at the end of term? It bores me now.'

She saw her grandfather's lips straighten and went on. 'I've learned it all before from Candida, and that doesn't help. You wouldn't believe how keen all the other students are, or how well they paint.'

'Well, if you're sure, you can start in the mill after the New Year holiday.'

'Thank you, Gramps. You won't regret this, I promise.'

'I hope *you* won't regret it. That's more to the point.'

CHAPTER EIGHTEEN

W HEN WALTER CAME HOME the following evening, Prudence was up and dressed, though with the face of a long-suffering martyr. As usual, Aimee brought him the post and his glass of whisky, then went to the kitchen to help get their evening meal on the table.

The first letter he opened gave him such a shock that he spilled his drink down his pullover and the cold liquid soaked through his shirt and made him yelp with surprise. Aimee came running in to see what had happened. 'What is it, Gramps?' She pulled him to the kitchen to mop him dry with a tea towel.

He waved the letter at her and slumped onto a chair. 'Armand did tell me that your paintings were insured with a French company and the policy had a few more months to run.'

'Yes,' Aimee said. 'He said we'd need to think about what we wanted to do about insurance after that.' Prudence had picked up the letter to read.

Walter said, 'He's now written and enclosed a bill from the French insurers for the next year.' His mouth still felt dry; it was an enormous sum.

'I didn't realise your mother was spending money like this on insurance,' Prudence said. 'You must pay it, of course.' She helped herself to more sherry. 'It can be settled from Aimee's funds, can't it?'

'Prudence, she doesn't have funds until the pictures are sold. I wonder if it's sensible to keep such valuable items here. They could be stolen.'

'How would thieves know they were here?' Aimee asked.

Walter got to his feet. 'Let's look at those pictures again.' He led the way back to the sitting room to stare at them. 'Which one is the Chagall?'

'There are two by him, this one and this. He was a friend of Maman's, but I don't much care for his work.'

'Neither do I,' Walter said.

'This is by André Masson. The only one I really like is this by Degas.'

'Well, that's a relief. The insurers are asking what security arrangements we have for them, and the answer is none. Armand is suggesting we might prefer to put them into safe storage and have prints made to hang here. You want to keep just the Degas, then?'

'No, Gramps,' Aimee said. 'Let's sell them all. It would be a worry as well as an expense to keep them here.'

Prudence had followed them in; she was aghast. 'They're a last gift from your mother, Aimee. You must keep them.'

'No,' Aimee said. 'I find pictures aren't important in my life after all. I don't think I take after my mother, though you've both been telling me I do since I was a baby. I've been trained to be exactly like her, but I'm not. I'm more like you, Gramps, a practical sort of person, quite down-to-earth.'

Grandma was shocked. 'For goodness' sake, Aimee, no! Your mother made a success of her life. You can do that too.'

'I hope I can be a success,' she said, 'but I doubt it will come from painting pictures.'

Walter sighed. 'I just want you to be happy, content with whatever life brings you.'

He'd always had a soft spot for Aimee, but he was afraid he wasn't doing a good job of looking after her interests. In fact, he wasn't doing a good job anywhere. He had so many problems of his own.

Candida was no longer going to Fairholme on Saturdays, and was missing the small income it had given her. It had made her realise that her only route to survival was to follow in her father's footsteps and paint fake pictures. She was enjoying being able to concentrate on them.

The smaller picture was a view across the village of Dignac on market day, with stalls in the square and red pantiles on the roofs baking in the summer heat. She'd managed to fill it with golden sunlight in just the way Micheline would have done. Once it was finished to her satisfaction, she'd forged Micheline's signature on the bottom. It was typical of the work her friend had produced. The larger painting, of the pool in the river where she'd swum with Micheline in those long-ago summer holidays, would fetch a higher price.

She was pleased with what she'd done so far, but she'd have to sell them to gain any reward, and that was the worry. She was reluctant to involve Armand, because he knew her well and would no doubt have all the facts regarding her father's conviction for fraud at his fingertips. That was not something he was likely to forget, and she was afraid he might suspect she was doing the same.

But on the other hand, Armand had been Micheline's husband and he had the gallery, through which he was selling all manner of paintings. She knew the art world; if she had anything to sell, that would be the route she'd be expected to take. Common sense told her it would be more likely that their authenticity would be questioned if she tried to sell them elsewhere.

Another problem was that Armand knew Micheline's style more intimately than anyone else, and was the most likely person to suspect they were not genuine. Candida's advantage lay in the fact that she had been friendly with Micheline for years before he'd married her. He'd never have seen or heard of her fraudulent pictures, so almost certainly he'd ask her when exactly they'd been painted. She tried to work out the dates he'd be most likely to believe, and that showed up a problem she should have thought of sooner. She knew she was copying Micheline's style in her mature days, but now she feared that Micheline would not have painted quite as confidently as that as early as 1922. Would Armand think of that?

Walter was at his desk later that evening when Armand rang to give him news of the Renoir. 'Sorry about the delay,' he said. 'I went to a sale of fine art in a nearby gallery and it was a disaster. Very few of the pictures reached their reserve. I'm afraid in the present economic climate few people have the money to pay high prices for pictures, and those who do prefer to hang onto it. So I've cancelled the sale I was going to put it in. I think things may have improved by late November or early December, when everybody starts to think of Christmas.

I understand things are no better in London, or anywhere else in Europe come to that.'

'There's very little money in Liverpool at the moment, that's all I know.'

'In the meantime, I've hung the Renoir in my gallery along with several other important pictures; and if you're agreeable, I'd like to offer it for private sale at a price the equivalent of fifty-three and a half thousand pounds.'

Walter gasped. 'Good gracious me, is anybody likely to pay that? It's a fortune!'

'Actually, I'd put the value a little higher, but it's more likely to find a buyer if it seems a bargain.'

'You must surely mean a relative bargain, Armand! Of course I'm agreeable. Good Lord, this shows my ignorance of the art world.'

It was only a week later that Armand phoned him again. 'I've had an offer for your Renoir,' he said. 'I can't believe the speed of it; the sale I cancelled would not have been held until next month. A dealer has offered fifty-three thousand pounds for it; in other words, he's knocked five hundred pounds off my price.'

'That's good, isn't it?'

'It's worth more, but it's unlikely to make its real price in this depression; nothing is doing that. Do you want to accept his offer?'

Walter hesitated; after all, they were selling this on Aimee's behalf and he wanted to do the best for her. 'What would you advise? I know nothing about fine art.'

'It's a good offer in the present financial climate. It's not easy to sell high-value items like this.'

'Should we consult Aimee?'

'Only if you want to. There's no legal need because she's a minor. Hasn't she already said she'd prefer to sell it?'

'Yes. Accept the offer then, Armand.'

'I think that's wise. What are you proposing to do with the money?'

'I'll ask my stockbroker to invest it for her.'

'Good, that'll give her a regular allowance to spend on clothes and personal items, and it's only right she should have that now. You do know you could fund her art school fees from it, and any other expenses you have to pay on her behalf?'

'Yes, though unfortunately she wants to leave art school now. She doesn't think she has the talent for it. She wants to come and help me at the mill.'

'*Mon Dieu!* Whatever would her mother say?'

'I shudder to think, but that's her choice. Thank you for selling this picture for her; I had no idea it was worth that much.'

'Not difficult for me, Walter, my trade is selling pictures. Let me know if there's anything else you want me to do.'

Walter put the phone down thinking that in spite of Candida's misgivings, Armand had discharged his duties to Aimee to the letter. He sat back in his chair and thought of what he could do with that life-changing sum, the improvements he could make at his mill. But no. He reminded himself it was Aimee's money, not his, and went to find her.

'She's gone out to see that lad again,' Prudence complained. 'I knew it was a mistake to let him come in to share her lessons. He's a very unsuitable friend for her.'

Walter felt so stunned by the value of the painting that he

ignored Prudence's worries. 'Armand has sold the Renoir for fifty-three thousand pounds,' he told her.

'Good gracious me!' Prudence's mouth fell open. 'How marvellous for Aimee, but it proves my point that that lad is far too close to her. She's an heiress now; he'll use her to get at her money. And it's not just this fifty-three thousand pounds; she's got all these other pictures as well.'

'I know, it's a sobering thought.'

'I'm sure Aimee will be glad to pay for a bit to be done to the house. The roof needs mending and the place needs repainting throughout, as well as new carpets and curtains. It's really rather shabby.'

'It's Aimee's money, not ours,' Walter said abruptly, 'and we have to look after it for her. Armand has acted honourably over this and so must we. The money will be invested in her name, and until she's twenty-one she'll have a small monthly allowance to buy her clothes and meet her personal needs.'

'She could afford to pay us for her keep,' Prudence said sharply.

'No,' said Walter. 'She's our granddaughter. We've brought her up and I don't think we should start taking money from her now.'

'I've never heard of anything more ridiculous.' Prudence was bitter. 'You keep me desperately short of money.'

'Aimee's mother has given her this; it's not from our side of the family.'

'She's got so much, she won't mind. This house is run on a shoestring, it's hardly a place for an heiress to live. There's no comfort here. Aimee and I have to work like skivvies to provide what little we do have.'

Aimee returned home shortly afterwards and laughed with delight when Walter told her of the phone call and the sale of the Renoir. 'Good,' she said. 'I'm going to make a cup of cocoa. Shall I make some for you too?'

Walter said, 'We were shocked at the price it sold for, but you don't seem surprised.'

She beamed at them. 'Armand told me he expected it to make somewhere around sixty to sixty-five thousand, so it's less than I expected, but I'm absolutely delighted, couldn't be happier.'

Prudence gave a squeal of irritation. 'So you knew all along?'

'Fifty-three thousand pounds is a fortune. It makes me feel like a princess to have all that money.'

'Right, how about that cocoa?' Walter smiled. 'Better make some for us all.'

It was Saturday, and Frankie was helping his grandad weed the flower beds in the Greenings' front garden when Lydia came home with two carrier bags advertising a dress shop in Birkenhead.

She beamed at him. 'No shop job, Frankie? This is a bit of a come-down for you. Aimee must feel she's scraping the bottom of the barrel to go out with a jobbing gardener.'

That did Frankie's confidence no good, but he said, 'This is just a hobby now, Lydia. Her grandfather has given me a job in his mill. I'm designing patterns to print on his fabric.' He told himself he should be used to her jibes by now, but he felt hot and sticky and his trouser knees were muddy and damp because he'd been kneeling on the grass.

Ten minutes later, Aimee came up from the ferry on her

way home; she too had carrier bags and came tiptoeing across the lawn to him. 'I've had the most splendid news about that Renoir,' she whispered, because his grandad was close by. 'It sold for fifty-three thousand pounds. I can't believe it. I'll be rich! Isn't that out of this world? See you later.'

She was gone, and Frankie sank back on his haunches feeling devastated. He'd known all along that Aimee was beyond his reach. It was one thing for Mr Kendrick to give him a job in his mill, and quite another to accept him as her suitor. He'd been dreaming of something that had always been out of his reach, and the fact that she'd inherited this fortune confirmed it.

Everybody would think it was her money he was after. He'd fallen in love with her and she was free with her kisses and hugs and said she loved him too, but this must surely be death to his hopes. She could marry anyone now.

CHAPTER NINETEEN

T HE WEEKS WERE PASSING slowly for Esther. She was looking more beautiful than ever, but her slim figure was thickening and soon her pregnancy was more noticeable.

'It was bound to happen sooner or later,' she said to Walter, and buried her head in her hands.

She was very subdued the next time he saw her. 'Sister Superior summoned me to her office to ask me about my condition. It seems my colleagues had noticed and were horrified. She said, "You know I'll have to ask you to leave. You are such a bad example to our girls; what would their parents say?"'

Walter was guilt-stricken. He was to blame for the fact that the woman he loved was having to face embarrassment and the loss of her career. She'd never asked him for money, and didn't now. He decided that he would leave it on her mantelpiece on the last day of each month.

The following Saturday morning they went shopping for baby clothes and napkins, and he ordered a cot and a pram. 'I'm thrilled,' Esther said. 'I'm getting excited about it now.'

For Walter, the waiting was nerve-racking. He offered to book her into a nursing home and pay for a nurse to look after them both for the first month, but she was having none of that. 'Waste of money.' She smiled at him. 'I've seen the doctor and been to the maternity clinic. Everything is going well. I'll be delivered in Grange Mount, our local maternity hospital, and they'll keep me in for three weeks afterwards. I should be fine and able to manage at home by then.'

Walter was dreading the birth. He didn't know how he could look after Esther, appease Prudence and still run his business. He hadn't the time or the energy to do more than he already did. The nearer the time of Esther's confinement came, the more nervous he became. He'd never felt lower, anxious for her and her child and fearful for the future.

Late one night, as he tried to creep quietly through Prue's room to his bed in the dressing room, she gave him a jolt by suddenly sitting up. 'Sorry, Prue,' he said. 'Did I wake you?'

'Wake me? How can I possibly get to sleep? Don't you realise what you're doing to me and Aimee? What an insult to us,' she said bitterly, 'taking up with that woman.'

He supported himself on the bottom rail of her bed. 'I didn't mean to hurt you. I'm sorry, very sorry.'

'Sorry? Is that the best you can do? You're having a child with her and have set her up in a house. You've rejected me, ruined my life, and as for Aimee, you've spoiled her prospects of a decent marriage; her reputation will be tarred with yours.'

'Nonsense, Prue, that might have happened when you were young, but not these days.'

'Well, it should, for a girl in her position. And you should never have let that Hopkins lad come into the house and join her lessons.' Her voice was rising, and he crept back to make sure the door was closed; he didn't want Aimee to hear all this. 'He's manoeuvred himself far too close to her. You should have had more sense.'

'Prue, please, nothing need change, nobody need know.'

'*I* know,' she shrieked at him. 'Aimee knows; she'll tell the neighbours. Soon everybody will know.'

'She won't.'

'Stop seeing that woman; spend more time with us.'

Walter stifled a groan; she couldn't see that she was asking the impossible. He loved Esther and must take care of her too. 'Do you want a divorce?'

'So you can marry her? No thank you. What would I do, alone at my age?'

Walter felt even worse. He'd loved Prue once and couldn't bear to see what he'd done to her. What a fool he'd been to get into this mess. He wasn't earning enough money to keep one family in comfort, and soon he'd have two. 'This is getting us nowhere; let's leave it until the morning. Goodnight, Prue.'

'Don't shut yourself away from me in that room,' she shouted, but he ignored her, closing the dressing room door carefully and switching on the light.

He was late getting up the next morning and felt half comatose when he crept past Prue's bed. She was snoring gently, deeply asleep. Aimee did her best to liven him up over breakfast. He knew the post had come and there was a letter for him, but he couldn't be bothered to look at it before he had to rush to catch the ferry.

Prudence felt cross and out of sorts. She was being slighted and shut out of family life. She'd told Walter calmly and politely what she thought of Esther Kerr, and where he was going wrong with Aimee, but it had been like water off a duck's back.

She'd explained to him many times that Aimee needed

guidance and help to make the right start in life, but he wouldn't listen. He had always tried to keep her and Aimee apart, and now that she was at art school and travelling over to Liverpool with him, the two of them spent even more time together. Now he'd convinced her he needed her help in his business. For goodness' sake, he'd been running it all his life and should have it under control by now.

He was allowing Aimee far too much freedom, and by taking that Hopkins lad into the business, he'd brought them even closer. Aimee was seeing far too much of him, and that could only lead to disaster. He was far too forward and would surely get her into the trouble Verity had got herself into. And all the time they left Prue to her own devices, neglected and alone. Neither thought she might like to be taken to a concert or the theatre.

She felt like crying.

Last night Walter had told her he was working late and she'd thought seriously of going up to Esther Kerr's house and confronting them both, because she was certain she'd find him there. But it had been drizzling all day, and after she'd cooked dinner for Aimee, the rain looked as though it had set in for the night, so it seemed sensible to put it off to another evening.

Of course, going there would embarrass her as well as them, and anyway, embarrassment was far too light a punishment for Walter. What she should do was think of some way to really hurt him. He deserved the worst.

CHAPTER TWENTY

CANDIDA HAD RECEIVED A note from Walter yesterday telling her of the need to re-insure Aimee's paintings, and asking her to come over on Sunday afternoon to discuss the best thing to do. In the sitting room at Fairholme, he said, 'Keeping them here is hardly an option. I suppose you knew it would cost a fortune to insure them?'

Candida lifted her eyes from the tea and raspberry buns in front of her to look at the pictures hanging on the wall. 'Well, I knew it wouldn't be cheap, but Micheline must have thought it worthwhile.' She'd guessed Walter would be in favour of selling them; he was a down-to-earth businessman who took little interest in art. 'What about you, Aimee? It must fill you with pride to have paintings of this quality here in your home. Don't you want to keep them?'

'No, these should be in art galleries for everybody to see. Anyway, I find when I look at them every day that they lose their punch and begin to seem ordinary. Gramps is worried about thieves coming in, and there are so many more important things to spend money on.'

Candida tried to smile; she hoped she didn't look as nervous as she felt. 'I have two pictures that Micheline gave me years ago,' she said, 'and though I love them dearly, I've decided to sell them too.'

'Because of the cost of insurance?' Walter asked.

'No, I've never insured them; when Micheline gave them to me, her career was just beginning. They weren't worth much then, but I'm in need of money now.'

'Oh!' Walter said. 'You know the Paris market is very depressed at the moment? Armand delayed the auction for the Renoir but managed to sell it privately.'

'I know only too well. You're lucky it sold so quickly,' Candida said. 'Here's hoping I have the same luck.'

'Well it seems these others will have to wait until December if we want Armand to sell them,' Walter went on. 'So the question is the same as it was over the Renoir. Would we sell more quickly in London and get better prices for them there, d'you think?'

Candida had argued the other way over the Renoir, but now that she had her own pictures to sell, she needed to steer Walter towards using Armand again. She wanted Aimee's pictures by more famous artists put on sale at the same time. They would take attention from Micheline's pictures. 'You said Armand charged very little commission last time?'

'Indeed, but can we trust him? Fifty-three thousand pounds is an enormous sum, but this would be even bigger. He's secretive, isn't he? None of us ever heard so much as a whisper about his first wife or the two boys he seems to have had with her. With these paintings we'll be putting a huge amount of business through his gallery.'

'It will result in a fortune by anyone's standards,' Prudence agreed.

Walter put his cup and saucer down. 'Would we even know if he took a share of that for himself?'

'Gramps,' Aimee protested, 'you're being too hard on Armand. He made sure I saw everything Maman willed to me and that I took what I wanted. He couldn't have behaved better over the sale of the Renoir, could he?'

'I know nothing about buying and selling art in France,' Walter grumbled. 'It's a foreign country after all.'

'It would be much easier to go the same way again,' Candida said. 'If I were you, I'd only insure the pictures until they're sold, six months or whatever.'

'Yes, all right. I'll ring Armand this evening.'

Candida relaxed. So far so good. She cut her raspberry bun into dainty pieces and popped one into her mouth. 'These are absolutely delicious.'

'I made them,' Aimee said. 'My first attempt and I'm quite pleased with them.'

When Candida left them, Walter tried to telephone Armand at his flat, but there was no answer. It was Sunday, but perhaps he had reason to be at his gallery, so he asked the operator to try that number. The phone was lifted immediately and Walter strained to understand the strong Paris accent at the other end of the line. He wished he'd asked Aimee to sit beside him. He gathered Armand had been there but had now left.

In his halting French, he gave his name and number, and said that he needed to speak Armand. 'Tomorrow evening will be soon enough,' he added. He told Aimee that he'd tried to contact Armand and had asked him to ring back.

She was always home an hour or so before him and was not

surprised when she lifted the phone the following afternoon and found she was speaking to her stepfather. 'Hello,' she said, and explained about the renewal notice for insuring the paintings. 'It's really put Gramps off them. We've decided it would be better to sell them all.'

He laughed but said, 'Are you sure, Aimee?'

'Yes. I'm not cut out to follow in Maman's footsteps. I don't think I've got what it takes to be a painter. I'm more like my father's side of the family, down-to-earth and practical.'

'But you've just started at art school, haven't you?'

'I have, but it's a mistake and I plan to leave. I'm wasting everybody's time there. I'd rather work in Gramps's mill.'

'Well, I suppose you're old enough to know what you want in your life. I'd better have a word with Walter first, but of course I'll be happy to sell the paintings for you if that's what you've decided. You do know that it isn't easy to sell anything at the moment and it might take a long time?'

'The sale of the Renoir taught us all that,' Aimee said, 'but you're probably better placed to do it than anyone else.'

'Right, well I'm coming to London at the beginning of next month. I could travel to Liverpool to pack up the pictures and take them back with me.' '

'Oh, lovely, you must come and stay with us. We have plenty of space here.'

'Do you still have the packaging material that Candida used to send them to you?'

'No, but she'll know what you need. I'll talk to her about getting more. Have you ever been to Liverpool?'

'No, never.'

'I'll show you round, take you to the art galleries and—'

'Aimee, I won't be able to stay long. I have to get back to Paris; the gallery doesn't run itself.'

She sighed. 'Well, at least you're coming. I'll get Gramps to ring you to confirm everything.'

Having a guest to stay was a rare treat, and Aimee took an afternoon off art school to meet Armand at Lime Street station. She recognised him easily amongst the passengers streaming off the train, taller and smarter than most, and looking decidedly French. He kissed her on both cheeks. She led him to the taxi rank and they rode down to the ferry in style, while she clutched a handful of coins; Gramps had reminded her to have the fare ready to pay.

'This way you can see our river,' she told him. 'The Mersey is very different from the Dordogne, much wider, and tidal where we live. It's a pleasant trip across and an easy walk from the ferry terminal when we get off.'

Once back at Fairholme, she showed him all over the house and then to the room she had prepared for him. 'Very English,' Armand said as he looked round.

Prudence called for Dora to bring in a tray of tea, but at first she had little to say to him. These days she wasn't saying much to anybody. Armand set out to charm them all; he had brought wine for Gramps, flowers for Grandma and chocolate for Aimee. Soon Gran was chatting away and acting as hostess; she looked as though she was enjoying Armand's company.

Dinner was to be a much more elaborate meal than usual. Grandma had said grumpily that she wanted nothing to do with it, so Aimee and Gramps had had to decide on what they could produce. There was always soup at dinner time, and they decided they'd have roast beef and Yorkshire pudding, followed by apple pie and cream. It was what they often had for Sunday lunch, and Aimee knew they could cope with it. She helped Dora with the preparations and left her in the kitchen to cook it while she set the dining room table with their best silver, china and glass.

Prudence felt better when she was going to bed that night, although they were later than usual. It had been a pleasant evening. At one time they'd frequently dined out and given dinner parties, but recently Walter had said he had no energy for such things. He was sleep-sodden and silent now, though he'd been the life and soul of the party earlier. Since he'd taken up with that woman, Prudence had felt starved of social occasions like this. She'd had no company at all.

She'd always enjoyed her visits to France, and Armand's company, but with Micheline's death those had stopped too. To see him again reminded her of the lovely house in Dignac, complete with servants and every luxury under the sun, while Walter spent his money on other women and she was deprived of even basic comforts. This was not the life she'd been used to; her family had provided better than this. Certainly it was not the life he'd promised her on marriage.

She'd decided she'd try to get Armand to support her. As she handed him a cup of coffee after dinner, she looked into his handsome dark eyes and said, 'An heiress like Aimee shouldn't be living in a place like this. It needs smartening up, modernising, to provide more comfort, but Walter won't spend Aimee's money on anything like that. I think he should, don't you agree?'

She was put out to hear him say, 'I'm sure Aimee is happy enough living here. It's where she was brought up, and she has the love and devotion of you and Walter.' He smiled. 'This is what she's used to, and she's old enough to make up her own mind about what she wants. Just give her time, Prudence.'

That infuriated her more than ever. It was clear that Walter had been talking to him. He was turning everybody against her, cutting her out; she was being ignored.

Aimee decided that because Armand was staying, she'd take another day off. She was clearing the kitchen table when he came down. 'Am I late?'

'No, Gramps has to get off to work.'

'I'll need your help. Do you know where in Liverpool I can get packing materials for these pictures? I've told Walter I'll take them back with me.'

'Candida knows all about that sort of thing and will take us there. I've arranged that we'll meet her for lunch today.'

Armand said, 'That'll be a great help, thank you.'

'What would you like for breakfast?' she asked.

'Just coffee and bread,' he said. 'That's all I ever have.'

'We eat toast here because we don't have your fresh bread.' He sat at the table and watched her make it. 'I'll have a second breakfast with you this morning,' she said, and slid the butter and marmalade in front of him. Last night he'd been telling them about his work in Paris. 'I'm so glad you could come and stay,' she went on. 'I feel we're getting to know you now.'

He smiled at her. 'And I feel you're beginning to accept me as your stepfather. That pleases me; we all need family.'

The coffee pot was percolating and she had four slices of

bread under the grill. She was feeling so at ease in his company that she found herself saying, 'But you have another family, don't you?' His smile disappeared; she could see his sudden dismay. 'Sorry. Candida and I, well, we came across photographs at La Coutancie of your first wife and two children.'

'Yes.' His hands covered his face. 'I'd forgotten about those photographs when I said you could take what you wanted from our bedroom.'

'But why make it a secret?'

'Oh dear, it wasn't meant to be. I couldn't bear to talk about it, think about it even. It was such a devastating shock. Even now . . .' Aimee could see his face twisting. 'Eulalie, my first wife, was ill, mentally ill, I mean, and it took me ages to realise that. I discussed it with our doctor more than once, but I don't think he realised how severe her condition was.'

'But your children?'

He couldn't look at her. 'Eulalie smothered them and then killed herself.' She could see his agony. 'I was at work. I feel I let them down. I should have been there. I could see she was getting worse but I never imagined she'd do such a thing. It never entered my head.'

Aimee threw her arms round him in a hug. 'How could you have known? How absolutely terrible. I'm so, so sorry.'

'She loved the boys, everybody did.' He was blinking hard. 'I almost sank. Micheline was a marvellous support to me. She dragged me back to the real world. I owe a great deal to her.'

A pall of black smoke alerted Aimee to the burning toast. By the time she'd dealt with that and opened a window, they'd both recovered. She could see Armand had genuinely suffered.

CHAPTER TWENTY-ONE

CANDIDA WAS VERY MUCH on edge as the time grew near to show off her fakes. 'I can't wait to see them,' Armand had said. Aimee had added, 'Neither can I. These are pictures Maman has painted that none of us has yet seen.'

That had horrified her. Alone at home with them, it was easy to believe they'd fool everybody, but she knew that was just her opinion. Were they as good as she thought? As good as she hoped?

Her whole future depended on whether Armand believed the paintings were Micheline's work. If she was to gain anything from them, she had to look relaxed, show them off and seem proud to own them.

They met Candida at midday in Liverpool and she took them to the shop where she bought all her art materials. Armand chose what he needed and left his purchases to be collected later. 'Where is the best place to have lunch?' he asked.

Candida hailed a passing taxi and told the driver where to go.

'I was quite surprised to hear you had two paintings Micheline had given you that were worth selling,' he said once they were seated in the restaurant. 'I don't know why I should be, as I know you were close friends all through art school. I'll be glad to sell them for you. The way you described them, they sounded quite impressive.'

'One is,' she choked out.

'You must come to Paris to see them sold,' he told them both.

'I'd love to,' Candida said, then pulled a face. 'No, I really can't afford holidays.'

He laughed. 'I can advance you enough to cover the fare and you can pay me back when I sell the pictures.'

'No, I mustn't be tempted. How long d'you think it'll take?'

'Three or four months, maybe more. Everything is taking longer at the moment.' Candida was sucking her lip. 'I'll speed it up if I can,' Armand added.

Aimee squeezed her arm. It had taken an age for her own money to come through, but Gramps said he had it now and it was being invested in her name. She'd already told Candida that she could lend her money to tide her over, but Candida had said she couldn't possibly accept it. Aimee invited her to come for dinner that evening and bring her pictures over so Armand could pack them with hers and take them back with him.

'I can't wait to see them,' he smiled.

Candida stood on the front doorstep of Fairholme, clutching her portfolio. She was shaking with nerves, taking deep steadying breaths to calm herself.

Aimee answered the doorbell. 'Hello, do come in.' She was as bubbly as ever. 'Glad you've come early.'

Candida took her coat off, shivering as she hung it in the

usual place, then followed Aimee to the sitting room. Armand leapt to his feet as she entered and kissed her on both cheeks. He was smiling. 'Ah, your pictures, let's have a look at them.'

Candida opened her portfolio with stiff fingers. 'Sorry, I never got round to framing them; couldn't afford . . .' She knew they'd need to be framed before they could be put up for sale, but she'd wanted to avoid going deeper into debt for that.

'They can be framed now,' he said as he lifted them out and propped them side by side on the sofa, then stepped back to look at them.

Candida felt her heart turn over and found she was holding her breath. Walter handed her a glass of sherry. She gulped it back before she realised what she was doing.

'It's that pool in the river where we swim, isn't it?'

She pulled herself together; she'd prepared a few words to say about that. 'Yes, Micheline painted me in that red swimsuit; I think that's why she gave me the picture.'

'I recognise the picnic hamper on the bank too.' He continued to stare at it. 'The sunlight dappling the water gives the sense of a sweltering day in the Dordogne. It's a good size too, quite an important painting. I hadn't dared hope for anything this good.'

'I love it,' Aimee said. 'It's the sort of picture you'd want to hang in your house – to remind you of summer on a cold winter's day.'

'I think an ornate guilt frame would show it off to its best advantage.' Armand went closer to appraise it. 'How long have you had this, Candida? I mean, when did Micheline paint it? Often she dated her pictures, but not this one.'

'Nor the other smaller one,' Candida managed.

'Can you remember when it was?'

'It must have been . . . let me see, 1922 or '23.'

'We were all at the École des Beaux-Arts then, weren't we?'

'Yes, she used to invite me to La Coutancie in the summer holidays.'

Looking at the picture now, she also asked herself whether it would have aged more in ten years. She wasn't sure. Her father had aged his fakes by baking them in the oven, timing them at a precise temperature to allow for the passage of a century or so. She'd left this one in the sun for a while, but sun was notoriously fitful in Liverpool.

Armand said, 'It's a very attractive picture, very saleable. Micheline would have been proud of painting it, especially back then. I'm surprised she gave it to you.'

'I did model for it.'

'Yes, but even so. She might have made her name sooner if she'd sold it instead.'

That left Candida with a thudding heart; had Armand picked up that it was painted in Micheline's later style at a time when she was unlikely to have developed it? His words seemed to indicate that he had.

Aimee knew that Frankie was keen to see her mother's paintings, and there'd be little opportunity before they were packed. Later that evening, she climbed over the wall to the stables. 'Come and see the pictures my mother painted and gave to Candida,' she said. 'It's now or never; Armand and I will pack them in the morning.'

'I'd love to.'

He followed her down the garden and through the kitchen

door. He always hoped to avoid being seen by Mrs Kendrick when he went inside Fairholme. He knew she'd tried to ban him from coming, and now that Aimee had inherited a fortune, she was even more keen to keep them apart.

They crept across the hall and upstairs. The pictures were propped against the schoolroom wall. 'I really like this.' Frankie took his time to look closely at the painting of swimmers in the Dordogne.

'Candida says she modelled for that,' Aimee told him. 'That's why Maman gave it to her.'

'Gosh, I wish I could paint like your mother.' He continued to stare at it.

'I wanted you to see it,' Aimee said. 'There's something about it that bothers me.'

'What? It's a really lovely picture.'

'It is, but . . . Do you remember that large canvas that was here, all bleak broken trees like no-man's-land in the war?'

'Yes, you offered it to me, if you remember.'

'Well, it's gone. I haven't given it to anybody else. I thought perhaps you'd taken it after all.'

'No, Aimee, I wouldn't take anything from here without asking you first. My grandad says it isn't enough for us to be honest; we have to be absolutely transparently honest, or we won't get any more work in Rock Park. When did you notice it wasn't here?'

'Almost straight away; and now, looking at Candida's picture, I have to say I think it was the same size.'

Frankie was shocked. 'Not Candida!' He felt grateful to Miss Rathbone; she'd taught him all he knew about art. She'd even helped him get the job at the mill he was so proud of.

'It's a terrible thought,' Aimee agreed, 'but nobody else has been here.'

'Dora? She cleans in here.'

'I know. I had to ask her. She laughed and said, "What would I want with a canvas? Painting pictures is for children; everybody but you gives up that sort of thing by ten years of age." I'm pretty sure she didn't take it.'

'Your grandmother?'

Aimee shook her head. 'She never goes near the school-room.'

'But that means . . .'

'I know, it doesn't bear thinking about. Were these pictures really painted by my mother?'

'Why would Candida take that canvas? She could easily have bought one.'

'It came from my mother's studio; one bought here could possibly be identified as British.'

'Oh my goodness! Are you going to tell your stepfather?'

She shook her head again. 'I don't know. If we're right, and he sells it, he could find himself in terrible trouble. What would you do, Frankie?'

It was his turn to shake his head. 'I find it very hard to believe it of her. I'd have thought she wouldn't dare, not after what happened to her father.'

'I know she's short of cash; she told me she's been trying to get a teaching job. Now she's even lost her Saturday job teaching us.'

'Hang on,' Frankie said, 'we're just surmising. We might have the wrong end of the stick here.'

They went back to staring at the picture. 'Everything about

it seems right to me,' Aimee said. 'Maman painted this, I'm sure.'

Frankie went to look at Micheline's paintings of Aimee that decorated the wall of the staircase. The first one, at the bottom of the stairs, showed her as a toddler; after that, she'd painted one almost every year, and each one was dated. 'Look, Aimee,' he said, 'can't you see how her brushstrokes show more confidence in the later pictures? Everything about that last one is strong and well defined.'

Aimee looked again. 'Perhaps you're right.' Why had he seen that and she had not? Of course he was right.

'Now look again at the paintings Candida says were done by your mother. What do you see?'

'Superb confidence, masterly definition. I wish I could paint like that.'

'So do I,' Frankie said, 'but Candida says they were painted in 1922 or '23.'

'Yes, and that suggests . . . Oh my goodness, what d'you think we should do?'

'Nothing. Let's just wait and see what happens.'

CHAPTER TWENTY-TWO

CHRISTMAS WAS APPROACHING, AND though Aimee had always loved this time of year, it was bringing back the grief of Micheline's death. Without Maman, Christmas could never be as she'd known it; instead, she tried to welcome English traditions.

On Christmas Eve, Frankie asked her to meet him under the leafless pear tree in the garden after dinner, and she knew it was to give her a present. She'd thought of buying him another suit, as she knew he was anxious about having very little to wear to work, but she was afraid he'd think she was throwing money at him. She'd bought him a relatively cheap watch instead, as he didn't have one.

She left the fire Gramps had banked halfway up the chimney to run up the garden. It was a very cold night, but Frankie was waiting for her and pulled her into his arms.

'Happy Christmas,' he said, slipping something onto her finger and holding it there as he kissed her. 'My gift to you is a ring. I want you to look upon it as a pledge for an engagement ring. It's the best I can give you at the moment.'

'What sort of a ring?' she laughed. 'It's too dark for me to see.'

'Do you remember us finding a gold ring on our way to the Palace Cinema, years ago?'

'Yes, I do. It had lost its stone. You went back to the police station and found it hadn't been claimed?'

'I did. It's real gold, eighteen carat, I think, though I might be wrong about that.'

'It's got a stone in it now, I can feel it.'

'It's not a stone, just a piece of red glass I picked up when Dad was mending a stained-glass panel in somebody's front door. He's got a lot of craft tools and I've been fiddling around with it for the last month. It's my third attempt, a pretend ruby, and to me it looks OK. Well, not bad.'

'Thank you, I shall treasure it because you've spent so much time fixing it. I wish I could see it.'

'This is just a pledge. I promise to redeem it with a real stone one day.'

'Thank you. Gran mustn't know. I shall wear it on my right hand and call it a dress ring. Only we will know it's an engagement ring.'

'Another one of those secrets,' Frankie said, and took her into his arms for a proper kiss.

Once back under the kitchen light, Aimee was absolutely thrilled. Frankie had done a marvellous job. It was a pretty ring and looked convincingly real.

It was Boxing Day when Frankie said, 'Not only are we keeping our suspicions about Candida faking pictures a dark secret, but now we're not telling your grandfather that I'm taking every opportunity to kiss you and tell you I love you and that I'm hoping to marry you one day. He's been very kind to me; I feel beholden to him. He'll be cross if he finds out that I've taken things this far and we haven't told him.'

Aimee smiled up at him. 'I find myself thinking of you all

the time. It gives me a warm feeling to know you love me. Don't worry, Gramps will be on our side; anyway, you're creating patterns for him. He needs you.'

'It's not just that. I was upset when I heard you'd come into a fortune. I wish you hadn't. He'll think I'm marrying you for your money. It will keep us apart.'

'It needn't, Frankie. We mustn't let it.' She threw her arms round him and kissed him. 'I'm in love and very happy about it, thrilled, excited . . .'

'So am I, but we mustn't let other people notice, especially not at work. You know how they gossip. We don't want him to hear it first in an office rumour.'

'That's the last thing we want, but it isn't going to be easy. I feel love shining out of me like a beacon, telling everybody how I feel.' Aimee felt a little frisson of delight run down her spine and kissed him again. She laughed. 'You'll have to keep your hands in your pockets and your eyes away from me.'

'These things have a way of leaking out,' Frankie said. 'I dread to think what your grandmother would do if she knew.'

Prudence was still appalled at Aimee's decision to go and work at the mill. 'It's no place for a young lady,' she said. 'I don't think you'll like it.'

'It's my choice, Grandma.'

'You can always change your mind if you don't enjoy it,' Gramps said.

'I want to take my father's place in the business,' she said firmly. 'My mind is made up.'

'All right,' Walter said. 'As I said, I'll put you in each department in turn, where you'll work in a junior position to

197

learn how the business functions from the bottom up. Unless you understand that, you won't be able to help me. The hours will be a lot longer than at art school, and I don't think you'll find it easy.'

'I think you're being very silly,' Prudence said.

'My family have owned and run this mill for over a hundred years,' Walter said. 'You'll know something of its history, but I want to make things clear to you. Cotton spinning has been carried on in Lancashire since the Industrial Revolution, and our company, Alfred Kendrick and Sons, was founded in Rochdale in 1802. We bought raw cotton from America and started spinning and weaving it to make fabric.

'In the middle of the nineteenth century, one of my forebears split the management between his twin sons, Mathew and Maurice, who couldn't get on together. Thereafter Mathew bought the raw cotton and took charge of the spinning and weaving, and Maurice took on the dyeing, finishing and marketing. It remained one company, of course, and the profit was split equally between them.

'The business thrived like that for half a century, and when it outgrew its original premises in Rochdale and no land was available close by, our site on the outskirts of Liverpool was bought and Maurice's dyeing and finishing machines were moved there. Since then, all the fabric produced in Rochdale has come to Liverpool to be dyed and finished. It's closer to the docks and the markets for selling the cloth on.

'My father managed it all and that's what I inherited. Today I employ a manager to run the Rochdale end, but I visit when I can and try to keep an eye on what he's doing. I'll take you with me next time.'

'Isn't it more difficult to run a mill when it's split between two sites that are miles apart?' Aimee asked.

'It is indeed. Those twin sons did us no favours, but it's too late to put the two halves together again.'

Aimee started her apprenticeship in the mill after the New Year holiday, and felt a little apprehensive as she set out with Gramps. Frankie was waiting for them at the ferry house and accompanied them to the mill door, chatting all the way. He told Aimee he'd found everybody very friendly and had soon settled in.

'I'm glad to hear it,' Gramps said, 'and I'm sure Aimee will do the same.'

On the first morning, she was taken round the various departments, and Gramps introduced her to everybody as his granddaughter and told them he was planning to train her to manage the mill so he could retire. She noticed that he knew all the foremen by name. She herself already knew a few of the managers but found it a struggle to remember the rest, as well as take in the jobs they were doing. She decided she must get herself a notebook and write it all down.

Gramps showed her all the machines, and explained exactly what each one did. After an hour, she found the clatter and noise almost overpowering and was glad to return to the comparative quiet of the office.

In the personnel department, he introduced her to the young manager, Charles Hibbert, and his very much older deputy, Mrs Perry.

Aimee shook Mrs Perry's hand and said to Gramps, 'I didn't know you employed ladies in senior positions.'

'Mrs Perry is the one exception,' he told her. 'She manages

the cleaning team who come in every evening at five o'clock when the rest of us go home. Everyone speaks very highly of her.'

She was slightly built and plainly dressed, the sort of person who could fade into the background and not be noticed, but her head was held high as though she was in command here rather than the youthful Mr Hibbert. Her grey eyes darted around; nothing evaded her notice. Aimee didn't know what to make of her.

'What I'd like,' Aimee said, 'is a list of everyone employed here, with a brief description of their jobs. It's what I need to get an overall picture. I hope I'm not putting you to too much trouble?'

'Not at all.' Mrs Perry spoke softly. 'I'll do that for you.'

'Thank you.' Aimee smiled. 'I have so much to learn if I'm to be any help to my grandfather.'

In the accounts department, Gramps said, 'Do you remember Neville Sanderson, our chief accountant? He's a relative of Grandma's.'

Sanderson stood over six feet tall, with broad shoulders, and wore a suit that was easily the smartest in the office; nobody could forget him. 'How d'you do,' he said, putting out his hand. Aimee took it and found he had a bruising grip. 'How is Aunt Prudence?'

'Very well, thank you. We've met before, Mr Sanderson.' She smiled. 'You're in charge of the company accounts?'

'I am indeed, and I stand in for your grandfather when he isn't here – second in command, you might say.'

'I'll know where to come when I need advice, then,' she said politely, but there was something in his manner she found offputting.

When she was back in Gramps's office, he said, 'Sanderson is not the right person to ask for advice. When he was pleading for a job, he told me he was sitting his accountancy exams, and he asked if I'd train him in management as I'd trained Alec. He was always telling me he was grateful and how much he was learning. Later, he asked to be put in charge of the Rochdale mill, and I thought he'd have it working at top efficiency in next to no time. He was in charge there for six years or so, and I can only say things were no better at the end than when he started.'

'Then why did you put him in charge of the accounts department?'

'He asked me to. He said that really he was an accountant and he wanted to devote all his time to figures rather than managerial work. He was brimming with energy and enthusiasm and said he'd sort the business out for me in no time. On past showing, I was a fool to believe him; he's not done any better here.'

'It sounds as though he's been telling you where he wants to work and you've let him do exactly what he wants.'

'Yes, but I don't really trust him.'

'Gramps, you should sack him.'

'Dispensing with the services of a senior member of staff can be difficult.'

'Couldn't you demote him to a job in the background, out of the way?'

'Then I'd have to find another man to fill his present position.' Walter sighed. 'Things have become more difficult since old Ben Hibbert retired. He was a friend to me and a very good accountant. Do you remember him?'

'No, but haven't you just introduced me to someone with

the name Hibbert? The young manager in personnel, would that be his son?'

'His grandson, I believe. We have more than one generation of some families working here. Things were easier back in Ben Hibbert's time. I hired a young fellow to replace him as chief accountant, but he couldn't get on with Sanderson; they were at each other's throats, and it caused unrest all round. Within months he gave in his notice.'

'Gramps! Did Sanderson drive him out? Why d'you put up with him?'

'He pleaded for another chance. I suppose I felt sorry for him, and he is a relative.'

'It sounds as though he's playing on that.' Aimee was horrified. 'You need a chief accountant you can rely on.'

'I should have tried to fill the position again, but the truth is it's all got a bit beyond me.'

'You needed help years ago, when you took Sanderson on, but he hasn't provided it.'

'Well, I have you now.' He took several sheets of figures from his drawer and gave them to her. 'A copy of last year's company accounts. You'll need to study them.'

Aimee sighed. 'I'm not likely to be much help yet. I need to find my feet first.'

'Of course you do, love, and I've a lot more to explain.' A buzzer sounded through the building. 'That signals lunchtime. Get your coat and we'll go and eat. I expect you're hungry.'

He took her to the café where he'd taken her before. 'Do you always have lunch here?' she asked.

'There are two or three places I go, but I like this one best, so mostly I come here.'

'It's kind of you to take me out to lunch,' she said, 'but you'll not want to do this every day. I'll get a sandwich or something and eat with my colleagues.'

She meant Frankie; he'd told her he brought sandwiches with him, and she knew she'd find his company more restful. She was appalled at what Gramps had been telling her and felt she'd need to keep a close watch on Neville Sanderson.

But he wasn't giving her time to think. As they ate lunch, he carried on telling her facts about the business that she needed to remember. Afterwards, they walked back to the mill and he took her to see some of his latest machines, then showed her round the laboratory.

'Getting the raw cotton has always been difficult, and in times of war it's almost impossible. For the last few years lots of firms have been trying to make a thread from chemicals. We aren't near anything usable yet, but I'm investing a lot in research, probably more than we can afford. That could be our future.'

'That's fascinating, I had no idea,' she told him, but he was moving her along and already telling her about the rainbow array of dyes they used, their qualities and costs. 'I'll just show you the pattern department,' he said, 'and then we'll leave the rest for tomorrow.'

As soon as he opened the door, Frankie looked up. Aimee gave him a wink. 'This is where the apprentices work, and of course you know Frankie Hopkins.' They stopped for a few moments to study the pattern he was working on. 'Do you think it needs more contrast between the shades?' Gramps asked.

'Yes, sir, I was going to add narrow curving lines in here.' Frankie showed him the number of a dye.

'That should do it, yes. It could turn out very well.' Gramps glanced at what John Hampton, the other apprentice, was working on, then asked, 'Is Bruce Stanley not in today?'

'Just gone to the bog,' Hampton muttered.

'Stanley is the senior here,' Gramps told Aimee, and swept her back to his office. 'I'm glad to sit down after that.'

Aimee was too, but he kept giving her more sheets of figures and explaining their significance until she felt her head was swimming.

'I'm overdoing it, aren't I?' He was suddenly concerned.

She laughed. 'There's a limit to what I can take in at one sitting,' she said. 'I think I've reached it.'

'It's only half four, but I'll ask that Hopkins lad to see you safely home. You look exhausted.'

Aimee felt immediately revived.

At breakfast the next morning, Gramps said, 'I'm thinking of going to the Rochdale mill this morning; would you like to come with me?'

'Yes, I'd love to. I want to see where it all started.'

'Good.'

'Can Frankie come too?'

'If you carry on like this, that lad will get too big for his boots.'

Aimee laughed. 'Didn't you tell Grandma he was polite and well mannered?'

'He is, but there are no patterns to show him in Rochdale, no dyes either. What good would it do to take him?'

'He notices more than you or I do. He questions everything and wants to know why it's being done. If you want to find out exactly what's going on there, he should come.'

'All right then. He's certainly a bright lad.'

She found it a very tiring day. Gramps asked Bill Smith, the manager, to walk them round the mill and explain every machine and process to them. The noise from the clacking looms was deafening, and the girls tending the machines had to communicate with sign language, as normal speech could not be heard.

On the return journey to Liverpool, Aimee said, 'My ears feel terrible after that. I wouldn't like to spend every day there.'

'No,' Walter said. 'Well, young man, did you notice anything unusual going on?'

Frankie shook his head. 'No, sir. It's impossible on the first visit to know what's usual and what isn't. What I did see were great rolls of cloth being loaded into a van.'

'To be taken to our mill in Liverpool.' Walter nodded. 'That's how the system works. What was woven in Rochdale yesterday comes to us today. That van will make more than one trip a day.'

'Would that provide an opportunity to lose some on the way?' Frankie asked. 'Is there a market for it? I mean, it's unfinished fabric, isn't it? If it was stolen, could it be sold?'

Walter sighed. 'Only to another cotton mill. It would have to be finished before the general market would be interested.'

Once back in Liverpool, Frankie spent a considerable time checking how many rolls came daily, and studying the paper-work to see how many were later routinely sold by Tom Tasker, the sales manager.

'I think it's unlikely that stock is being stolen at that point,' he told Aimee.

CHAPTER TWENTY-THREE

CANDIDA HAD NEVER FELT in such a dither before. The fate of her two fraudulent paintings seemed to hang in the balance. Armand had taken them and said he'd put them in a sale in the spring, possibly March or April, which meant she'd have to wait another three months or more. They would need certificates of authenticity, and she hadn't asked him whether he would do that himself or get someone who was accepted as an expert to do it. She was terrified that something not quite right would be spotted, and the sale would be held up or worse still refused. Could anybody be certain that everything was perfect?

She couldn't stop worrying about it, but of course it might help that they were being sold through a long-established gallery like Armand's, and that there would be several of the fine pictures that Aimee had inherited in the same sale. She'd handled all the paperwork for those and knew everything was in order, and so fortunately nobody would question their authenticity.

It made it harder to bear that she no longer had anybody to talk to about it. She missed Aimee and Walter's company, and she was nervous about bothering Armand in case he should suspect something. Besides, it cost a lot to ring him.

She was relieved to receive a letter from him saying he'd authenticated her pictures and was now planning to put them in a sale of fine art to be held in May. She rang Aimee to let her know because her paintings were involved too.

'We've heard nothing,' Aimee said. 'Come over on Sunday for tea. I'll talk to Gramps about it; he'll want to phone Armand, I expect.'

Candida was pleased with the invitation. It was Dora's slab cake today, but it was still very nice. Eventually Walter decided to make the call. Candida's heart was pounding as she followed him to his study and sat down in front of the desk. He got through without any trouble, and she could hear Armand's voice. He sounded excited.

Walter was soon in difficulties with the language and handed the phone across to her in exasperation. 'He can speak English well enough,' he complained irritably. 'I don't know why he doesn't use it with me.'

Candida could see her hand shaking as she reached for the receiver. 'Armand?'

She was met with a torrent of rapid French that even she found hard to understand.

'What is it?' Aimee had perched on the corner of the desk and was getting impatient.

Candida put her hand over the mouthpiece for just long enough to whisper, 'Bad news. Armand has had to delay the auction.' All the time she could feel fear tightening its grip on her. She had good reason to be terrified now.

'What?' Walter was shocked. 'Not again. Why?'

Finally Armand asked to speak to Aimee, and Candida handed the phone over to her.

'Candida, is this more trouble?' Walter's eyes were on her.

'I'm afraid so.' She felt she was touching bottom; this was the sort of trouble she feared most. 'Armand says your Renoir is the cause. As you know, he sold it privately to another dealer, who tried to sell it on hoping to make a profit. He thought he'd found a buyer, a big collector of fine art in Vienna, but then another very similar picture by Renoir came on the market and he was questioned about the authenticity of your painting. Some expert has denounced it as a fake.'

'It can't be,' Walter said. 'That was Micheline's picture.'

'Its previous history is being investigated.' Candida could hardly get the words out. Her tongue had gone dry, and she felt frozen in horror.

'So Armand's known of this problem for some time and hasn't told us?'

'Since last week, he says; he apologised for not telling us sooner.' Candida's voice shook. 'The vendor of the other painting has been charged with attempted fraud, but his case will not be heard until the autumn, probably October. In the meantime, the sale of our pictures has been stopped and all the works in Armand's gallery are to be reassessed by experts.'

She was conscious of Aimee getting increasingly worked up on the phone; now she said, 'Gramps, Armand wants to talk to you again,' and pushed the receiver at him.

She was almost in tears. 'That Renoir had belonged to Maman since May 1926; she had a receipted bill for the amount she paid. She knew she had to keep things like that and had its history going back through the years. She even knew which exhibitions had displayed it. I've seen it all and I just know it was above board.'

'Do you know who she bought it from?' Candida asked. 'If so, it can be traced further back.'

'From Armand, he's just told me.'

'What? I didn't realise . . .' Candida was fighting to stay calm. She must watch what she said, not let them see that panic was threatening to engulf her.

'Maman wouldn't have had anything to do with fraud.'

Candida pulled herself together. 'No, she'd have had no reason to fake it. Micheline's own paintings were selling at prices that gave her a good living. She just wanted a beautiful picture as a mark of her success. I think that's why she chose the Renoir; she wanted the best.' But what would this mean for her?

Walter finally put the phone down and sighed. 'It's all very difficult. Armand is upset; it reflects badly on his reputation. It's been reported in the French newspapers that the Renoir vase came from his gallery, and all his stock is now suspect.'

'What are we going to do?' Aimee wailed.

Candida gritted her teeth; she'd been through all this before with her father. 'We'll have to wait and find out if this man is found guilty, and what the art experts finally decide about your painting.' And that would mean more waiting and worrying for them all. It was turning into a nightmare.

The phone rang again, silencing them all. Candida could see Walter signalling to her to pick it up. It was Armand again, his voice calmer now. 'I wrote to you a couple of days ago, Candida. The letter will still be in the post, and I want to tell you the rest of the story or you'll think I'm keeping things from you.

'I think you might know the man who has been accused of faking the Renoir. It's Edouard Watteau. Do you remember him?'

'Oh my God, yes! He was at the École des Beaux-Arts with us.' Candida had once counted him her boyfriend! 'That's terrible.' Somehow it hammered home that they were all fraudsters and in this together.

'He was held up to us as one of the most talented in his year,' Armand said. 'Didn't he fancy you at one time?'

'Yes,' and like a fool she'd fancied him.

'What went wrong?'

She sighed. 'He had a huge ego, and really believed he was the most talented art student in the world and heading for fame and fortune. I remember him trying to put Micheline down, saying she was only average.'

'Looks as though he's heading for a sticky end now, though,' Armand said, 'and it's doing my reputation no good. Nobody's likely to buy anything from me until all this is over and the fuss dies down. All my pictures are suspected of being fakes. Everything stops so that they can be reassessed.'

Candida choked out, 'And that includes my paintings as well as those inherited by Aimee?'

'I'm afraid so. Do you know a Dr Eugene Fouche?'

'I've heard of him; he's another of those experts. Isn't he in charge of some art school?'

'The Académie de le Grande Chaumière here in Paris. He is convinced that the two Chagalls are fakes too.'

'They can't be, absolutely not,' Candida said. 'Micheline told me she knew Marc Chagall and he'd given them to her. All we have to do is ask him.'

'Yes, but you have no need to worry, Candida. You know yours are all right.'

She swallowed hard. 'There is that,' she managed, but once again she was fighting panic.

Once she had hung up, Walter said, 'Let's go back to the sitting room where it's more comfortable.' She could see how worried he was. 'Did Armand know this all along? Or has it come as a shock to him too?'

Candida said, 'That's what worries me. And it's bad news that another artist has been charged with faking pictures, not only by Renoir but by other artists.'

'This really bothers me.' Aimee returned with a fresh pot of tea and started to pour it. 'Do you think Maman knew? The thought of her being part of this fraud is awful.'

'I'm sure she did not,' Walter assured her. 'I always found Micheline completely honest. You mustn't think such things.'

'Impossible not to,' Aimee wailed, 'when she's caught up in the midst of it.'

Candida sat back in her chair and tried to breathe deeply. When she could trust herself, she said reassuringly, 'Micheline was not the instigator of this fraud, but she might be the victim. She paid a large sum for that Renoir and I've been trying to piece together in my mind what I know of those years.'

'It was not dated,' Walter said.

'But Aimee has said the receipt is dated May 1926. What do you remember of those years, Walter?'

'Nothing much. I was more concerned about my business.'

'All I remember is Micheline telling me about a new boyfriend, and that everything was turning out well for her.' That year Micheline had not invited her over for the August holiday; her time was being taken up with her new boyfriend, and to be honest, Candida had resented Armand ever since. She felt he'd taken her place in Micheline's affections, and pushed her away from her long-term friend. She had tried to hide her envy that everything good was happening in her friend's life while she was left waiting and hoping on the sidelines.

In no time at all, Micheline had been writing in thrilling terms of marriage to Armand, and the invitation to their wedding followed shortly afterwards, to be propped on her mantelpiece. The memories of the wedding were painfully bittersweet. Aimee had been eleven years old, and her only bridesmaid, in a bespoke Parisian dress. 'I first saw the Renoir hanging on the wall at La Coutancie when I was over for the wedding.'

'The fact that Micheline bought it from Armand worries me,' Walter said. 'What if he knew it was a fake all those years ago?'

'Gramps, you sound awfully suspicious,' Aimee said. 'He says he gave her its full history and it's all above board.'

'Difficult not to be suspicious,' Candida said. 'Did he deliberately sell it to Micheline to get at her money? Then, when she fell in love with him, did he think he'd have a permanent meal ticket if he were to marry her?' She immediately felt ashamed; she must have an evil streak in her to think such things of Armand. 'I never liked him,' she said.

'He made me like him,' Aimee said. 'I felt really sorry for him when he told me how he lost his first wife and children.'

Not for the first time, Candida wondered if that story was true.

* * *

The next morning, Aimee went to the mill with Gramps again, and after another session going through the figures he'd given her yesterday, he said, 'I want you to work in our sales department for the next three months. It's a good place for you to start, and I see our sales as very important. Come with me and I'll introduce you to Tom Tasker, our manager. He has to sell everything we make, otherwise it's a loss to the company, and he'll teach you the basics of marketing.'

She followed him down a corridor and through a room with a table piled high with samples to a cubbyhole of an office. 'Good morning, Tom,' Gramps said. 'I've told you all about Aimee, my granddaughter. I'm going to leave her here with you and in three months' time I'll expect her to know everything there is to know about marketing.'

Tom Tasker got up from his desk; Aimee thought he looked relaxed. 'Hello, Aimee,' he said, and shook her hand. 'I've seen you from time to time when you've come to choose dress lengths, and now you're grown up and you want to join us.'

'I want to help my grandfather.'

'Well, welcome to the fold; don't forget you can come and talk to me at any time, about anything. I knew you were going to start with me, so I've had this desk brought up and put in amongst the rest of the sales staff. This is Bob Davies next to you; he'll explain our routine and show you where things are kept. I'll be taking both of you out this morning to sell our latest patterns. Give me half an hour or so.'

Bob Davies had a friendly smile and was nearer her age. 'I'll begin by showing you the first essentials: where we make the tea. We'll all need a cup before we go out.'

Half an hour later, Tom Tasker began driving them round a number of small clothing factories. Bob Davies was kept busy fetching rolls of cloth from the van and spreading them out to show off the details of the current designs. Tom knew all the managers by name and chatted and joked as he explained the finer points of his wares. Afterwards, Aimee helped Bob roll the cloth up and reload the van. She could see the customers were interested in the samples they left with them. Most said they'd work out their needs and future production and send in their order later, but one gave Tom a big order straight away. Aimee felt a little thrill run down her spine when for the first time she saw their fabrics made up into items of clothing ready to go to the shops.

On the way back, Tom stopped outside a baker's shop. 'I need to get something for my lunch,' he said. He bought a sandwich and then chose a selection of cream cakes. Bob decided on a couple of sausage rolls, and as Aimee was getting hungry, she bought a meat pie.

Lunch break in the mill was usually from one o'clock until two; it was almost over by the time they returned. Tom's secretary, Phyllis, made cups of tea for them all and they sat down to eat in the office. Tom opened up the box of cakes he'd bought. 'This doesn't happen every day,' he said to Aimee. 'It's to celebrate the New Year and see it in in style. We're a team here; we all pull together, and I like to provide a bit of cement to keep it that way.'

They were chatting and laughing when suddenly Neville Sanderson blocked the doorway. 'What a racket you're making,' he barked, eyeing the now nearly empty box of cakes with disfavour. 'You should all be working at your desks instead of horsing around. The lunch hour is long since over; you should have settled down to work again like the rest of us.'

'My watch makes it half past two,' Tom Tasker said in a relaxed drawl. 'We've been out working all morning and partly through the lunch break too. We're owed another fifteen minutes to eat our lunch.' He held out the box. 'Can I offer you the last cake, Neville?'

Sanderson left, slamming the door. Aimee thought he hadn't even noticed her.

Gramps told her that he'd be working late this evening, and she was to leave with the rest of the junior staff. She was delighted when Frankie came to find her a few minutes before the buzzer sounded at five thirty, and they travelled home together.

She found Grandma in a bad mood. 'Walter says he needs to stay late? What can he possibly find to do at this hour?'

'I must be taking up a lot of his time,' Aimee said. 'He's explaining everything to me.'

Prue sniffed. 'You shouldn't be working there in the first place. Whatever would your mother say if she knew?'

Grandma had little to say during the meal. Dora had made them Aimee's favourite pudding: Manchester tart, a cold raspberry jam tart with a covering of set Bird's custard. Aimee ate two pieces but kept her mind on what she'd planned to do. 'Grandma,' she said, 'do you know Neville Sanderson? He's Gramps's chief accountant and I understand he's a cousin of yours.'

'I remember Walter saying something about him, but I don't know if I've met him. A cousin, you said?'

'Gramps was pretty vague, but when I asked him again, he said he thought he was a cousin once removed of your mother's.'

'I don't think so; probably he was just angling for a job. I told Walter he shouldn't have employed him; he's never been happy with his work. My mother died many years ago; you and Walter are my only living relatives now.'

'But Sanderson was your maiden name, so he could be related. Did your mother have aunts or uncles?'

'Not that I know of. We were a small family. I did have one younger sister, but Verity never married; she always had a bad chest and died in her twenties.'

'Tell me about her, Gran, was she much younger?'

'Yes, more than four years. She was very pretty. Attracted a lot of attention from gentlemen.' There was a note in Prue's voice that told Aimee she'd heartily disapproved of her sister.

'It's terrible that she died so young. Do you have any photographs of her?'

'No.' Aimee could see she would get no more information from Grandma; it looked more and more as though Sanderson had invented the relationship for his own purposes.

Aimee's first thoughts when she woke up the next morning were of Frankie. These days she was getting up a little earlier to make herself a sandwich to eat with him at lunchtime. He was always waiting at the ferry for her and Gramps, and as soon as they drew near, her eyes would dart through the assembling passengers seeking him out. To see him waiting for her, meeting his gaze, knowing he loved her made a thrill run down her spine.

This morning she was very conscious of his shoulder

touching hers as all three of them leaned against the rail looking down at the turbulent brown water. She recounted to Gramps every detail of her sales trip the day before. 'I think Tom Tasker enjoys his work, and I really enjoyed my trip out with him. He's a jolly person.'

Walter smiled. 'He's doing really well. I have no worries about the sales department and can safely say we have no problems there.'

She went on to tell him about Neville Sanderson coming to complain about the noise at lunchtime. 'He was really throwing his weight about, acting as though he owned the place,' she added.

'Tom can look after himself,' Gramps chuckled. 'I don't suppose it bothered him.'

'It didn't, but I don't understand why you put up with Sanderson. He swaggers round as though he's the boss and drives himself to work in a flashy American car, while you come by public transport. I asked Grandma about him last night, and she doesn't even think he's a relative. I worry that he's in a position of trust and seems to have lots of money.'

'The Sandersons were never short of money. Prudence's father was known locally as the Sausage King. He set up a factory making the best pork sausages and sold them all over Merseyside. He had a fleet of vans taking them round the butchers' and grocers' shops.'

'I didn't know that,' Aimee laughed.

'No, Grandma would have preferred her family wealth to have been earned elsewhere. We don't talk about sausages, even though the business was sold after the war.'

'We don't ever eat them either.'

'No, she doesn't care for them.'

'That's a bit extreme, isn't it? Anyway, I'm going to ask Sanderson to explain the relationship.'

Up to that moment Frankie had been staring down at the creamy wake left by the ferry. Now he spoke. 'I've heard rumours going round that Sanderson is making a lot of money for himself by running a little business on the side.'

'What sort of business?' Gramps demanded.

'I did ask, but people were vague about it. I get the impression it's something allied to cotton, but I don't know if there's any truth in it. Nobody seems to like him; I think they resent him because he treats them in such a lordly fashion.'

'He's rude and he's harsh with all the juniors,' Aimee said. 'He's not very kind to me.'

'So it might be that they're suggesting reasons for his apparent wealth that aren't true, to ridicule him,' Frankie said.

'But the rumours could still be right,' Aimee said. 'Gramps, you're telling me that he tried hard to get a job with you, and harder still to be in charge of your company accounts, and during the years he's worked here he's started to look increasingly prosperous, while your company profits have slipped.'

'Yes, that's about it, but it could be this depression; it's hurting every business.'

'But he's in a position where he can manipulate the figures,' Frankie said. 'Wouldn't it be wise to check through the accounts carefully to see if we can find any discrepancies? To see if there's any foundation for these rumours?'

'I do check them,' Walter said indignantly. 'Of course I do.'

'Are you paying him a salary that allows him to live in such a fashion?' Aimee asked.

'Probably not, but to check through the accounts would be a mammoth task. Who do you suggest should do that?'

'You,' Aimee said. 'We don't have the knowledge or experience.'

'No,' Walter sighed, 'and I don't have the time or energy. You do realise that by law the company accounts have to be audited, but I'll be more than happy to get out all the figures for the last few years so you two can look through them again. After all, you could be right.'

When Aimee travelled home with Frankie that evening, they were each carrying a bundle of documents. 'I upset your grandfather this morning,' he said, 'by suggesting he hadn't studied his company accounts.'

'Yes, you put your foot in it, but Gramps won't hold that against you.'

'I've glanced at these this afternoon and I have to tell you they mean absolutely nothing to me.'

'Nor me,' Aimee sighed, 'but I feel Neville Sanderson wanted a job here for some reason of his own. He's told lies about being related to Grandma, and he keeps reminding everybody of it in order to make sure he keeps his job.'

'Well,' Frankie said. 'We aren't the only ones who wonder if he could be taking money out of the business to run his fancy American car, but it's just surmising; nobody really knows. He could be as honest as the day is long.'

'I'll come over to your house after dinner tonight,' Aimee said, 'and we'll take a good look through these figures together.'

When she got there, Frankie's grandad was asleep in the armchair drawn up to the living room fire. 'Won't we disturb him?' Aimee sat down at the table and they spread the documents out.

'Not if we whisper. He usually dozes off at this time.' Within ten minutes, though, Frankie had pushed the papers aside. 'It's no good us studying these; we don't understand the first thing about them, and people who do have checked them and found nothing wrong. If he's doing anything illegal, it must be happening in some other way.'

'Yes, openly, in front of everybody's eyes, and we take no notice because it's always gone on.'

Frankie put an arm round her waist and pulled her closer. 'Let's go out for a walk along the prom. It's getting dark now and there won't be many people about.'

They tiptoed out, leaving the documents behind. They got no further than Aimee's back garden. It was totally secluded there, and she was able to melt into his arms.

The next morning Aimee sat at her desk in the sales department feeling very much on edge. Tom Tasker had given her a job to do checking his sales figures, but she couldn't put her mind to it. She'd keyed herself up to ask Neville Sanderson just how he was related to Grandma, and there was only one way to do it. She got to her feet and went along the corridor to his office.

She'd thought this through. He'd tell her the story about his mother being a vague cousin, and she would tell him that Grandma said that wasn't true. That ought to give her the upper hand, and to think of it gave her a little frisson of triumph. She could see Sanderson being cowed and she could point out that he'd got his job on false pretences. She knocked on his door and went in. 'Hello, could you spare a minute? There's something that's been bothering me.'

'Of course, have a seat. How can I help?'

Her mouth was dry, but she managed to sound confident. 'I don't understand your relationship to my grandmother; perhaps you would explain it.'

He smiled at her for the first time. 'Hasn't she told you?'

Instantly Aimee had misgivings. 'Well, I've heard her version . . .'

'Yes, even after all this time Aunt Prudence is likely to be cagey about it. My mother is her younger sister Verity. She wasn't married, so I'm from the wrong side of the blanket.'

Aimee could feel a hot flush running up her cheeks. She'd got this very wrong.

He went on. 'Once her pregnancy became noticeable, she was cast out of her home, cut off from her family and left to fend for herself.'

'You mean cut off without funds?'

'Not exactly. I meant she was cut off from all family support and left to make her own way at a time when she was in great need. She was not entirely without money, because when she was eighteen her father gave her a dress allowance and he continued to pay that. It didn't go very far; I had a fairly austere upbringing.'

Aimee felt as though the ground had been cut from under her feet. This sounded like the gospel truth. It was Gran who had been telling fibs. 'I'm shocked, horrified. Sorry, I didn't know. What about your father?' Oh gosh, had she gone too far?

'I never knew him. He went down with his ship HMS

Audacious when it hit a German mine in October 1914. That was before they could be married.'

'I'm so sorry.' Aimee felt her toes curl with embarrassment. 'So that makes you my father's first cousin?'

'Yes, but clearly your family still want nothing to do with us.'

'Except Gramps.'

'Yes, at least he was kind enough to give me a job when I needed it. Since I've had that, things haven't been too bad.'

'And what about your mother?'

'She's well, thank you.' He looked embarrassed too now. 'It's all ancient history, water under the bridge.'

'Yes, sorry to have raked it up, forgive me.'

Aimee got out as quickly as she could. Her stomach was churning; the exchange with Sanderson had definitely not gone as she'd expected, and she felt mortified and angry. Typical of Grandma to dress it up. Her sister had had an illegitimate baby; why hadn't she told Aimee the truth when she'd asked? She'd said Verity had died in her twenties, when she was clearly very much alive. Gramps too must have known that Verity wasn't dead, and they both must have been aware that Neville was her son. They'd been telling Aimee a load of fairy tales, treating her like a child.

CHAPTER TWENTY-FOUR

THAT AFTERNOON, WALTER SAT at his desk worrying about whether there was any truth in the rumours Frankie Hopkins had recounted about Neville Sanderson.

He was very surprised that after a rap on the door, Sanderson's head came round it. 'I've brought you the latest production figures,' he said, coming forward and putting them on his desk. 'Slightly down again, I'm afraid, sir.'

It took Walter a few moments to take them in. He stared at them in disbelief. They were drifting down month by month. Last month he'd paced regularly round the production department and kept a closer watch on what was going on. The machines had been running almost at full tilt. He'd been reassured that they were busy again, and turning out more.

'Right,' he said, dismissing the accountant; he couldn't bear to see his expression of concern. It must be assumed; no actor could do it better. 'I must talk to production about this.'

Could it be fraud, and was Sanderson responsible? How and when was it taking place? He had to stop it and he needed to be quick about it, but he had no idea how to do that. He felt he was losing control of his business; it was slipping away from him. He must take time and give it more thought.

His afternoon tea was growing cold in the cup when his

phone rang. It took him a few moments to grasp what the youthful voice was telling him. 'Nurse Watts?'

'Yes, from Grange Mount Maternity Hospital in Birkenhead.'

That was like a spark. 'Oh yes?'

'Mrs Kerr has asked me to let you know that she's had a little girl, born at two this afternoon. Both mother and baby are well, and our visiting hours are seven thirty to eight o'clock every evening.'

'Oh yes, thank you.' Walter felt new vigour running through his veins and sat up straighter. 'Can I come this evening?'

'Yes, of course.'

He put the phone down and wanted to laugh. The waiting was over and Esther and the baby were fine. A baby girl! He'd been hoping for a son, but no matter. It must have gone smoothly; it seemed some things did work out in his favour. He phoned Prudence and told her he'd be working late tonight and probably wouldn't be home before eight or nine. 'Don't bother to keep a meal for me. I'll get something to eat here.'

He locked his desk and put on his hat. He'd go into central Liverpool to buy some flowers and some chocolates for Esther before the shops closed. He felt like singing. He'd treat himself to a drink and a slap-up dinner in town. He really had something to celebrate now.

He was at the hospital fifteen minutes before the appointed time, and that gave him the chance to find out which ward Esther was on. He was at the door before it was opened, along with many other fathers bearing flowers and gifts. It shocked him to see how young they were.

On the dot of seven thirty, the waiting crowd flooded in.

There were beds ranged down both sides of the ward, and he was at a loss looking from one side to the other for Esther. At last he spotted her, beaming at him with her hair neatly combed and wearing a pretty nightgown and negligee. He kissed her, and could see that she looked happy but tired. 'I can't believe you've done it, that it's all over.'

The baby was in a cot attached to the foot of her bed. He could hardly see anything of it in the swaddling hospital bedding, and he put an exploratory finger in to loosen it. 'You can pick her up,' Esther said.

Walter wasn't sure he felt capable of that. It was a very long time since he'd seen a baby as small as this. 'She's asleep.'

Esther climbed out of bed and lifted the baby, unwrapping the covers so he could see her tiny limbs. 'She weighed in at seven pounds eight ounces,' she said proudly. 'Isn't she gorgeous?'

'We thought it would be a boy and we'd call him Rex, but what did we decide for a girl?'

'Daisy.' She was laughing. 'Daisy May.'

'Did you have a hard time?'

'No, the pains started about five o'clock this morning. It was quicker than I expected, easier too.'

'How did you manage?'

'I told you about Kitty, who lives on the corner of our road. She's a ward orderly here and I remembered she told me that her shift starts at seven, so I got dressed, picked up the bag I'd packed and went round to her place. We came together on the workmen's bus. She's been back to see Daisy.'

'Oh my goodness! You were in labour and you came on the bus?'

'It was all right. Kitty was a great escort and she knew exactly where I had to come.'

A short while later, a strict-looking sister came into the ward and rang a handbell. 'Time's up, gentlemen,' she called. 'Will you all please leave now.'

Walter couldn't believe he'd passed half an hour in wonder and joy at the miracle of his new daughter.

It was striking ten when Walter let himself into the hall at Fairholme and saw Aimee at the kitchen stove. 'Hello, Gramps,' she said. 'I'm making cocoa for myself and Gran; shall I make a cup for you too?'

'No thanks.' He'd had a wonderful evening and felt full of happiness. 'I think I'll go straight up to bed.'

'No, don't do that. I've been waiting for you to come home. I'd like a word.' Aimee put two cups and saucers on a tray and led the way into the sitting room.

As Walter followed, he noticed Prudence pull herself upright in her chair. 'Oh, you've come home at last,' she said nastily.

He ignored her and said to Aimee, 'Did something happen at the office?'

'Yes, I asked Neville Sanderson to explain his relationship to Gran and was shocked to find he really is related, closely related.' He could see she had Prudence's full attention. 'Gran, he's your sister Verity's son, your nephew and first cousin to my father.'

Prudence's face was turning brick red with rage. 'Verity's illegitimate son,' she spat. 'My father did not wish us to recognise her men friends or her children. She cut my family's reputation to shreds.'

Walter spoke up. 'Only one man, Prudence, and only one child.'

Aimee said, 'I'm horrified. I can't believe you'd cut off your own sister because she had a baby. How heartless that was!'

'An illegitimate baby,' Prue said stiffly. 'Things were different when I was young. My reputation was ruined too. It meant I could no longer hope to marry into a better circle.'

'We were engaged before it happened,' Walter reminded her. 'You intended to marry me anyway, so that made no difference to you.' Prudence flashed him a look of pure hatred.

'But you told me Verity had died in her twenties,' Aimee protested, 'and left me to find out from Neville Sanderson that she's alive and well. I can hardly believe that you haven't spoken to her in over thirty years. I didn't know what to say when he told me. You led me to suppose that he was telling a string of lies about being related to us to further his own ends, when it was you who was telling the lies.'

'My father cut her off. He decided we must have no further contact with her, that she was a bad influence on me.'

Walter could see that Aimee was upset. 'Between the two you,' she said, 'you dropped me in it, made me feel a real fool.'

'I'm sorry—' he began.

Aimee held up her hand. 'I can't believe it of you, Gramps. You repeated the same string of lies to me. You're just as bad. You knew Neville Sanderson's father went down with his ship in the Great War and his mother was alone and would be in need of help.'

Grandma broke in furiously. 'Verity could always give a good sob story.'

'Gran,' Aimee said, 'the truth is that her fiancé was unable to come home and marry her because he was in the navy and the country was at war. I think that's a very sad story. Like my father, he gave his life to defend us all.'

'Well, Prudence,' Walter said, 'Aimee deserves to know the rest of your family history; you might as well tell her everything.'

'You are insufferable,' Prudence spat out. 'I've had enough of this, I'm going to bed.' She leapt to her feet, knocking over her untouched cup of cocoa. Hissing with vexation at the mess on the carpet, she rushed out, slamming the door behind her.

'Oh dear.' Walter lay back in his chair. 'Get a cloth, Aimee, would you? And if you'd get me a whisky too, I'd very much appreciate it.'

When she'd done what was needed, Aimee sat down. 'I hope you're going to tell me the rest of the Sanderson history now you've whetted my appetite for it.'

'That is my intention.' He paused to collect his thoughts.

'Gran's father was known in the district as the Sausage King,' she prompted. 'You told me that.'

'Yes, and this house was nicknamed Sanderson's Castle. The family was wealthy, but polite society was rigid in Victorian days, and the Sandersons were not received by the foremost Liverpool families. I think Prudence has always resented that. They lived amongst the professional classes here, but he'd worked his way up from a stall in the market, and trade can be a dirty word, particularly when associated with sausages.'

'But what about the cotton trade?'

He smiled. 'I have to tell you, cotton is somewhat upmarket compared with sausages. The cotton trade has been well established in Lancashire for generations and many have made fortunes from it. The Cotton Exchange in Liverpool and its merchants are venerated here.'

'So the only difference is that Gran's father made his money from sausages?'

'That's about it. He died suddenly of a heart attack before we were married, and her mother sold the business afterwards. This had been her family home for years, and rather than be left on her own, her mother invited us to live here with her.'

'Yes, Gran told me that. She's proud of this house.'

'In her later years, your great-grandmother was an invalid, and Prudence looked after her. Well, she had a personal maid, but Grandma used to read to her, buy her books and embroidery thread, that sort of thing. She expected to be left the family fortune, but her mother changed her will without telling us. I think she must have felt guilty about Verity and went against her husband's wishes by leaving her all her money.'

'Goodness! All of it?'

'Yes. Prue was absolutely furious and felt slighted. "I looked after Mother in her old age," she said to me. "Clearly she didn't appreciate all I did for her. Verity never came near but she got all the money." She thought it was extremely unfair.'

'But Gran was given this house.'

'And her mother's personal possessions. All her silver and expensive crockery, and a lot of jewellery too.'

'Oh gosh.' Aimee was biting her lip. 'So that's where Neville Sanderson gets his money. It's family wealth that his mother inherited. Gramps, you should have told me the truth about that. I thought you believed he was involved in some sort of fraud that was running the company profits down. I thought you expected me to watch him like a hawk and find out how he was doing it. And look what you've done to Frankie: your staff will think you brought him in to spy on them.'

'Well, I'm almost sure that stock is being taken. All is not well in the business. I still want you both to keep your eyes open. I didn't mean to make you cross, I'm sorry.'

'Oh, Gramps,' she said, and flung her arms round him in a hug. 'Together we've made Gran very angry.'

Aimee had found it difficult to get to sleep after the argument between her grandparents and was late getting up the next morning. Gramps was more lethargic than usual and they only caught the ferry because Frankie was doing his best to make it wait for them.

During the morning, Mrs Perry brought her the information she'd asked her for: a list of the staff at the mill together with a brief description of the jobs they did. 'Every employee is on this list?' she asked. It ran to many pages.

'Yes,' Mrs Perry confirmed. 'There are two lists really, one for Rochdale and one for Liverpool.'

During their lunch break, she and Frankie studied them, and with a note of wonder in his voice he said, 'If fraud is taking place, then the names of the fraudsters must be on this list, and from the jobs they do, we might be able to work out who might be involved. Neville Sanderson could still be one of them. His job seems to be to fix the company accounts so they not only look correct but can withstand examination.'

'Yes, but he'd need help. To move rolls of cloth is hard physical work. They're big and heavy, and it takes time to fill a van. How do they do that without anybody seeing them?'

'Vans are being loaded all the time in the yard outside,'

Frankie said. 'Who is likely to notice that some vans are transporting fraudulent orders?'

'Wouldn't Sanderson need a crony in the production department to falsify the number of rolls they're making?' Aimee pondered. 'Yet Gramps thinks the manager, Douglas Tate, is sound.'

Frankie ran his finger down the list. 'His deputy is a Mr Oswald Perry, aged fifty-nine, who's been in the job for the last sixteen years.'

'Perry? I wonder if he's married to Mrs Perry . . .' She found her name on the list: Hilda Jane Perry, aged fifty-seven. 'There's no way of knowing if they are married, but they could be. Gramps says he often takes on a second family member. Mrs Perry wouldn't be much help lifting heavy rolls of cloth – there's nothing brawny about her but she works from one o'clock till eight in the evening and oversees the office cleaning.'

'Easier to help yourself to stock when most people have gone home for the night,' Frankie said thoughtfully.

The buzzer sounded through the offices signalling it was time to return to work. Frankie gathered up all the sheets of paper and gave them to her.

'I'm putting Mrs Perry on the list of suspects,' Aimee said. 'I'll ask Gramps if she's married to Oswald Perry in production, and if so, his name must go on it too.'

'We ought to stay late and see what happens after hours,' Frankie said.

'I've usually had enough by five o'clock,' Aimee retorted, 'and I expect you have too.'

'Yes, but if we want to make more progress, we should.'

* * *

Aimee felt she was learning a lot from Tom Tasker and enjoying her time in the sales department, but her feelings for Frankie now dominated her life. The two other apprentice pattern makers usually went out in the lunch break; even so, eating lunch at his office desk somehow inhibited them both. He couldn't throw his arms round her there in case someone came in, and his kisses were reduced to a few quick pecks, but at least it gave them a welcome opportunity to be together to talk of their future.

They now took it for granted that they'd get married, but they'd agreed they'd have to wait because they were young. 'Your grandfather won't agree to it,' Frankie said.

'It'll take me at least three years to learn how to run the mill, and perhaps longer to convince Gramps that I can do it. We'll buy a house here in Liverpool and cut down on the time we spend travelling back and forth to work.'

'Yes, a small modern house that's manageable,' Frankie agreed.

'We'll buy a car too, and we'll both have to learn to drive.'

'You are ambitious,' he laughed. 'It'll take an age to do all that.'

'No it won't, you're forgetting my inheritance. I don't know why you've taken against that. It gives us the money to buy things when we need them.'

'Put it down to my misplaced masculine pride,' he sighed. 'I can't help feeling I should be providing those things for us.'

'Well you're making a good start and I'm sure eventually you could,' she said slowly, 'but Maman has given me this and I want to share it with you.'

'Then that's our future all mapped out,' Frankie said, 'exactly as we want it. I'm very happy about it, but I feel we should tell your grandfather our plans. He won't think kindly of me if he hears them from office gossip.'

'But so far it's still our secret, and the time we spend together is totally ours.' Aimee smiled. 'Let's keep it that way for a bit longer.'

Frankie felt he had to agree. Drawing up plans like this was all they could do at the moment, but it was more of a wish list than a plan. He couldn't possibly leave Dad in the old stables and move over to Liverpool, and he was afraid the old man wouldn't want to move. He was a creature of habit and very much set in his ways. He'd been born in the old stables and would probably want to die there.

At lunchtime the next day, Frankie showed her another pattern he'd started to paint. 'You told me you were getting on fine when you first started to work here,' she said, 'but I understand more of the set-up now. Tell me what's going on in dyes and patterns. How are they treating you?'

Frankie beamed at her. 'Pretty much as I expected. They think I'm working too hard and turning out far too many patterns, especially Bruce Stanley, who's my immediate boss. When I started here, he was asked to break me in, show me round, that sort of thing; now he's saying, "Ease off, take a rest, you're showing us up."'

'So they aren't working hard, and Gramps isn't getting the patterns he needs. Are you making yourself unpopular?'

'Let's say I don't seem to be making any good friends. My difficulty is that the first pattern I did of swirling colours has gone into production, and they think success has come far too soon for me. I'm thought to be big-headed.'

She smiled. 'I don't think you are. So you're not happy working here?'

'I'm thrilled to have the chance, you know I am. I'm fascinated by all the dyes that are used to print the patterns on fabric. Some are better than others, and some cheaper; some fade and some will run if washed. I have to bear all that in mind when I'm creating a pattern.'

'That's why Gramps takes people on as apprentices, to give them time to learn.'

'Yes, I know, but it's different for me. I'm hoping my work will win your grandfather over. I want him to approve of me as a husband for you. So I'm trying to absorb it all at once. It's not easy, because there's no simple system, but there could be.

'We use water-based paints to create our patterns and John Hampton spends hours matching the colours to the dyes and writing their numbers on the pattern so they can be used when it goes into production. But it seems to me that if instead we had the colours of the dyes in mind when we were creating our patterns, it would save a lot of time and be easier for all of us. I've started to make a catalogue of the dyes by using them to colour bits of cloth and attaching a note to each one with the number of the dye, its current price, whether it fades or runs easily, and what type of cloth it works best on, all the facts that have already been worked out in the laboratory.'

'Frankie, that's a marvellous idea.'

'Then when I create a new pattern, I can look at the catalogue of dyed colours and see how it will actually look on cloth, and so can everybody else at every stage of production.'

'You cut out the watercolours altogether?'

'Yes, and I have all the information at my fingertips which simplifies things for me.'

'I suppose artists have traditionally used watercolours to create patterns.' She bit into her ham and lettuce sandwich. 'Where is this catalogue you're making? I want to see it.'

'It's just a few bits of dyed cloth and some notes at the moment.'

Aimee looked at them one by one. 'We should tell Gramps about this idea and show him these right away.'

'Oh, and that's not all. I was working on this pattern this morning.' He took it from his easel and put it in front of her.

'Geometric.' Aimee finished her sandwiches and rolled up the greaseproof paper. 'A lovely shade of green.'

'Bruce Stanley thinks so too. I can't get over what he said to me. He wants to take this pattern and pass it off as his own. He's offered me money if I'll let him do it.'

'What? Gramps needs to know about that as well. He'll be out having lunch at the moment, but as soon as he's back . . .'

Aimee watched his office and saw her grandfather return from lunch with a visitor. It was mid-afternoon before they were able to talk to him.

'What's this?' he asked when she ushered Frankie in and laid the geometric pattern and the dyed cloths out on the desk in front of him. She watched his face change as Frankie recounted the idea again.

He was amazed. 'This catalogue is a brilliant idea, Frankie. What made you think of it?'

'I was trying to make things easier for myself, cut the routine jobs so I'd have more time to work on patterns, but then I saw that changing the system would make things easier for every-body. I've only catalogued the dyes I use most. There are a lot more for me to do.'

'Carry on with it. It'll make for efficiency all round. It's exactly what is needed.'

'Thank you, sir.'

'And Bruce Stanley wants to pass this pattern off as his own work? I've noticed he isn't always in the office.'

'He goes out occasionally.'

'For how long? Out of the building, you mean?'

'I think so. He was missing for a couple of hours yesterday, and when he came back, his hair was wet. He started painting patterns then but he was half-hearted about it and tore the first couple up. I wanted to show him how he could improve his work, but he wouldn't take that sort of advice from me. Then he came over to look at what I'd done and offered me a couple of pounds to let him pretend that this pattern was his work.'

'Well, I'm glad you've told me instead of accepting his cash.' Walter was frowning.

'Not a chance. But it shows he wants to keep his job here, doesn't it?'

Walter sat back in his chair. 'It certainly does. What about Hampton?'

'He stays in and he does try to create patterns, but with this catalogue, a lot of what he's been doing will no longer be needed. He doesn't like me either.'

'He's been here two years and I don't have much hope he'll succeed. Rather a lacklustre lad.'

'I could get him to help me dye the bits of cloth.'

'You keep him busy on that then.'

'My problem with the two of them is that I haven't been here very long. They think I know nothing.'

'But you use your brain and they don't,' Walter said. 'I'm going to mark this pattern.' He turned it over and put three red dots in one corner. 'I want you to accept Stanley's offer of cash and sell it to him. If he puts this in as his work, I'll get rid of him.'

Aimee giggled. 'Gramps, isn't that entrapment?'

Frankie stifled a laugh. 'And they'll think I've been planted to spy on them.'

'I'm paying their wages, so I'm entitled to expect them to work.' Walter was not amused.

After dinner that evening, Walter said to Aimee, 'Bring your coffee to my study; I need a word.' She sat down on the opposite side of his desk and he went on, 'I've been looking at the latest figures from Tom Tasker, and they're up a little. Frankie Hopkins' patterns are selling well.'

'I'm so glad, he'll be delighted to hear that.'

'And another bit of news. John Hampton gave in his notice today. He said he'd decided he wasn't cut out for pattern making after all, and he'd found another job.'

'Oh! Frankie did wonder if he was hand in glove with Bruce Stanley, and he didn't think either was very interested in pattern making.'

'They weren't much good at it, probably thought it would be easy. Aimee, I know I said you should stay three months with Tom, but I think it's time I moved you on.'

She smiled. 'I've enjoyed being in sales, and I've learned a lot. I've told Tom he's broken me in to working at the mill.'

'I knew you were happy there.' He lifted his eyes to meet her gaze. 'No doubt you've learned a lot about patterns and dyes too.'

'I have, Gramps.' She recognised that as a hint. 'But that's not exactly what you mean, is it?'

'No. You're starry-eyed about Frankie Hopkins, and I gather he feels the same way about you.'

'He does, and his conscience is troubling him because we haven't told you. We kept it a secret because Grandma will be dead against it. She doesn't like Frankie and she'll say we're too young. I knew I should tell you, Gramps; you do understand?'

'I've nothing against him, Aimee, quite the reverse. He's a nice lad and you've been friendly with him for many years. I'm paying him as an apprentice, but he's already producing patterns I can use and that sell well. He's also altering the way patterns are created in the business; he's made it more efficient with his catalogue of dyes. Don't say anything to him: I'll call him into my office tomorrow and tell him myself. I must pay him a reasonable wage, and he ought to know that I appreciate what he's doing. I like his grandfather too; he's a good worker, does a good job and does it when he says he will.'

'I'm so glad you've taken it like this, Gramps. It'll be a weight off Frankie's mind. He's very sensible . . .'

'So are you. I've arranged for you to move to the accounts department next week. I want you to think about how that can be made more efficient, because right now, it isn't. I'm afraid a lot of my problems might stem from there.'

'Oh dear.'

Gramps looked up and smiled. 'You knew this would be coming sooner or later.'

'I did, but I'm not looking forward to coping with Neville Sanderson. I bet he wasn't pleased to hear I was coming.'

'He wasn't, but I told him I wanted you to learn the routine work of his department from the bottom up. Make sure he explains everything to you, and keep on asking questions.'

The following week, Sanderson seemed his usual grandiose self as he welcomed her to his department. He gave her yet another copy of the annual accounts and said, 'You need to familiarise yourself with these.' He introduced her to the man who worked at the desk next to hers, but she was so distracted, she didn't register his name.

All was silent as she stared at the figures in front of her. She felt isolated in a quiet corner from which she could see very little. Before long, her neighbour left and she was completely alone. She was really missing the friendly atmosphere of the sales department. Eventually she could stand it no longer and started to walk round, stopping here and there to interrupt a clerk working on an adding machine. She didn't find any of them forthcoming.

She could see that Sanderson's office was deserted, but just outside was a girl busily typing. Aimee introduced herself and learned she was his secretary. 'He's quite strict,' the girl told her. 'He doesn't like us wasting time and doesn't encourage us to talk.'

At that moment Sanderson returned and Aimee followed him into his office. 'I'm here to learn what goes on in your department,' she told him. 'I want to try my hand at everybody's job so I know exactly what they do.'

'Yes, of course, your grandfather did tell me.'

'I'd like to have my desk moved here where the action is. I feel a bit cut off over there.'

'I thought you'd like a quiet spot,' he said. 'More private.'

Just as she'd suspected, he wanted her out of the way where she'd see and hear little. 'No, I need to be in the thick of things. Somewhere near your secretary would be fine, and I want a job to do.'

'Of course.' He introduced her then to a young clerk called Donald and told him to teach her to do his job.

'How long have you worked here?' Aimee asked as she followed him to a loading bay where the Rochdale van was about to unload rolls of unfinished fabric.

'Three months.' He showed her his ledger and how he recorded the number of rolls being delivered. 'I'm glad you've come to take over this job,' he told her. 'It's boring work, totally mind-numbing, and I'd go mad if I had to do it for ever.'

'How often do these vans come?'

'Usually there's one in the morning and one in the afternoon, sometimes more.'

Aimee set about the task and had to agree that it would be a desperately boring job for anyone. She watched and made a tick in the ledger every time a roll came off. Surely one of the men unloading the van could do this. Or she thought she'd heard of a machine that just needed to be touched and it would add the numbers up. She'd never been more pleased to hear the buzzer signalling the lunch break. Everybody stopped that instant and disappeared. She went to unload her frustrations on Frankie.

'Well,' he said, 'if it's your job to count the rolls of unfinished cloth coming in, at least we can be sure that number is correct.'

'Yes,' Aimee said, 'and I've discovered that everything stops for lunch. They just walk away from what they're doing, and presumably return an hour later and carry on.'

Frankie's egg sandwich was suspended halfway to his mouth while he thought about that. 'If the same thing is happening when the finished rolls of cloth leave the machines, it provides an excellent opportunity for a thief. I'm going to keep tabs on the finished product, see what happens to that.'

Late the following afternoon, when the buzzer signalled that it was time to go home, they met up and Frankie said, 'I've spent most of today watching what happens to the finished stock, but as far as I can see, nothing has been stolen. However, there are lots of opportunities to fake the numbers. The whole system needs to be reorganised. The number of rolls is being recorded in two different ledgers, and I should have asked what happens to those figures. Presumably they go to a clerk in accounts to be totalled up.'

'I can find that out,' Aimee said.

'But I feel we're making progress now,' Frankie said.

'Yes, the fact that Neville Sanderson is a close family member doesn't mean he isn't involved in some fraudulent scheme as well.'

'It gives him a motive,' Frankie said. 'He's righting a wrong done to his mother.'

'And a wrong done to him when he was a baby. I think Gramps suspects Sanderson because he went to so much trouble to get that chief accountant job, and it puts him in a position where he can adjust the figures so a loss won't be seen.'

'Your grandfather thinks he's not much good at it,' Frankie said. 'Is that just an act Sanderson is putting on to deliberately give the wrong impression? I get the feeling that he knows exactly what he's doing, and is actually a couple of jumps ahead of us. What d'you think?'

'I think he's pretty astute. There was nothing slow about him when I asked about his relationship to Grandma. He was quick to sort out my previous misconceptions and put me in the wrong. I'm sure he intended me to feel a complete fool. I blame Grandma for not telling me the truth.'

Frankie smiled. 'It's not difficult to guess why she didn't.'

'Oh, I know. She brought me up to believe that having a baby born out of wedlock is the worst sin a young girl can commit, and a blot on the family reputation.'

'That's why I have to be very careful to keep my feelings for you damped down.' Frankie kissed her forehead. 'I've more warm blood than I dare show.'

She squeezed his arm. 'I know.'

CHAPTER TWENTY-FIVE

O N THE FERRY GOING TO work the next morning, Walter said, 'I'm thinking of paying another visit to Rochdale tomorrow. Just for the morning. Do you both want to come with me?'

'Yes, sir,' Frankie said. 'I'd like to look round again now that I know something of what goes on there.'

'Is the manager reporting problems?' Aimee asked.

'There are always problems,' Walter said. 'Water pressure is low, but he's asked the Water Board to turn it up and he's coping. The weavers are asking for more money and I can't really afford it, but they haven't had a rise for some years so I suppose I'll have to improve their rates.'

'Then I'd like to come in with you when you talk to the manager, to see how you negotiate this.'

'Yes, that's a good idea. Frankie, I suggest you walk round and look closely at what is going on. Is all the cloth they weave coming to Liverpool? Does the place look busy, or are there employees standing about?'

'Yes, sir,' Frankie said. 'I'll be better doing that alone with nothing to distract me.'

'That's how you get the reputation of being my spy,' Walter told him.

Frankie smiled. 'Somebody needs to do the job if you want to cut waste and make production more efficient. I'll be good at it; I've done my share of looking busy in shops and restaurants when I've had nothing to do.'

Walter couldn't stop a smile spreading across his face.

Later that morning, he was sipping his mid-morning cup of coffee at his desk, still worrying that stock was somehow leaking out of his premises, when he heard a knock on his door. 'Come in,' he called.

Bruce Stanley's head came round the door. 'I've brought one of my patterns to show you, sir. I think you might like this one.' With a flourish it came down in front of him.

'Yes,' Walter said, 'I do like it; I might well put it into production.'

'I'm so pleased. I've numbered the dyes and collected all the information about them, in accordance with your latest instructions.'

'And I see you've signed it too.' Walter surveyed the youth with distaste. 'I've seen this pattern before. I went to your department last week and saw Mr Hopkins working on it. You were not there; I gather you go out quite a lot.'

That noticeably sapped Stanley's confidence. 'Er . . . no, sir, hardly ever. I must have been studying the dyes or attending to something else.'

'It's the second time I've noticed your absence when I've been in your office.' Walter could see the apprentice was now completely rattled. He turned the pattern over to check for the three red dots. 'Why have you signed somebody else's work and brought it here to claim it as your own?'

The youth had no answer; he was flushed and had

pinpricks of sweat across his face.

'I must draw my own conclusions then. You obviously don't have time to work on patterns for me; what is it that takes you away from your desk?'

He had no answer to that either.

'Are you just bored and lazy, or are you doing something else?'

'I'm sorry, sir, I'll work harder . . .'

'Right.' Walter stood up. 'I think you know what to expect. I can't allow you to appropriate another person's work. Come with me to the payroll clerk. I'll ask him to pay you to the end of the week, and then you'll be escorted to your office to collect your personal possessions before you leave the premises.'

Walter felt reduced to a wreck after that. According to Frankie Hopkins, this lad was going out for an hour or so at a time. He'd sacked him, but others were probably involved, so he hadn't necessarily stopped the loss. It was a worry that wouldn't go away.

Prudence was fuming silently for days after Walter had raked up her family history. He knew very well how much that upset her. She'd believed him to be an honourable man, but now he was neglecting her completely. She felt full of hate and curiosity for Esther Kerr, and for the house he'd provided for her. Aimee had told her she was living near Victoria Park; she'd forgotten the name of the road, but it might come to her if she saw it. It was a sunny afternoon. She'd go out for a walk and see if she could find the place.

She hadn't gone far before she found it; Aimee had definitely said Southdale Road. It wasn't at all the sort of area she herself would consider living in: small terraced houses with just privet hedges in front and no gardens. It looked rather downmarket, and anything but comfortable. She was very surprised that Walter would consider this a suitable district for his paramour to live. Esther must have been desperate to consider it.

She didn't know the number, so she strolled slowly along the terrace, peering at each house. She heard a front door opening just as she passed it and turned to look. Esther Kerr was struggling to get a squeaking pram down the front step and out onto the pavement. That jolted Prudence's nerves; had the woman seen her? Embarrassing to be caught spying. Hurriedly she turned her back and moved on, pretending to study a board outside a similar house advertised for rent. When she risked another glance, Esther was walking briskly, skirt swinging. Victoria Park was at the top of the road.

Once she'd disappeared, Prudence turned to check there was no one else in the road, then picked up a stone and flung it at Esther's front window. It bounced straight back into the hedge, making her fume even more. It was too small to break the glass and there were no other stones around here, but she'd find a bigger one in her rockery and come back to break her window.

She walked up to the park. Esther was sitting on a bench chatting to another young woman with a pram. When her baby started to cry, she lifted it out and cradled it in her arms. The bitch! The sight of contented motherhood filled Prue with such fury she wanted to scream. How dare Walter do this to her? She'd wanted more children but they hadn't come to her. And this was outright rejection; he'd thrown her over for a younger woman. Cast her off.

Boiling with indignation, she turned for home, striding as fast as she could. She'd get even with Walter. He wasn't going to get away with this.

She brooded all evening, trying to work out what she could do. Hurting him wouldn't be enough.

On the morning Walter planned to go to the Rochdale mill, he said, 'We'll take a taxi direct from the Pier Head.'

'Gramps, doesn't your business make enough for you to have a car and driver at your disposal? He could meet you from the ferry every day and take you back again. It would make life easier for you.'

'It would, and I think I'll have to come to it eventually.'

When they reached the Rochdale mill, Walter sent Frankie off alone, and took Aimee to see Bill Smith, the manager, in his office. The union bosses filed in and gave him a hard morning. He ended up increasing their rates by more than he'd intended. When he and Aimee were left alone for a few moments, she told him he should have been tougher. 'In the present labour market they'd have settled for less,' she berated him. She was probably right; he was a pushover for everybody these days.

'You and Frankie had better go,' he told her. 'Nothing more will happen here today.'

'I'm sorry if I've upset you, Gramps, but I've got to say what I think. You want to get rid of me?'

'No, of course not. I'm going to take Bill out to lunch; he wants to discuss a personal problem with me, and it probably won't help him to have you sitting in on that.'

Frankie joined them. 'How did you get on?' Walter asked. 'See any signs of fraud? Or anywhere I could cut down?'

'No, sir, no sign of fraud. The weavers have to keep up with the looms, so they're all busy, but you have a lot of staff in the office who are standing around talking and seem to have plenty of time; you could probably cut down there. I've asked to have the duties of each one set out so we can see which jobs could be combined.'

'I'll look at it, but it's very hard to do that,' Walter said. 'It would put men on the dole, and many have worked for us all their lives and have families to support. They'd find it almost impossible to get another job at the moment.'

'You're very kind to your workers,' Frankie said.

'I have to bear in mind the decades of loyal service they've given.'

'Yes, well other than that, there's a bit of waste fabric, sir; you might ask them to cut off more carefully, but otherwise I could see nothing wrong.'

'Right, thank you. You two go back to Liverpool. I'll be late home tonight, Aimee, don't wait dinner for me. Gracious, was that thunder? Suddenly it's quite dark; it looks as though we might have a storm.'

They set out to walk to the station. 'It's going to rain, and if Gramps was with us we'd have been rolling along in a taxi,' Aimee grumbled.

They'd reached the shopping centre when suddenly Frankie glimpsed a swathe of fabric draped across a shop window. He caught at Aimee's arm and pulled her to a halt. 'Look at this; it's my swirling pattern of greens and blues.'

Aimee stared at it in surprise. 'I didn't know our fabrics were sold here. Tom Tasker didn't take me round all his customers, but I spent a lot of time helping with his paperwork and I don't remember an address in Rochdale.' The shop window was displaying home furnishings; there was a notice offering upholstery work, and another saying: *We could turn your home into a little palace. Let us redesign and refurnish it for you.*

'A posh place,' Frankie said. 'It seems strange that there are people happy to pay others to design their homes. Surely everybody has their own ideas about that?'

'No,' Aimee said, 'the Greenings had somebody to redesign their sitting room, and it looks very nice indeed. The point is,' she went on, 'where did this shop get that curtaining? Was it through Tom Tasker or did it come from somebody else? I wish Gramps was with us; he'd know.'

'We'll have to go back and ask,' Frankie said. 'We can't go in and make a fuss and then find it's all above board. But in case that material did fall off a lorry, we might as well find out all we can about this business. Have you got pencil and paper? We need to write down the address.'

'No,' Aimee said. 'My notebook's back in my desk in Liverpool.'

'Same here,' Frankie said. 'There's a newsagent across the road; he'll sell small notebooks.'

They bought a notebook and pencil, then noticed that right next door to the newsagent was a small café. 'I can smell toast,' Aimee said, 'and I'm starving. My sandwiches are in Liverpool too. Let's have a snack to keep us going.'

It was early in the lunch hour and they sat at a table in the window. Frankie ordered tea and cheese on toast. Aimee had a good view of the business opposite and wrote down *The Rochdale Furnishing and Design Centre*, together with the number, 84. They had to ask the girl who served them the name of the road, and then she wrote that down too.

'Eat up,' Frankie said. 'It's just occurred to me that the shop might close for lunch before we have a chance to go in.'

'We need time to work out what we should ask,' Aimee said.

'We'll pretend to be customers and enquire about that fabric to start with,' Frankie said, 'then hope to find out something about the business.'

When they went into the shop, there were no other customers. A pretty girl greeted them from behind the counter.

'We're interested in the green and blue curtaining in your window,' Aimee said. 'Could you tell me how much it costs?'

'It is lovely, isn't it?' She opened up the back of the window so they could see it more closely. 'You can feel the quality.' She demonstrated with her finger and thumb. Aimee followed suit. 'The cost depends on how much fabric you need for your windows, and whether you want us to make up the curtains for you.'

Frankie said, 'Our problem is that we haven't measured up and we come from Liverpool. Do you have another branch that's nearer?'

'I don't think so, but there are several in Lancashire and Yorkshire. Would you want to use our full service? If so, I can arrange for one of our designers to visit you and measure up.'

'I don't know if we could afford that. It's just that the fabric caught our eye. How much would it cost by the yard?'

The girl reached for a record book under the counter and gave him a price.

'That's quite expensive,' Aimee said.

'Do you have a catalogue showing your prices?' Frankie asked.

'No, I'm sorry.'

'Could we have a word with your manager?' Aimee asked, knowing they were fast running out of questions a customer might reasonably be expected to ask.

'No, I'm afraid he's out on a job. If you leave your name, address and phone number . . .'

'Thank you,' Frankie said. 'I'm afraid it was wishful thinking on my part.' He turned back to the material and fingered it again. 'I do really like this. It's the colour of the ocean.'

They could talk of nothing else until they were back at the Liverpool mill. Aimee led the way to Tom Tasker's office and pushed her new notebook in front of him. 'Do you know this address?' she asked, and together they told him what had happened.

'The Rochdale Furnishing and Design Centre? No they aren't customers of mine, but I do supply agents who work further afield selling our fabrics on our behalf. I'll need to telephone them.'

'But Rochdale isn't that far away,' Aimee said.

'I know, and that does make it look rather suspicious.'

CHAPTER TWENTY-SIX

THE NEXT MORNING, AIMEE enjoyed a few minutes' extra snooze time and then had to get up in a hurry. Gramps had been late again last night and she'd gone to bed before he came home. She didn't mention seeing their curtaining in Rochdale at breakfast, because they were running a little late. She knew that if Gramps had to give his full attention to something, he'd stop eating.

She waited until they'd walked to the ferry house and met up with Frankie. 'Gramps, we discovered something yesterday,' she said. 'Frankie noticed some of our fabric in a shop window when we were coming back to Liverpool. Tell him about it, Frankie.'

Frankie explained what they'd seen and done. 'By the time we were ready to leave work yesterday,' he went on, 'Tom Tasker was able to confirm that the shop where we saw the fabric did not get it from a legitimate source. He has no idea how they came by it.'

'What?' Walter was aghast. 'So that means it's been taken fraudulently from our stock. But how?'

The ferry had arrived; Aimee had to steer him on board. 'Isn't that what you suspected, Gramps?'

'It is. Well done for spotting the fabric.'

'I couldn't miss it, sir,' Frankie beamed. 'That pattern was my first success.'

'We'd all have come back by taxi if I hadn't stayed on,' Walter said. 'It was sheer chance that you saw it.'

'It seems this fabric must have been taken from our mill,' Aimee said. 'What should we watch out for?'

'It must have been finished in our premises, so it disappeared somewhere between the machine that printed it and the warehouse.' Walter sat back to think. 'The rolls are counted and the number checked as they're removed from the machines. Find out who does that, Frankie. They'll be recording them in a ledger, so I want to see that. Don't tell anybody why you want it, or what you're doing.'

'I've already checked the ledgers, sir. They show totals that all seem accurate.'

'So this is proof that fraud is taking place. It's clear evidence.'

'How can we help, Gramps?'

He sighed. 'You must keep an eye on your colleagues working in accounts. Someone there must be altering those figures. I'm going to have a word with Tom Tasker. Perhaps get him to go up to Rochdale. There are identifying marks on each roll and he'll be familiar with them. It's a horrible feeling. I think of my workforce almost as family, and to find they're stealing from me . . . I'll have to call in the police. Yes, I'll do that right away. This is a criminal matter.'

Walter spent the evening in his study thinking about the theft from his mill. He'd been visited in the office by two plain-clothes policemen, and he'd had to ask Aimee and that lad to join them to help explain the problem. He was ashamed to think he'd left most of the work to them.

The police officers had listened carefully and one took notes. After they'd left, a more senior officer came. He'd told Walter that while they accepted that fraud could be taking place, they had nobody in the force who was qualified to understand his accounting system, nor how his mill functioned, so they would have to ask him to keep a closer eye on his staff and come up with solid facts or proof against individuals before they could take action.

He didn't like it. They were telling him it was his job to watch things more closely and report anything unusual or out of the ordinary. And all the time his stock was being stolen, and putting a stop to that that looked pretty hopeless.

The next day, Frankie felt he'd wasted a lot of time wandering around watching rolls of fabric being moved and loaded into vans. It all looked perfectly normal to him. From time to time he caught sight of Aimee doing the same thing.

At the same time he was playing about with some new shades of cream and fawn. He wanted to design a really handsome curtain fabric, but what he drew looked very similar to his previous patterns. It left him tired and frustrated, and on the train going home with Aimee his worries surfaced. 'Your grandfather ought to have some backup to ensure he always has a competent pattern maker. He shouldn't be relying entirely on me. I could be killed crossing the road tomorrow and then where would he be?'

'Don't say such things,' she cried. 'You'll tempt fate.'

'No, I'm thinking it might be a good idea if he asked Candida to work on patterns with me. It certainly wouldn't take her three years to learn; she'll be fine with a little practice.'

'She desperately wants to earn some money.'

'I know she does, so I'm sure she'll welcome the idea. Will you put it to your grandfather?'

'No, it's your idea, you do it. I want you to get the credit if it turns out to be a good one.'

The next morning on the ferry, Frankie pointed out to Mr Kendrick that he was the only pattern maker he currently employed. 'If something happens to me, you could be in difficulties now those two apprentices have gone. You should take on someone else.'

'I've been somewhat disheartened by those two. I'm relying on you now. Where did you get your talent from?'

'It's a knack; I seem to understand what's needed, but what if I can't go on doing it? What if the market changes and you want something different? You really should have another pattern maker.'

'It's finding somebody who is keen and willing to learn.'

'May I suggest you think about Candida, sir? She knows a great deal about designing patterns and about colours, and it wouldn't take her long to learn about your dyes. And just as importantly, if she were in the office we'd have someone there to help us track down the fraud.'

'Yes, but Candida lives for the pleasures of the art world: all pictures, Paris fashions and the social scene. She wouldn't want to work in the dust and grind of a mill like mine.'

Aimee said, 'She'll jump at it, Gramps. She's looking for a job and finding it very hard to get one. She needs a regular income. She's very good at organising things; the sort of person who sees what needs doing and does it. She'll pull her weight.'

'I know that; she always has. So you need an ally in the office you can trust?'

'Exactly,' they chorused.

'I'm sure she'll soon be making patterns to suit you,' Frankie added. 'And as for tracking down these thieves, we really do need her.'

'In that case, you'd better ask her to tea on Sunday, Aimee, and we'll put it to her.'

Prue had felt anger building up inside her for the last day or so. She was edgy and bad-tempered; she blamed that on Walter. He was carrying on exactly as he always had, wrapped up in that woman and his business affairs. He shouldn't have allowed Aimee to work at the mill, and she was seeing far too much of that Hopkins lad. It made her boil with fury every time she thought of it. She wished she could think of some way to get her own back on Walter.

As she stood gazing out of the window, deep in thought, she noticed that old Bob Hopkins was at the far end of her garden, hacking viciously at some plant. In her raw mood, the sight of him was enough to upset her. She went outside. 'What are you doing?' she asked irritably. 'You're making a dreadful mess.'

He stopped. 'Afternoon, Mrs Kendrick. I'm trying to kill this off. I've tried for the last year or so, but it always comes up again.'

'What is it?'

'Belladonna, they call it. Or deadly nightshade. It's better out of here in case someone gets poisoned. I'll burn it later together with these other weeds.' He had a bare patch at the far end of the garden where he lit his bonfires.

Prudence went back inside to ponder on her problem. Would it be possible to poison Walter? Wasn't this what she was seeking, a way to get her own back? It seemed she had the means to do it right here in the garden. She waited until Hopkins had gone for a cup of tea, then sauntered up to inspect the bonfire he'd been building. She pushed away the dandelion roots and grass and saw the small black berries gleaming amongst green leaves.

It took her only a moment to decide. She dropped her handkerchief over the stalks and gingerly picked up a generous bunch. Nobody must see this; it needed to be taken straight upstairs and hidden in her wardrobe. They kept old newspapers for lighting fires by the back door in the scullery. She paused long enough to pick one up and wrap the belladonna before taking it through the kitchen. Dora was busy at the sink and didn't turn round.

Once she had it safely out of sight, Prudence felt she had time to think. She needed to find out more about the plant, because for a start she had no idea how much it would take to kill a man. She'd have to go to the library and see if she could find a book about it. It had better be Birkenhead library, as there was a reference room there.

She had to ask a library assistant to help her find information about poisons, and that meant she had to make up a cock-and-bull story about why she needed it. Within minutes she was seated at a writing table and a large tome was put in front of her. She'd take no notes; the last thing she wanted was to keep proof of what she was doing, just in case something went wrong.

She flicked through the pages until she found it: *Atropa belladonna*. She groped in her handbag for her glasses and read on: *More commonly known as deadly nightshade, belladonna is one of the most poisonous plants growing in Britain. It is the source of atropine and used for medical purposes. It is soluble in fats but not in water.* Oh dear. She'd thought of making a jelly to put it in – Walter was fond of jelly – and serving it in separate dishes. But that wouldn't do if it wasn't soluble in water. *It has a bitter taste and can easily be detected in food.* And she'd have to disguise that somehow.

It dilates the pupils of the eyes and signs are easily recognised and treated by doctors, but it is rapidly broken down after death and leaves no detectable signs post mortem. There was nothing she could do about dilated pupils, but at least the doctor wouldn't be aware of the need to look for such a sign, and it would soon be gone. But should she use the leaves or the berries? And how much would it take to kill him? She could find no advice about that and it wasn't something she could ask.

She would use a generous amount of the berries – they looked more deadly than the leaves – and would have to hope it would be enough.

When Dora brought up her breakfast the following morning, Prudence asked her to pass her aspirins as she had a headache. She meant to stay in bed a little longer than usual as she needed to put her mind to how best to poison Walter, and there were fewer distractions in bed. It would be their wedding anniversary tomorrow; she could make a special pudding to celebrate. She'd devoted forty-two years to Walter and she wasn't planning to give him much more time.

There were plenty of early raspberries ripening in the garden. She decided she would make a raspberry fool. She'd add plenty of sugar to counteract the bitter taste, and perhaps a slug of brandy would help too. She'd use her individual cut-glass serving dishes, as she couldn't risk eating any of it herself, and she had to protect Aimee. She'd squeeze the juice and pips from the deadly nightshade berries and mix them with fresh cream; that should be fatty enough to absorb them.

She could see another problem. If Walter did notice the bitter flavour, he'd almost certainly stop eating. She'd read in that book that it would make him feel very ill, even if it didn't kill him. Making him ill would go some way to getting her own back on him, but she couldn't afford to let that happen. She'd also read that a doctor would easily recognise the signs of atropine poisoning and could treat it. If Walter survived and complained of symptoms, suspicion would almost certainly fall on her. Once he was dead, the doctor could well miss the signs, as they wouldn't be present for all that long. She would have to make sure Walter consumed enough poison to kill him in the first mouthful or so.

With her plans made, she got dressed and went downstairs. Dora was mopping the kitchen floor. 'Put a note out for the milkman tomorrow and ask him to leave half a pint of double cream,' Prue told her. But would half a pint be enough? She had little idea how much her recipe would need. She'd never concerned herself with food. 'Better make that a pint.'

Dora was reaching for the notepad. 'A pint?' Her eyebrows went up.

Clearly a pint was quite a lot, but no matter. 'Yes, I'm going to make a special celebration meal tomorrow evening.'

Prudence put on her hat and coat. She had to go to a hardware shop and buy a pair of rubber gloves. She thought she'd read in that book that belladonna could also be absorbed through the skin, but she wasn't sure, and she couldn't afford to take any risks while she was crushing the berries.

On the way, she passed a bakery with a mouth-watering display of cakes in the window. Her gaze fastened on a plate of meringues. She could crumble those into her raspberries and cream to add sweetness; Walter had a sweet tooth and would enjoy that. She went in and bought three.

Oh, she mustn't forget the main course. Walter liked steak but she didn't care much for it. Perhaps as this would be his last meal she should indulge him. She called in to her regular butcher and asked him to deliver three of his best Scottish fillet steaks tomorrow morning. She'd roast them in the oven with some potatoes.

Once back in her own kitchen, she looked in the cupboard for something in which to crush the berries. She found an almost empty honey jar with a screw top and sent Dora to the sitting room to fetch her spectacles so she wouldn't see her pop it in her bag together with a spoon. Then she went upstairs to begin her preparations.

She picked the berries off the stems of belladonna and crushed them against the side of the jar with the spoon. She separated out the skins and put them down the lavatory; the resulting fluid had a lot of seeds in it. Should she strain them out, or was most of the poison in them? Perhaps he'd mistake them for raspberry pips. Again she wished she knew how many it would take, because she hadn't the slightest idea. She added a few more berries to be on the safe side, then put the jar in the back of her wardrobe, where nobody would be likely to see it.

She took the bunch of dying leaves and stems still wrapped in newspaper out into the garden and buried them deeply in the bonfire Bob Hopkins had built. Then she sat down and enjoyed the lunch Dora had prepared for her.

She expected Walter not to return home until late – it was what he usually did on Wednesdays – but she didn't get the customary phone call to warn her of this and he came home with Aimee. She was sorry she hadn't got her dessert ready for him tonight. Just to see him doing what he always did, ignoring her completely, made her anger boil up. She hated his indifference, loathed him discussing what had happened at the mill, particularly with Aimee, though at least Aimee had the manners to explain what they were talking about.

'Gramps thinks we're being defrauded. Rolls of finished fabric are disappearing. He's called in the police to investigate.'

'What did they say?' Prue asked.

'Proving fraud is very difficult,' he told her.

Prudence knew she must not allow herself to be distracted; she must make sure he would be home for dinner tomorrow. 'Walter,' she said, 'tomorrow is our wedding anniversary.'

'Tomorrow?'

Clearly he'd forgotten about it: typical. 'Yes, forty-two years. I'm planning a special dinner to celebrate.'

'Lovely,' Aimee said. 'What are you going to give us?'

Walter was blinking at her, looking as though he didn't think there was anything to celebrate. 'Yes, of course. We usually go to the Royal Rock for dinner, don't we?'

'We used to when we were young,' Prudence said frostily. 'I thought a quieter dinner at home this year. You will be home tomorrow if I make something special, won't you?'

'Of course, Prudence, yes, of course. I'll look forward to it.'

She sniffed; Walter knew how to lie as though he meant it.

* * *

Prudence didn't sleep well that night; she was nervous, a bit edgy, but she mustn't lose her nerve, not now she'd got to this point. Everything must be done exactly as she'd planned if she was to be above suspicion.

In the middle of the afternoon she started to prepare her raspberry fool. She brought the fruit to the boil for a few moments to soften it and bring out the flavour, and crumbled the meringues. She gave Dora the job of whipping the cream into stiff peaks; that was a rather tedious task, but Prue herself took pleasure in mixing the other ingredients and adding a generous splash of Angostura bitters to help disguise the taste. She rather wished she hadn't, because it spoiled the colour somewhat.

While Dora had been making the beds this morning, Prudence had taken the precaution of removing the tin of mustard from the kitchen cupboard. She needed a reason to send the girl away so she could deal with the belladonna. She washed and dried her cut-glass dessert flutes – a wedding present from her mother but unused for years – and was now ready to fill them.

Dora was peeling potatoes at the sink. Prue rummaged around in the cupboard.

'Do we have any mustard?' she asked. 'I can't see any, and we must have mustard with steak. Dora, perhaps you could run round to the shops and get a tin.'

'Now?'

'Yes please. The shops will be shutting soon.'

Once the girl had left, Prudence started to fill the flutes; she'd do the first two, and then add the poison to the mixture before filling the third. Her hands were trembling as she felt for the bag she'd kept out of sight with everything she'd need. She put on her rubber gloves and unscrewed the top of the honey jar.

The contents looked absolutely harmless and had no smell; she hoped she wasn't going to all this trouble for nothing. It didn't mix with the cream as easily as she'd expected, but she did her best and filled the third flute. They looked identical, which was what she was aiming for, but she must mark the poisoned one so she could be sure Walter would get it. She put a small blob of cream on the outside of the flute.

Before touching anything else, she tipped the remains of the poison and the cream mixture down the lavatory, even scooping the last of the honey from the jar. She pushed the point of the scissors through both rubber gloves and took them and the jar out to the bin. Then she washed her hands and scrubbed the mixing bowl and spoon thoroughly. She must leave nothing that might incriminate her if anything went wrong.

When Dora returned with the mustard, she was decorating her desserts with the three raspberries and two mint leaves she'd kept for each. Finally she slid the matching glass saucer beneath each flute and set them on a small tray.

She straightened up feeling totally spent. Had she remembered to do everything? The desserts looked identical; only she knew which was which, so she'd have to serve them herself. It would give her great satisfaction to put Walter's in front of him and watch him eat.

'They look beautiful,' Dora said.

'I'm going to lie down on my bed for half an hour,' Prudence said. She needed to pull herself together. 'I don't feel very well.'

CHAPTER TWENTY-SEVEN

A IMEE LEFT THE MILL with Frankie, but for once they met up with Gramps as they were boarding the ferry. He was carrying a great bunch of hothouse flowers and a box of chocolates. They arrived home together. Savoury smells met them as they went in.

'Dora, you're still here? It's well after six,' Walter said.

'Mrs Kendrick didn't feel well and had to go and lie down,' Dora said, 'and as it's a special dinner tonight, I didn't like to leave.'

'Oh dear, I'll have to pay you overtime,' he said.

'What's the matter with Grandma?'

'I don't know, she didn't say exactly. Do you want me to start the roast potatoes?'

'No, you can leave it all to me now,' Aimee said as she put the kettle on. 'I'll make some tea and take Grandma a cup. D'you want one, Gramps?'

'No, I'll get myself a whisky. Thank you for staying, Dora, you run along now. I hope Prudence has some appetite for this feast.'

Before he could head to the sitting room, Aimee said, 'Gramps, take the flowers up to Gran first; you know she likes you to make a fuss of her.'

'She likes everybody to make a fuss of her.'

While she waited for the tea to brew, Aimee surveyed the three dessert flutes that had been left on the kitchen table. It was a bit hot for them here; they should have been put in the larder. As she went to move them, she noticed a blob of cream on the outside of one of them. Grandma would be the first to complain about that. She dampened the corner of a tea towel and wiped it off, then polished the glass dry and took the tray to the larder. She was starving hungry, but it looked like being a good spread tonight.

She poured two cups of tea and headed upstairs. Grandma was sitting on the side of the bed looking hunched and tense.

'Lovely flowers,' Aimee said, moving them so she could sit down.

'Yes, it's the least he should do.'

'Sorry to hear you aren't well, Grandma.'

She sighed. 'I must have fallen asleep. I tired myself out making a feast for our wedding anniversary. I shall be fine after this cup of tea, dear. Please take the flowers down when you go, and put them in water for me.'

Prudence was glad when Aimee took the flowers away; they'd made her boil with rage. Walter had bestowed them on her as if he was giving her the Crown Jewels, and no doubt he'd expect her to be everlastingly grateful.

He'd betrayed her and turned to another woman. He'd be with that French teacher tonight, enjoying himself, if she hadn't made an effort to keep him at home. He'd pretended to be concerned about her health: 'I do hope you'll be able to enjoy this lovely meal you're making for our anniversary,' he'd said, knowing very well she had nothing to celebrate in being married to him. She loathed him, but he was going to get his come-uppance tonight.

She had to calm herself; she'd need a clear head to see this meal through. Whatever effect it had on Walter, Aimee must see her acting completely normally. She must never suspect.

She washed her face in cold water, changed her dress and, feeling a little more in control, went downstairs. Aimee was fiddling around in the kitchen, getting the first course ready. She'd turned out to be quite a good cook.

Prue went to the sitting room. Walter was nursing a glass of whisky in his armchair, looking weighed down with the cares of the world. What a pity she couldn't tell him his worries would soon be over. She sat down on the opposite side of the empty grate.

'Feeling better?' he asked. 'Shall I pour you a glass of sherry?'

It was taking Aimee an age to dish up and call them to the dining room. Prue had set three places at one end of the six-foot mahogany table with embroidered place mats and their best china to make it seem like a celebration. Walter's vase of flowers had the other end to itself. Whatever had made him think she'd want flowers when the garden was full of them? He was just going through the motions. There were lots of things she did want, but he'd never asked her. No, it would never occur to him to think further than flowers.

He raised his whisky glass. 'Here's to our anniversary.'

She knew he was making an effort to sound jolly, but even his smile looked false. There was a plate of asparagus with butter sauce in front of her, but her throat felt tight and she could hardly swallow.

Aimee took an interminable time to bring the steak to the table. It was a bit rare for Prue's taste, but cooked as Walter liked it, and he was full of praise. They were chatting together about business matters, which they must know would exclude her, but now that this was nearly over, she didn't mind so much.

Walter's praise continued. 'This steak cuts like butter; it's very tasty, moist and tender.'

'It is Aimee, you're a good cook,' Prudence agreed.

When Aimee took the remains of the vegetables to the kitchen, Prudence collected up the dirty plates and followed, knowing the moment was on her. Her last task would be to place the poisoned dessert in front of her husband.

In the kitchen, she stared at the table. 'Where is it? What's happened to the special desserts I made?' She knew she sounded panic-stricken.

'I put them in the larder, Gran. It's very hot in here tonight and I didn't want the cream to curdle.'

Prudence felt quite fluttery, and her knees were weak taking those few steps, but there was the tray just as she'd left it. She put it down on the kitchen table.

'There are lots of vegetables left over,' Aimee said. 'Plenty to make a salad for us tomorrow night.'

Especially as Walter won't be here, Prue thought, looking round wildly. 'I had some finger biscuits to serve with these.'

'They're here, Gran.' Aimee opened the tin and put it beside her.

'Thank you, dear.' As she put a biscuit on each glass saucer, she suddenly realised she couldn't see the mark she'd made on the poisoned flute. Panic was rising in her throat. Aimee was holding the kitchen door open for her. She groped for the tray and followed her back to the dining room. Where was the blob of cream? Her head was swimming as she set the tray down on the sideboard, but she mustn't lose her nerve now.

She looked more carefully, turned each dessert glass round. Was that it? It must be, but it was more a smear than a blob. She'd thought the mark she'd made was more obvious, but of course the idea had been to make all three look identical. She picked it up and smiled at Walter. 'My special dessert,' she said, placing the flute in front of him with a flourish. She put the second flute in her own place and the other in front of Aimee.

'This looks absolutely marvellous, Gran. What is it?'

'Raspberry fool.'

Walter's spoon was scooping a generous amount into his mouth, and then another, but Prudence didn't dare watch him. She took a deep breath and picked up her own spoon with shaking fingers.

'This is gorgeous, Gran, I love it.' Aimee was pleased it had turned out so well. 'You're a good cook.' Gran usually left any work in the kitchen to others.

'It's excellent,' Gramps agreed. 'You must make this again.'

But Prue was clutching her throat, and her choking cough turned into a scream.

'Gran, what's the matter?'

Prue's dessert flute narrowly missed Aimee as she hurled it across the room. It hit the skirting board with a crash and shattered in a creamy mess. She was waving her arms about and shouting at the top of her voice. Aimee couldn't understand what she was saying; the odd words she could make out sounded full of hatred.

She watched Gran totter, arm outstretched, towards the vase of flowers, her intention clear, but Gramps stepped in front of her and swept it safely onto the sideboard. 'Prudence, what are you doing? What's the matter? You treasure this glassware; it was your mother's.'

She would have slumped to the floor, but Aimee held her upright. 'Are you sick? What's happened?' she asked anxiously. 'Gramps, let's get her up to her bed.'

Walter took her arm. 'Come on, perhaps you'll feel better if you lie down.'

It wasn't easy, but the fight had gone out of Grandma now and she felt limp. They took her upstairs and laid her on top of her bed. Aimee was puffing. 'She feels very hot, and her face is crimson.'

Gramps was leaning against the bedstead, struggling to get his breath. 'At least she's gone quiet,' he said. 'Perhaps she'll go to sleep.'

Prudence was breathing noisily. 'She's ill, Gramps, had we better call the doctor?'

'Yes, yes, we should. You do it, love.'

Aimee ran down to the hall and snatched up the phone.

'He's out on a call,' the doctor's wife told her. 'I'll let him know as soon as he gets back.'

'Will he be long?'

'Hopefully not.'

She shot back upstairs. 'How is she?'

'I think she's going to sleep. Let's leave her and see. Should I cover her?'

'She's very hot, Gramps, I wouldn't.'

They went down to the dining room. 'What a shambles.' Aimee sat down in front of her dessert. 'I think I'll finish this first, it's too good to waste.'

Walter tried to do the same. 'It's very rich,' he said, 'and she's given us huge helpings.'

'It's delicious, I love it.'

'I wonder what upset her; it came on very suddenly, didn't it?'

'Very.' Aimee stood up. 'I'll get some paper and clear up the broken glass.' She brought a shovel from the kitchen and scooped up the mess onto several sheets of newspaper. 'Lucky she missed the carpet.' It was a highly patterned square with polished floorboards round the edge. She used more newspaper to rub at the sticky patch, then wrapped them into a ball, which Gramps took out to the bin near the back gate.

Aimee cleared the table, then covered the dirty dishes in the sink with water. She couldn't resist finishing the rest of Gramps's dessert, and then that dish went into the sink too. Dora would wash up when she came to work in the morning. Perhaps Gran might like a cup of tea? She went upstairs to ask her, but she seemed to be asleep.

While they were waiting for the doctor, Gramps said he'd like some coffee, so she made some. He was restless and she could see he was very worried; he kept going up to see if Prudence was all right. 'She's still fast asleep. I'm sorry we sent for the doctor now; it means he'll wake her.'

Almost two hours passed before the doorbell rang. Aimee

let the doctor in and was leading him upstairs when Gramps joined them. Once in the bedroom, she switched on the light because it was getting dark now. 'Gran,' she said. 'Dr Ellis has come to see how you are.'

The doctor stepped in front of her and had his stethoscope on Prue's chest in moments. He looked up, shocked. 'When did she last speak to you? I'm afraid Mrs Kendrick has gone.'

'What?' Walter asked.

'I'm sorry. Your wife has passed away.'

CHAPTER TWENTY-EIGHT

WALTER HAD TO HOLD onto the bedstead for support. 'Dead? I can't believe it. She ate a good dinner, didn't she, Aimee?' He felt poleaxed and looked to her for support, but Aimee had had the wind knocked out of her.

'I'm very sorry.' The doctor was biting his lip. 'I'm afraid there's no doubt about it.'

They both stared at him. 'Surely she can't be dead?' Aimee wailed. 'Not just like that. She was fine, absolutely fine. What could have made her die so suddenly?' She went closer to touch her shoulder. 'Gran?'

'Aimee, love.' Walter put an arm round her shoulders. 'Come away, let's go downstairs. We need to talk to Dr Ellis, hear what he has to say about this.' Once in the sitting room, he collapsed onto his armchair and closed his eyes.

'I think perhaps you both need a brandy. Medicinal purposes.'

Aimee got the bottle out and poured a generous amount into each of three whisky glasses. She handed one to the doctor. 'I'm afraid the brandy balloons are dusty; we haven't used them for ages.'

'Why didn't you tell me?' Walter demanded. 'I had no idea she was really ill, not like this.'

'I'm as shocked as you are,' the doctor told him.

'But she went to see you only last week.'

'Perhaps the week before.' Aimee took a sip of brandy and recoiled. It was like swallowing fire.

'She was always going to see you, or calling for you to come here. Every few weeks.' Walter's glass was empty; he waved it at Aimee, who got up and refilled it, then went to top up the doctor's glass.

'No thank you,' he said. 'It could be the result of a heart attack, but she never gave me any reason to suspect she had a weakness like that. She complained of nervous problems: lack of sleep and always feeling tired and having no energy. No appetite, but nothing that led me to think she might die.'

Aimee wiped the tears from her eyes. 'She was bustling around at dinner time, more alive than usual. She'd made a special celebration meal and wanted everything to be exactly right.'

'Our wedding anniversary,' Walter said. The ground seemed to be giving way beneath his feet. His conscience pricked; he knew he'd neglected her.

'So tell me what happened? Mrs Kendrick was well at dinner time and had cooked the meal?'

'No.' Walter felt confused. 'It was all very quick. Dora usually has everything prepared when we come home, but Aimee does most of the cooking, and she did it tonight. Prudence ate the asparagus and then the steak, but she did seem more edgy than usual. I didn't realise she was unwell.'

'Gran helped me take the dirty plates to the kitchen after the main course, and brought back the raspberry fools she'd made earlier in the day. We all began to eat, but suddenly she started screaming and coughing. Then she leapt to her feet and threw her dessert flute across the room, and it shattered against the skirting board.'

'As though it wasn't to her liking, not what she'd expected?'

'Yes,' Aimee said, 'but it was absolutely delicious.'

'Then what did she do?'

'She was crying and obviously very upset, so we took her upstairs to lie on her bed.'

'Was she speaking?'

'Yes,' Walter said, 'but not clearly.'

'What did she say?'

'She was all muddled up,' Aimee said.

Walter didn't want to think about that; it had seemed like a stream of hatred directed at him. Numbly he shook his head.

'We'll have to finish this in the morning,' Dr Ellis said. 'It's getting very late. Because her death is unexpected, I'm afraid I'll have to ask for a post-mortem, and that might well be followed by a coroner's inquest. I'll arrange for Mrs Kendrick to be taken to the hospital morgue first thing tomorrow. Would you like something to help you sleep?'

Aimee said, 'No thank you.'

'Mr Kendrick?'

Walter accepted two pills but felt he'd never sleep again. He couldn't understand why Prudence had slid into the next world so unexpectedly, but he had the feeling he was to blame.

'Gramps, I'll have to make up a bed for you. Which room do you want?'

'No, don't bother; I have a little bed in my dressing room, I'll sleep there.' Prudence was filling his mind and the shock of her sudden death had left him shaken and bewildered. They had married with such high hopes for future happiness, but it hadn't been a success.

He went through the bedroom towards his dressing room and paused at the bed. The doctor had come back in here before he'd left and pulled the counterpane up to cover Prudence's face. Walter turned it back. Her pale eyes were open but the piercing gaze that in life had demanded so much attention was gone. She stared sightlessly up and through him. Walter shivered, closed her eyes and covered her face again.

He'd let her down once more. Whatever had caused her death must have been his fault, and now everything was going to change. Despite the pills, Walter couldn't get to sleep; he tossed and turned for ages.

Aimee was exhausted and fell asleep immediately, but she woke up shortly before five o'clock and already it was daylight. That Gran was dead seemed unbelievable, even surreal in the grey light of dawn.

She tiptoed into Prue's bedroom to convince herself it had really happened and folded the counterpane back to see her face. Poor Gran, she looked younger than she used to, but at the same time it seemed her death had been as much of a shock to her as it had to them. Aimee kissed her cheek; it was to Gran she used to run as a child when she'd scraped her knees. Prue had tried to mother her. Poor Gramps, too; she could hear him snoring in his dressing room. How were they going to manage on their own?

She shuddered, wanting Frankie, wanting the comfort of his arms round her. She got dressed and went up the garden and over the wall to the old stables. No light showed, but she could see that Frankie's window was open. She picked up a small stone from the border and tossed it up to the glass.

Nothing happened, so she tried again, and this time it went right through into his room. Seconds later he came to the window, rubbing the sleep from his eyes. 'Aimee? What's the matter?' She started to cry. 'I'll come right down and let you in.'

Within seconds he was at the kitchen door in his pyjamas. She felt his arms tighten round her in a hug as she put her head down against his shoulder and choked out, 'Gran died in the night.'

She stayed with Frankie for the best part of three hours. He made tea and toast and they had it at the kitchen table while Aimee poured out her torrent of anguish and told him everything that had happened, some of it more than once. 'Gramps went to pieces; he was confused, didn't seem to know what he was saying.'

'I don't think he should go to work today,' Frankie said, 'and neither should you. This must have been an enormous shock, and you won't have had much sleep. I'll go in but I'll not say anything about Mrs Kendrick. Unless you think Neville Sanderson should know?'

'Relative or not, he hasn't been near Gran for years. I'll tell him when I go back to work.' Aimee took another gulp of tea. 'I can't believe that yesterday all I was concerned about was that roll of curtaining we saw in Rochdale. It seems very little to get worked up about in comparison with Grandma's death.'

'But it's still important,' Frankie said gently. 'It's the first evidence we've had that fraud really is taking place. Your grandfather's worried about it, but you'll have to leave it with me over the next few days. You two will have more than enough to do at home.'

'Yes, I know, Gramps wanted me to check the number of fabric rolls completed against what Tom Tasker has available to sell. He'll help you; at least we can be sure his figures are correct.'

'I'll see if I can do that today. Listen, can you hear the ceiling creaking? Well, it's the floor in Dad's room really; it means he's getting dressed. I'd better put the kettle on for more tea.'

Aimee was back home when the ambulance arrived to take Gran to the hospital. She led the men upstairs with their stretcher, and Gramps met them at the bedroom door wearing his dressing gown. Together they watched Prue being loaded onto the ambulance. Then the men came back with a collection of forms they were required to fill in, and the questions started. When did she die? What had caused it? Had she been ill in the days leading up to her death?

Dora arrived for work at that point and was horrified when she found out what had happened. She told them, 'Mrs Kendrick complained of feeling ill early yesterday afternoon, and had to go to her bed to lie down. She was acting strangely all day.'

'In what way?' Walter wanted to know.

'She was a bag of nerves and in and out of the kitchen when normally she never came near. She only showed her face if she wanted me to do something for her.'

'She was restless then?' he asked.

'Well, more excited I'd say. She was making a special meal

to celebrate your wedding anniversary, and was very fussy about getting every detail exactly right.'

'She wanted you to help her?'

'Normally she leaves everything to me, but she wouldn't let me near her raspberry fool.' Dora turned her attention to washing up the detritus of the meal while Aimee made tea and toast and sat Gramps down at the kitchen table. She wanted to do for him what Frankie had done for her, because it had made her feel better.

Before he'd finished eating, Dr Ellis arrived and enquired how they were, then the questions began again. 'Was there any of the raspberry fool left over? I've been wondering if I should send some to the lab. You said she seemed normal until she ate that.'

'Well, yes, except Dora has just told us she was ill early in the afternoon,' Aimee said. 'There's nothing left anyway. After we'd taken Gran upstairs, we came down and finished ours. Well, Gramps left some, but I finished that off too. It was lovely, absolutely gorgeous, and I feel all right.'

He seemed to be taking them through every detail of what had happened last night over and over again. They were left exhausted and sat around unable to think of anything else, trying to make sense of it.

That night, Gramps said, 'A sad day, Aimee. I thank God you've grown up and you're able to help me.'

CHAPTER TWENTY-NINE

THE FOLLOWING DAYS WERE the hardest of Aimee's life. She felt haunted by what had happened to her grandmother, and Gramps seemed positively tortured. He sat hunched in his armchair and hardly noticed when she spoke to him; he seemed shut off in a world of his own.

Frankie called in on his way home from work. 'I'm keeping my eye on the fraud problem,' he told Gramps.

Later, when Aimee walked up the garden with him on his way home, she said, 'Gramps seems depressed; this has hit him really hard. He's sunk in gloom. I'm wondering if I should ring Esther. He hasn't mentioned her.'

'Well he wouldn't, would he?'

'But I don't know whether she knows what's happened. Gramps thinks Gran's death is his fault.'

'What could he have done to cause it?'

'Nothing, I'm sure. I'm thinking it could be guilt because he took up with Esther. Gran was always complaining he neglected her.'

'Was she? Well, he's just the sort to have a heavy conscience about that. If Esther doesn't know, she needs to be told. Ring her, or ask him to do it. Better if you can move things on; she'll have to know sooner or later.'

Aimee went back indoors and found Gramps still hunched in his chair in exactly the same position. She went straight to the phone in the study and rang Esther.

'Aimee? Is everything all right?'

'No, Gran died last night. It's turned everything on its head. I'll get Gramps to come and talk to you. Hold on.'

She ran to him. 'Esther's on the phone. She wants to talk to you.' She had to help him to his feet and felt she was towing him to the phone.

'Esther?' he said. Aimee closed the door softly and went to see about their supper.

Candida saw the telegraph boy cycle up to the front door, but there were other flats in her building so she didn't know if it would be for her. The strident tone of her doorbell sent a shiver of panic through her. Telegrams brought bad news, didn't they?

She ripped open the envelope and leaned against the wall for support. My God! Prudence was dead? This was unbeliev-able! She staggered back and collapsed on the nearest chair. The woman was always complaining of aches, pains and biliousness, but she'd looked in reasonable health. It was a real shock. Aimee wanted her to go to Fairholme to help there.

It was a rather tearful Aimee who opened the door to her and told her at length about Prudence's death and that there would have to be a post-mortem. Poor girl, she was in quite a state. It had been such a shock; none of them seemed to know what they were doing. Walter thought they needed help but couldn't say what sort.

'Perhaps you could organise the funeral for us?' he said

before going off to see Esther. Candida didn't feel there was much she could do until they set a date. She helped with the meals but felt at a loss for most of the day.

Gramps was very grumpy the next morning, and snapped when Aimee asked how he was. 'I'm upset, of course. I'm shocked to the core that Prudence died like that, and I feel guilty because I didn't realise she was so ill.'

They had been told that the post-mortem would take place this morning, and they were waiting for Dr Ellis to ring and tell them what had been discovered. Aimee felt they were caught in limbo because they could do nothing to arrange the funeral until the cause of her death had been settled. Gramps was like a cat on hot bricks, wandering round the house and in and out of the garden, unable to settle to anything.

They were eating lunch when the phone rang, and he sent her to answer it.

'No diagnosable cause of death has been found,' Dr Ellis told her. 'The coroner will hold his inquest tomorrow morning at eleven o'clock. Can you and your grandfather be there?'

Aimee assured him they would be, and was quite pleased to see Walter go off to spend the rest of the day with Esther.

Walter felt confused and hardly knew what he was doing. What had happened to Prue was a nightmare. Spending time with Esther and their baby daughter comforted him.

'That's the effect of shock,' she told him. 'A death in the family always brings upset. Tomorrow, if all goes well at the inquest, you might be able to relax a little.'

'What if it doesn't go well?'

'You've no reason to suppose it won't.'

'But I still have to face her funeral.'

'Yes, but Candida will do all that for you, and she knows how to comfort Aimee. I'm afraid you won't find it easy to relax until it's all over, and even then you'll need a few quiet days before you recover and begin to see things differently.'

Walter knew Esther was taking a wider view. For her, Prudence had always been a stumbling block, and he couldn't blame her. She'd see that now he'd be free to spend more time with her, and even move into her little house to live with her. They'd fantasised about it in the past, and he'd told her it was what he wanted too.

Her beautiful green eyes met his. 'What are you going to do when everything settles down?' she asked him. 'This changes everything, doesn't it? We can make a new start.'

'Yes,' he agreed. Esther thought it was decision time, but his mind was numb; the changes had been too sudden and too big. It was like a black hole in the ground opening up in front of him.

'We've talked it all over several times, haven't we?' she said. That had been easy when it was impossible to do anything. They'd talked of getting married too, a very quiet wedding, of course.

He'd told her he didn't like Fairholme; it was too big and old-fashioned, he couldn't afford to maintain it, and it was in quite the wrong place. They'd discussed selling it and buying a smaller modern house in Liverpool, near the mill.

'That would be far enough away from Rock Park for us to do it almost straight away,' Esther said now. 'Nobody would know us there.'

'What about Aimee?' he said. That was a problem they hadn't factored in.

'You said she was keen to marry Frankie Hopkins. You'd be able to release money from her fund so that they can buy themselves a little house somewhere.'

'She's nineteen, Esther, far too young. She's never had a boyfriend before Frankie, never known any other men.'

'She can come and live with us if you think that's best. Aimee and I get on very well; we were good friends.'

'The problem is these are big decisions.' He felt he was living in no-man's-land and couldn't make progress with anything. 'I feel all muddled and I don't know what would be for the best.'

'We both need to think carefully,' she said soothingly as she put Daisy in his arms. 'I'm going to make some tea.'

The baby nestled her head into his shoulder and he tightened his arms round her. Esther was a very patient person, restful and easy to live with. Whatever was the matter with him? He wanted what she wanted, and this was a decision he would have to make sooner or later.

Aimee knew that Frankie would call in to see her on his way home from work, and she intended to read her book in the garden until he did, but she couldn't sit still and went in to drink tea and chat to Dora. She sent the maid home early and walked down to the ferry to meet Frankie. She felt a little shiver of pleasure run down her spine when she saw him come striding up the pier. Recently he'd broadened out across the shoulders; he held his head high and looked a confident young man. He was growing more handsome, too. When he caught sight of her waiting beyond the ticket barrier, he lifted his hand in greeting and his face lit up with a smile. He kissed her there in full public view.

'I don't care who sees us now that your grandfather knows,' he told her.

On the walk home, he tried to bring her up to date with the situation at the mill.

'I can't think of anything but Grandma,' she told him.

'Come on,' he said. 'It might help your grandad if you do.'

'Go on then, what's new?'

'Nothing much. I don't feel I'm making progress. I've been wondering about Bruce Stanley: did your grandfather suspect he was involved in this fraud and set out to trap him so he could get rid of him?'

'You'll have to ask Gramps.'

'I know, but now the question is: has it stopped or it still going on? If it's still happening, I'm afraid more senior staff must be involved. I asked Tom Tasker for hard figures on the stock completed by the production department and available for him to sell. I've checked and they tally with the official figures Neville Sanderson is using in the company accounts.'

'Ah, so if fraud is going on, he must be involved?'

'Yes, and it would be a help to know you were watching inside his department.'

'One more day and I'll be back at work,' she said.

As she opened the front door, they could hear the phone ringing. She ran to pick it up. 'Hello, Gramps,' she said. 'Yes, fine. Of course I don't mind. I'll feed Frankie your share.'

She put the phone down and smiled at him. 'Gramps isn't coming home for dinner tonight. Can I persuade you to stay here and eat with me?'

He laughed. 'I'd love to, but I can't. I have to think of my grandad. We were going to have sausages.'

Aimee led the way to the kitchen and showed him the four lamb chops the butcher had brought that morning.

'Four chops between three isn't easy,' he said.

'It is,' she laughed. 'They're quite big, so one chop each and we split the fourth between us. Dora has prepared mint sauce, new potatoes and cabbage to go with them. She's also made a bread and butter pudding, and told me to put it into the oven when I'm cooking the chops.'

'Sounds good. Can we take it all over the wall and cook it at our house? We can put our sausages in the oven at the same time.'

'Why not? Tip the water out of the saucepans, and find a lid to put on that pudding dish. I'll fetch the picnic basket; most of this stuff will fit into that. We can come back here afterwards and have the house to ourselves.' She beamed at him.

It was very late when Walter arrived home. The light had been left on in the hall so he could see his way in, but the rest of the house was in darkness. He paused on the landing. Aimee ought to be asleep, but he had to make sure. He opened her bedroom door as quietly as he could. Yes, he could see her outline in the bed and hear her soft regular breathing.

He crept to his own room and switched on the light. Prudence's room really. He stared at the luxurious double bed he was supposed to have shared with her during the forty-two years of their marriage. Dora had stripped it bare and sent the sheets to the laundry. She understood the situation. For many of those nights he'd sought refuge on the narrow couch in his dressing room, and felt more at home there than he did in the big bed.

He must put the inquest out of his mind and remember his duty to Prudence. Eventually he'd have to see that she was laid to rest properly, with all the formality and dignity she would have wanted, but Candida would understand what needed to be done.

He couldn't stop thinking about the night she'd died. He'd never known her go to the kitchen to prepare food if there was somebody else to do it for her; neither had she ever got up from the table to help clear away the dirty plates. The more he thought about it, the more convinced he was that she had put some deadly poison into her portion of that raspberry fool. She'd expected her end to be painless but she'd died in agony. The shock on her dead face was evidence of that. It was quite in character for her to turn it all into a huge drama and commit suicide in the midst of their anniversary. Dr Ellis had thought she might have been poisoned, otherwise he would not have asked about leftovers, nor would the coroner have had to be consulted.

If she had committed suicide, then Walter had driven her to it by taking up with Esther. That was weighing heavily on his conscience and it would do for ever more.

The inquest was being held in Birkenhead, so Walter called a taxi to take them. Aimee could see he was knotted with tension. 'What are you worrying about?' she asked.

His tired blue eyes stared into hers. 'I blame myself.'

'Gramps, there's no reason for you to feel responsible. These days you blame yourself for everything that goes wrong.'

When they arrived, the hall was already filling up. Esther and Candida were both there, as was Dr Ellis.

The coroner began. Aimee thought him slow and pedantic as he examined every detail of what had happened on the night Grandma had died. It was all painfully familiar. Possible poisoning as a cause of death was discussed; the coroner said this was a case that was difficult to determine, but eventually, in the absence of hard evidence, he ordered her death be recorded as due to natural causes.

Aimee relaxed and expected Gramps to do the same when he heard that, but he still seemed worried. He invited Candida and Esther to have lunch with them, but Esther said, 'I can't, Walter. I've left Daisy with a neighbour and need to get back. I can't presume on her kindness for too long.'

Aimee was afraid Gramps would feel that was his fault too. Her mind was already on what might be available in the pantry for them to eat, but he swept her and Candida to a nearby café of the sort that provided a substantial meal for workers at an economical price. It was the kind of lunch he ate regularly, but today he was only picking at it.

Aimee turned to Candida. 'Gramps believes Gran killed herself deliberately.'

'Suicide?' Candida seemed to be thinking about it. 'It would be like her to choose a moment of high drama to do that, but if she didn't leave a note, it doesn't seem likely.'

'I looked everywhere,' Walter confirmed, 'but no, she left no note.'

Candida was frowning. 'Please don't take offence; I know I shouldn't speak ill of the dead, and I'm sorry to do it, Walter, but Prudence would never have killed herself in that way without letting us all know what had driven her to it. If she thought you were responsible, she'd have heaped blame on your head and would certainly have left a note. In fact it would have been an epistle, you know it would. She'd have milked the occasion for all it was worth. If she's left no letter, it could not have happened that way.'

'I think Candida's right,' Aimee said firmly. 'I know you've been pondering this since it happened, Gramps, and so have I, but the coroner has ruled and now we need to put it out of our minds and make arrangements for Gran's funeral.'

'I'm afraid I have another problem I haven't mentioned yet,' – Walter was shaking his head – 'and I'll need your help with that too, Candida.'

'Of course,' she said. 'You want me to help with the funeral arrangements, is that it?'

'I do, but the coroner tells me I need to take Prue's birth certificate and marriage lines to the registrar so that her death can be registered and her body released for burial, and I can't find them. I've searched through my study, my desk and the safe, but only my personal papers are there. I've been wondering where she'd be likely to have kept them.'

'In her room?' Aimee said.

'Yes, but she kept everything locked up, and I can't find her keys. Do you know what she did with those?'

'She always seemed to have them on her, in her pocket.'

Candida turned her attention to her serving of spotted dick and custard. 'When we've eaten, we'll go and have a good look round her room. They're bound to be somewhere in there.'

He'd put off asking for Candida's help with this as he knew Prue would have hated the idea of anyone going through her personal possessions, but he had to find her keys. He was feeling better since the coroner had ruled her death to be due to natural causes and the girls had dismissed his idea about her taking her own life.

When they got home, he led them up to her bedroom and threw open the door. 'Prue's parents used to sleep in this room and she changed nothing.'

'Very Victorian.' Candida was staring round at the beautifully moulded ceiling, the lush carpet and ornate curtaining. 'It's vast, isn't it?'

'I think the most likely place for her to have kept documents is in this blanket chest.' He pointed to a massive piece of mahogany furniture that stood at the foot of the bed. He knew she kept some of her valuables in it; she had a few shares she'd inherited from her parents, and a bank book of her own, but she'd never divulged any information about that sort of thing, and she'd given him to believe that the income she derived from them was negligible. She'd always needed a regular allowance for clothes and another for the housekeeping, and he'd provided it.

'She always kept that locked,' Aimee said. 'She didn't want me to touch it.'

Walter tried her wardrobe and the drawers in her dressing table, but they were all locked too.

Candida said, 'Isn't that Prue's handbag?' She pointed to a large lizard bag standing on the corner of the dressing table. 'She rarely went anywhere without it; have you looked inside?'

Walter had it open in seconds. 'You're right, Candida, bless you. Why didn't I think of that?'

He unlocked the chest and lifted the lid. He recognised

Prue's document case immediately and opened it eagerly. Yes, here were the certificates he'd been searching for, hidden amongst her financial documents. Before he could investigate any further, his attention was caught by a silver teapot he knew intimately. He lifted it out and held it aloft. It was one of a four-piece set by Paul Storr and had been handed down through his mother's family; she'd been proud to serve afternoon tea in it. He delved deeper into the chest; yes, here were the coffee pot, milk jug and sugar bowl.

He stared at them, shivering with shock; these should not be amongst Prudence's possessions. A few years ago, she had accused a predecessor of Dora's called Martha Smith of stealing the tea set. She'd sacked and dismissed the girl without a reference, and without telling him.

A ray of sunlight was glinting on gold coins in a half-open red velvet pouch – a lot of gold coins. He'd found a treasure trove, and there was no mistaking the interest Candida and Aimee were taking as they peered inside. He put the teapot back, slammed the lid of the chest down and turned the key in the lock, 'I'll deal with the rest of it later,' he said.

After a few moments of stunned silence, Candida said, 'Well, now you've found Prue's documents, hadn't we better take them to the registrar and get on with what needs to be done?'

With obvious effort, Walter pulled himself together. 'Yes, of course. Aimee, would you ring for a taxi?'

Gramps was in a bit of a state; he seemed unable to make any decisions. Aimee was glad to find that Candida had lost none of her driving force. She took charge and dealt with everything in the registrar's office, after which she asked what sort of funeral he wanted for Prue. When Gramps shook his head, she suggested taking another taxi and going to the premises of a funeral director in Rock Ferry. There she made them both concentrate on coffins and wreaths and flowers.

'Prudence would expect me to provide a lavish funeral,' Walter said as they came out.

'She'll have no grounds to complain about what you've just arranged,' Candida told him. 'What do you want to do about the refreshments afterwards? Shall I organise that too?'

'Yes,' he said, 'yes please. It needn't be fancy.'

'Right, I'll do that, but I think we've all had enough for one day. I know I have. I'll come over tomorrow and we'll decide then about what to serve and make a list of what we need to buy. What time would be convenient for you?'

Aimee had thought of going to work with Frankie tomorrow, but it seemed that would be too soon. 'Come and share a salad with us at lunchtime,' she said. 'Say half twelve to one, then we'll think about funeral refreshments in the afternoon.'

Candida set off towards the train station, and Aimee and Gramps walked down to Rock Park. 'I'm glad that's over,' he said, 'and that the arrangements have been put in hand. Things will get easier for us soon.'

Back at the house, he went to lie down on his bed. Aimee herself felt in limbo. Time seemed to be standing still, Grandma's sudden death a heavy weight hanging over her.

Walter woke up at four o'clock in the morning with the treasures in Prue's blanket chest very much on his mind. Although he felt heavy-eyed with sleep, he got up, put on his dressing gown and went back into the bedroom to take another look. Why hadn't he noticed before that she'd kept the room elegant with new carpets, curtains and bedding? He'd lived with her for forty-two years and he'd thought he knew her through and through, but what he'd seen in that chest proved him wrong. She'd nagged him often enough about having the rest of the house smartened up, so why hadn't she done it?

He unlocked the blanket chest and stared again at what it contained. There were enough gold coins here to pay for anything she could have wanted. He picked up a few guineas and let them run through his fingers: yes, legal tender.

Prudence had been a hoarder and a miser on a scale he'd never suspected. He flicked through a thick wedge of stock certificates, but had no way of knowing if these investments were still active or whether the companies even existed any longer.

He picked up her bank book and found that a tidy sum had accumulated. What had she intended to use this wealth for, if not to maintain the house? It certainly looked as though she had not expected to die. He'd need an accountant to evaluate her wealth. But not Neville Sanderson, absolutely not him.

After the tight financial control he exercised in his mill, Walter felt overwhelmed by the hoard hidden in Prue's blanket chest. What had he been doing for the last forty-odd years that he hadn't noticed what she was up to? Had she even been in her right mind? He'd never questioned her story to explain the loss of his mother's tea set. He took it out now. He'd get Dora to clean it and they'd use it. It was rightfully his.

Prue had nagged him for weeks to report the theft to the police, but he hadn't. He'd liked Martha Smith and hadn't wanted to land her with a criminal record. He'd put it off and put it off until it was too late to do anything. It seemed Prudence had known him better than he knew her.

More to the point, who did all the rest of this hoard belong to now, and what should he do about it? He couldn't remember seeing a will when he'd been searching through the papers in her document case. He himself had made a new one many years ago after Alec had been killed, as he'd had to think of Aimee as well as Prue. He'd tried to persuade her to do the same, but she'd refused to use the solicitor whose services he retained for his mill business. He thought he remembered her saying she had been to see a solicitor in Rock Ferry, but was that just a ruse to stop him pressing her to do it?

He tipped the contents of the document case onto the bed and spread the papers out, shuffling through them. Yes, thank goodness, here it was. He found his glasses and sat down to read. It was what he'd expected. She'd left a generous legacy to Aimee, and he was to receive the house and the residue.

It was almost five o'clock and he felt tired and cold. He got back into bed, but realised almost immediately that he had another problem. The solicitor he'd known and trusted for years had retired and he would have to find a new one. He needed guidance on legal problems at the mill from time to time, and Neville Sanderson had brought in a young man in a smart suit to deal with those, but he must avoid involving any crony of Sanderson's in his personal affairs. He'd talk to Esther about it. She might know of a local firm.

At breakfast that morning, Aimee slid his plate of scrambled egg on toast in front of him and said, 'Gramps, I was a bit surprised when I saw what was in Grandma's chest.'

'So was I,' he grunted.

'I could see you were as shocked as we were. There was a whole bag of guineas there; did Grandma have a lot of money?'

'It seems she did.' Walter had foreseen that Aimee would ask and had decided there was no point in keeping the facts from her, though he didn't mention the Paul Storr tea set because it showed Prudence in a bad light.

'So all that is yours now and you won't be pushed for cash any longer?'

'Not quite; nothing is that easy. There are a few formalities first, and I'll need the services of a solicitor to guide me through those. I must try and find one.'

'There's one living in that house right next to the toll gate; Riverview, it's called.'

'Yes, of course, Douglas Maynard, I spoke to him not so long ago.' They'd been coming home from work one evening and Maynard had waited a moment at the gate for Walter to walk up from the ferry. They'd talked about the display of roses all round Rock Park, and as the bugles from the *Conway* could be heard from its mooring in the river, they'd discussed that too. 'I suppose he'd be as good as any.'

When he spoke to Esther, she told him that Maynard had an office on the Old Chester Road in Rock Ferry. 'I've never used him, but my mother did and I think she was happy with what he did for her.' She found a piece of paper and wrote down the address and phone number.

'Thank you, that makes it easier than knocking on his front door out of business hours,' he told her.

Chapter Thirty

CANDIDA TOLD HERSELF SHE ought to feel more upset about Prudence's death, but weeks had gone by since they'd spoken to Armand and she was getting more and more worried that she'd heard nothing further from him about her paintings. She'd made up her mind to ask Walter if she might ring him again, but he was so distressed she didn't want to remind him and Aimee of additional problems. She'd exhausted her last scrap of patience; the longer she waited, the more frightened she became that something had gone very wrong.

She arrived at Fairholme at lunchtime to find Aimee more her usual self. 'I had to ask Gramps to stay here with us today,' she said. 'He's spending more time with Esther and I'm sure that's good for him, but I want him here so we can make decisions and get on with the arrangements.'

When Walter joined them he said, 'Prudence's body was released to the funeral directors yesterday, and we've agreed that the funeral will be on Friday morning at half past eleven.'

'That means you'll have the mourners collecting here at lunchtime,' Candida said, 'and they'll be hungry.'

'More likely they'll all need a stiff drink by then,' Walter grunted. 'Make sure there's plenty of whisky, and perhaps we should we get some sherry in for the ladies.'

'We have quite a stock of that already; Gran liked it, both sweet and dry.'

Walter look at Candida. 'Would you like a glass now? Dry, isn't it?'

'Yes please.'

'I'll get it, Gramps.'

'Bring me a small whisky too.'

'At midday, some will prefer tea or coffee.' Candida put her mind to the arrangements. 'How many do you think will come?'

'Not many. She didn't have a lot of friends; just a few ladies from the church.'

'Better not get them drunk,' she said, but it didn't raise a smile. 'How many do you want to cater for?'

'There'll be a few neighbours too,' Aimee said. 'Mrs Greening will come. Maybe twenty at most.'

Dora came to the door and said, 'I've got lunch all set out for you, Aimee.'

'Thanks. Are you ready to eat, Gramps? Not that there's any hurry; it's all cold.'

Walter said, 'We could have a salad on the day of the funeral; they won't want anything substantial.'

'A sit-down meal?' Candida was surprised.

'No, Gramps,' Aimee said. 'Finger food: little sandwiches, meat pies, that sort of thing.'

'That would be easier,' Candida agreed. She was ravenous and was glad when Aimee led the way to the dining room. She could see she was being treated as an honoured guest. In front of Walter was a silver salver with a piece of poached salmon that Aimee had decorated with slices of lemon and green grapes. He served generous helpings and passed the plates round. There was cucumber sauce, a mixed salad and crusty bread to go with it. When Candida was offered a second helping of salmon, she accepted it gratefully. It was a long time since she'd eaten food like this.

Aimee cleared the plates and brought in a sponge and cream confection for dessert. 'Delicious,' Walter said. 'You've become a good cook, Aimee.'

By then they'd all relaxed, and Candida felt this would be a good moment to bring up her problem. 'Have you heard from Armand?' she asked. 'He keeps putting off this auction to sell our paintings. Last we heard it was going to be in May, but I've heard no more. Do you know if he's changed his plans?'

'We've heard nothing from him recently,' Aimee said. 'We surely should have been given the exact date if it was going ahead.'

'Last year Armand had to delay the sale he'd put the Renoir in,' Walter said, 'but then he displayed it on his walls and it sold very quickly. I'm sure that sooner or later your sale will take place.'

Candida realised then that between Prudence's death and the fraud at the mill he was finding it impossible to think of anything else. She'd had to sell two of Micheline's evening dresses, and was sure they were worth more than the shop gave her, but the money had paid her electricity bill and a week's rent.

Frankie was missing Aimee's company at the mill. Many people had enquired about why she and her grandfather had not come in. 'They aren't very well,' he told everybody. 'Something they ate, a digestive upset.'

Now that they had proof that rolls of cloth were being stolen, he didn't like being the only one trying to figure out how it was being done. It seemed an impossible task and he felt responsible. Of course he didn't expect Walter and Aimee to be here; for them it was more urgent to deal with the aftermath of Mrs Kendrick's death. But should he have told everybody that they were ill? He might have alerted the thieves that the coast would be clear for increased activity. Fear kept him prowling round the mill, but he saw only routine work going on.

He'd arranged to call and see Aimee on his way home. As he walked up from the ferry to knock on the front door of Fairholme, he marvelled at how much his position with her family had changed. He was ushered into the sitting room to find that Candida was there with them.

'May I remind you about the problems at the mill, sir?' he said. 'You were going to ask Candida . . . ?'

'Oh! Yes, I'm sorry. Everything's going wrong at once; I hardly know which way to turn. Candida, as you know, I've long suspected that stock has been going missing from the mill . . .' He brought her up to date about what they'd found at the shop in Rochdale. 'Frankie has asked me to offer you a job. He reckons he needs your help, but you can say no if you think the mill is too noisy and dirty for you.'

'No, no, it won't be.' They could all see she was keen on the idea.

'The thing is,' Frankie said, 'the police need proof before they can arrest anybody, and in cases of fraud it's very hard to get. This is not the work of one person; to move this amount of stock and not be seen means there must be a gang, and we don't know who they are. Aimee and I are keeping our eyes open and prowling round, but so far no luck. We need someone we can trust: would you be willing to come and give us a hand with this?'

Candida was smiling. 'It isn't what I was expecting, but I'm happy to try if you think I could be of any help.'

'I know you could,' Frankie said, 'but there's another thing. I'm the only pattern maker at the mill, and there's a perennial need for new ideas. I know you could do that too.'

'Draw patterns for you?' Candida looked at Walter. 'I tried once, didn't I? You thought Frankie's work was better.'

'The thing is,' Frankie said, 'we didn't really know then what sort of patterns Mr Kendrick wanted. With all due respect, sir, you didn't explain fully or tell us what the patterns were to be used for. If you'd said curtains or children's night-clothes, they might have been nearer the mark. You did say both Candida and Aimee did well for a first effort. I was lucky that my pattern was a mixture of green shades, and green is a good furnishing colour. Candida's was blue, and in England's climate a cold colour like that isn't likely to be a bestseller.'

'Well, that is true,' Walter agreed.

Frankie went on. 'Candida, you taught me most of what I know about patterns and colours, and I'm sure you'll meet the requirements in half the time it would take anybody else.'

Candida was all red cheeks and looked as though she didn't know whether to laugh or cry. Walter said to her, 'I should have taken this lad into my office long ago; he sorts us all out. I really do need more than one person to create patterns. Are you happy to come and work for me?'

'More than happy, Walter. I shall enjoy painting patterns. I'm delighted about it.'

'And happy about watching for fraud in the mill too? We've got to find some way to stop that.'

'Of course. I've done a lot of strange jobs for you, haven't I?'

'In that case, come to my study and let me explain my pay rates. I can't take you on as an apprentice, not when you are capable of doing so many other things.'

CHAPTER THIRTY-ONE

CANDIDA LISTENED WHILE WALTER explained what he wanted her to do. She felt her head was spinning. She'd agreed to help with the arrangements for Prudence's funeral on Friday, and once she'd done that, she'd cease to be employed informally as and when Walter needed help. She'd have the weekend to relax before starting at the mill on Monday, and there she'd become a full-time member of the staff.

Armand had opened up a deep pit of worry that was keeping her awake at night, but this development had gone some way to restore her sense of security. She should have been more patient.

Walter sent her off to find Aimee and Frankie, who were drinking tea in the kitchen, and she poured a cup for herself before she sat down. She was delighted with the salary Walter had offered; it meant that soon she'd be able to eat properly and start paying off her overdraft.

'I'm so pleased you've decided to join us,' Frankie said politely. 'I have a lot to explain to you, both about the fraud at the mill and about pattern making. Which will you have first?'

'I know nothing about the fraud; you'd better start there.'

'We have proof that rolls of cloth are being stolen,' Aimee

said. 'What we need to find out is who is responsible and how they're doing it. I feel they're wary of me and Frankie and careful to stop us seeing anything suspicious, but possibly they won't be of you, not to start with. Would you be willing to work late in the evenings?'

'Yes, whatever hours you suggest.'

'We've both been keeping our eyes and ears open, and we don't think anything illicit is being sent out of the mill during the working day,' Aimee went on, 'but at five o'clock the hooter sounds and everything comes to a full stop; the mill and the office empty, though some of the bosses work on occasionally. The cleaners come in, but they only stay for two or three hours. It would seem that late evening is the most likely time of the day for stock to be stolen.'

'There is a nightwatchman,' Frankie said, 'and security staff over the weekend. I've thought of staying late myself, but I'm shattered by five, though I'll need to come in with you for the first few nights until you know your way round. It's a warren of a place. I think the best thing is for us both to start work at lunchtime on Monday. I'll introduce you as the new pattern maker and show you the dyes, and you can get started on that. I'm hoping the rest of the staff will assume we'll both leave at five.'

'It'll just be to start with,' Aimee said, 'to see if you can find out how these thefts are taking place. Don't come to work in your Paris fashions; I'm hoping the thieves will think you're one of the cleaners if they see you after five. I'll give you one of Dora's overalls to put over your dress. You'll need to stay out of the way till Gramps's office is cleaned; usually they lock it afterwards, but I can give you a master key. His office is right above the loading bay, and there's a good view over the yard from his window.'

'In fact,' Frankie said, 'I might stay late tomorrow to see what the routine is after five o'clock.'

Aimee said, 'I'll come into work tomorrow morning, Frankie, but I'll not stay on. Gramps thinks I should tell Neville Sanderson about Grandma, in case he wants to come to the funeral.'

'I don't suppose it's likely,' Frankie said, 'if he's had no contact for all these years. Come up to the old schoolroom, Candida. I need to show you the list of employees so you'll know what job they're all doing and be able to put a face to them. That's not too easy when there are so many. If you need more mental exercise, we have copies of the company reports for the last few years.'

'To tell you the truth,' – Aimee pulled a face – 'I'll be relieved when the funeral is over. It's hanging like a weight over everything. Poor Gran, what a thing to say, but I will be glad to go to work.'

Candida went home feeling that the afternoon had moved things along at a breathless pace. The job she'd been desperately seeking for years was suddenly hers. It was a job that could be permanent, a job painting patterns, a job she could get her teeth into and would enjoy. But she was more worried than ever about the fraudulent pictures she'd painted. She'd known for months that all Armand's pictures were going to be scrutinised and she'd been shaking with panic ever since. She wished she'd fought the temptation to fake; she should never have done that.

* * *

303

Aimee went to work alone the next morning. She did the monotonous job she was given and kept a lookout for Neville Sanderson, but he was not in his office, nor did he appear to be anywhere about the building.

When the hooter sounded for lunch, all work stopped instantly and many of her colleagues disappeared. Frankie appeared and she was glad to see him. She made mugs of tea and they sat at his desk. 'Just like old times,' he said.

After the two o'clock hooter signalled the return to work, the desks filled instantly and Aimee could see Sanderson deep in paperwork in his office. She watched one of the managers go in with some documents, and they pored over them for some time. When she saw him leave, she got to her feet and was about to go in, but Sanderson pressed a bell and Mrs Perry from the personnel department walked to his door and entered ahead of her. Aimee hesitated. Should she wait her turn? No, this was not a time for good manners; she needed to know exactly what he was up to.

She tapped on the door and walked straight in. 'I hope I'm not interrupting?' she said, as though surprised not to find him alone. Mrs Perry didn't turn round. 'I've just come to tell you that my grandmother died suddenly on Wednesday.'

Aimee didn't miss the woman's startled jerk; she spun round to look at her, her face white with shock, then scrambled to her feet. 'Excuse me, I have to go.' She whisked past her and closed the door quietly.

'Died? Oh my goodness,' Sanderson said. 'I'm very sorry to hear that. Come and sit down.' His tone was soothing, sympathetic. 'It must have been a terrible shock for you.'

Aimee slid onto the vacant chair. 'It was. I find it hard to believe even now.' She launched into the story of the wedding anniversary celebration, Gran's sudden death, the post-mortem result and the coroner's verdict at the inquest. 'Poor Gramps is very upset.'

'It's wise of him to stay home and rest. Should you be here, my dear?'

'The funeral is at eleven thirty tomorrow at St Peter's. Gramps wanted me to tell you in case you wanted to come.'

'That was very kind, very kind. If there's anything I can do to help . . .'

She had no more to say and got herself out of his office as soon as she could.

Frankie came to see her before it was time for her to go home, and she told him about her visit to Sanderson's office. 'Mrs Perry seemed quite shocked to hear that Grandma was dead, as though she knew her. And Gramps is wrong about Sanderson being slow-witted. I think he's got a brain that works like lightning. It must have come as a shock to him too, but he said all the right things without turning a hair. Didn't Gramps say that Mrs Perry looks after the cleaning staff?'

'Did he?'

'I'll leave you his keys; you could open the files and find out more about her. I won't be in tomorrow; it's the funeral.'

'Of course. I want to be with you and feel I should come out of respect for your grandmother, but I suspect you think I'd be more useful here at work.'

'I just wish it was all over.' She bent and kissed him and he gave her a hug. 'I'm sorry I'm not staying with you now, but I have a lot to do for the funeral and I think Gramps is worried we won't cope. You'll call in on your way home and tell us anything you discover?'

'I could be very late,' he said. 'If I'm not back by ten, it would be better for you to go to bed and sleep.'

'Perhaps it would,' she agreed, 'but Gramps will want to hear your news. If that happens, come over and have breakfast with us instead.'

Another hug and she was gone. The distant whirr of machinery was dying down and his fellow workers were leaving as quickly as they could, laughing, chattering and shouting to each other, banging doors and thundering along the corridors. The torrent slowed to a trickle and then there was silence.

Frankie felt very much alone in this vast building; it seemed spooky now without busy people all round him. He locked his desk, picked up his mackintosh and the bag into which he'd packed essentials for his vigil, and made his way warily to Walter's office, meeting no one. He used the keys he'd been given to get inside and locked the door again behind him.

He went straight to the large window above the loading bay, which would give him a good view if any theft took place. He could see across the yard to the back wall and the now closed gate. He turned and surveyed the office itself. Once it had been fitted out expensively, but that must have been many years ago, as the decor was looking a little faded now. It was conspicuously clean and tidy because Walter hadn't been in for the last few days, but he was afraid the cleaners might come to check that he hadn't come today, so he needed somewhere to hide. He'd thought perhaps under the desk, but there was a door on the far wall he hadn't noticed before and he needed to know where it led.

He found he was in a private cloakroom, where one of

Walter's coats still hung. Excellent. He hung his own coat up next to it, and after taking out the sandwich he'd made, left his bag there too and came to sit at Walter's desk, leaving the cloakroom door open so that if he heard a key turning in the lock he could rush straight inside and hopefully be out of sight. No sooner had he taken his first bite than he heard a faint rattle of buckets in the corridor. He darted back to the cloakroom and hadn't quite closed the door when he saw a cleaner come in. He held his breath, but she just looked round and was gone again, locking the door behind her.

Flooded with relief, he crept back and flung himself into Walter's chair. He was shaking, which was silly, but the urgent need to hide had unnerved him. He found he'd left crumbs on the carpet. He picked them up carefully and threw them down the toilet, but stopped before flushing it in case the sound of running water should betray his presence.

He looked round the room again and his gaze settled on the bank of filing cabinets. He found the key amongst the bunch Aimee had given him and unlocked the drawers, picking out the files of the staff members on his list. He took a chair to the window, where he could watch the yard while he read through the files in the hope of learning more about their suspects.

Time was dragging on; it seemed nothing was going to happen tonight and he felt he was wasting his time. Surely by now the cleaners would be gone and it was the safest time for a theft to take place? He was losing patience.

Daylight had faded and Frankie decided he'd creep down to get a closer view of the loading bay and see if anything was happening. He met no one and everything was locked up for the night, dark and silent. There was no sign of the nightwatchman; presumably he was stationed somewhere and would do occasional rounds. It looked as though nothing had been planned for tonight. He might as well go home.

Back in Walter's office, he put on his mac. Heavens, it was half ten and he was already too late to make the last ferry. What a fool he'd been to wait all this time; he could have left much earlier. He used Walter's master key to get out of the building, leaving by a side door, then caught a train and made the last connection to Rock Ferry, from where he could walk home.

He was too late to call in to tell the Kendricks that nothing had happened, but it hadn't been entirely a waste of time.

The next morning, Frankie's alarm woke him early, but he felt sleep-sodden and lethargic. He got dressed quickly, ready to go to Aimee's for breakfast. The smell of frying bacon as he approached their back door and the sight of Aimee wide awake and smiling brought him round.

'Good morning, Frankie.' Her grandfather was already sitting at the kitchen table. 'Did anything take place last night?'

'No, I'm afraid not. As a vantage point, your office is not the best. I must try and find a better one. I missed the last ferry home and had to walk from Rock Ferry station.'

'Rather a waste of your time then?' Walter asked.

'Not altogether. I've brought you the Perrys' personal files; I'm pretty sure they must be involved.'

He put the files on the table beside Walter, who said, 'I ought to be back at work helping with all this. I'm falling behind with everything, losing touch.'

'There's no rush, Gramps,' Aimee said. 'We're keeping you up to date, aren't we?'

'I'll come to the funeral this morning,' Frankie told them, 'then I'll go to work after lunch and stay late again tonight. I've told Candida to have a lie-in on Monday and come to work at one o'clock. Between us we'll get this sorted, Mr Kendrick, don't you worry.'

CHAPTER THIRTY-TWO

AIMEE WAS GLAD TO see Candida arrive at Fairholme later that morning. She'd been up early to start preparing the refreshments for the funeral guests, and she now had it all in hand. 'Come in,' she said. 'I was just thinking of having a cup of coffee.'

She led the way to the kitchen, where Dora was buttering finger rolls. 'I've made a dozen with ham and I'll have another dozen to use up that roast beef. I've done small sandwiches too, some with cucumber and some with egg. Will that be enough?'

'With all the meat pies and sausage rolls, yes, I think so.' Aimee made three cups of coffee. 'Come and sit down, you must need a break.'

'I feel a bit rushed today,' Dora said as she sat at the table with them. 'The funeral is a big occasion and there'll be lots of guests here.'

Aimee said, 'I know, we're all on edge. Poor Gramps, he's been in a real tizz since Grandma died. I wanted him to have his breakfast in bed this morning, but he was up by half six and prowling everywhere. I didn't want him to go to Esther's this morning, but he rang for a taxi to take him. I've told him he must be back in plenty of time to change for the funeral. He's ordered the cars to be here by eleven twenty.'

'I'm sure he will be,' Candida comforted.

'I'll be going up to change after this.' Aimee grimaced. 'I've decided to borrow a black hat and coat from Gran's wardrobe. It'll make me look like a crow, but Gramps thought I should wear black as a sign of respect.'

'I'll give you a hand setting the food out on the dining table, Dora. What else is there to do?'

'Thank goodness you're both here to cope with all this,' Aimee said.

Later, full of trepidation, she held onto Gramps's arm as they followed the coffin into the church, with Candida and Esther behind them. She thought Gramps felt quite shaky. Frankie was sitting at the back of the church with his father. Aimee was comforted by his sympathetic nod and half-smile as they walked slowly past.

They sat down in the front pew. Aimee couldn't take her eyes away from the coffin, which was right in front of her. It seemed unreal to think of Gran shut inside it, but she'd seen her with her head on the pillow set in folds of satin lining. She was wearing her best cambric nightdress decorated with rich lace ruffles. Now the lid had been screwed down and was heaped with flowers. Aimee shivered and Gramps squeezed her hand; that had always been his way of showing comfort.

The vicar began the service, with the curate in attendance. Gran's favourite hymn was announced, but the singing sounded reedy and slow and the organ was dragging the voices of the congregation along. Prayers, more hymns and a eulogy from the vicar, telling them that Prudence had worked tirelessly to raise funds for the church to help with its work in Africa. She'd been a leading member of the Mothers' Union, and they were very grateful for her help. More prayers for her soul followed, then at last they all stood and the coffin was wheeled to the door and hoisted onto the shoulders of six stalwart men.

Outside, the sun shone from a blue sky and the air felt fresh. Aimee took a deep breath and looked round. She thought she knew the ladies of the church by sight, but there was another woman keeping herself well apart from the rest of the congregation, her face covered with a lace veil. Gramps stumbled, but she kept him upright and they reached the newly prepared grave. She turned to look again for the stranger, but she'd gone.

At last they were back in the car, and then, with relief, Aimee saw their own front door. Gramps whispered, 'I could do with a whisky after that.'

The mourners were close behind; Gramps greeted the vicar and led them all to the sitting room. The Mothers' Union turned up in force to pay their respects, and Candida and Dora threaded their way through the throng carrying trays laden with glasses of sherry.

Aimee told herself to treat it like any other social occasion, especially those Grandma had taken her to at the church. It surprised her that the guests were talking about all sorts of things and seemed to have forgotten why they were here.

Frankie came and caught at her arm. 'Are you all right?'

'I'm fine now. Where's your grandad?'

'He went home, didn't want to come to the reception; he said he wouldn't be at ease.'

'Oh dear, I'd have made him welcome.'

'I know that, but he wasn't so sure. Look, I'm going to work now and I'll stay late again; the thefts must be taking place in the late evening, but it doesn't happen every night.'

'And you need to be there when it does. Don't go yet, Frankie. Stay and have something to eat. Dora and I have organised quite a feast and I haven't had time to speak to you. It doesn't matter what time you get there as long as it's before five.'

'It would be better if I went now,' he said. 'I'll call in on my way home if I'm not too late.' Then he was gone, and the curate was hovering close to have a word with her.

Aimee tried hard to be a good hostess. At last the guests were beginning to leave. Mrs Greening was saying goodbye. 'It was a lovely service,' she told Walter. 'I'm sure Prue would have been pleased with it. We'll all miss her.'

Lydia squeezed Aimee's arm. 'Sympathy and all that,' she said. 'Have you had a terrible time?'

Aimee nodded. 'It was so sudden and such a shock,' she said. But it was over now and life could go on; she would be able to think of something else once she'd closed the front door on them all.

Dora was washing up at the kitchen sink and Candida was clearing the dining room table. 'There's quite a lot of food left,' she said.

Aimee put a meat pie and a couple of sandwiches on a plate in the pantry. 'For a snack before I go to bed,' she said. 'Do you want to take some of it home? Gramps won't want to eat any more.'

'Yes please.'

'I expect Frankie and Dora will be happy to take some too. Divide it into three, Candida, while I find some bags to put it in.'

* * *

Frankie reached the mill before the two o'clock hooter sounded to bring his colleagues back from lunch. In the afternoon he tried to sketch out a pretty flower pattern for ladies' dress fabric, but he had no energy and couldn't put his mind to it.

At five he went along to Walter's office. One glance out of the window told him that tonight would be different. The yard gate stood open, and parked against the wall were two luxury American cars, one of which he recognised as belonging to Neville Sanderson. He suspected the other one belonged to Oswald Perry. It must mean they were still in the building, though possibly they were just working overtime.

The cleaner came again but he was ready for her this time, and as soon as she'd gone, he returned to the window. Time was going on and the cars had not moved; he was sure that must mean they intended to do something tonight.

Another hour dragged by. He sat with his nose pressed to the glass, but the office was directly above the loading bay, and there was a canopy over that to provide shelter from the weather, so it was difficult to see anything. As it grew darker outside, however, he became aware of a glow of light from below. He opened the small fanlight in the window and thought he could hear voices; yes, there were definitely people there.

He decided he'd creep down and try to get a closer view. He'd got as far as turning the key in the door when suddenly a burst of light filled the office. He shot to the window in time to see a van with headlights full on driving away.

'Oh my God!' Had it all gone on right under his nose and he'd missed it?

Three figures were crossing the yard to the cars, and there were three more behind them. The two cars drove out, also with headlights blazing, and the other group locked the gate behind them. Undoubtedly theft had taken place tonight, and Frankie felt a fool to have waited and waited and yet not seen enough to recognise anybody. He was afraid he'd lost a good opportunity and could have achieved much more.

He was surprised to find it had only just gone nine o'clock. He would be home quite early and able to call in at Fairholme and tell the Kendricks what had taken place. But when Aimee opened the front door to him, he found her grandfather had gone to see Esther and was not yet home.

Aimee led Frankie to the kitchen and they sat together at the table, drinking cocoa and eating cake. Once he'd recounted his sorry tale, they began daydreaming about their future. 'It would do no harm,' Aimee said, 'if we started looking round near the mill for a house that would suit us. Gramps is relying on you now to do so much for him that there's no reason for him to want to delay our marriage. I mean, you're twenty-one and showing responsibility, and I have enough money with which to set us up.'

'There is a difficulty for me.' Frankie was pursing his lips. 'I want us to get on with our life, and I'm desperate to marry you, you know that, but I have to think of Dad.'

'He can come and live with us. I won't mind in the least if it means I can have you as well.'

'He won't want to come, Aimee. I've put it to him. He said he was born in the old stables and he means to be carried out feet first. I know he'd be the first to urge me to go, and he says he'd be perfectly happy on his own, but he's been a father to me when I've had no other. Now that he's unwell and growing old, I can't possibly leave him on his own. Sorry.'

Aimee clung to him. 'I should have known. You're exactly the sort of person who'd want to show loyalty and affection; that's why I love you. We'll keep things as they are.'

When they heard the taxi outside, Aimee pulled out of Frankie's arms and went to open the door. Gramps brought a blast of cold air in with him. 'Hello, Frankie,' he said. 'It's late for you to be here.'

'Yes, sir, it is. I called in to tell you what happened at the mill tonight.'

'Of course, thank you. Let's go and sit down.' Walter led the way to the sitting room. 'I take it there have been developments?'

'Yes, but I missed an opportunity to find out a lot more, so I'm not pleased with my efforts.' Frankie went on to tell him that he believed another theft had taken place, but that he'd failed to see anything. 'I'm sorry.'

'Don't blame yourself.' Gramps sat back in his armchair to think. 'I'd say we've made a big step forward; it tells us when and how these thefts are taking place. At what time did this happen?'

'It was almost nine o'clock when the van drove away. Your office is a safe place for us to watch from a distance, but not a great deal can be seen from there. I need to look for a better spot on the ground floor, where we can hide and see exactly what is going on and who is involved.'

'Definitely Neville Sanderson,' Aimee said. 'Frankie saw his car parked in the yard.'

'Wait a moment,' Walter said. 'I'm going to ring the police right away. They need to know about this.' He got up and went to his study.

When he returned, he was holding a piece of paper. 'I've spoken to an Inspector John Hardy, and he agrees we've made good progress with this. He's said he'll post officers to keep the mill under surveillance as darkness falls, but they want me to have people watching too.'

'You will have,' Frankie assured him.

'And if you see any signs of the suspects loading a van at that time of night, he wants you to ring him immediately. He hopes that will give us the chance to catch them red-handed. I've written down his telephone number for you.' He gave the paper to Frankie.

'Gramps, with the funeral and everything, I haven't got round to telling you what happened yesterday. As you suggested, I went to Sanderson's office to tell him Gran had died. I wanted to hurt him, shock him. He's played on the family connection and I wanted him to know it was over. I knew that Mrs Perry was with him, and I wasn't going to let that stop me, but she gave such a start of surprise I thought she must have known Grandma. She couldn't hide her shock, whereas he showed no emotion and just switched smoothly into false concern for me.' She took a deep breath. 'And I glimpsed someone in the background today at the funeral who could have been her. If I'm right, then she must have known Grandma.'

'Mrs Perry is in charge of the cleaners,' Frankie said. 'It's been on my mind all afternoon. Neville Sanderson said his mother was alive and well; who better to assist in this theft?'

'You mean she's Grandma's sister?' Aimee asked. 'I suppose that would that give her a motive. She might have seen Prudence as her father's favourite, helping him to oust her from the family when she really needed their help. Perhaps she regards stealing your fabrics as a means of getting her own back. Did you know her, Gramps? What d'you think?'

Walter shook his head. 'When I first met Prue, I saw quite a lot of her family, but that was more than forty years ago.'

Frankie went on. 'Her husband, Oswald Perry, is the deputy manager in the production department, which is very convenient for them. One of his jobs will be to record the number of completed rolls of fabric they make.'

'But Verity didn't have a husband; she was an unmarried mother,' Aimee reminded them. 'That was her sin.'

That brought a defeated silence, until Frankie said, 'You lost touch with her forty years ago. She could have married in that time.'

'Of course she could,' Walter agreed, 'but her name . . .'

'Verity's an uncommon name. If she'd put that on her records, you'd immediately have known who she was. How did she get the job; did you interview her?'

'I wouldn't imagine so. The people in personnel don't normally involve me when they hire junior staff.'

'Hers is not a junior position,' Frankie said, 'but not to worry. If it is Verity, they would change her name, wouldn't they? They wouldn't want you to know.'

'It's a very successful method they've set up,' Walter said ruefully. 'Very successful.'

'But we're getting closer,' Frankie said. 'We can now see that they need a group in position to do this, and we may know some of them. When Candida starts on Monday, I'll stay on with her until ten o'clock or so to show her the ropes.'

'Yes,' Walter said, 'and I think it would be wiser if she appeared to be just another employee working in the pattern department, rather than a friend of yours and Aimee's. The staff will take less notice of her and perhaps reveal more.'

'I agree,' Frankie said. 'I'll take care that we aren't seen together too much around the office.'

Walter smiled. 'I feel better about this now we seem to be making progress.'

CHAPTER THIRTY-THREE

FRANKIE HAD ARRANGED WITH Candida to catch the same train to the mill at lunchtime on Monday, and told her he'd travel in the last coach. As it happened, he was hanging out of the window and looking out for her as the train pulled into Liverpool Central. She saw him and got straight in beside him.

They met Aimee and Walter returning from lunch. 'I'm glad to see you here, Candida,' Walter said. 'I hope you don't find working late hours too much.'

'I feel quite lazy getting up leisurely and coming to work at lunchtime,' she said.

'I'll keep you busy,' Frankie told her as they reached the pattern department. 'You can have Bruce Stanley's old desk here beside mine. But first I'll take you to the personnel department and introduce you to Mrs Perry. Do take a good look at her; she's a major suspect and you'll need to remember her face.'

Mrs Perry said, 'Mr Kendrick has telephoned us about you, Miss Rathbone. I understand you're an artist and a former art teacher? He says we are fortunate to be able to employ you to work on our patterns.' Frankie left her there to be enrolled.

Afterwards he walked her round the mill, explaining the

geography of the building, and they ended up in Neville Sanderson's office. He'd already explained Sanderson's relationship to Prudence. 'Remember his face too,' he said.

During the afternoon, he told her what he'd learned about patterns and showed her the dyes that would be used on the fabric. 'I'm very grateful to you, Frankie,' she said. 'I know you asked Walter to give me a job and now, like magic, I'm here.'

'I've owed you a favour for years.' He grinned at her. 'You persuaded him to allow me into Aimee's lessons. Without that, I'd still be cutting the neighbours' grass with Dad.'

'I suppose you could say one good turn deserves another.' She wore a broad smile too.

'But it's not just a question of favours,' Frankie went on. 'Walter really needs you here, and so do I. To thrive, this business needs regular new patterns, and I don't know whether I could keep that up on my own.'

At five o'clock, they heard their colleagues go home. Frankie made a cup of tea and they ate the sandwiches they'd brought. 'We'll go to Walter's office when we've had this,' he said. 'I'll take some paper so we can try out patterns, and you bring all that stuff I've given you about dyes, because if no cloth is stolen tonight we'll be bored out of our minds.'

'You don't think it'll happen tonight then?'

'It doesn't happen every night and there are no cars parked outside, so no managers here.'

They worked on their patterns and took turns to watch at the window. 'The cleaners are leaving now,' Frankie told her. 'I'll give it another ten minutes and then I'll go and see if anything is happening downstairs. They'll need to bring the rolls of cloth down to the loading bay in readiness before they can start putting them on the van. You stay here out of sight Candida, just in case there's anyone else here.'

Knowing he wasn't alone, Frankie found the building less spooky. He went warily down a narrow staircase he'd discovered and found the building deserted and all locked up for the night.

He went back to Candida. 'There's nothing doing tonight,' he told her, 'but at least it gives you the chance to find your way round this rabbit warren of a place. Come on, let's go and explore.'

Frankie found he had a lot more to learn about the building too. He discovered two more staircases, as well as a hoist from the ground floor. In the loading bay, there was a platform where vans could back up to be filled, and a space behind a partition where goods could wait.

'We need a safe hidey-hole where we can really see what they're doing.' He led her round opening doors where he could. 'This might do, if we could leave the door open, but there isn't anywhere safe with a decent view. Come on, we might as well tidy up Walter's office and go home.'

They caught a train that got Frankie to the Pier Head in good time for the ferry, which cut out a long walk at the other end. He could see the lights were still on in Fairholme, so he called in to see Aimee.

'Staying late was a waste of time then?' she asked.

'No,' he said, 'not entirely. Candida's learning her way round the mill, and we both had another go at pattern designing.'

On Tuesday night, the mill seemed to empty again as soon as the cleaners left, but on Wednesday, when Frankie and Candida went to Walter's office, they saw a car parked in the yard. 'Good,' Frankie said. 'I think that's Oswald Perry's car. It looks as though they mean business tonight.'

'A luxury motor,' Candida said. 'American. Looks like poor Walter might be footing the bill for that.'

'Let's pull a couple of chairs to the window and sit one each side behind the curtains so we can monitor developments.'

As they waited, they ate their sandwiches, and Frankie brought out the evening paper.

'I thought spying would be exciting,' Candida said.

'It's the most boring thing imaginable,' he said, offering her the newspaper.

She waved it away. 'I'll have another look at the colours of those dyes.' Frankie could see she was keen to absorb all the knowledge she'd need to paint patterns.

It had been an overcast day and it got dark earlier than usual. At eight o'clock, the car was still parked outside. Frankie let out a long, slow breath. 'I wish they'd get on with it before we die of boredom.'

'Be marvellous if we could nail them tonight.' Candida stood up and stretched. 'Walter would be delighted.'

'I'm tired of waiting,' Frankie said. 'I'm going to take a peep downstairs to see if anything's going on. You stay here,' he told her. 'I don't want to make any noise and let them know they're being watched. Lock the door behind me; I'll give three little taps so you'll know it's me.'

He crept to the top of the stairs and listened. He thought he could hear an engine running, and yes, voices too. He felt immediately invigorated. He was right: they were planning a move tonight. They seemed to be making no effort to be quiet, so they must believe they had the mill to themselves.

His heart was beating faster as he went down the stairs and along the passage until he could see into the area behind the loading bay. The lights were on and he recognised Oswald Perry driving a forklift truck. He was amazed to see Bruce Stanley and John Hampton there too; they were stacking rolls of finished fabric in mounds ready to be loaded onto the van when it arrived. Now he knew more about the gang involved in this theft.

Hardly daring to breathe, he crept back to Walter's office, fearful that every creak of the staircase might alert them to his presence. He tapped on the door and Candida let him in. She spoke in an excited whisper. 'Neville Sanderson has just parked his car and I saw him walk in through the loading bay. What did you see?'

'They're bringing the stock down ready to load. I'm going to ring that police inspector.'

He lifted the receiver, and a few moments later he was through to Inspector Hardy. 'We expect a theft to take place tonight,' he told him. 'The gang are getting the goods in position to load, but the van isn't here yet.'

'How long before they'll be ready?'

'Your guess is as good as mine,' Frankie said.

'How many men in the gang?'

'I've seen and recognised three, and we've just seen another arrive. There could be more.'

'Right, my officers are in position, but we'll stay out of sight for the time being. Watch for the arrival of the van, and as soon as you see it, ring again. It would be a great help if we could catch them red-handed; it would make getting a conviction easier.'

'All right,' Frankie said. He left the inspector's number pinned under the corner of the phone. His mouth felt dry. 'It's all about to happen,' he said to Candida. 'We're ready, aren't we?'

'Ready and waiting.'

Time passed slowly as they stood behind the curtains at the window; because they could see nothing happening, every minute seemed like ten. 'Do you think there could have been a van already backed up to the loading bay that you couldn't see?' Candida asked.

'I'm wondering the same thing myself.' Frankie hesitated. 'We don't want to be waiting up here if they're already working hard to load it. My senses tell me they're getting on with it, but I don't want to ring Hardy again unless I'm sure. I'm going down to take another look. You stay here, I won't be long.'

He went downstairs to the place where he'd watched them stacking the fabric rolls. The screen shutting off the loading bay from the building was now folded back, and under the electric lights he saw a busy scene laid out before him. One van was almost completely loaded with rolls of fabric, and more were neatly stacked and waiting in readiness. Why had he not thought to check beyond the screen? Logic should have told him that the vans might already be there. He turned, ready to run back upstairs, knowing he needed to make that second phone call urgently now.

'Good evening, Mr Hopkins.'

He spun round, and was gripped with horror to see both Neville Sanderson and Oswald Perry behind him. He knew he'd been trapped.

* * *

325

Candida was watching at the window and could see light shining up from the loading bay. Did that mean the partition was open now between the bay and that storage area behind? She was starting to feel very much on edge. Where was Frankie? He'd said he wouldn't be long and yet it seemed ages, and what was going on downstairs? A sudden movement outside caught her eye; an unmarked van had driven into the yard and was approaching the loading bay.

She was in a dilemma: should she telephone the police? She'd made so many wrong decisions recently and she didn't want to make another, but she mustn't do what Frankie had done on Friday night: just sit here and let them steal yet another load of Walter's fabric. With shaking fingers she lifted the phone and gave the number pinned beneath it to the operator. She tried to sound confident as she told the inspector that the thieves were in the act of loading up another van with Walter's stock.

When she'd put the phone down, she rushed back to the window and stood waiting with bated breath. It seemed an age before she saw three police cars drive into the yard. The last one stopped to let an officer out to close the gate. With a heavy sigh, she sank into a chair, still afraid she'd done the wrong thing. A minute later, stiff with stress, she pulled herself to her feet and ran to the stairs to see for herself what was going on.

The sudden bright lights dazzled and confused her. The thieves were angry and protesting noisily as the policemen struggled to line them up against the far wall. Candida counted them: Neville Sanderson, Mr and Mrs Perry and the two pattern apprentices. She could see two vans backed up against the loading platform, one almost filled to capacity with Walter's fabric. The gang had been caught red-handed. They were now handcuffed together, and it looked as though they were being escorted towards the police cars.

She felt weak at the knees with relief. Thank God she'd screwed herself up to make that phone call. It had certainly been the right thing to do. If Frankie hadn't left that number there . . . She glanced around frantically, then opened her mouth and bellowed, 'Hang on a minute. Where is Frankie Hopkins? He came down here twenty minutes ago to see what was going on. Where is he now?'

In the sudden hush, everything stopped and an officer came to talk to her. Candida could barely get the words out to explain. 'Frankie came down here to make sure they intended to steal the fabric. He said he'd come back to telephone but he didn't. They must have done something to stop him. Where is he?'

The gang was separated for questioning, as Candida imagined the worst. It was Bruce Stanley who broke down first and muttered, 'He's in Mr Perry's office.'

Candida was the only one who had any idea where that was. She charged along the corridor, but the door was locked. She used Walter's keys to open it and found Frankie crumpled on the floor in a pool of blood. He'd been beaten up and was losing consciousness.

An ambulance was summoned and she went with him to hospital, gazing in horror at the cuts and bruises on his face. She kept trying to talk to him. 'We caught them, it's all over,' she told him over and over. 'You're safe now and on the way to hospital.'

Once the doctors had started to work on him, she phoned

Aimee. 'I have news for you,' she said, 'but it's both good and bad.'

'Frankie's hurt?' Aimee screamed. 'How badly?'

'I don't know yet, the doctors are attending to him now.'

'Oh goodness! I'm coming over to see him. Hold on, Candida, while I tell Gramps.' Candida fed borrowed pennies into the payphone and hoped she'd not run out. Aimee returned. 'Gramps and I are coming straight away,' she said. 'Please wait until we get there.'

They came by taxi, and by then Candida could tell them that Frankie's right shoulder had been dislocated but had been put back in place, and that he'd now been taken to X-ray because they thought his left arm and left ankle might be fractured.

Walter was horrified. 'Thank you,' he said. 'You must go home and rest, you look exhausted. I'm very grateful; you've both done marvellously well. It's a huge relief to know you've caught these thieves at last.'

He walked to the hospital door with her and they saw a taxi dropping off another passenger. He put her inside and paid the driver to take her home. Candida sat hunched on the back seat feeling sick, unable to forget the blinding fear she'd felt.

CHAPTER THIRTY-FOUR

FEELING STIFF WITH WORRY, Aimee waited for Frankie to come back from the X-ray department. 'I had no idea I was putting them in danger like that.' Gramps squeezed her hand. 'I'm so sorry he's been hurt, but he's in the right place here and they'll do all they can for him.'

Frankie was wheeled back on a trolley and pushed into a small ward at the back of the casualty area. Only one other bed was in use and the occupant appeared to be asleep. 'It's just temporary while the doctors look at his X-rays and decide what needs to be done,' the nurse told them.

Aimee could see Frankie's eyes following her. 'You're awake?' she said.

It was the nurse who replied. 'He's had painkillers and he's now more himself, so you can talk to him.' She brought chairs so they could sit beside him. His face had been wiped clean of blood, but they could see it was covered with cuts and bruises.

'I'm so glad Candida managed it.' His smile was wobbly. 'They were caught red-handed.'

'You did it between you,' Walter told him, 'and I'm absolutely delighted. If you've stopped those regular losses, the mill will stand a reasonable chance of making a profit. Goodness knows how long this has been going on. I'm very grateful to both of you.'

A doctor came to speak to them. 'You've been quite lucky,' he told Frankie. 'You'll have a black eye by morning and your foot and ankle will be badly bruised, but the X-ray showed no fracture. Not so lucky with your left arm; that showed a break in the radius, so first thing in the morning it will have to be put in plaster. Now we're going to send you up to a ward, where you'll be able to get some sleep.'

'I want to go home. My grandfather isn't well and he's alone there.'

'I'm afraid you need to stay here for a day or two to make sure there's nothing else broken.'

Aimee sided with Frankie. 'We were hoping to take him home.'

'He's had a nasty knock on his head and he lost consciousness for a time. He needs to stay here to be safe.'

The doctor was gone and Frankie was biting his lip. 'Will you make sure Dad is all right? He hasn't been feeling too well for the last few days, unsteady on his feet, and he didn't go to work this morning, but he wouldn't let me send for the doctor. Not sick enough, he said.'

'Of course we will,' Aimee said.

'Our bathroom is on the ground floor and I'm afraid he might fall on the stairs. There's an old commode in Connie's room, but he didn't want to use that.'

'We'll make sure he has everything he needs,' Walter assured him.

The nurse returned with a porter. 'Right, we're taking you up to the ward now,' she told Frankie. She turned to Aimee and Walter. 'I have to ask you to leave now. It's late and the lights have been switched off in the ward so the patients can sleep.'

'Of course.' Aimee bent to kiss Frankie goodbye.

'I love you,' he whispered. With aching heart, she watched him being wheeled away.

'It's too late for public transport,' Walter worried, but the nurse directed them to a public phone box at the entrance and Aimee rang for a taxi to take them home.

Outside, it was dark and raining heavily. 'What would they have done to him,' Aimee asked, 'if the police hadn't come in the nick of time?'

'Luckily they did,' Walter said.

'Sanderson and his cronies had a well-organised plan that's been working for years, and it's clearly a paying proposition. Frankie knew them all and understood what they were doing.' Aimee shivered. 'Once they'd caught him spying on them, they knew they had to silence him.'

Walter looked grim. 'They certainly treated him roughly: got him on the floor, and it seems from his injuries that they kicked him.'

Aimee shivered again. 'Anger could have driven them to kill him and dispose of his body before they'd thought it through.'

'You read too many blood-and-thunder novels,' Walter said as their taxi arrived.

Once they reached Rock Ferry, Walter asked the driver to take them to the old stables to check on Frankie's grandad. 'It's after midnight,' he said, 'so he might be asleep.'

But when they drew up outside, the lights were on. 'We'd better call in and see him,' Aimee said.

She found the back door unlocked and Bob Hopkins sprawled in his battered armchair in the living room. 'That you, Frankie?' he asked.

'No, it's Walter Kendrick and Aimee.'

'Mr Kendrick?' Bob struggled to sit upright. 'Frankie hasn't come home, is that what's brought you here? What's happened to him?'

'Yes, he asked us to come and make sure you were all right,' Aimee told him.

'But where is he?'

'He was working late at the mill,' Walter said, 'and with his help the police have arrested the gang that have been thieving from me for a long time.'

'We're proud of what he's achieved,' Aimee told Bob, 'but the thieves caught him spying on them. They've broken his arm and he's in hospital. He's worried about you, says you're ill.'

'Aye, I'm very sick.'

'It's late,' Aimee said. 'We'll see you upstairs to bed. Are you hungry? I could get you some supper.'

'No, not hungry.' They helped him up. 'Bathroom first,' he said.

'I'll see to this,' Walter told Aimee. 'You make him a hot drink.'

'Would you like hot milk?' she asked.

'No, there won't be enough for Frankie's breakfast.'

'He won't be here for a day or two,' Walter said gently, 'and we can get you more.'

Aimee warmed a cup of milk, and took it up to find that Gramps had got Bob upstairs and half undressed. The old man was coughing. 'No more off,' he protested. 'Too cold.'

'We could ring for the doctor now,' Walter said. 'I think you're ill enough to justify that.'

'No doctor,' Bob said. 'A couple of aspirins and I'll be better by morning.'

They stayed with him while he drank the milk, then put him to bed in his long johns and woollen vest. 'Frankie's afraid you might fall on the stairs,' Aimee said. 'He says it would be safer for you to use the commode in Connie's room.'

'No, I couldn't. Anyway, it broke and she used it for something else. No good now.'

'Goodnight then,' Walter said, switching off the lights. 'Stay where you are until Aimee comes back in the morning.'

They found the key to the back door and locked up.

'He's not an easy patient,' Aimee said.

'An obstinate old man,' Walter said, 'and he's reeling all over the place. He could hardly get up the stairs and I was afraid he'd fall backwards. I'd feel happier if he'd let us ring for Dr Ellis.'

On the walk home, Aimee said, 'It's worked out well for the mill, Gramps. I'm delighted about that. Those losses will stop now, thank goodness.'

'Yes, such a relief.' Walter sighed. 'I should feel on top of the world, but actually I feel downright exhausted.'

'Stay in bed in the morning,' Aimee said firmly. 'I think you should take the rest of the week off. You can leave me in charge for a day or two; there's no need to rush back now the thieves have been caught.'

'I'm being very lazy leaving it all to you young ones, especially now that Frankie's been hurt.'

'I'll set my alarm an hour earlier in the morning,' Aimee said, 'so I'll have time to check on Mr Hopkins before I catch the ferry. Unless he's very much improved, I think we should ask Dr Ellis to call on him whether he likes it or not.'

'I quite agree,' Gramps said.

After her late night, Aimee felt a bit bleary-eyed in the morning as she ate a lonely breakfast of cereal. She intended to climb over the garden wall and took with her an old towel to place on top; she'd learned from experience that the soot-stained bricks could leave black stains on her clothes.

When she let herself into the kitchen, all was still and silent. 'Mr Hopkins, are you awake?' she called. 'It's Aimee, come to see if you're feeling any better.'

Nothing broke the silence.

At the bottom of the stairs she called again. 'Mr Hopkins? Can I come up and see you?' She hesitated. Gran would have had a fit at the thought of her going into his bedroom, but she couldn't go to work without seeing him. She was quite pleased when she heard him cough. 'It's Aimee,' she said. 'I'm coming up.'

He seemed quite distressed when she reached his bedside. 'Water,' he gasped. She ran downstairs to refill the glass she'd taken up last night. His bedroom curtains were closed; she flung them open and saw how ill he looked, pale and sweaty. 'Did you manage to get any sleep?'

'Couldn't stop coughing. Pains in the chest.'

'You need a doctor,' she told him. 'I'm going home to phone for Dr Ellis, then I'll come back and make you some breakfast.'

'Don't want the doctor. Don't want breakfast either.'

'You need them.' She went home and made the call, then took Gramps a cup of tea and brought him up to date with Bob's condition.

'You'll have to stay with him until the doctor has been,' he said. 'Don't go to work until you've made sure he's all right. That's the least we can do for Frankie when he's done so much for us.'

Aimee returned to the stables. 'The doctor will be coming when he's finished his breakfast. So what would you like? I've brought more milk over, and I see you have cereal and eggs in your cupboard; what about scrambled eggs?'

'Not hungry, just tea.'

'A slice of toast?'

'Just tea.' She turned to go, but Bob stopped her. 'That commode . . . I remember our Connie saying something about keeping it for Frankie.'

'Keeping it for him?'

'Yes.' The old man was shaken by another fit of coughing and at that moment she heard Dr Ellis calling from below. She ran to let him in.

The doctor sat down on the bed as though he had all the time in the world. 'Are you in any pain?' He took Bob's temperature and put his stethoscope over his chest until another fit of coughing made him pause. 'Pneumonia, I'm afraid.' He shook his head.

Aimee told him about Frankie being in hospital.

'Well, Mr Hopkins,' he said, 'you're too sick to be here by yourself. I think I'd better arrange for you to go to hospital too. I'll get an ambulance to come for you.'

'No, I don't want to go. I'd rather stay here.'

'Hospital is the best place for you when you have nobody to—'

'Our Frankie will be back soon. He'll look after me.'

The doctor was putting his instruments into his case. Aimee saw him to the door. 'I'll look after him until Frankie comes home,' she said.

'No,' he told her. 'He's seriously ill. You can't stay here day and night. He needs hospital care.'

She went slowly back upstairs. 'He says nothing but hospital will do for you,' she told Bob. 'I'll put a few things together for you to take: soap, towel and slippers, that sort of thing. Tell me where I'll find a bag to put them in.'

'No, listen.' Suddenly the old man seemed agitated. 'Tell Frankie about the commode.'

'Where is it?'

'In Connie's room.' He was kicking his feet out of bed. 'I'll show you.'

'No, just tell me. You shouldn't be out of bed.' He was swaying and she had to hold him upright, but there was no stopping him. She opened the door. 'Are you talking about that chair?'

'Commode, it was a commode. She wanted me to . . . to screw the seat down to hide something . . . to keep it safe for Frankie. He's been searching. Tell him to look there again.'

Aimee's heart was racing. 'When was this?'

'When she had to go away.'

'You mean years ago?'

'Yes, that's it.'

'Come on, you'd better get back to bed.' She could feel him sagging against her, and it took all her strength to help him

336

back under the covers. He lay there inert. She tried to talk to him about what he'd need in hospital, but he was no longer interested. She went round picking up what she thought he might want.

When the ambulance had pulled away, she locked the cottage door and went home. Gramps was up and dressed and Dora was making him some breakfast. 'I feel I have to let Frankie know that his father has pneumonia and is very ill,' Aimee said, 'but they told us there was no visiting allowed today.'

'Yes, I've just rung to ask how he is. They told me he's as well as can be expected. I'm going to ring them again and say we need to come in and talk to him. This is not something we can keep from him. Don't worry, they'll understand.'

He was on the phone for a long time, and eventually he said, 'Yes, we can see him.'

When they got to the hospital, the ward sister led them to Frankie's bed and drew the screens round it. His cuts and grazes stood out more noticeably on his pale face this morning. He had a swollen black eye and his left arm was in plaster, but he pulled himself up the bed when he saw them. 'How's Dad? I understand from Sister . . .'

'Yes, it's bad news, I'm afraid.' Walter recounted what had happened.

'Poor old Dad.' Frankie pursed his lips. 'But that settles it. I can't lie here knowing he's alone and ill in another hospital on the other side of the river.'

Under the circumstances, he was given painkillers and the doctor discharged him. 'I'm perfectly all right,' he assured everybody. 'On the mend now.'

They took him home to Fairholme by taxi. Aimee had asked Dora to make up a bed and prepare a room for him and to provide lunch for three. Frankie felt he was being welcomed like royalty, but he felt anything but well and was anxious about his grandad.

'I'll come with you to see him this afternoon,' Aimee told him.

CHAPTER THIRTY-FIVE

As FRANKIE LIMPED UP the ward clinging to Aimee, he caught sight of his grandad propped up on pillows and struggling for breath. His eyes were closed and his skin was parchment white.

'Hello, Dad. How are you feeling?'

Bob's watery eyes flickered open; it seemed a long moment before he said, 'Feel awful.' Frankie could hardly hear him. 'I'm finished.'

Aimee said, 'I'm going to have a word with Sister, see what she thinks.'

'They'll get you better with rest and medicine in here,' Frankie said.

'No, it's pneumonia this time. Old man's friend.'

'We'll get better together, Dad, you'll see. You'll be all right. '

'My time's up; this is going to see me off.' He had a bout of coughing. Frankie waited. 'One thing I remember now . . . Connie wanted you to look at that old commode . . .'

'What commode? Aimee did say something.'

'Chair in Connie's bedroom.'

'Oh yes. I'll take a look at it. What am I looking for?'

Bob sighed heavily. 'Don't know.'

Frankie thought he was nodding off when Aimee came back.

'What did Sister say?'

She shook her head and looked numb.

They sat with him a little while longer. Frankie held his hand and told him what had happened at the mill. From time to time the old man managed a single word in response.

Frankie ached all over, but in the taxi with Aimee beside him he said, 'Dad made a big effort to tell me to look at the old chair in Connie's bedroom, as though he'd remembered something important.'

'Let's go there now on the way home. You won't stop thinking about it unless we do.'

He found the familiar bare stairs more difficult to climb than he'd expected. The house smelled of damp; what must Aimee think of it? The chair looked no different to usual. 'Was it once a commode? Dad seemed to think it was.'

Aimee said, 'Looks as though there was once a lid that lifted up and down.' She touched a broken hinge.

'Yes.' He straightened up, feeling fully alive at last. 'Somebody has screwed this square of plywood over it. There could be something underneath.' He swept the cushion seat to the floor. Dust eddied upwards, but the screws were easy to see, one in each corner. 'We'll need a screwdriver.'

'I'll get it,' Aimee said. 'Where d'you keep that sort of thing?'

'Kitchen cupboard under the sink.' Frankie sank down on the bed to wait.

'I've brought three of different sizes,' Aimee said when she returned.

He had the piece of plywood off in moments to reveal a bundle of newspapers folded inside. Under his breath he gasped, 'Oh goodness.' He lifted out the fragile and yellowing papers and laid them on the bed. Aimee gently spread out a copy of the *Weekly News* dated 4 May 1914, showing a picture of a raging fire on the front page. The headline ran: *Flames tear through Sandiways House, the eighteenth-century home of Thomas Ingram, his wife Deborah and their children, Thomasina, Penelope and Francis, all of whom perished in the blaze.*

'So now you know who you are,' Aimee breathed.

Lost for words, Frankie went on reading: *The cause of the fire is thought to have been an electrical fault. Sandiways House was one of the first houses in the district to be wired for electricity.*

'Where is this place?' he asked.

'Er . . . it says this paper covers Great Altcar, Hightown and Ince Blundell, but I'm not sure where those places are. Lancashire somewhere. We'll have to go home and look at an atlas.'

They spent an hour reading every word in the newspapers and found that Thomas Ingram had been the curator of the Walker Art Gallery in Liverpool. 'That answers a lot of questions,' Aimee said. 'Now we know where you get your talent for painting; it's in your blood, in your family. If Grandma had known this, she'd have been proud to welcome you to the house. Delighted to have you as a son-in-law.' Her smile became outright laughter. 'I can hardly believe it.'

'Neither can I. It seems too good to be true.' Frankie was bundling the newspapers together. 'Let's go, I'm tired.'

Downstairs, he looked again at the photograph hanging on the living room wall. 'Does that baby look like me? I can't see much likeness.'

'It certainly shows Sandiways House,' Aimee said. 'How am I going to get you home? I can see you're not up to climbing over the wall, but I could go over and phone for a taxi to collect you.'

'No, I'll walk round. For heaven's sake, it's only a few hundred yards.'

Chapter Thirty-Six

FRANKIE HAD GONE TO bed after an early supper, and had lain awake thinking about the fire shown in those newspaper cuttings and the family it had killed. Aimee was convinced it was his family. He woke up in a comfortable double bed and it took him a moment to remember that he was at Fairholme.

He could hear water running, and knew that Aimee and Walter were getting up. He pulled himself painfully up the bed and reached for the painkillers he'd been given. For him it was just a question of taking time to recover, but there was Dad to think about too; he hadn't been so lucky.

There was a tap on his bedroom door and Aimee came in with a tray. 'Good morning, how are you? I've brought you tea and toast.'

'Thank you, you're being very kind.'

'You'll want to visit your grandad again.'

'Yes, he's gone downhill so fast and looks really sick.'

'Do you want me to come with you, or can you manage on your own?'

'I can manage. We mean a lot to each other, and I think it would be better if I went by myself. I'm afraid he's not going to get better this time.'

'He's your family and this is hard for you,' Aimee said sadly.

'Hard for us both,' Frankie said.

She dropped a kiss on his head. 'Dora will make some lunch for you. I'm going to the mill with Gramps, but we'll be back early.'

Frankie had been told he could visit any time because his grandfather was so ill, and he was at the hospital shortly after ten o'clock. The ward sister said, 'He's had a restless night, and he's not so good this morning.' Frankie's heart sank. He'd been hoping against hope that Dad might recover.

He saw there were screens round his bed as he limped up the ward and sank onto the chair he'd vacated last night. 'Hello, Dad.' He felt for his hand. 'I was hoping you'd feel better this morning and be able to talk to me.'

'Frankie lad,' Bob mumbled. 'I'm fine.'

'We found those newspaper cuttings in the commode in Connie's room. You knew they were there, didn't you?'

His weary half-smile confirmed it.

'Aimee thinks I'm that Francis Ingram, the boy who died in the fire.'

Dad almost sniggered. 'Connie's favourite, he was. Soft on him and wanted to bring him home.'

'What? But she didn't? It isn't me? I didn't think it was. I never looked anything like that baby.'

'Brought some of his clothes home, but not him. Couldn't; they'd never have let her. Fancied him as her own, though.'

'You're sure about that?'

'The fire . . . she was home with me that night. Two evenings off a month they gave her. It was a while after that that she brought you home.'

Frankie relaxed. That was clear enough. 'Why didn't you

tell me all this years ago? You said she'd told you nothing, but you've always known about it. Why the big mystery?' Bob's eyes were closed; he seemed to be slipping into sleep. 'Talk to me, Dad,' Frankie pleaded. 'I need to know when she brought me home. What did she do after the fire?'

'Lay on her bed, crying all day about the baby burned to death.'

'Did she get another job?'

'She tried, but she couldn't cope. Mooned round all day doing nothing.'

'But what about me?'

'Just came home with you one day.'

Frankie groaned. Wasn't this what he'd supposed all along? He took a deep breath. 'Dad, you must have asked her where she got me from.'

'Didn't want to tell me, could hardly talk for crying. She said . . . some street in Liverpool it was. Too many babies in the house so they didn't want you. Gave you to Connie.'

'Oh my God . . . How old was I?'

'Smiling up at us you were. She thought about six months.'

'But she didn't really know?'

'I wanted to take you to the Salvation Army or something but she wasn't having any of that. After what happened when I made her give up her own child . . . I couldn't go through it again. She wanted to give you a better life. She bathed you, dressed you in that dead baby's clothes, made you out to be a toff.'

Frankie could hardly get his breath. Poor Connie. He stared down at his grandad and watched him close his eyes. He'd tired him now. He pulled the bedclothes round him. 'Thank you for telling me,' he said. 'Have a little sleep now, Dad. I'll come and see you again.'

He had to get out of here, get the hospital smell out of his nose. He went downstairs and out into the street. It was raining again. He buttoned his mac and welcomed the cooling drops on his face. He'd not been in this part of the city before, but it didn't matter. He limped on, all aches and pains, until he saw a small steamy café. He went in and sat down, ordered a cup of tea and a cheese sandwich, and later a pork pie.

After an hour or so, he was feeling better and decided to go back to the hospital. There were many more questions he wanted to ask. If Dad was still sleepy and didn't want to talk, he'd go back to Fairholme and come again tomorrow.

When he reached the ward, his grandad was struggling for breath, slumped against his pillows. It scared Frankie to see him like this. 'Hello, Dad.' He felt for his hand. 'I was hoping you'd feel a bit better this afternoon.'

Dad groaned. 'Frankie.'

The ward sister bustled up. 'I thought you'd gone home. I'm glad you haven't; you'll be able to sit with him for a bit to comfort him. He been very restless and the doctor thought he could be in pain. He's written him up for a sedative. I'll give it to him now.'

Frankie watched her give his grandad an injection. 'There now, that didn't hurt, did it?' Dad didn't react, and Frankie knew now that he was never going to. He held his hand and sat with him until four o'clock, when he took his last breath.

When his taxi drew up at the front door of Fairholme, Walter and Aimee were just letting themselves in. 'How is he?' Aimee asked.

'He died earlier this afternoon.' Frankie was tight-lipped. 'He was more or less unconscious all afternoon, couldn't say a proper goodbye. But he's told me the facts of my life. The truth, I mean. That child in the fire wasn't me.'

They ushered him inside. 'You must have had a terrible day,' Walter said. 'Would you like a brandy?'

'A cup of tea is more my sort of thing.'

'Of course.' Dora produced it on a tray with dainty cups and saucers. Aimee was holding his hand, her eyes full of sympathy, but he was near to tears and he felt nothing would help him through this.

Aimee suggested Frankie use the same funeral director as they'd used for Grandma, and with absolutely no fuss it was all fixed up to take place four days later.

There were few mourners at the church apart from the Kendricks; just a handful of neighbours who had employed Bob. 'I don't think I need invite anyone back for refreshments,' Frankie said. So the family returned to Fairholme to lunch alone. 'I only remember Dad having one good friend,' he said. 'Bert Smith used to keep the café on New Ferry Road, but he died last year.'

That afternoon, he decided to go round to the old stables and pick up some more clothes, along with a few personal bits and pieces. He was still stiff, and with his arm in plaster he couldn't climb over the wall. Aimee brought two bags in which they could pack his belongings and walked round with him.

It was a dull, dark day; he looked round the living room and thought how shabby it all was. He shivered; it was cold here too, as no fire had been lit in the last few days. 'I want my clothes and alarm clock, and I have a few books in my bedroom. Let's start there.'

It took Aimee only a few minutes to push his clothes into the bags. Frankie put the alarm clock on top and then had a look round Dad's room, but he couldn't face that today. 'Let's go down.'

Back in the living room, Aimee said, 'Do you want to take that photograph of Connie?'

'Yes, I must take that. It's the best photograph we had of her.'

Aimee lifted it down to the table and studied it. 'Frankie, I've had a thought. Have you ever taken the back off this photograph? There could be something hidden behind it in the frame. A letter, more photos perhaps.'

Frankie took it from her. It was a cheap frame with simple clips holding the picture against the glass. 'It's pretty dusty; I'd better wipe it.' He took it to the kitchen and bounded back a moment later galvanised by his find. 'There is something here, yes, a letter.' He pulled it out with shaking fingers and took it to the window, where the light was better. *Dear Frankie, it's breaking my heart to leave you, but they tell me I must or you will catch this terrible disease and might die from it.* 'It's from Connie.'

'I was sure she wouldn't go away without leaving a note for you.'

Frankie was reading again: *I wanted a son and I stole you because you smiled up at me. I do believe I rescued you from worse and I hope you've been happy with us. Dad and I soon loved you and wanted to keep you always. I know what I did was wrong so I must ask you to forgive me.*

I meant to give you so much more. I tried to give you a posh background like Francis Ingram's so you'd have a better life, but Dad and I couldn't

348

afford much. All I could ever give you was my love. You brought me such joy.

Aimee's eyes were heavy with unshed tears and she could see Frankie was blinking hard. She threw her arms round him in a hug.

Chapter Thirty-Seven

THAT EVENING, AIMEE SAID, 'Gramps, can Frankie stay here with us? He's not in a fit state to look after himself.'

'Of course,' Walter replied. 'Frankie, you're very welcome to stay here until you're back on your feet.'

'I meant permanently,' Aimee said quickly. 'When he's back working at the mill, what's the sense in him having to return to a cold house and cook his own dinner? It takes a lot of energy to do that, and shop for it and light fires. I would like him to be here with us.'

'Oh dear, sorry,' Walter said. 'I wasn't thinking . . .'

Frankie curled up with embarrassment. 'Aimee, that's a very kind thought, but I'll be able to manage. I'm used to looking after myself. I'll be perfectly all right in the old stables; that's my home.'

'No,' Aimee said firmly. 'Everything is changing; it's time you and I thought of our future. You've lost your dad and now we're the only family you have. We want to be together, Gramps, we want to be married. Oh, you tell him, Frankie.'

Frankie took a deep breath. 'Mr Kendrick, I've been trying very hard to show you that I'm a responsible person and capable of looking after Aimee. We've both tried to act sensibly and in a grown-up manner, and it would make us very happy if you would give us your permission to marry.'

'Without us having to wait until I'm twenty-one,' Aimee burst out. 'Frankie and I have been soulmates since we were children. We want to get on with life. I've got the money to buy a house; what's the point of waiting?'

That brought Walter up short. 'What have I been thinking of? Really you've been looking after me all this year. You've sorted out my problems for me. How could I refuse?'

'So we can?' Aimee threw her arms round his neck. 'Thank you, Gramps.'

'It should be me thanking you and Frankie. My brain no longer seems to work properly and everything is happening at once.' Walter had that terrible feeling of being overwhelmed.

The youngsters began to chatter like birds. Frankie had a permanent smile on his face and Aimee was bubbling with joy. Eventually she got to her feet and said, 'I'll make us some coffee.'

'Not for me,' Walter said. 'I'll ring for a taxi and go and tell Esther the news. You must make a big day of it in church: white gown, big cake and champagne. All the trimmings. How soon will it be?'

'Just as soon as we can arrange it,' Aimee said, 'but we don't want many trimmings. We're going to look for a house within easy reach of the mill, so before long you'll be here on your own.' She turned to look him in the eye. 'Will you marry Esther?'

Walter had been wondering how to tell her. He said awkwardly, 'Yes, I feel I have to make an honest woman of her, but really I ought to wait a decent length of time.'

'Nonsense, Gramps, stop dithering. Esther will be good for you. Just go ahead and marry her. Why worry about what everyone else thinks?'

Walter knew Prue would have been loud in her condemnation. 'You're right. I'll take her to the registry office as soon as I can. All we want is to be legally married with no fuss.'

'Excellent,' Frankie said. 'Looks like you could be hitched before us.'

Once the front door had closed behind Walter, Frankie pulled Aimee into a hug. 'At last,' he murmured.

Aimee kissed him and took the ring he'd given her last Christmas from her right hand. 'Now that we have Gramps's blessing, I'm going to shout this from the rooftops.'

Frankie slid it onto the third finger of her left hand. 'We can now tell everybody that we're officially engaged, but I promised to buy you a proper engagement ring when the time came. What sort of a ring would you like, diamonds or a sapphire or what?'

She laughed. 'I like this one,' she said, twisting it round her finger. 'You worked on it to turn it into a thing of beauty. That means more to me than anything you could buy. I know it's red glass, but everyone thinks it's a ruby. What I really want now is a wedding ring.'

'Then that's what I shall get you,' he said, taking her in his arms again.

They made their plans: a quiet wedding at St Peter's, the local church, as soon as it could be arranged, and they'd be searching for a first home near the mill as soon as Frankie felt better.

At the start of the new week, Walter pulled himself together and went in to work with Aimee to find the mill operating just as it always had. He'd left far too much to the youngsters and they'd succeeded beyond everything he could have hoped for, but it had made him feel more frail and helpless than ever.

Aimee told him, 'The news has gone round. Half the staff knew or suspected it was happening, and they're glad we've caught the thieves. Neville Sanderson was not popular. He threw his weight around too much.'

Walter was hugely relieved to know those big losses had been stopped. After only an hour at work, he realised the whole atmosphere in the mill had changed for the better. He heard Frankie being talked about as a hero and was delighted to find that Aimee had earned respect; he was beginning to see that she would be able to run the business eventually. She really was a chip off the old block.

He'd come to work this morning determined to get his life back to normal and fully sorted before he remarried. He'd meant to seek help from a solicitor to deal with Prue's estate, but he'd been putting it off. Now, determined to get on, he pulled his phone nearer and drew out the slip of paper Esther had given him on which she'd written Douglas Maynard's office address and phone number.

'Douglas, you've heard that Prudence . . . ?'

'Yes indeed, I was very sorry to hear it.'

No doubt the news had gone round Rock Park like wildfire and been much discussed.

'Will you act for me? I need to obtain probate for her estate.'

'Of course, Walter, I'll be glad to. When would it be convenient for you to come in and see me?'

'Well . . . early in the morning before I come to work, or better still, late in the afternoon before you finish.'

'Yes, let me see . . . What about tomorrow afternoon at four o'clock?'

'Excellent,' Walter said.

That evening, he said to Aimee, 'Would you like to come with me to see Douglas Maynard tomorrow afternoon? I've asked him to do what's needed about Grandma's will.'

'Yes, yes, I would.' He could see she was surprised to be asked.

'You suggested I should use him,' he said, 'and I have to start treating you like an adult. We'll leave work early to do it.'

When they arrived the following afternoon, they were ushered into Douglas's office and offered cups of tea. 'I've brought our granddaughter with me,' Walter said. 'I feel she should hear about the legal details from you.'

'An excellent idea.' Douglas smiled.

'I've told her that she is to receive a generous legacy, while Prue has left the house and the residue of her estate to me.' He'd always thought the residue would be negligible, but with the hoard in the blanket chest, it promised to be more than lavish. 'I've brought a copy of the will.' He took it from his document case and pushed it across the desk.

Douglas picked it up and glanced at it, then his head jerked up and he gave Walter a piercing look. 'This isn't it.'

'Yes it is, I found it in—'

'I mean she revoked this one and made a new one.' He opened his desk drawer, took out a document and pushed it in front of him.

Walter felt stunned. 'She made another one?'

'Yes, she came in here last month to see me.'

'She said nothing to me.' Walter couldn't believe it. 'Has she changed something?'

'Yes indeed, you'll see on the next page that Aimee is to be her sole heir.'

'What?' Aimee said. 'That isn't fair.'

Walter felt his mouth go dry, and the print danced before his eyes as he tried to read. He was turning the pages with numb fingers, but he couldn't see his own name anywhere.

'Oh my God!' He'd been planning to invest some of that wealth in his business, buy new machines, make it more efficient.

The solicitor said, 'This is the legal will. Aimee is to inherit the house along with everything else.'

'No.' Aimee's voice cut in. 'No, this is nonsense. I want Gramps to have these things. I've already inherited all I need from my mother.'

Walter took a deep breath and pushed the document away. 'There is a complication you need to know about. You tell him, Aimee.'

'Oh goodness, well we were looking through Prue's belongings for her personal documents after she died, birth certificate and suchlike, and we came across quite a hoard of valuables in a blanket chest.'

'Oh! What sort of valuables?'

'Bags of gold coins,' Aimee said, 'her bank books and quite a lot of jewellery.'

'Share certificates too,' added Walter, 'but they're old and I don't know if they still have any value. I'm afraid I'll need professional help to assess the worth.'

'I can arrange that.' Douglas stared at him. 'Where is this hoard; in a blanket chest, you said?'

'Yes, in her bedroom.'

'Did she have these things insured? If so, they'd be listed and possibly valued.'

'I haven't the slightest idea. We've not seen any policies, so probably not.'

Douglas scratched his chin. 'Perhaps when we finish here I could drive you home and look at what you've found. Probably most of the contents will need to be taken to her bank for them to estimate the value, and I'll look at the jewellery and decide if we'll need a valuation for that too, but as I said, this is the legal will and it's what I have to act on.'

'But I don't want the house in Rock Park,' Aimee said. 'I want to buy a new one near the mill. Surely I can give it all to Gramps?'

'Of course you can, my dear, but you'll have to wait until it legally belongs to you. Then I can draw up a document for you to gift these things to your grandfather, though you'll have to reach the age of twenty-one to do that, and I understand that is not yet the case.'

Aimee was on her feet and almost jumping with impatience. 'Grandma knew I was well provided for. I don't want her things; why did she do this?'

Douglas said, 'Aimee, your grandmother wanted to take care of you. She must have loved you very much.'

That made Walter catch his breath; he knew it was more a case of how much Prudence had hated him. She must have really loathed him; he knew that now without a doubt. It made him feel absolutely awful, because this he did deserve. He'd taken up with Esther and made Prue feel like a woman scorned.

CHAPTER THIRTY-EIGHT

CANDIDA WAS AT HER desk in the pattern department trying out new designs. She'd been thrilled when Walter had told her he liked her work and picked out two patterns he might use. He'd since said both would be put into production, and the machines were already printing her dress fabric.

She felt that she was achieving success at last, and her years at art school had not been wasted. She had a job she was enjoying and for the first time ever she was earning enough to support herself in reasonable comfort, but she kept having nightmares when she thought about the auction Armand had been ordered to put on hold, and the fraudulent pictures she'd painted. She'd wished many times that she'd had more patience and waited for what had now come.

The case of the dealer accused of fraud was due to be heard in Paris this month. Candida asked Aimee if she had heard from Armand. 'No, not a word. He must know we're anxious.' If Armand was reluctant to tell them the news, it could only be bad. 'I'll ring him when I go home tonight.'

That had given Candida a disturbed night. Now she looked up from her desk and saw Aimee heading towards her. 'How is Frankie?' she asked.

'He's better and insisted on coming to work this morning.'

Aimee lowered her voice so as not to be heard by others. 'I rang Armand last night. Come to Gramps's office; we need to talk about what's happening.'

Candida shuddered. She found that more chairs had been taken into Walter's office so they could be comfortable; he waved his hand towards a tray of coffee on his desk. 'Help yourself.'

'What has Armand told you?' she asked.

Aimee pulled a face. 'My Renoir is now definitely classed as a fake. Some of the paints used, those shades of pink, were not manufactured before the turn of the century. Proof positive.'

Candida closed her eyes. 'Oh!' She'd been expecting something dreadful like this.

'Surely they had pink paint before then?' Walter sounded irritable.

'They probably did,' she agreed, 'and it could always be made by mixing red and white, but the paint used on that particular canvas will have been found to have been unavailable in Renoir's lifetime.'

'The case against the man accused of painting it opened yesterday,' Frankie said. Candida was glad to see he looked well, though his left arm was still encased in plaster. 'He's denying it, of course. He says he hasn't the skill to do that sort of work.'

Candida bit into a chocolate biscuit. She couldn't stop wondering how long it would be before she was accused of faking too. It must surely be coming.

'Armand is being pressed to pay back the fifty-three thousand pounds the dealer paid him for it.' Aimee pulled a face. 'Frankie and I saw a lovely house we could have bought with that,' she mourned.

'You'll have to pay up if the court rules it,' Walter said. 'Luckily I invested it for you with my stockbroker instead of spending it.'

'I've been spending my allowance,' Aimee said. 'Will I have to give that up too?'

'Well, you'll not have an allowance in future,' – Walter looked grim – 'but the interest will more than cover what you've spent so far. We might even have a bit of cash in hand, unless . . . Will they ask for interest to be repaid on that money, Candida?'

'I don't know, sometimes they do.'

'Armand is extremely upset,' Walter said. 'He's complaining that this is very bad for his gallery; it's in turmoil, crawling with officials and experts and not a hope of selling anything.'

Candida felt sick and pushed the dry crumbs of her second biscuit round her mouth, unable to swallow.

Candida was having nightmares and couldn't let it rest there. She also needed to talk to Walter about work, so a few days later she knocked on his office door. 'Can you spare me a minute?'

'Of course, Candida, come in.'

'I've brought some of the patterns I've been working on, and I'd like your opinion.' She spread them out on his desk. 'Are they anyway near what you're looking for?'

He studied them silently one by one. 'Yes, yes, they are. I like this small flower print, it's pretty and fresh. It might suit summer dresses for little girls. Soft muslin-type fabric.'

'There's another pattern here with different flowers.' She pushed it in front of him.

'These flowers are too big for little girls. This pattern would be more suitable for curtain material, but the patterns I need now are for children's clothes.'

'For home dressmaking material?'

'Yes, but Tom Tasker sells it to clothing factories too. Have another go at this small print, Candida. I need three or four different colourways. Get Frankie to show you the dyes we use.'

'He already has.' Frankie was keeping her busy trying out patterns.

'Then choose the shade you have in mind and mark their numbers on the pattern. Keep them dainty.'

Candida was heartened by this. 'Thank you, I will.'

Walter smiled. 'Frankie said you'd be much better at pattern making than any new apprentice, that you knew most of what was needed already. It seems he was right.'

That was even better. She smiled. 'I hope so.'

'Do it in different colour combinations and I'll use it for the summer season's new styles.'

'That's marvellous.' She could feel a tide of colour spreading up her cheeks. She took a deep breath. 'Walter, have you heard any more from Armand about the sale of our pictures?'

'No, I haven't. Why don't you ring him now from the office? He should be at work too, shouldn't he?'

That was the permission Candida had been waiting for, and within twenty minutes she had Frankie and Aimee with her beside the phone in the patterns office. Aimee agreed to make the call, and was quickly through to the gallery receptionist.

'She says Armand has been called away and isn't expected back today,' she whispered.

'What does she mean, called away?'

'This is Aimee, his stepdaughter.' The receptionist spoke quickly and for quite some time. 'All right,' Aimee said eventually. 'Thanks, I'll have to speak to him at home tonight.'

Candida said, 'What did she say?'

Aimee put the phone down and stared at it. 'I think something must have gone wrong. They don't know what to say to me. They're cagey, rattled.'

Scared stiff, Candida stood leaning on the back of a chair, afraid that her neck was on the block and the axe was about to fall. 'I could try and have a word with his assistant, if she's working there this morning. She's bound to know more about this.'

'Yes,' Aimee said, 'yes, I remember her. You seemed to hit it off when we met. What was her name?'

'Dominique Dupois. You liked her too, didn't you?'

'Yes,' Aimee said. 'Yes, you ring her. Do it now.'

A chair was pulled out for her and the phone pushed nearer. Within a few minutes she was through to the gallery again and was able to indicate to Aimee and Frankie that she'd been told Dominique was there. Another wait for her to come to the phone, then Dominique's voice. '*Allo.*'

Candida explained who she was.

'I remember you and Aimee. It's been a terrible week here.'

'What is happening? What's going on? Where is Armand?'

'He was taken to the police station to answer questions, but I believe he's gone home now. Everything has been closing in on him, but he says we are not to worry; that he is being falsely accused and it's all lies.' Her voice broke. 'It's in the newspapers today, all sorts of stuff. It's awful.'

'What kind of stuff? What are they saying?'

'That Armand was charged with a similar offence ten years ago, but he says he was cleared of it. And that he could be another crooked dealer selling faked pictures.'

'Oh my God,' Candida said. She felt she was being swept off her feet by a wave of horror. Surely not Armand? Panic was rising in her throat; she'd never even considered . . .

'Experts and officials are going through everything here,' Dominique went on. 'Poor Armand, he . . .' She gave up her struggle with English and lapsed into French. Candida gripped the phone harder. This was terrible, worse than she'd ever imagined.

Walter had come into the room and was frowning at her. 'What is she saying? Give me the phone. I'll make her tell us what's happening; we aren't going to be fobbed off like this.'

Candida passed the receiver across, and the three of them listened intently to Walter's half of the conversation. When he ended the call, Aimee asked, 'What did she say?'

Walter looked grim. 'Watteau's fraud trial opened yesterday, and today half of Armand's staff have been there to watch. I've had to bully that assistant of his, but we need to know what's going on.' He took out his handkerchief to mop at his face.

'Go on, Gramps.'

'Dominique said that after a barrage of hard questioning, Watteau broke down and finally admitted that his wife had faked Aimee's Renoir. All Armand's stock is to be re-examined by experts and sales halted until pictures are approved as genuine.'

'This is getting beyond me,' Frankie said. 'Did Armand know that it was a fake?'

'He must have done,' Walter fumed. 'He sold it to her in the first place. Armand is not at all the sort of man we thought him.'

'He took advantage of my mother,' Aimee said, 'and there's nothing we can do about it.'

They were all talking at once and getting nowhere when the phone rang on the desk. Walter picked it up. 'It's Dominique, asking to speak to you,' he said to Candida. She stifled a groan and prayed this didn't mean the end she was dreading.

'Candida, I forgot to tell you,' Dominique said. 'The Micheline Durameau Lepage paintings you put in the sale were given the stamp of approval last week.' Candida straightened up. 'I thought Armand was worried about them – well, we all were – but they were confirmed to be absolutely genuine.'

'They were?'

'But of course you knew they were all right.'

'Yes,' Candida laughed, 'yes, of course.' She was off the hook, all her tension floating away. She felt as though she was flying.

'We received an offer for the equivalent of two and a half thousand pounds for the small picture last Tuesday, and Armand decided to accept on your behalf. He thought you would be happy with that.'

'Yes, yes, I am, very happy.'

'All this trouble is driving prices down and a Micheline Durameau Lepage used to make more than that. Armand has written to you about your paintings, and also about the Chagalls; they're in the clear too. Chagall confirmed they were a gift he'd given Micheline, and that he owns a couple of hers. Have you not received the letter?'

'Not yet.' She laughed again. Christmas had come early.

'We'll keep the big picture on the wall here. I'm sure that will sell soon. We all think it's lovely.'

'No,' Candida said. She was having second thoughts. 'I don't think I'll sell it after all. Please can you arrange for that to be sent back to me?'

She was a successful faker of art. She could fool the experts, she could competently handle any sort of art work, but she was doing no more faking. That had given her the fright of her life. She'd really believed she'd end up in prison as her father had.

She put the phone down and looked up.

'What made you laugh?' Aimee asked.

Her smile dissolved into another laugh. 'Last week the experts appraised those paintings your mother gave me. They've been confirmed as genuine, and she's already sold the small one.' She told them the good news about the Chagalls.

'Well that's something,' Walter said. 'I think I'll go to see Esther.'

That evening, Aimee was curled up with Frankie on the sofa. 'I find it hard to believe Armand was capable of such villainy,' she said. 'He must have known all along that the Renoir was a fake, but I still don't understand how Maman could have been taken in.'

'Armand is a con man. He took you in too, didn't he?'

'Yes, he made me like him; he was kind to me, generous and quite fatherly.'

'He made everybody like him. He needed people to trust

him, and believe in what he was selling them. He was very good at it.' Frankie pursed his lips. 'Faking is more common than I thought,' he said. 'That's because people want what other people value. They don't just look at a picture and decide they like it enough to hang in their homes. If the artist is famous, they see his work as an investment and will pay a lot more. They hope that others will think the same way and it will increase in value. Also it will mark them out as rich and able to appreciate the finer things in life.'

'Poor Maman, she must have loved Armand. Do you think he felt the same way, or was he just trying to live at her expense?'

'He must have loved her,' Frankie said. 'He did marry her, after all.'

CHAPTER THIRTY-NINE

WALTER HAD BEEN PLANNING to take Esther to Southport for a short honeymoon, but now that the case of fraud was being heard in Paris, they were all on edge. Esther said, 'Wouldn't you rather go to Paris for a few days?'

'Well, what's going on there is very much on our minds. What about you?'

She laughed. 'Do you have to ask? The English seaside out of season, or Paris? Like Aimee, I had a French mother but was brought up in England; the big difference is that I've only rarely been to France. I'd love to go to Paris.'

'That settles it then. Candida, could you please book the journey and a hotel for us? It had better be near the court, since we'll want to see what's going on there.'

Esther said, 'I don't want to leave Daisy behind; can you try and get a cot for her?' To Candida, it didn't sound like the romantic honeymoon she herself would want.

Walter locked up his desk, hoping he hadn't forgotten anything, because he wouldn't be coming to work for the next few days. Tomorrow he was to marry for the second time.

Aimee tapped on his door and walked in. 'Come on, Gramps, you can't work overtime tonight. Esther and Daisy are coming over and Dora is putting on a celebration meal for us all.'

Walter pulled himself to his feet. 'I'm ready to leave now.'

'Good. Frankie and I want a word with you on the way home.'

They set out to walk to the train more briskly than was comfortable for him; he deliberately made them slow their step. 'This isn't more trouble at the mill?' he asked.

'No, Gramps. Frankie has been nagging me to take a look at your laboratory, and we've spent this afternoon talking to the chemist in charge.'

'Ah yes, a clever fellow; can't pronounce his name. He's German, I believe. He does the normal lab work and in addition he's experimenting with synthetic fibres. When I was younger, I used to dream about how synthetic cloth would free us from buying in cotton.'

'Yes, it's his personal interest,' Frankie said, 'and he's full of enthusiasm.'

'He reckons that in another five years or so we might be able to producing a completely new type of fabric made from chemicals,' Aimee said.

'Within five years? I doubt that, but he did tell me he was making progress.'

'Would it be like rayon?' Frankie asked. 'I see that in the shops now.'

'No, completely different to rayon. Completely new.'

'Well according to him, it looks as though your mill will be the first in the field to make it.' Frankie smiled. 'That shows great foresight on your part.'

Walter laughed. 'You're making me feel much better about how I've managed the business.'

'I'm very impressed with this man,' Aimee said. 'He said he would like to have an assistant to give him more time to spend on his synthetic fabric. Would you be willing to take on another chemist, Gramps?'

'What do you think?'

'If he believes we can be the first in the field, then I think we should go all out for it.'

'He has someone in mind he used to work with,' Frankie said. 'Shall we arrange for him to come and see you when you get back?'

'Yes. If that happened, I could see our mill making a reasonable profit in the future.'

'It needs to make a good profit, Gramps, not just a reasonable one.'

Aimee was trying to persuade Dora to join them in the sitting room to have a glass of champagne when the doorbell rang. 'I need to watch the food,' Dora protested. 'You won't like it if the dinner burns.'

Aimee went to see who it was and found Douglas Maynard, their solicitor, on the step. 'I have a valuation of the goods in your grandmother's blanket chest,' he said. 'I thought I'd drop it off on the way home. You'll be surprised.'

'Come in, Douglas,' Walter said. 'This is very kind of you. I shall be more than glad to have all this business settled. Come and have a drink; we were just about to have a little celebration. Aimee, bring Dora back in here with two more glasses, and make her sit down.'

Frankie poured the champagne and handed it round. As soon as the solicitor was seated, Walter looked at the document showing the valuation. He blinked at it, unable to take the figures in. 'Surely this can't be right?'

'I can assure you it is,' Douglas said. 'Some of those shares belonging to your wife have prospered over the years. Sanderson's Sausages, for instance.'

Walter handed the document to Aimee, who said, 'Heavens, I can hardly envisage a sum like this.'

She showed it to Frankie. 'Oh my goodness!' he said. 'Unbelievable.'

'No worries now about returning the money we received for the Renoir.' Walter smiled at Aimee and plucked the paper from her fingers to give to Esther. 'You'll be part of the family by this time tomorrow, so you might as well know what we're talking about.'

'Sanderson's Sizzling Sausages,' Esther said. 'Everybody's favourite; they're sold everywhere.'

'I love them,' Dora agreed. 'Bangers and mash with onion gravy, but you never have them here.'

'No, we don't eat sausages in this house,' Aimee said. 'Grandma would have nothing to do with them. Gramps, there's going to be plenty of money for both of us. We'll split it between us, and we need to think about how best we can use it.'

'As I explained, Aimee,' Douglas said, 'you'll have to wait until the will is settled and the money is yours. You'll have plenty of time to consider how you'll use it.'

'Of course we will,' Aimee said. 'Let's drink a toast to Grandma, who has made everything possible for us.'

Walter raised his glass. 'To Prudence,' he said with a wry smile; making everything possible for him was probably the last thing she had intended.

* * *

Candida felt that Walter and Esther's wedding day was on her when she barely had the arrangements in place. She had been invited to the ceremony in the registry office and afterwards to share the celebratory lunch at the Adelphi Hotel. When she put on her best hat that morning, she felt again the thrilling surge of confidence she'd had when Walter had told her he'd use her patterns.

There were only to be the five of them, and the ceremony was held in a small panelled room made elegant with flowers. Like her, Esther was wearing one of Micheline's Paris confections, and looked fabulous in it. The ceremony was brief, and it seemed no time at all before the bride and groom were signing the register. Outside on the steps, Walter handed Frankie a camera to take photos while they waited for a taxi to take them to the Adelphi Hotel.

Over the champagne they could talk of little else but Watteau's trial. The newly-weds planned to spend the night in town and travel to Paris tomorrow morning.

'I want you to phone me every evening,' Aimee told her grandfather as she kissed him goodbye, 'so that we are all kept up to date with what is happening.'

'There won't be much news tomorrow,' he told her, 'because we won't get there until the afternoon.'

Two days later, Candida was at her desk early when Frankie and Aimee breezed in. 'Gramps is in Paris now and says all France is scandalised by this fraud. It's hitting the headlines in the newspapers. Esther is taking cuttings and will send them to you. We want to read them too, so please bring them to work.

They say this accused dealer, Edouard Watteau, is handsome and smartly dressed; a man about town.'

'Apparently he's fifteen years younger than his wife,' Frankie added. 'She is a painter of considerable ability and experience. The implication is that she's been providing a champagne lifestyle for them both by faking pictures that he's been selling.'

'Gramps says Armand is in a terrible state because his gallery has been caught up in it.'

Candida felt no sympathy for him. 'Anything else?'

'They say Watteau's wife is a very sophisticated lady who spends a small fortune on beauty products, hairdressing and clothes, and that they've been living together for several years.'

Frankie went on. 'He's been insisting he's innocent and that he withheld information about her because he was trying to protect her, but actually it was his own lifestyle he was protecting. He broke down under questioning and blamed her, so now they are jointly accused of faking.'

'He sounds the worst sort of rat,' Candida said. She pondered on the narrow escape she'd had when she'd ditched Watteau.

'She was put in the witness box today and questioned about my Renoir. She denied faking it, denied faking anything, but the lawyers are asking questions that are laying bare her background. She said Watteau was a weak man; clearly she feels he's let her down. Apparently she has two young sons, but she says Watteau is not their father. The newspapers are saying that she is a free spender, a master forger, and likes to have a man in attendance.'

Frankie wore a wry smile. 'It seems the journalists don't think highly of her character.'

Now that Walter and Esther were married and on their honeymoon, Aimee's attention turned to her own wedding. 'Candida, I'd like you to come with me to choose my wedding dress this afternoon. I know traditionally the mother of the bride does it, but we've always called on you for help.'

'I'm flattered,' Candida said.

'The wedding is to be at St Peter's, just as Gramps wanted it,' Aimee said. 'He's signed the forms giving me permission, and there's time enough for the banns to be called.'

'Really it's as your grandmother would have insisted,' Frankie smiled, 'though she wouldn't have approved of the house we've chosen.' He turned to Candida. 'It's an almost new semi-detached in an ordinary street about twenty minutes' walk from the mill. I've given up the tenancy on the old stables and rented this instead. Everything in our new house is fresh and clean and up to date.'

'It sounds great for a first home,' Candida said.

Aimee smiled at Frankie. 'After we've chosen my dress, I want to go with Frankie when he's measured for his morning suit. Gramps says it's what Grandma would have wanted, but I think he does too.'

Frankie laughed self-consciously. 'If one of the conditions of marrying you is that I wear morning dress, then I will.'

'I've ordered a three-tier wedding cake because we haven't the time to make one, but Candida, I'd like you to organise the wedding cars and talk to Dora about the menu for our wedding breakfast. Gramps will expect an extravagant spread.'

Candida was pleased. 'How many guests?'

'I'll invite some of the neighbours and a few people from school. Say twenty-five to thirty.'

Candida was pleased to be able to help. It was easier to relax and enjoy things now she knew she was in the clear. She was determined not to think of the trouble Armand had got them into.

Candida was at the house all afternoon the next day, and between them she and Dora managed to get the wedding organised. She was invited to stay on for supper, and they were just getting up from the table when the telephone rang. Aimee said, 'That'll be Gramps,' and they all rushed to his study, where she slid onto the chair behind the desk to speak to him. Candida and Frankie craned forward eagerly, trying to follow the conversation.

They were both astounded when Aimee broke off to say, 'Watteau's wife has claimed that Armand Duchamp is the father of her boys, and that she was married to him from 1920 to 1926. Her name is Eulalie Deverzy. But Armand told me that she and the boys were all dead. I just can't believe this.'

Candida gasped. 'Oh my God!' Poor Micheline. How she'd envied her her handsome new husband and her extravagant wedding. But now it was looking as though her whole married life had been a sham.

Aimee was listening to Walter again and Candida could see from her face that there was something else. Eventually she looked up, shocked. 'Armand has been arrested,' she said. 'He's been charged with selling fake paintings with the intention to defraud. It was announced in court in the middle of the afternoon and the trial was promptly adjourned until Monday morning.' She was cradling the phone against her neck. 'Gramps and Esther had intended to come home tomorrow but have decided to stay on to see what happens on Monday.'

Once Aimee had ended the call, Frankie stood up. 'Come on,' he said, 'we need to consider what this means.' They followed him back to the sitting room to talk it over, repeating themselves half a dozen times and growing more frustrated.

'I'm just so shocked,' Aimee said. 'I can't believe Armand is so evil.'

'Why didn't one of us notice what was going on at La Coutancie?' Candida asked. 'Why didn't Micheline?'

'Oh! Perhaps she did,' Aimee wailed, clutching her head in her hands. 'Was that really an accident she had, or was it a deliberate attempt to end everything?'

'Aimee, no.' Frankie leaned over to pull her close. 'Don't think like that.'

'But what a terrible life she had. Did she realise what Armand was doing?'

Frankie tightened his arms round her. 'Your mother's death was ruled an accident; we have to accept that and put it all behind us.'

Candida was glad to be alone on the walk to the train station. She'd been lucky, much luckier than Micheline. She'd had an almighty fright but she'd avoided disaster. She had a job she enjoyed, she had friends she could trust and she had a future.

CHAPTER FORTY

AIMEE WOKE EARLY ON her wedding day and got out of bed to open her curtains. She felt a curl of anticipation. The weather was cold and grey, but it was predicted to brighten up this afternoon, with little chance of rain.

Everything was ready. She opened her wardrobe door to peep at her wedding dress of oyster silk taffeta, styled traditionally on princess lines with long sleeves and a collar that stood up to frame her face. 'It will show off your slim figure,' Candida had told her.

She put on her dressing gown and went out onto the landing Gramps was already dressed and heading downstairs. 'I've asked Dora to bring your breakfast upstairs today,' he said. 'Grandma would say you need a peaceful start to keep wedding-day nerves at bay.'

Dear Gramps: throughout her childhood he'd been her prop and support, and she loved him dearly. She laughed. 'I'm not likely to get wedding nerves. I've never been so certain of anything before. Tell Dora I'm going to have a bath and I'll be down to have breakfast with you.'

'And Frankie? The groom isn't supposed to see you today until I walk you down the aisle.'

She laughed. 'Not possible when he's living in the same

house. You'll have to tell him to close his eyes. Anyway, I'll just be in my old dressing gown.'

Down in the kitchen, Dora was at the stove. She'd been part of Aimee's childhood too, a friend who had given her the cake and biscuits that Grandma forbade. 'I'm making egg and bacon all round,' she said. 'You'll all need something solid in your stomachs today.'

Frankie was already at the table with a cup of tea in front of him. He stood up and kissed Aimee's cheek. 'Good morning. Shall I pour you some tea?'

She took pleasure from the thought that from now on he'd always be at her breakfast table.

The morning went on like no other. Candida arrived and took her to her room to get her ready. She'd had more practice at dressing for big occasions than Aimee had and was good at hairdressing and make-up. Aimee really felt like a bride when she'd finished.

'Mind you don't trip on the stairs,' Candida warned. She guided her to the sitting room to find Grandpa dressed in his finery, with Esther in one of the Paris fashions and Daisy wearing the pink party dress she'd worn for her parents' wedding.

'Frankie's gone up to get ready,' Gramps told her. 'I think we should have a glass of champagne, just one each, to set the day on a congratulatory course.'

Candida joined them looking chic and sophisticated, followed by Dora dressed in her best hat and coat. 'I'm coming too,' she said, smiling at Aimee.

Gramps said, 'I knew you'd like Dora to be there; we've got caterers in to do the work today.'

'It's a lovely idea,' Aimee said. 'You've been part of the family for as long as I can remember.'

Esther got up to open a window. 'Listen,' she said. Aimee could hear the distant sound of church bells pealing a carillon. 'They're ringing for you.'

Gramps said, 'Prudence worked hard for St Peter's and was well thought of by all at the church. The vicar told me they wanted to ring the bells for you, and his wife has insisted on playing the organ at the wedding as a thank you to your grandma. They feel she was one of them.'

'How kind everybody is,' Aimee said.

She and Frankie had decided on a wedding without fuss. 'It's the married state we want,' Frankie had said, 'rather than a big party.'

Aimee had smiled. 'But it is lovely to have both.'

Candida leapt to her feet. 'Here's the car to take Frankie to church. You must stay in here out of sight.' She went out, closing the door firmly behind her.

Before it was Aimee's turn to set out, Candida rearranged her short veil, and Esther put a black velvet cloak round her shoulders. 'To keep you warm on the journey,' she said. Maman had given it to her one Christmas. She'd worn it to walk to Rock Park parties for years.

'Poor Maman,' Aimee said. 'She chose the wrong husband.' She knew that she herself had made a much better choice.

Yesterday Frankie had found Grandma's prayer book and suggested they read through the ceremony together. That was his way with everything; he needed to know exactly what he was doing. She'd known for years that his love was rock solid, but today they would be showing family and friends the extent of their commitment. They were already a team and they could rely utterly on each other.

The car pulled up again at the front door, and Esther wrapped Daisy in a shawl. Candida said, 'We're going now; the car will be back for you and Walter in ten minutes.'

They waited together in silence, and Aimee felt very grand in her finery. In the car, Gramps squeezed her hand, showing support and comfort as he had so many times in her life. She was glad he was happily settled with Esther and Daisy; she wouldn't have liked to leave him alone when he'd been so troubled earlier in the year.

As she approached the porch of St Peter's, she could hear the organ playing and Candida was waiting to slide the cloak from her shoulders. The church had been a familiar part of her childhood; Grandma had brought her here most Sundays. How could she forget the mint imperials Gran had slipped her to make sure she sat completely still during the service? Yes, she'd had an upbringing filled with love, even though she hadn't been brought up by her mother.

Frankie was waiting at the front of the church. He turned to welcome her with the half-smile she knew so well, and they stood shoulder to shoulder as the service started.

'Dearly beloved, we are gathered together to join together this man and this woman in holy matrimony,' intoned the vicar, and just at that moment, the sun broke through the clouds and shone through the stained-glass window high up on the west wall, bathing them all in a brilliant shaft of coloured light. To Aimee, it seemed like a blessing from God.